Copyright © [2023] by [F. Miguel Da Costa]

All rights reserved.

No portion of this book may be reproduced in any form without written permission from the publisher or author except as permitted by U.S. copyright law.

These are works of fiction. Names, characters, incidents or places are either a product of the author's imagination or are used fictiously. Any resemblance to actual persons, living or dead, business establishments, events or locales is entirely coincidental.

If this book has been purchased without a cover, you should know that it is considered stolen Property. It was reported as "unsold or destroyed" to the publisher and author, and neither the publisher nor the author has received any payment for this.

Scanning, uploading, and distributing this book via the Internet or any other means without the publisher's or author's express written consent is illegal and punishable by law. Please purchase only authorized electronic editions, and do not participate in or encourage electronic piracy or copyrighted materials. Your support of the author's rights is appreciated. Without limiting the rights of the copyright reserved above, no part of this publication may be reproduced, stored in or introduced into a retrieval system, or transmitted, in any form, or by any means (mechanical, electronic, photocopying, recording or otherwise, without the express written consent of the copyright holder above or the publisher of this book. Your support of the author's rights is appreciated.

Disclaimer

This work contains sensitive subject matter that has no intention, by the author, publisher or collaborators, of causing malicious intent or personal offence to anyone who may find this subject matter distasteful or disrespectful. The views or subject matter expressed in this work is not reflective of anyone involved in the production or publication of this book.

For Vitalia, Soraiyah and Mila

THE SHADOWS IN THE PINES

F. MIGUEL DA COSTA

Contents

1. Orange Belly Voodoo — 1
2. Sketch — 31
3. The Sawdust Of Loretto — 63
4. Show Me the Way — 87
5. Broken Promises — 113
6. Bitches Brew — 125
7. Looking For Roger — 165
8. Walking With Ghosts — 189
9. Comforting Places — 215
10. 1918 — 237
11. The Masks We Wear — 249
12. A Deal They Can't Refuse — 272
13. Mother's Milk — 299
14. Acknowledgements — 338
15. Author Bio — 339

1

ORANGE BELLY VOODOO

Her ankle shattered when she fell. She clutched it in both hands, rocking back and forth, clenching her jaws in excruciating pain. The hurt had not been agonizing until she looked down on her ankle and saw the bone jutting out the side of it. The rest of her body throbbed while she gripped the bottom of her foot to realize it dangled loosely in her hand. The moaning and desperate weeping of her cries had been spent the last three hours trapped in the well. Her tears had dried on her dark skin leaving faint white streaks running down her cheeks. The pleas for help disappeared when she realized nobody was coming to help her.

She sat in soft mud that collapsed on her weight and crawled up her sides with their dark grassy mounds of wet sod and broken twigs. The sun was at its afternoon height, and its rays shined only halfway down the circular stone-entrenched water well. Fruit flies had gathered and clouded the opening of the abandoned hole. The Louisiana heat had burned a stench at the bottom that resembled decaying animal hides and dank rotted foliage.

In the bottomless pits of her mind, she heard Auntie Celine's bracelets' jingling sounds and saw the vases of brightly coloured Acacias that sat atop her Aunt's mantle. The balloon-shaped wine glasses were filled to the brim with Port wine – what she thought was *Papa Legba's* favourite. Most offered Rum, but Celine was adamant that she had spoken to Papa Legba in her dream – and he told her he wanted the darkest red Tawny, the only kind that left a sweet sensation on his lips. Cuban cigars smouldered in the glass ashtrays, and a thin smoke streak rose to the ceiling almost every evening.

When she was a child, Marie snatched a half-burning cigar from the mantle and took a drag only to hack harshly, leaving Celine to punish the young girl for stealing from *Papa Legba*. She now smelled the thick tobacco smoke in the well as she sat in the cold mud. Her nostril flickered at the harsh smoke as it travelled up her nostrils.

"Don't look at it, *chérie*. It hurts worse when you look at it."

She heard Auntie Celine's voice like she was beside her in the dark abandoned water well tending to her foot. Marie thought she could feel her elderly Aunt's gentle fingers glide along her leg, tenderly brushing like she was working to soothe the pain.

Marie thought of Celine often. She remembered being five years old. Auntie Celine had gently wrapped the stain-faded bandage around her forearm after scratching it on the chain-linked fence bordering Celine's property line and the adjoining dirt road that led to the major highway.

She heard the rustling of dried leaves beside her and saw one of the dried mounds of dead grass shift over. The sound of rustling had pulled Marie out of her memories, leaving Auntie Celine to vanish just as quickly as she appeared in the dark hole.

A snake's head came out with its tongue flicking wildly; it slithered toward Marie with its head propped up. The throbbing of her ankle had ceased for a moment as she held her hand out and smiled. The snake slithered up her arm and reached her shoulder as Marie extended her arm out to marvel at the coloured scales. The snake was black from the top – its underside a bright orange with speckled black dots running the length of its body. The patterns resembled brail, or random domino dots splattered along its scales. Its eyes were tiny black beads, its tongue flicking in large swoops.

Marie felt her leg throbbing. The aching pain shot up her leg every time she moved. She guided the snake to her ankle and coaxed the reptile to bite her – which it did. Its mouth gaped open, and its fangs dripped with toxic venom. It latched down on her foot and pumped the venom into her. She sat back, her head slightly thumping against the Well's stone wall, and closed her eyes. The overwhelming feeling of a heated blanket enveloped her, and she exhaled with relief as she felt the venom travel up her bloodstream. Her leg didn't ache anymore – the pain had ceased. The snake slithered its way up her navel toward her chest, where Marie unconsciously toiled with the snake around her fingertips in unbridled ecstasy.

She quickly fell asleep in the dark and damp well. Her new friend slithered around its new host until it coiled beside her and rested.

※

Her hand glazed against the smooth and polished surface of the oak table in the middle of the riverside cabin. The platter of Breadfruit steamed and reached Marie's nostrils when she reached for the knife and sliced it in half. The warm buttery scent exploded when she tore the fruit open. She grasped a chunk of the innards and placed it in her mouth. She grabbed another few chunks in her hand and strolled over to the kitchen, where Auntie Celine stood ahead of a dark wood stove, stirring the boiling pot of Salted Cod that nearly floated to the water's surface.

"You have to let in sit in cold water," she said as Marie's pattering footsteps reached her. "*Sortie le sel* (get the salt out). If you don't – won't be right," she said in French.

Marie learned how to speak French as a primary language as well as English. She had failed her third grade in Beaconsfield Middle School because of her confusion regarding the two languages' pronunciation, usage, and grammar. She came home with lash marks and bruises on her hand, proving too much for Celine's tolerance to accept. In response to the chatter and gossip around the Haitian community about the child's embarrassing failure and the physical abuse Marie was getting at school from her teachers, – Celine fell to home-schooling the girl herself.

"Is that for *Papa Legba*, Auntie?"

"*Non*."

"It is for us, then?"

"*Oui chérie.* It is for us. We will give *Papa Legba* something when the sun goes down."

"I brought Rum." Another voice from the entrance of the cabin said.

A white man stood at the door and meagrely stepped inside the cabin holding out a bottle of dark Rum. He was bald and thirty pounds overweight. He wore large-brimmed glasses that mirrored tiny brown eyes dampened from recent sobbing. He hadn't shaved in weeks, and the facial hair began to grow in long thin strands from his chin. He resembled a man down on his luck and nearly gave up at meagre attempts to present himself as a responsible, family man. He clutched the bottle with both hands and tilted his head forward like a beckoning admirer.

"I understand this is what you prefer, madam," he said.

Celine placed the wooden spoon to the side, looked at the doorway, and saw a familiar face. She stomped, clapping her hands excitedly, and nearly danced her way to him. He smiled at her, and Marie saw the white man's shoulders slouch and loosen.

"*Merci, merci, Monsieur* Bennett"

"No, thank you. What you did...." He shuddered.

"*Non, Por favour.*" Then she said in a thick French-accented English, "She is an n-nice girl. She is well?"

"Yes, she is doing better. The fever went down considerably, and she had awoken." He held back from crying, "My wife is grateful. We are grateful."

Auntie Celine placed the bottle of Rum on the side mantle and cusped the white man's hands,

"Say - Uhm, to family, send love." She smiled after completing her words, and Marie felt a warmth in her chest that the warm breadfruit couldn't create.

The man broke down and sobbed, holding Celine's hands to his wet face. He kissed her withered hand. The oversized golden rings with shining amulets adorning their surface were smothered in the man's lips. Celine bowed slightly, her long necklaces of pearls and beads hanging from her skinny neck. She looked over to Marie and smiled.

The sight was a foreign one to Marie. A white man expressing vulnerability to a black woman, thanking her, grovelling on his knees, the tears of his pain and anguish pooling on the floor, the genuine gratitude that had been so foreign for the blacks in the *bayou*. Moments like this left Marie with an admiration for her great Aunt that enshrined an acceptance of what wasn't a common occurrence in her community. The acceptance of others, no matter their skin colour, ethnicity or customs. Celine had shown her to accept those different from her, occasionally adding, "*même s'ils ne nous acceptent pas, amour*"

"Even if they don't accept us, love."

"Wake up." The loud echoing voice said, raining down the opening of the well. "Wake up, bitch. If you don't – I'll bury you. Do you hear me?"

Marie woke sweating profusely. Her eyeball stung when the salty sweat dripped into it. She looked to the opening of the well and was blinded by the sunlight that shone over her now that the midday sun was at its peak. She saw the flies and mosquitoes buzzing around in the illumination of the sunlight. The stone wall was blackened with burnet soot and streaked up the side halfway to the top.

That's when she thought that she hadn't been the only one trapped in here – that there had been others, and like cave paintings of the past, the scratch marks on the stones through the black soot were like pictorials of the souls that were lost in this dank and dreadful place once upon a time. The walls showed themselves to be a time capsule of the past lives who were desperately clawing at the hard stone, trying to escape but ultimately burning away until they couldn't dig in with their nails anymore.

"Please," was all she could muster. Her hands hung limply to her sides and sunk into the thick mud she lay in.

"You in there for a reason. It's what you get. It's what all you people get."

"Please," she whispered.

"What?" He looked down into the dark hole, amused. He saw a double of Marie's silhouette along the wall and nearly stumbled into the well himself if he stayed standing in one spot too long. He teetered for a moment, then regained his balance. He belched loudly and could taste the acidic vomit mingled with cheap Rum on his breath.

Marie saw the fat, bald man that stood above her looking down. His eyeglasses sparkled in the sun, and she could make out the sunburn on his bald head. Her eyelids drooped heavily, and she lowered her head, exhausted, feeling like it weighed the same as a cannonball. Sleeping would have been a relief if it weren't for the man staring down at her.

"I shouldn't have gone to her, you know." He said, slurring some of the words. "It's my own fault."

The large bottle of Rum toppled over into the yellowed grass beside the opening to the well. He had drunk most of it that morning when he decided to kidnap the girl and prove to that *Swamp Witch* that her magic was evil – and there was punishment for that, especially when it involved his little girl.

Bill Bennett slumped over, picked up the half-empty bottle of Rum, and took a large swig. He looked down at the girl in the well and tossed the bottle into the well. It flipped in the air until it finally landed on Marie's forehead with a loud thumping sound, leaving a large welt that looked like a baseball had been implanted under Marie's skin.

From the top of the well, Marie heard the drunken laughter of the man who had pushed her inside.

This man called her over, looking to gift Auntie Celine another bottle of Rum to sacrifice to *Papa Legba* – he said he was grateful and felt that one bottle was not enough to show his gratitude. He had offered little Marie a job - picking the fields of strawberries for a pretty penny. She heard his voice as she faded away.

"Yes. I have a job for the girl – I'll pay her well. I will also feed her, and she can have plenty of water."

※───◆───※

"Good morning, Deputy."

"Jack. How are you this fine morning?" Deputy Frank Wilders sat leaning back in his chair with a newspaper, his feet perched on the edge of his desk.

"Just fine. Just fine, indeed," Jack Hollingsworth said.

"It's hotter than the devil's asshole out there, I'll tell ya," Frank continued while reading the news articles.

"Yes, sir, it is." He said. "What's the day's business? Any calls?" Jack asked,

"No. I just got in myself. Didn't hear any phone ring or anything about the town." Frank said.

"Well, I just came from the market on 5th Street."

"What are you doing there?" Frank asked, "Nancy takes care of that kind of thing, doesn't she?"

"Well, I got up good and early. Couldn't help it, I just woke up ready to go and full of energy, so I figured I'd help the old lady out. Nancy wanted those fresh Mangoes just brought in from the docks. They just came from Bolivia or someplace – nearly half rotten – but I managed to pick a few good ones for her. Anyhow, I heard a few things from Mrs. Dewey and Fredrick Boucher."

"What kind of things?"

"Nothing concrete. Probably just blabbering and gossiping. I did hear them speak about the Bennett girl. Did you hear about that? I heard some talk about Mr. Bennett taking his little girl to the bayou to see that witch doctor. God-damn despicable if you ask me. Those people are like swamp rats; I couldn't imagine ever going to those folks for anything."

"I don't know where you're going with this." Frank lowed the paper exposing his light blue eyes and the furry white eyebrows that accompanied them.

"I suspect the *Witch* had something to do with the Bennett girl," Jack said.

"How so?" Frank sat up in his chair.

"I can't pinpoint it, sir. I just got a Hunch about it."

"A hunch?" Frank's brow raised, and his eyelids became slits. "A what?"

"They call it a *hunch* Deputy."

"Who's they?" Frank smiled. "What are you thinking, young buck?"

"I think I could go by the woods and talk to Celine, Sir."

"Not sure how far you'll get with that. Those people have their *own* way of doing things. I'm not sure we should interfere."

"All the more reason to, I think. That's the beauty with policing – we can pretty much do what we want around these parts."

Frank had a sudden sickening feeling in his gut. "Not without my permission, you don't." Frank tapped his fingernails on his wooden desk. "Listen, I'll tell you what. How about you go check out Bennett's farm? I was thinking of checking up on the poor bastard. Just lost his little girl – not sure how any man could handle that, not with his wife gone and all."

"Okay, I suppose I can stop in on Bill."

"Yes. In the meantime – I'll take a trip to the bayou and scope things out, maybe ask a few questions. I'm not sure where you're going with your *hunches* – but if there's anything there, I'll sniff it out. Sound good?"

"I'm not saying the lady did anything wrong – just a feeling." Jack chimed in,

"And it will satisfy you if I check it out?" Frank asked,

"Yes."

"Right then."

Frank got up from his desk, rolled his chair into the hutch, and picked up his coffee mug, strolling to the front door of the police station. Jack stood at the counter and turned on the coffee pot for a fresh batch. When he turned to Frank,

"Hey, Deputy."

"Yes, Jack?"

"Why do you think Bennett took his little girl to that witch?" Jack asked.

"He must have been desperate, Jack. I heard the doctors couldn't help." Wilders looked towards the tiles on the floor, "he's a father with hope and nothing but bad news coming from everywhere around him. Maybe he put his hope in the wrong hands – maybe not. We'll see."

Frank wore his large, brimmed hat and stepped outside into the blistering sunlight. The town was noiseless and serene except for the odd chirping of crickets. He stood and listened to their song for a moment. He rubbed the center of his forehead, trying to smother the sharp pain from the sudden sunlight. Then he strolled down the steps of the police station to his cruiser and got in.

※

Bill Bennett sat in his leather chair, rocking back and forth. The tears flowed down his cheeks as he looked towards the fireplace's mantle and stared at the framed pictures of his little girl. She smiled brighter than the southern Louisiana sunlight and showed the adorable gap between her two front teeth. Little dimples indented themselves on her cheeks when she smiled so brightly. Bennett sobbed at the thought of how he pinched those cheeks frequently when she was a baby – when Susan was still around.

He could hear Susan's voice occasionally and thought he saw her sometimes in the yard picking rhubarb and carrots from the garden he dug for her. She had begged Bennett for a little garden for years before he built her that garden bed. Time had passed, and the plants were dead now. The Basil had withered, and the Oregano had dried up and blown away in the wind. The Marigolds that once sprung up mightily was now a deteriorated shroud of the glory they once had, left with single stalks that found themselves tilted over. He thought of the garden now and then, making a point to avoid it when he went on his way to tend the fields. It had brought him too many bad memories, and he regretted the damn garden and ever having built it. Bill Bennett shuddered at the irony that; the once exotic flower bed and garden was a cemetery for the one who cherished that land more than anyone else.

He couldn't satisfy himself with the relief that she wasn't around anymore. The lies he told others of her leaving him - and how she had gotten addicted to Opium, had her travelling to the west coast, where she probably had shacked up with some Asian brothel, where they pimped her out, paying her in Laudanum and Heroin. That's what he told them. He knew the truth that she was still with him – still nearby.

He saw her face smashed in and her teeth missing from the rapid oncoming blows. He saw her skin rotting away, larvae feeding on her dead flesh, the torn tissue on her forehead exposing her skull, and her withered fingers degenerating into boney tips. The nightmares he had almost every night since he killed her, of her hands sticking out from the bed and pulling herself out, kept him up until morning when he was too tired of regret and shame, finally dozing off on the living room couch he sat on.

"You have to show them love, or they'll never grow tall," Susan had said.

"Yeah, Daddy – you have to love the plants the way you love me."

"I s-shouldn't have taken her there." He muttered aloud to himself. "That fucking witch. She killed my baby. That god-damn Papa Legba, that God damn *hoodoo* shit killed you, sweetheart." He wept aloud to himself.

He took the ashtray on the coffee table and flung it into the fireplace, where the glass smashed and littered the floor with tiny crystals and smothered cigarette buts. He felt a moment of satisfaction. He looked up at the framed pictures of Betty-Lou and shunned the thought that she wasn't with him anymore. He clenched his jaws, and his face turned a bright cherry red.

"I'll get payback for you, my baby." He stood up and looked through the dirty shades of his kitchen towards the well in the backyard next to Susan's Garden. "I'll get my payback for you, sweetheart."

◆

Marie awoke to the spray of dirt that landed on her face. She spit out the thick grains of sand with the only energy she had left. Rolling her eyes upwards, the sunlight was still blinding her. She saw the dark figure at the entrance to the well shovelling mounds of dirt on top of her. Her eyes glanced toward her legs and feet, and she saw that he had started burying her already, as her legs were nearly covered with mounds of dirt.

She felt the shiver travel up her spine with every landing. It was cold, like the dirt had been in a freezer overnight. Marie shivered uncontrollably as she heard the groaning and chatter over her. Bennett was drunkenly talking to himself and grunting with every shovel. Marie would have panicked if she had the energy to do so. She thought of ways to survive – maybe she could pack herself above the dirt with enough effort to stay afloat – if she had the effort – if she didn't have a shattered ankle.

The cold sweat trickled from her brow at the thought. Her headscarf, a dark magenta adorned with a silver chain around the brim, had turned black and wet with sweat. Her hands had disappeared into the dirt as she looked down at them. The snake had disappeared as she saw the slithering tail bury itself in the dark mounds.

She thought to herself that Auntie Celine could hear her. She prayed that Celine was telepathic and could listen to Marie's thoughts of panic and sorrow. She groaned Celine's name with a shallow mutter. She didn't realize that her words had been incoherent and knew the sound was too mild for her Great Aunt to hear so far away.

"Shut up down there!" He shouted. "You're like that bitch; you just won't shut up!" Bennett scooped another shovel load and dumped it into the well, hearing the thumping splatter of the dirt landing on the teenager trapped below. Bennett took a breather and wiped his brow. He glared at the sky and huffed shallow breaths when he heard the voice coming from the side of his farmhouse.

"Hey, Bill. How are you?"

Constable Jack Hollingsworth entered the backyard and shut the wooden gate behind him. He strolled over with his head down, contemplating how to address a grieving man who had just lost his daughter to cancer and a missing wife who had disappeared a year before. He'd rather scope out the *swamp rats* in the *bayou* – he'd rather the inevitable conflict to the feeling of awkwardness.

"Jack," Bennett said as he heard the mild groaning from the well. He immediately picked up the shovel and flew a couple of scoops of dirt into the hole until the sound disappeared.

"Bill, I wanted to come by and check up on you. I have to admit; I don't know how to go about it – never done this sort of thing before." Jack said. He stood five feet from Bennett with his hands on his hips.

"It's fine, Jack. It's been tough."

"I can't imagine. Frank is a bit occupied this morning. I wish he were here – he's better at this than I am."

"Jack. I'm swamped here. Not much has been doing good – Missus ain't around; I'm sure you heard she left me." Bill said. "Now, the God damn cattle fell into the well and spoiled the drinking water. I should figure something out, don't you worry."

"I heard something like that, yeah. That sort of thing ain't none of my business, but I feel for you, brother. I do." Jack said. The chickens flapped their wings and hopped around Jack's feet as he stood talking to Bill.

"Don't mind the chickens, stay a foot away, and they won't shit on you – or bother you none." Bennett wiped his brow; a fresh splatter of sweat fell to the ground as he flicked it away.

"You filling it up, then?" Jack asked. "Need a hand?"

"No," Bennett responded almost faster than he should have - leaving Jack with a cutting eye that stank with suspicion.

"Let's go inside. I'll fix you a fresh lemonade – it's blistering out here." Bennett said.

"Bill Bennett – when have you ever made lemonade for anybody?" Jack chuckled.

"Since Susan left, Jack. Since Susan left." Bennett stuck the spade in the dirt and walked toward the back screen door until Jack stopped him in his tracks,

"I won't be staying long, Bill – I appreciate the offer, but I have other duties, you understand? If you want help filling the well – I can come back after hours and help."

"Yes. Well, I don't want to keep you, Jack. No need for the help either, buts it's appreciated."

"If you need anything, Bill – not just coming from a cop – but from a friend...." Jack said,

"I'll give you a holler, Jack. It goes a long way, you know? Coming out here. I appreciate it, but I got much work ahead of me, you understand."

"Yeah, of course, I'm not holding nothin' against you, Bill."

Bill Bennett wobbled on his feet slightly, leaving Jack with pity for the man who had taken to the drink to ease the sorrows he had in his life. He didn't doubt or blame him for it – he knew he would do the same. He knew a man kept it all inside and took to the drink as a reprieve from the burdens he held from providing and tolerating his family, who caused him more grief than he took for granted. He saw himself in Bennett's shoes, slugging along and trying to keep busy to avoid the memories and hallucinations of his lost family still with him. Against his better judgment, Bennett let more drunken words slip from his mouth that changed the innocence of the conversation.

"You better get, Jack – those damn chickens will stink up the well soon. I better get back to it."

Jack Hollingsworth froze in place, glaring around, noticing there weren't any cattle around; he then peered at the stone opening of the hole in the dirt.

"Why don't you come down here for a minute Bill? Show me what fell in there."

"I told you already," Bennett responded.

"Come on down, Bill," Jack said sternly.

Bennett looked to his feet, shook his head, and spit on the floor. He slowly walked over to the policeman like a boy who had stolen and guiltily walked over to the stork clerk. Jack peered over and stepped back from the intense heat and stench of the opening. Bennett had come closer behind Jack and stopped his feet from dragging in the dirt - then took a few more steps toward Jack silently like a predator lurking after its prey.

"The fuck, Bill?" Jack said with a finger under his nose. He retook a step toward the opening, and just as he peered down – Marie saw the man's face explode, his body toppling down on top of her. She let out a loud shriek that had dampened the ringing in her ears from the gunshot that awoke her from nearly passing out again.

The dirt had not covered her nose and eyes, and she saw the face in her lap that stared back at her. The wide gaping mouth that hung open and the crater in the man's face where his left eye used to be. The blood poured like an open tap from the hole in the man's face and soaked into the dirt, leaving it a darker hue than the wet dirt originally was. Then Marie saw – and felt - the weight of dense earth piling on her again.

For Marie, the astonishing reality set in immediately – there was no floating to the top, not with the extra weight on top of her. There was the only outcome and the frightening realization of being buried alive with the murdered policeman on top of her. She closed her eyes and thought of the snake's venom pulsing through her veins. She relished the feeling of the numbing venom coursing through her and wished it would reach her heart and stop it from beating before the dreadful white man above buried her while she was still conscience. Marie closed her eyes as the dirt covered her face. She finally took one last gasp of breath before her entire head was covered.

⇝ •◆• ⇜

Deputy Frank Wilders thought he had gotten lost while he walked the overgrown footpath to Celine's shack. He occasionally looked to the shoreline for the Alligators on his left, hovering under the surface of the algae growth, waiting for him to take a wrong step and fall in. Geckos scattered at his feet. The sound of the constant screeching of Cicadas was loud and intense. The heat from the deep brush and humidity had him sweating more profusely than he should have, even in the dark and cooling shade of the towering Cypress' and Cottongums surrounding him.

He could hear the beating of drums from the path, which didn't surprise him. He knew of all the Rumours from folks in town about the people who lived here. The hermits of the swamp, the loners, the outcasts, and the poverty-stricken. Of how their customs and religion had malicious intent and of *Witches* that spoke to the devil. Frank never took the Rumours and speculation seriously, but the resounding thumping of the drum skins couldn't help but convince him that everything in this place wasn't entirely Christian – and he didn't like that. It made him feel foreign in a place he was obligated and employed to patrol and police. A district where he grew up, went to school and met his wife. A place he garnered much admiration and profound satisfaction from the community that lived there.

He finally reached an opening in the tall grass and came upon Celine's cabin. The rotten wooden dock from her sloping shoreline had become dilapidated; however, a canoe was still tied to the only mooring hook left on the pier. He immediately saw the crowd of black farm workers who crowded the cabin's front porch. Some sat on the steps chatting with each other in a low tone, shuffling cards. Another man, over six feet tall, leaned against the screen door, propping it open while he smoked a cigarette. Most of the farm hands stood and peered inside the front door while children sat in a perfect circle on the burnt yellow grass carving wooden dolls that gave Frank Wilders the shivers at the thought of their intended use.

Frank managed to make his way to the porch. A circle of Haitian women stood inside the doorway and took up the small room. Mosquitos flew around their heads, and Dragonflies could be heard buzzing on the floor. They all stood with their heads down, chanting while looking down on Celine, who was withering and flailing her arms about as if she had become possessed.

Frank had seen this kind of ritual before, except at the local tent church functions where the pastor claimed he healed the disabled and gave words to the mute with the drizzle of holy water and a sudden slap to the forehead. He hadn't bought the counterfeit miracles before, and he didn't buy them now – regardless if it was Christian or otherwise.

Celine flailed at an altar decorated with long colourful cloth of Maroon and Violet. The mantle held glass vases with giant Sunflowers, some with yellow petals and some with thick stocks but dark red pedals instead. Atop the mantle sat ashtrays with burning cigars, glasses of dark red wine, and bottles of white and black Rum. What put off Frank were the miniature skulls that lay scattered along the floor – he wondered if they were human or some tiny Monkey or Ape species. He stood and watched, speechless, until Jacques spoke from behind him.

"Bad *juju,*" he said. Frank turned his head and returned to the porch steps where the tall black man stood.

"I don't know how to ask, "Frank muttered to the man.

He wore dirty linen that served as farmhand outfits, his nails were stuffed with dirt, and his legs had been splattered with wet mud thigh-high – probably from walking through the swamp. As the other farmhands did, Jacques wore a straw hat that cast a cooling shade on his wet face.

"Celine had a dream. She saw bad *juju* happen to Marie." He spoke with a thick French accent but was the best English speaker in the community. "She saw the earth rise. She saw a bad white man. She heard Marie's voice. She does the *Riri* now, a bad *Riri*. The kind of evil *Riri*," Jacques explained.

"A dream?" Frank asked

"She saw a serpent with an orange stomach. It is meant to take the pain – give death. *Liberte*", it was the best way of explaining it to Frank.

"What is she doing in there?" Frank asked.

"She is calling on da *Guede.*" He said. "Spirit."

"I don't like the sound of that. Which spirits, you said, bad ones?" Frank asked.

"Yes. Bad, bad spirit." He said with a sombre tone. "You must go – don't be involved."

"That's a hard thing to say to a Deputy Jacques." Frank placed his hands on his hips and kissed his teeth at the thought.

"Damn hard thing." Frank nodded his head and walked back to the doorway.

Celine sat before the altar and had several Gardner snakes lying around her. She held a black feathered rooster by the neck and poured Rum all over it. The wings flapped, and spits of Rum flew around, the loose feathers gently floating back to the snake-infested floor that Frank hadn't noticed before. Frank shuddered at the sight – the sound of the rooster screaming froze him, and his eyes enlarged broadly.

Celine then took a knife and cut off the rooster's head. The women jumped and shouted in celebration, and the men started dancing on the porch clapping their hands. The drum beating grew louder. Frank thought the young black man pounding on them would break through the skins.

Celine pierced a menacing glare at Frank while the decapitated rooster kicked in the air, its wings still flapping. Her chilling gaze horrified Frank. The rooster flapped furiously in her face, and she didn't even blink. She shouted something in French at him that he didn't understand, and he could see the anger, the pain on her face. He couldn't help but feel a sense of shocking sorrow the same way he felt attending so many funerals where widows or mothers would shriek angrily at the sky—cursing and shouting but expressing the unbearable grief of a depressive sadness.

Frank felt the large fingers grip his shoulder. Jacques pulled him away from the doorway and turned him towards his face, grasping the Deputy by both shoulders.

"You must go now. The *Loa* will come soon."

"What the hell is that?" Frank said, his eyes still nearly bulging,

"Da Papa. *Papa Legba* is coming."

Bill Bennett had sobered up after filling the well. He had a throbbing headache, his temples pulsing, his legs were exhausted, and he felt like they would give out when he reached the couch – but he didn't see double anymore, and his speech had returned to being legible again. He walked to the candle holders on his living room wall and lit them with a shaking hand. Then after he had enough of the flickering yellow candlelight for him to see – he stopped at the ice box and pulled out a cold beer.

The chair had felt comfortable on his back and legs now that he had finished the grunt work. He didn't think of the little girl buried alive in the well. He didn't ponder his wife buried in the garden or the nosy cop that shouldn't have come around in the first place – he thought of the satisfaction of the leather cushions blanketing his ass from the rigid frame of the couch—the dizzying relief of his feet in the air.

The gunshot crack had kept ringing in his ears since he shot Jack Hollingsworth in the back of the head. His dirty white undershirt, now a wet, light brown, had blood splatter marks on his gut. Bill wore it with pride as he took a long swig from the beer bottle. He looked at the old radio atop the mantle above the wood stove and contemplated dialling it. He didn't move. His exhaustion overtook his thought and stayed sinking into the couch – the same way Marie sunk into the dark wet mud in the well – he sighed at the idea of the little effort it would take to stand up, reach out, and turn the dial.

He took another swig of his beer, and upon resting the bottle on his knee, his eyes enlarged at the frightening figure looking through the kitchen window from outside in the dark. The blank and beady stare of his dead wife, Susan, shocked Bill when he observed the tiny black pebbles she had for eyes and how they looked like the glass beads taxidermists use to imitate the soulful life-filled eyes of squirrels or raccoons. They were dark, but still had a shine that sent a chill running down Bill Bennett's sweaty dirt-caked arm. She stood in the dark, still wearing her kitchen apron (the one she *disappeared* in), staring a chilling glance at Bill. He blinked for three solid seconds, and when he opened his eyes – she was gone.

He looked down at his beer and thought it had taken its toll on his sanity. So much had happened in the day – the past month- that convinced him of the anxiety and paranoia mixed with the beer and earlier morning Rum that he saw things that weren't there. The radio wouldn't be a bad idea in terms of providing a welcoming distraction, and the effort didn't seem so much after all.

He took another swig from his beer, then the candlelight blew out, leaving him in the dark.

"Who's there?" he shouted. A faint creaking of the floorboard came from the kitchen before him. He immediately thought of Susan and shrivelled into the leather cushion.

"Who's there, I said." He yelled again. Another long creaking footstep grew louder than before.

"So, help me, God – I'll put a fucking hole in you. I swear it."

A candle flame flickered and appeared on the candle holder above Bill's head. With the light barely illuminating the room, he felt a sense of relief at the dim flickering. As Bennett looked around the room, he saw he had been transported to a place that held the familiar stench of damp and soggy logs, the look of withered wooden panels and fruit flies buzzing in clouds above his head. He heard the croaks of toads and the buzzing of dragonflies.

The humidity was unbearable. Bill Bennett felt the intense heat surround him and cause him to pour in warm sweat.

The cabin interior was familiar – the carpet on the floor, the long oak table leading to the kitchen (too far in the dark to see), and that altar. That haunting and unimaginable alter was responsible for many bad things in his life. Where he had begun sitting in his living room – he astoundingly found himself in Auntie Celine's riverside cabin.

The candlelight flickered more intensely, and the brightness of the flame grew more immense as if it wanted to show Bennett more. The walls were stained with streaks of blood from the ceiling, and the floorboards tilted upwards at the ends, cracked at the edges and splintering apart. Bill Bennett hadn't heard the hissing and deep huffing of the snakes on the floor, but as he looked down, he saw the floor in front of him littered with piles of black and white striped Gardner snakes entangled in mounds at his feet. Bennett shrieked in horror and shooed away the flies landing on his face. He saw black roosters around galloping between snakes, and an altar where his fireplace should have been – was replaced with Celine's, decorated with embroideries and bottles of Rum and wine, a crystal ashtray on either end with smouldering cigars burning a dying ember.

The snakes hissed and huffed deeply at the creaking steps that drew closer to Bennett from the dark. He couldn't make out who was there but could see the figure standing tall and wearing what looked like a stove pipe hat in the dark.

"Who are you? Where am I?" Bennett shrieked.

Those were the most obvious questions he could ask, but he didn't acknowledge thinking of the words in his mind – they just came out naturally. His mind ran blank without a single thought, only being replaced with a frozen shrill of horror at the giant man approaching him. He didn't feel his hand tremble or his chin quivering, he couldn't feel the hot air soaking into his pores anymore, and he didn't feel the warm piss flowing between his thighs.

"I'm here, Daddy," a voice said.

"Betty, baby?" Bennett mouthed the words, but the sound didn't come out.

"Yes, Daddy. I'm here. Don't you miss me?" The voice from the shadows responded.

The prominent figure drew closer to the borderline of the candlelight. It was at least seven feet tall with the stove hat, the ivory skulls adorned the brim faintly appearing in the darkness as he stepped closer.

"What the hell are you?" Bill shuddered. He heard the faint beating of drums in the distance, gradually becoming louder and louder, reaching closer and closer. He looked over his shoulders and to the ceiling, trying to figure out where the drumming was coming from.

Could it be in my head? He thought. Who was beating it, shaking the tambourine and clapping their hands? Bennett wasn't alone in this place. It wasn't just him and the monster. He had been surrounded by others who weren't here visibly, but they stood over him, chanting and breathing hot air down on him, beating that haunting drum louder and louder.

The figure stepped into the light slightly and showed its horrifying appearance. The looming black man had darker skin than any shade of skin if the whiter face paint didn't shroud it. He wore a slender-fitting dark purple tuxedo with several long necklaces made of finger bones and scalps that hung to his waist, chiming its hellish sounds as it wavered side to side with his steps. The man's dreadlocks fell to his knees, adorned with rotting flesh and tiny snakes slithering through his locks. He smiled at Bennett, and his golden teeth speckled in the candlelight. They seemed like they floated in his mouth as his gums were dark and black. His eyes burned like the furnaces of hell and glowed a bright fiery red with the same appearance of tiny beads amongst a black, deeply socketed brow. The man held a tall cane that looked like a piece of rotting deadfall decorated with black rooster feathers and a skull that sat atop the butt of the handle. His fingers were long and wrinkled – like he had submerged them underwater for hours showing every line and channel in his skin.

"What do you want?" Bill whimpered.

"The man placed a cigar in his mouth, and his gold-encrusted teeth crunched down on the end of it. The cigar began to smoke; then it lit ablaze by itself as the towering figure held his free hand out – a tiny Gardner snake peering out from his puff sleeves. He watched the snake gracefully slither to his hand and work between his fingers like a child observing a dog chewing on its toy. He seemed enthused and distracted by the snake – as if Bill was unimportant or wasn't there at all.

"What do you want?" Bill shouted at the demon standing in front of him.

Papa Legba smiled at the man, and his bloody tongue then reached down, the blood dripping from the tip as it grew longer until the end nearly touched the sizeable black bow tie neatly tied at his collar.

"I'm here, Daddy," the child's voice said again.

"I'm here to take you."

"They will be rolling in Bill Bennett soon, sir." Wilma Burrows said. She sat behind the desk before the large, refrigerated Coronors autopsy room doors.

"Dr. Conners is inside with the three other bodies. I believe he is expecting you, Deputy."

"I don't think he is, Wilma. I thought I'd come by and see for myself. Three bodies?" Frank asked, surprised.

"Yes. A teenage black girl...." she looked down at the pad in front of her and read,

"...Susan Louise Bennett, the wife. She was found buried in the flower garden," She said. "Also, another little girl, Betty Lou Bennett."

"Jesus. Where was *she* found?" He asked.

"In the Well, sir, along with Jack." She said gravely. "Constable Jack Hollingsworth is here, Deputy. I'm very sorry; I realize this must be difficult."

Frank nodded his head and took a deep breath.

"Yes, it is. I spoke to his wife already. It's...yes, it's tough."

"I can imagine. If you wish, I'm sure Dr. Conners wouldn't mind. I know he is in there doing a preliminary analysis – but I'll pretend he was expecting you."

"Thank you, Wilma; I'm sure it's fine."

Frank walked through the heavy metal door, and when walking through, he could feel the cold air hit his skin like walking into a mild autumn evening. He saw the three long slabs rolled out from the drawers in the wall. All three bodies lay beside each other on their cold metal bed with white sheets drooped over them.

"Hi, Frank. Suppose Wilma let you in?" Dr. Conners asked.

"Yes."

"It's no problem; I need you here anyway – to identify the bodies."

"Don't think it's right for me to I.D. Celine's girl. I'm sure Jacques or Celine would reserve that right."

"Agreed," Conners said. "But Jack and the Bennett girl – I'm afraid you're the only one."

"Yes. That's fine." Frank walked over to the last slab on the left, and Conners met him, reaching down to the white sheet and raising it, exposing Jack's pale, lifeless face. The hole in his eye had turned black from the coagulated blood. The hole's edges were still moist with red, but Frank shied away from the wound as soon as he saw it. He looked at Jack's brows and saw how they were frozen in arches – like he was surprised and the tiny hairs stuck in that manner. His mouth was closed, and his thin pink lips had turned a pale blue. Frank closed his eyes and shook his head at seeing his friend lying dead on the cold metal slab.

"It was quick, Frank. I know it's rough – but it was quick. Single gunshot wound to the head, I estimate a .40 calibre round, but I'm still awaiting ballistics results." Conners said as he lay the white sheet back over the dead policeman's face.

"I'll give him a good burial. I'll pay for it myself." Frank said solemnly.

"Yeah, I'll chat with Nick Carruthers at Holy Mary's. He will make a space for a plot – a good one – even if there isn't any more room; I'm sure he will help. Jack was a good man." Dr. Conners said. "A damn good man."

They walked over to the tiny mound shaped like a child on the next slab. Frank hesitated.

"I don't know. I'm not sure I'm.... "

"Nobody ever is Frank. It must be done. You knew the girl, right?"

"I've seen her at the summer Carnival and community BBQs. She was a girl like any other girl. Running around, chasing balloons. I'm afraid I might not recognize her if I see her now."

"Is that the truth?"

"No." Frank sighed. "I'm afraid *I will* recognize her – that's the problem."

"I see," Conners said. He sighed and asked Frank one more time. "Are you ready?"

"Yes."

Conners raised the sheet and exposed the child's face. She was still beautiful. Her skin had grown pale and lifeless as any other corpse, but her long lashes lay gently on her cheeks, her forehead was smooth like her skin was made of velvet, and her lips were still a shade of pink, which was astounding to Conners and the Deputy. However, her little pale arms had the stiffness and tense feeling of early set *Rigor mortis* that concluded she had been dead for about a week.

"That's enough," Frank said. Conners dropped the sheet abruptly.

"Yes. That's her." Frank said. He took a few steps from the slabs and turned away from Dr. Conners, where he snivelled and wiped the tears from his eyelids.

"I'll put the word out to Celine that Marie was found. That she will need to come down," He tried to sound assertive, pushing the sorrow to his gut. "How did the Bennett girl – "Frank asked.

"Cancer. She passed about a week ago." Conners said. "She had a tumour in her brain that grew to the size of a golf ball. Poor girl, to think of all the life she didn't get to live."

"And she was found in the Well?"

"Yes."

"Jesus."

The Large metal door swung open, and Benjamin "Benny" Sanders, an intern at the Coroners, popped his head in. He had a smile on his face as if he was listening to the comedy hour special in his headset. Benjamin was the son of Lucas Sanders, the town butcher who had had enough of his son's macabre fascination with meat, finding his son constantly arranging different cuts of animals into some grotesque *Frankenstein* creature and giving his creations names. After firing him and countless nights of beatings – Benjamin finally found his place at the underground basement morgue of the Coroners' office.

"Hey, Doc. We got the Bennett guy here." Benny Sanders said.

"Yes. Bring him in." Conners responded.

Sanders rolled the gurney to the middle of the room where Dr. Conners and Frank stood waiting. The white sheet draped over Bill's body had puddles of dried blood around its surface. Sanders kicked on the brakes and chewed his giant wad of bubble gum. The headphones covering his ears blared Heavy Metal music, and Sanders turned to leave, blowing giant balloons of gum in front of his face as he walked out nonchalantly – like he was wrapping a loin with his dad at the Butchers shop—just another day.

"All right, here we go," Conners said. He reached over and pulled the sheet exposing Bennett's horrifying naked corpse. They both jumped back and let out a shrill gasp. Conners had seen malicious injury before, but nothing like this. Frank ran to the can in the corner of the room and hurled chunks of his lunch into it. The heat from the body rose like a mirage and let out a stink that didn't resemble a corpse or rotting flesh but burnt cigars mingled with the thick musk of shit and urine.

"My Lord," Conners said under his breath as he stared at Bill's body. His hand trembled as he held it out for no reason. He was shocked at the state of Bennett's body and had no practical explanation for why he held it out, pointing.

Bennett's entire body was littered with shallow slits and deep papercuts, like someone had taken a knife and slivered thin incisions into Bill's flesh. The slits encompassed his whole body, front to back, under his armpits, and behind his knees. Slits in the webbings of his fingers that made the digits of his hands look longer than they were – even knife slits at the soles of his feet – any available space had been occupied with shallow cuts that had darkened with dried blood. Bennett's face was the most tortuous and disfigured of all.

He had been cut down the middle of his face, and his skin was pulled back and secured with two large nails embedded deeply in his temples. The meat was still a bright red, and every sinew and muscle that made up the underlying structure of Bennett's face could be seen. Patches of the white skull appeared in some spots like the surgeon had gone too deep with his knife while cutting, or the skin itself, while being pulled back, ripped chunks of meat from Bill's face exposing the bone.

Bennett's eyes were also missing. The dark hollowed holes left behind where his eyes once occupied were now replaced with two fat burnt cigars protruding outwards. Frank stared across the room, holding the garbage can in his hand, staring in disbelief at what happened to Bill Bennett. The thoughts and questions raced through his mind, but the words couldn't develop enough to escape his lips. He stood with the soles of his feet planted on the white tiled floor of the room.

Conners' hand was still outstretched, and he took a few steps closer to Bill Bennett's body; he placed his fingers on Bennett's neck and noticed the dead man's lip quiver slightly. Conners' brow furrowed, and he leaned closer, trying to feel a pulse and examine the quivering lip.

He drew his ear close to Bennett's mouth and then felt the hot air shoot him with a burst in his face. Bennett gaped his mouth wide and let out a terrifying scream. Conners jumped again and saw Bill Bennett's arms flailing all around and his feet kicked against the cushion and side rails of the gurney.

"My God. He's still alive!" Conners shrieked.

Frank dropped the garbage can and heard the loud *clack* against the floor in the background of the agonizing screams. Bennett's hands felt around his face and grasped the jutted cigars from his eyes. He pulled them out, and a slimy blood mucus trailed behind the ends of the cigars. Bennett screamed louder at the realization of his state.

The bloody cigars rolled on the floor and began to smoulder when they finally rested. The smoke rose from the tips, and the ember got brighter as Bennett's screams grew agonizingly rampant. The desperate cries fueled the cigars to catch with life – until Bill Bennett's screams eventually smouldered into ash.

Bill Bennett's lifeless body lay lifeless on the gurney; his arms hung on either side, and his mouth gaped limp and open.

To Their horror, Dr. Conners and Deputy Frank watched as a black snake with an orange belly made its way out of Bill Bennett's mouth and slithered onto his chest and stomach, where it, too, died.

2

SKETCH

"Liana Worthington is here for her sketch. She sounded a little down on the phone, so try to be more patient with this one than you were with the last." Shondra said.

He yawned, stretching his arms out above his head. The loud knocking at the door woke him up from his afternoon slumber. Bryce Harper could hear shuffling feet nearby; laying in his hospital bed in his penthouse Atlanta apartment, he drew curiosity to the visitor at the door - his eyes opened slowly, blurred with sticky eyelashes and sleep crumbs; he wiped them away and felt the morsels roll off his cheek. Harper heard his live-at-home nurse turn the doorknob and open the door.

"Oh yes, please come in; Mr. Harper has been expecting you."

Shondra had been his live-in nurse for five years since the car accident; Shonny has been loyal to him and grew close since the police unions fundraised a "Go Fund Me" page to have her hired to care for Harper. She was an elegant and kind-hearted woman from Georgia with a mini afro she always kept perfectly manicured and greased. She wasn't a big fan of the fake hair or weaves most women spend countless dollars on to try to fit in with society's idea of "beauty" standards. She was born in Senegal and moved to Atlanta as a little girl. She was proud of her African heritage and how places in the south – like Atlanta – had provided her with the freedom to express her ethnicity, celebrate it, and indulge in Atlanta's Afro / Caribbean heritage, cuisine, and the liberty of shopping at black-owned businesses that Atlanta had an abundance of.

She peered over to Harper, shook him on his shoulder, and snapped him out of his afternoon haze. Her lips moved, but the sound delayed as Harper quickly snapped back to attention, finally trying to shuffle himself into a sitting position.

"Come on - I told her you were waiting for her. Don't make me look bad now," she said with a slight Southern accent,

"Oh, I could never make *you* look bad, Shonny," he replied sarcastically. She stood straight up, arching her back with her hand on her hip. She gave him that look. The one that said,

I know you didn't just give me that attitude.

She didn't have to say it. Harper got the picture; he overstepped and gave her a sly grin,

"Ok, send her in, please. Oh, and can you please hand me my sketch pad...and...."

He thought hard, deciding which graphite drawing pencil to use, and felt his stomach drop with utter uselessness when he didn't immediately spot what he was looking for. He aimlessly looked around and finally landed his gaze on the pencil. He leaned forward slightly, peering over at his writing desk to the left of his bed in front of the giant glass window overlooking Atlanta's skyline.

"...and maybe the hb4 Shondra? That one there. Thank you," he added.

Shonny pressed the button on the side panel of the bed, raising and adjusting the back of the bed to accommodate Harper's sitting position, with the heart monitor beside him beeping like a metronome at one-second intervals in the background. She leaned over him to check the intravenous bag that hung from the skinny metal pole. Harper could smell the scent of her body butter and tried to hide his perverted gaze when looking down at her blouse as the collar of her scrubs opened slightly.

Hmmm, coconut today, huh, Shonny? Nice choice. He thought.

She gently squeezed the translucent bag and watched the bubbles float to the top. She flicked the lines with her finger, checking that the lines were open and flowing.

He looked at her lovingly as she straightened up and spun in place, almost like a giddy child. She walked to the office desk beside the hospital bed, cocking her hips like a runway model to exaggerate her sly, sarcastic wickedness.

"You go, girl," Harper said teasing,

"You know I got it." She responded over her shoulder.

To have a beautiful woman with him, tending to his needs, was a foreign reality to Harper. His ex-wife had been verbally abusive to Bryce and had developed into a radical feminist over the years.

She began having animosity toward Bryce for his over-abundant masculinity that she saw as degrading to her nature and unnecessary to humanity. She took out her frustration on him with insults, threw fits and constantly threw random objects at him. He was glad to be rid of her, *but so many wasted years*, he thought. *So many years could have been happier with someone like Shonny.*

Shonny provided the satisfaction no other woman presented to him. As a caregiver. He only wished he could return the favour. To be a better man to her, avoid the bouts of depression and anger towards her, and instead take her out dancing on the weekend, and buy her makeup, encouraging her to feel beautiful in front of the bathroom mirror – even if it was just for herself. He ached for the gentle touch of a woman's fingertips on his skin, her lips on his, her heavy breaths as he satisfied her, the look in her eyes of surprised astonishment when she climaxed sitting on top of him.

Harper yearned for feeling. A feeling that seemed so distant and felt like an icepick in his forehead every time he reminded himself that he wouldn't get to experience anything like that for the rest of his life.

"Mrs. Worthington, I'm ready for you now," Harper said. He sat in his hospital bed, now with the top half adjusted to have him in an upright sitting position. His 12 x 18 sketching pad sat on his lap with a few different graphite pencils beside him on the nightstand—his handy HB4 in his right hand.

"You have a wonderful view of the city Mr. Harper...." She said,

"Please, call me Bryce." He said, "I'd like this to go as easily as possible. I know this was a traumatic event, and I understand if some memories are a bit hazy or traumatic. Just keep in mind that we are safe here, and I'm on your side, right? I want to catch this guy, too; get your car back."

"Yeah, that's great,"

"Just try your best, and we will see what we come up with."

"The police said you were the best they had and recommended you. The sergeant said it was policy for him to suggest using a sketch artist from the station, but another policeman mentioned you were good."

"Howard?"

"I'm not sure of his name. He had a mustache and a little gap between his teeth, and he talked nice and seemed kind."

"Yeah, that's Howie," Harper chuckled,

"I, too, would like this to go easy. I'll do my best to describe the asshole who stole my car".

"Not a problem...Mrs. Worthington, is it?"

"I'm not married, and you can call me Liana, please." She said, batting her long fake eyelashes at Harper. He could see where this was going and didn't mind it.

Harper was a police sketch artist who worked for the Atlanta Metro Sheriff's office. These days after the accident, he told himself frequently that he wasn't interested in taking on any more cases for the department.

Still, he felt obligated to the Police department, which had cared for him for so many years - before and after the accident. Although they had been good to him, and he appreiciated the goodwill, he was regretful that his skills were left to catching petty robbers and low-life criminals, and he got the sense that the department pitied him for being paralyzed, giving him the *easy stuff* that almost insulted his intelligence. He would much rather help with more insidious murders and kidnappings *if* he were going to help at all. He much rather draw the latest serial killer, gang member, child abductor, or terrorist suspect, not so much the low-level crimes, like carjacking pretty blond girls or mugging little old ladies for their dusty old purses.

Just collect on the insurance policy, lady. Cut me some slack here, would ya? He thought.

Worthington started to describe the assailant as she closed her eyes. Her head propped up, her eyelids squeezed tight, exposing lines and wrinkles not previously apparent. She sat upright with her hands patiently folded in her lap, her chest out, and her back straight. She gave the impression that she was taught to sit upright correctly at the dinner table as a kid or almost looked like she was praying as her forehead tilted to the ceiling. Her thin lips moved as she described the man who had taken her car. She seemed as if she was in a meditative trance, hypnotized in reliving her traumatic experience, yet, Harper got the impression that she wasn't going through a hard time at all because of the carjacking. Reliving the ordeal as she sat calmly in the chair beside his bed didn't seem tumultuous for her, like other victims of violent carjackings had been.

He always started with the eyes. He asked her about shapes and compared them to what she might recognize to make them easier to imagine.

"Were his eyes shaped like almonds or more rounded?"

"Do you remember the colour? Were his eyelids droopy like a stoner that was always high?"

"His eyelashes: could you describe them? Did you notice any little details about them? Were they obnoxiously long or not so much?"

Moving on to the nose, he continued,

"Short, stubby, long, thin, pointy at the tip?"

"The nostrils...did they flair out naturally like he constantly took in large gasps of air through them?"

They sat for approximately half an hour as she continued to describe the assailant. She stayed in the same sitting position, gleefully telling Harper about the man who ripped her out of her car at gunpoint and took off in the brand-new Lexus. She spoke fast with the manner of a young, privileged girl from the Hamptons and was much too fast for Harper to keep up with. Harper occasionally switched pencils as he was quick to complete drawing the lines and would switch to another darker tint pencil and continue shading.

"Oh my God, Bryce. It's him. It's the guy." She exclaimed, "My goodness, you are amazing! You did all this by just description?"

"I'll send the sketch to the commanding officer in charge of your case. I'm sure he will get right to it, Ms. Worthington." He concluded, trying to cut the conversation short, hoping she would be on her way.

"Can I hire you for your talents, Bryce? I work for a movie studio in the city, and we could use your talent for our CG animation films. The sketches would be fantastic for character development, and I'm sure you would be handsomely rewarded," she asked as she handed the pad back to Bryce. She got up from her seat to collect her jacket that hung on the back of the chair. She didn't take her eyes off him.

"No, I think I'm good. Thanks for coming over, Ms. Worthington. I hope they catch this guy soon."

"Liana. Thanks for having me, Bryce." She flung on her long grey winter jacket, tossed her hair over her shoulders, and gave him a suggesting glare that would have flattered most men.

"I hope you reconsider, Bryce; I wouldn't mind seeing you again...." Catching herself being a bit too forward, she walked over to the apartment door while mumbling her goodbyes to Shondra as she saw herself out.

Well, what a naughty girl. Harper thought. He was slightly aroused and then tilted his head forward, muttering to himself,

"Knock it off – since you can't do anything about it anyway."

Some things were more important now. Some things held more meaning. The serenity of his apartment, the scent of coffee that sat beside him on his nightstand, the steam dancing upwards from the lid of his cup, the grip of his graphite pencils, the texture of his sketching paper when his palm gently glided on its surface were the last remaining feelings Harper had that he didn't take for granted anymore.

Most of all, he found solace in the drawings—the hours of line drawing and erasing, shading every surface of the faces, contextualizing every feature. Harper would exaggerate every valley, every skin pore, every pimple, every bump with the skill he had developed over the years at the department. That was the good stuff. Any feature that was specific to the person he drew, he accomplished it. The final result of every completed face would give him a genuine appreciation for the simple passions art brought to his soul. It was his form of Buddhist meditation; he could get lost in his drawings, the hours dwindling until the sunlight that blared through his window turned dark and starry with the evening night. That's all he needed these days. To be lost in his drawings and the feeling of accomplishment when he stared at the pad and saw the strange face looking back at him. When he was especially impressed with his work, He pondered to himself,

To think – it all started with a blank page,'

He looked down at the drawing he held before him and considered the artwork pretty good. As he examined it, judging his work and contemplating, he spoke up, asking Shondra,

"Shonny, can you please get Howie on the phone for me?"

Handing the phone to Harper, Shonny stood beside his bed, looking at the page. Yet again, impressed by Harper's exceptional talent, she nodded her head in silent approval,

"Hey, Howie, it's Bryce. Yeah, I'm just fine. Listen, that Worthington lady, the carjacking victim you sent over…yeah, that's the one, listen," he continued,

"There's no carjacker. She's trying to do an insurance fraud scam, buddy. Yup…yeah, I know. Well, the thing is, Howie, I didn't draw what she described. Still, she told me it looked just like the guy." Harper closed his eyes and thought twice about what he would say. He didn't want to damn the poor lady after all. She was pleasant and the flirtation had made an impact on him, though minor as it was, he reminded himself that he was only a sketch artist – It wasn't his place to play the judge or executioner.

"I'll tell you what, I'm not a cop. I just draw faces for a living. I don't want to accuse anybody without proof...but my Spidey sense is tingling". He nodded his head as Howie spoke on the other end. The mumbling and incoherent sounds coming from the receiver resembled a surprising tone from Howie,

"Maybe look into it – but I got a pretty good feeling. I'll have Shonny send the copy over right away and do what you do, buddy... Yup...okay, thanks. I'll talk to you later. Bye," he handed the phone to Shonny. She grabbed it from his hand,

"Goddamn! Bitch had me fooled."

"Do you mind sending this over to Howard?" He ripped the page off from the seam and handed it to Shondra.

"Sure will. I would never have figured." She said,

"Yeah, I got some sneaking suspicions early on."

"What would the world be like without you in it, Harp?"

"A better one?"

"You stop it." She lightly slapped him on the shoulder, "I'll fax this over to Howard."

"Thanks a bunch."

Harper had much respect for Shondra. She took good care of Harper after the accident and although she was a stunningly beautiful woman, he had a more profound admiration for her that flew well past sexual desires. He appreciated Shondra and the many hours she spent with him. Constantly reading to him and telling him stories, bitching, and whining about family members and their grievances. The good stuff.

Shondra had a room in the apartment she could stay in, but chose not to most nights. She had a young son in an apartment on the south side of the city, and no matter how much Bryce begged for her to stay and offered to make room for Danny, she valued her independence and privacy.

"You think I want to live at work?" she once asked. He reminisced about the conversation. At the time, she was two years in. Trying to hide that he was offended by being referred to as "work," he knew she didn't mean it that way.

"Both of you could take the two rooms." He insisted, "Danny's getting big now and could use his own room soon, you know? I'm stuck in this bed all the time anyway, Shonny. I promise you will have privacy; the kitchen is yours, the washer and dryer…well, you know where they are. I know you will say *no*, but understand that my home is always open to you. You take care of me, and with all the money I received from the liability case, I want to take care of you too; show my appreciation".

"And that's why you pay me so well! I don't need help, Harper."

"Well, I can't spend all this money alone,"

"I don't need the money, Harp." She said, "I have much love for you – you're a wonderful man but don't think I'm the one to take advantage of you because you struck it rich. I'm here to help you, mend you. I want God and my son to see that….and I hope you do too!"

"Oh, Shondra…"

"It's nice, Harp – it really is – but you need to know not everyone in your life is here to milk you. It's important you know that."

"I know. You're a good one, Shonny."

It was good to know she wouldn't suck him dry. All the friends from his past wanted handouts from him now that he had money. Phone calls from the best friend in third grade he hadn't seen in thirty years, asking for twenty grand to cover major surgery, or the long-lost college girlfriend that ditched him for his roommate during freshman year, who needed a down payment for a property up north (an investment opportunity, she said. Of course). He would get random calls begging for money for one reason or another. Family members, too, regrettably. He learned quickly after the settlement that blood was thick but not as thick as green paper bills.

Shondra was right, he thought; her boy didn't deserve to be around that type of thing. Boys should be boys and live in the blissful ignorance of childhood – not surrounded by adult griefs. He felt ashamed at the offer of her moving in with him. Felt embarrassed at how selfish he was to keep her in his life and his home, not allowing her to live her own life with her own successes and regrets.

He reached over to the table ledge for the hot coffee and took a sip. He enjoyed the milk foam stuck to his lip and swallowed the dark espresso with a warm satisfaction that matched the accomplishment he felt with his drawings. The little things. He glanced over at Shondra, who was folding the rest of the laundry in the living room, thinking to himself,

She has her own life, Harp – she doesn't need to live yours.

The following day was Saturday when Harper would be alone except for the occasional phone call from Shondra checking up on him. The weekends brought the solace he relished, and he saw the opportunity to master his craft and passion for drawing the faces he *wanted* to draw in privacy and without interruption.

He didn't enjoy picking faces from a crowd of pictures or even having people dictate to him as he drew. He enjoyed the challenge of starting with a blank page, working the eyes, then the nose, the chiselled features of the mouth and lips, and seeing where the drawing ended. The surprise he would get at the completion of the sketch would present him with a blissful surprise. It was like discovering a new person that didn't exist yet, giving birth to a human on his page. Someone that had aspirations and misgivings, a life, a job, someone that was loved and cherished. Whether it was a child or an elderly man, a skateboarding teenager with overgrown locks of hair sticking out from under his ball cap, or a Rastafarian black man with his long thick dreadlocks falling over his shoulders and his long scraggly beard hanging from his chin - he excitedly obsessed over the anticipation of seeing where blind creativity took him.

As the hours passed, Harper completed four drawings of random faces he created out of thin air. Around his bed, he had papers with previous sketches floating like mythic gods and angels that watched over him, thumbtacked to the bulletin board behind his head on the wall. One sheet tacked over another sheet, every page encompassing the entire corked surface area. Some pages lay scattered on his lifeless legs - others lay dormant on the floor around the bed that housed him.

He thought of publishing a book of sketches at times but needed to be more confident that people would react positively to his faces. To Harper, it was an unattainable dream. His overbearing doubts overtook his reasoning, and he would constantly shudder at the conscience voice in his head telling him that they weren't good enough,

A daydream, like Alice in Wonderland. Imagine falling down the rabbit hole, tumbling, spinning within my fantasy. It'll never happen, Bryce. You might be good, but nobody wants to buy a book of faces. Wake up. They have their own to look at in the mirror. He thought.

Harper called it the 'Achilles Syndrome.' A self-diagnosed disease of the mind, of wanting his name to carry on throughout the ages, even if he was cursed to die young in order to acheive it. The idea had a sense of mysticism, to be remembered for his talent through his drawings long after he was gone. He told himself that the idea wasn't egotistical, but after all that had happened, he realized how one second could change his life forever, and in one second, he could vanish just as quickly. He didn't want to disappear. He wasn't afraid of death or the finality of it - he feared what was left behind. How would he be remembered?

"Draw, man. Just draw." He muttered aloud. "Who will it be today?"

He scratched at his chest from a sudden itch, reminding himself with a soothing thought that he was grateful to feel an itch at all. He constantly researched new treatments or the newest discoveries in Stem Cell research. In Switzerland, he talked with researchers who had an experimental procedure that would offer a high probability chance of a slight feeling in his legs again. The 10% was astounding to Harper. He would take what he would get. A slight tingle would be enough to knock back his depressive bouts.

He often cut himself with sharp utensils, just hoping to feel something. It was a secret he tried to keep from Shondra – but it didn't last long after her morning examinations. Both his legs were littered with scars, deep carvings, and shallow slits. The wounds healed badly, nearly becoming infected and left visible marks resembling skin-toned leeches or fat worms sitting on the surface of his quadriceps. Once the local police union and his buddies at the dept (especially Howie) found out what Harper was doing to himself, they shelled out their own money wherever they could to hire therapists until Harper stopped the cutting.

The first drawing of the day was completed by noon. It was of an adult man of Hispanic ethnicity. His long dark curls were bundled up in a ponytail behind his head; he had thick, calloused skin that hung from his jowls like a bulldog. The man's eyebrows were wide and bushy, with a freshly razored space between his brows. His skin was like worn leather, and his face grimaced back at Harper with an unsettling look of skepticism.

He closed the sketch pad and placed it on his side nightstand. Harper then reached for the remote control to turn on the day's recent events and headlines on the morning news. Turning on the giant 50-inch television that hung in front of him on his wall, he turned to *Channel Five News*. He sat quietly in his bed, reading the headlines on the lower right side of the screen while listening to the personalities (who jokingly called themselves reporters) debate the current political climate in the country.

Harper decided on a fresh cup of coffee as the channel cut to a commercial break. He reached over and lowered the side rail from his bed; it swung down gently, and he grabbed one leg at a time. He clenched at his trousers and pulled his legs over the edge of the bed, reaching over as he held himself upright with one hand; like a pillar or column on the mattress supporting his weight, he rolled the wheelchair over that was conveniently beside his hospital bed. Placing the chair where he desired to transfer himself to his seat, he pressed the button on the side of the bed's control panel that lowered the level of the bed horizontally. It made a quiet buzzing sound as the mechanical belts and pulleys within the bed structure lowered the bed frame to a reasonable height, placing the mattress on an even plane with the chair's seat.

He then grabbed onto the wheelchair, took a breath, and used his arms like a gymnast balancing himself over a swing bar, leveraging himself into his wheelchair. Placing his legs on the footrests, he unlocked the brake and rolled over to the kitchen, where all the bottom cupboards were conveniently stored with coffee bags and other dry goods for him to treat himself to.

He swung open the cupboard, grabbed the coffee filters, and prepared himself a fresh pot of Decaf in the easily accessible (and costly) coffee machine on the lowered countertop. Scouring through the bottom cupboard looking for those white vanilla wafer *Oreo* cookies they just came out with. He overheard the news broadcast back on the television report breaking news,

"*This just in, multiple wounded and some feared dead in downtown Atlanta this morning. Multiple EMTs and police on the scene, attending to many injured pedestrians.*" Harper listened to the broadcast over his shoulder and shuddered, "*Witnesses reported a man driving wildly on the sidewalk in a U-Haul van and running over multiple people, including women and children, who stood in line outside a local Starbucks coffee shop. More on this story to come.*"

Again? Jesus, what has this world come to? School shootings, now this type of shit? He thought.

He grabbed the Oreo cookies from the back of the cupboard and proceeded to pour himself a fresh mug of coffee. He rolled to his desk for a fresh pack of graphite pencils, shading tools, and a pencil sharpener.

Harper glanced toward the screen, looking up to see multiple ambulances and Police cruisers scattered around the coffee shop blocking off the street. Red and blue lights illuminated the tall downtown skyscrapers' concrete and glass walls. His eyes squinted at the bright screen; that ice-pick feeling was coming back, piercing him in the forehead as the bright glare from the TV started to give him an oncoming headache. A picture of the man then appeared on the screen. Harper sat quietly, his brows lifted, causing wrinkles on his forehead. His pencils rolled off his lap and rolled on the hardwood floor.

"Just coming in. We have more witness testimony and police accounts as the chaos dwindles. We want to warn viewers that this is quite graphic, and viewer discretion is advised.

"This should be good."

"The suspect in question is Eduardo Miguel De Santos. A Brazilian immigrant who recently emigrated from Rio de Janeiro last year.

His wife called the police screaming that she received a call from De Santos. She explained to the police that he was angry and very distraught. He had just gotten fired from his job at Home Depot for stealing tools, carjacked a local man of a U-Haul truck, and proceeded downtown where this tragedy occurred...

The reporter continued,

"... local authorities arrived on the scene, and a deadly stand-off occurred after the truck abruptly stopped, smashing into a light pole, toppling it, and causing damage to oncoming cars.

Local authorities report De Santos succumbed to self-inflicted injuries at the scene.

Carol Dupree, the Chief Superintendent of Atlanta Metro Police Department 523, disclosed to Channel Five, that police recovered a screwdriver at the scene, which appears to be De Santos's weapon, as local police drew their weapons on him. EMS and Emergency Response units are on the scene.

"Brutal," Harper said aloud to himself.

With a screwdriver, that must have hurt like hell. Wonder if it was a flathead...

He grimaced suddenly and rushed back toward his nightstand. He opened his sketching pad and flipped the pages revealing his latest drawing,

It looks just like him; it's uncanny. Eyebrows and everything. He thought.

He shook his head in disappointment at the terrible news. The aching was getting worse. He rolled back to where he dropped his pencils. Realizing it was too much work to try and pick them up, he clicked his cheek with annoyance and then proceeded to his desk for a fresh pack. Trying to avoid feeling glum, the pounding headache had started to come on strong. He became distracted by his cell phone on top of his desk vibrating. He reached over and answered it,

"Hey, Shonny, what's up? He chirped,

"Hey, did you hear about that crazy guy downtown? Insane." She asked, "Anyway, I'm just checking, you know. Same as usual. Did you see the pot of Gumbo I left on the stovetop? It's got the Andouille sausage you like."

"I see it."

"Just turn the stove on low for about 10 minutes, and it should be hot enough for you, honey". She said with her slight Georgian accent. Harper could hear Danny playing in the background. A little grin appeared on his face.

He's a good kid, he thought.

"I left some bowls on the counter, and forks are cleaned up, and I already put them in the drawer—also, some deli meats and fresh bread in the fridge for you." She was out of breath. "I picked them up yesterday while you were napping. In case you want a sandwich. Everything else cool?" she asked,

"Yup, I'm all good, Shonny. Did you get the Salami I like?" he asked as he rolled to the fridge in curiosity, pulling the fridge door open with a sudden grunt. He was reaching for the pack of wrapped deli meat. He shoved his writing tools under his armpit as he balanced the phone on his shoulder, gorging on the deli meat that he had folded and placed in his mouth.

"You know I did; what you take me for?" he could hear her smile through the receiver, "I can hear that you found it. Didn't your Mama teach you to chew with your mouth closed?"

"Sweet. Thanks, Shonny; I don't know what I would do without you." He said, barely able to pronounce the words with a mouthful of Genoa Salami.

"Okay, I got to let you go now. If you need anything, you know who to call....911, not me. I'm off." She laughed louder now.

"Okay, thanks for checking up. Say 'Hi' to Danny for me."

"Will do - talk to ya later, Harp."

"Bye, Harp." He heard Danny yell from the background.

Damn, good kid.

Hanging up the phone, harper rolled back to his bedside, climbing back up and covering his legs with the wool blanket Shondra's mother had made for him. He turned off the television, closed his eyes, and took a deep breath.

"All right," he muttered, "let's do another."

As the drawing of random faces continued well into the late afternoon, Bryce Harper tossed aside one completed sketch after another until he grew weary from staring at the eggshell paper for so long. He decided to take another break and check to see if the *Twilight Zone* marathon was on, forgetting when it started on the *Space* channel. Opening the package of Oreo cookies, he turned on the television and saw the news channel he had left off on. He was about to switch channels until a brief snippet came onto the headline,

A Developing story here, in downtown Atlanta. A terrifying car accident occurred earlier today; a man who ran over several pedestrians

died from self-inflicted wounds after a police standoff. Four dead, ten wounded—more at 11.

Harper was curiously perplexed at the news story earlier in the day; although he was initially dismissive of the similarity between the Hispanic man's picture and his drawing, the skeptical voice in the back of his mind prodded him like an annoying muscle spasm,

Right down to the scruff on his face. He thought, *What are the odd's he could be someone else?*

There is no way he could have known what the suspect of the deadly van killing would look like. He drew the face on paper well before the accident.

Realizing there wasn't any newer information regarding the carnage downtown (other than the dead and wound count), Harper shrugged and flipped the television channels. One channel after another, he couldn't find anything interesting until he landed on the *Twilight Zone* on the *Space* network,

Excellent. Looks like a new episode. Great timing, Harp.

He sat watching the half-hour sci-fi special until the last episode grabbed his attention. It was about an Army sniper who obtained a cursed gun. With every shot of his rifle, every terrorist killed – someone he loved died. It was interesting, and Harper began to wonder,

Man, what if I drew that Brazilian guy's death? Wouldn't that be creepy? That would be a good episode, I'm sure – if it didn't involve me.

He looked down to see his belly protruding like a pregnant woman and his pack of Oreo cookies sitting at his side. Empty. Nothing but crumbs were left behind. Checking his catheter bag, it was full and needed to be emptied. He had gotten into the habit of wheeling himself to the bathroom to empty his bag. It was a sense of normalcy. A feeling that he wanted privacy like everyone else and a sense of ritual that he was used to before the accident. He tried to keep that, even if it meant the hassle of getting back into the wheelchair. He clicked the television off and tossed the remote to the foot of the bed.

On his way out of the bathroom, with the toilet flushing in the background muffled by the soundproofing of the bathroom door closing behind him, he noticed something quite peculiar as he rolled slowly toward his bed. The television was back on, and not only that - but the channel was also flipped back onto the news.

Funny, I'm pretty sure I turned off the television. How the hell did it get back to the news? He asked himself, perturbed.

"Got to rest, old man," he said, pulling up to the side of the bed.

Still sitting in his wheelchair, he reached onto the top of the mattress, grabbed the remote control, pointed it at the TV, and turned it off. Tossing the remote and spinning around to go to the kitchen to get more snacks now that his bladder was emptied, the television turned on again.

....

He looked over at the remote on his bed mattress facing the television. He stared at the screen and read the news channel's little headline on the bottom right.

Six dead, 12 wounded—more at 11.

He couldn't get over the fact that the television had turned on by itself, almost like the inanimate object wanted him to see it.

Batteries are dying. That's it, what else could it be? he thought.

He was slightly curious about the death toll slowly rising but didn't want to become depressed simultaneously from the senseless loss of life. He knew he was emotionally vulnerable. The most tragic parts of a television series had him blubbering like a child, the conflict in his favourite action movies stirred him up like he was the main character in the film, and the happiest endings had him nearly falling off the bed, rolling around with joy. There was no middle ground – just the extremes of feelings he couldn't control.

He kept the television on as he rolled to the kitchen for a water bottle and a bowl of that hearty Gumbo Shonny left him. After turning on the stove to the low setting, as Shonny said, he sat in his chair in the kitchen, slowly waiting for the Gumbo to warm up and come to a light simmer. Reaching up and stirring the gumbo with a wooden spoon, he could start to smell the dark, rich gravy in the air. It was delightful. Andouille had developed into his favourite sausage during his trip to New Orleans when he was still married to Susan.

She didn't have a good time. She always complained of the heat and the smell of beer and vomit in the French Quarter during Mardi Gras. She had flown home early using the excuse of an emergency work meeting; when Harper later came to find out, she left to see the man she was having an affair with. She broke him to pieces when he found that sex tape of her and her new lover; he was still ashamed that he had let it get so far, and he still hated her for doing that to him.

He gave the Gumbo one last stir until he turned off the stove. He rolled back to bed with a hot bowl and proceeded to lay in bed, cupping the bowl in his hands. It was hot, and he unconsciously slipped a rag under the bowl in his lap just in case he would cause severe burns on his crotch. He couldn't feel any sensation after all and had learned this from the cutting phase during his intense bouts of depression.

He pulled himself back into the bed and decided to keep the television on while he continued to feed himself spoonful after spoonful of hot Gumbo, with a child-like amusement that he was living in a real-life *Twilight Zone* with the child-like imagination of the haunted TV turning itself on - he told himself that his *imagination* had gotten the best of him. There was no rational explanation for an inanimate object with a life of its own. It had to be dying batteries.

The day's top story is coming up at 11. He was looking down at his watch—10:15 pm.

Getting there, he thought,

He placed his empty bowl on the countertop beside him. He reached over to grab his sketch pad, flipping the pages and admiring the most recent drawings of today and the night before. The faces of two elderly European ladies wearing headscarves, a couple of teenagers, and a few professional-looking older men.

Wow, 15 sketches. He thought, *all pretty good too. If I keep this up, I might still have a book on my hands. Maybe a few more for the day, and I'll call it quits.* He concluded.

He looked down and proceeded to sketch. At this rate, he was on fire. Like a basketball player in the zone, hitting three-pointers after three-pointers, Harper was in the midst of an MVP season. He sketched quickly and accurately, completing three more sketches in half an hour, and looking at the sketches - he realized that the last one he was completing looked like Ms. Worthington.

Her long blond locks streamed over her shoulders, and she had thin lips and a pointy nose. Her cheekbones protruded exaggeratingly, and her thin long eyelashes (the fake kind) reminded him of her perfume while she sat beside him just the day before. It didn't take much shading, her skin was fair, and the makeup caked on her face hid all her skin pores and irregularities. The little mole hiding under the blush on her cheek, her mascara disguising the lines that would indicate she was getting older, was regretful to Harper, as he appreciated blemished faces. The kind of beauty that didn't need to hide the lines or the freckles. He completed her and stared at her. She seemed more beautiful on the page than she did in real life. He couldn't help but think to himself,

Should I have taken her up on that offer? I don't need the money, but it gets pretty lonely. I could do the job to keep busy. And to boot, I might be good at drawing the next Shrek or striking it big, developing the newest Disney character. I'm sure the money would be helpful in Switzerland. God knows how expensive that treatment is.

He continued working on a new face when he heard the news in the background. Harper glanced at his wristwatch and read that it was finally 11 pm.

A horrifying story today as a man ran over multiple pedestrians in line at a local Starbucks coffee shop in downtown Atlanta today.

The driver Eduardo de Santos was fired earlier in the day, accused by his employers at Home Depot of stealing tools over the past few weeks, including a screwdriver that would ultimately lead to the suspect's self-inflicted death during a stand-off with police.

Eyewitnesses at the scene report that De Santos barged out of his former employer and proceeded to carjack a U-Haul truck, then barrelling towards downtown as police searched for what was known at the time as a carjacker.

De Santos made it downtown when he barrelled over multiple people, leaving 15 dead and 18 wounded, including men, women, and children. Investigators are still on the scene.

The mass killing has made the national press, with the President commenting on the incident earlier today, calling it "an inhumane act of terrorism..." and saying that he regrets "...that he suspect didn't meet the full extent of the law".

Loved ones of the victims are still being notified, and the coroners have a significant job on their hands with forensic investigators combing over evidence as we speak.

De Santos stopped after losing control of the vehicle and crashing into a light post, which in turn, toppled over, causing damage to multiple cars in the nearby area.

De Santos was reported exiting the vehicle as police approached him, drawing their weapons in a tense standoff among the confusion. De Santos then proceeded to mutilate himself with a screwdriver killing himself at the scene. EMTs reached de Santos, but he lost too much blood and died shortly after on the way to the local hospital.

Investigators are not confident of De Santo's motive, and further investigations are pending regarding what led to this horrific crime.

This is a sad day for the city of Atlanta, with an ever-growing homicide rate reaching record-breaking numbers this year; this mass killing dawns a terrible shadow on the city, with multiple protesters speaking out at the crash scene. Many celebrities have been speaking out on social media, including....

"15 dead, damn, that's terrible," Harper said aloud. His eyelashes grew heavy and blurred with a salty wetness. His tears dropped onto his collar and left water blots on the fabric. He snivelled the loose snot hanging from his nostril back into his nose.

... we at channel four news would like to show pictures of the victims in Memoriam and pay honour for the terrible loss their loved ones must endure. Later tonight, a vigil is planned at the site of the crash.

The news channel then started showing pictures of the victims in better times. Some held their husbands in front of waterfalls and scenic backdrops; others had their high school yearbook pictures shown, social media posts, and selfies taken previously. The deceased's name was written underneath the image in a romantic cursive font with each shot.

Harper looked at the pictures of the victims. He suddenly became aware of their resemblance. He watched closely until Liana

Worthington's photograph was shown with her name under it. He couldn't believe it. He closed his eyes tightly and opened them again, hoping he imagined her face on the television screen. The same lady sitting before him trying to get a quick insurance scam buck was one of the victims. After their meeting, she must have walked to *Starbucks* and stood in line.

Shocked at the coincidence, he rubbed his eyes in disbelief, then watched as the following picture showed a little girl. She was around seven years old. Her curly red hair was in pigtails, and her freckles were plastered on her smooth milky face. Her bright blue eyes were hypnotizing, leaving Harper breathless at the familiarity of the little girl's eyes.

Harper flipped through the pages on his sketch pad until he landed on the little girl's drawing. He looked up at the screen, then back down at his pad in horror. The next face was shown on the channel. A middle-aged East Indian man with short black hair parted down the middle, an exaggerated lump on the bridge of his nose like it was previously broken. Harper flipped the pages, growing more confused as each face glared at the screen.

Jesus Christ....

He sketched the same man. Every detail was accurate, the nose, the hair, the pimple on his chin, everything.

The following image came on the television. A high school photo of a young Vietnamese man wearing circular glasses, the type Janis Joplin liked to wear in the sixties. Horrified, he flipped more pages and landed on the same face as the television.

He didn't have to flip the pages any longer as each face was shown on the screen; he knew all too well. He sketched every one of them on his pad. He dropped the pad of sketches in front of him as if it was burning his hands, feeling like if he didn't look, it wouldn't be real; he wanted the pad far away from him. The pad landed between his feet on the bed.

This can't be real; what the hell is going on? Is this a dream? He thought.

The depression kicked in as quickly as the headache, which was sudden and overbearing. All these years of trying to help people and save lives with his drawings now had the opposite effect, killing people with the same talent he thought was a gift.

The burden of the responsibility he held with his pencil quickly set in. He sat shocked, staring at the television, a teardrop slid down his face, and he felt a sharp pain in his chest. His breath was short, like he ran a marathon. The faces he drew were not random at all. Each face staring back at him *did* exist. They had children who loved them and parents who worried about them. They had wives and husbands, boyfriends who lusted and loved them. They had friends, distant relatives, co-workers, lovers, and neighbors.

How many more deaths was he responsible for? Were all the faces of the people he drew, dead now?

He pressed the button as his bed slowly fell into a lying position. Harper sobbed and drooled until his eyes closed. His eyelids became heavier until the sobs persisted, then he quietly slept.

The following morning Harper woke up wondering if the night before was real. Looking down at his shirt, he noticed that the collar was wet. He must have been sweating while having that nightmare. Pressing the button on the control panel, his bed sat him up.

Wait a minute. In the dream, I pressed the button to bring me down.... No, it was nothing. He thought, he looked over to his Catheter bag to see it was filled.

Damn. Almost made me piss myself. He chuckled to himself.

He wondered when he fell asleep last night. Was it before the television mysteriously turned itself on…. or after? Did it, in fact, turn itself on, or was that part of the dream too? It was all so blurry and confusing for Harper as he aimlessly looked over at his wheelchair to find it on the other side of the room - in the kitchen.

How the hell? How did it end up over there? He shuddered at the thought.

A slight fear set in, sending chills down his neck. There was no explanation for why the wheelchair was so far away. Suddenly, Harper sat in his bed contemplating all the possible ways it could have gotten so far, trying to convince himself of why the chair was in the kitchen, leaving himself devoid of any logical reasoning.

He froze as the television turned on. The volume was at the maximum level. Harper stared at the screen in horror as he watched the television switch channels by itself, finally landing on Channel Five News.

The pictures were on the screen again, like in his dream. The fear had set in full bore as he began to scream. He pleaded aloud,

"No! No! It's not real, No*!*" he continually screamed and began to whine mournfully again.

He could hardly hear his voice as his lungs burned from breathing so hard. The back of his throat tingled and felt raspy and sore from the screaming.

The sketch pad at the foot of his bed sat on his paralyzed feet. Its cover quickly flew open, and pages flipped by themselves as each picture was shown simultaneously with the images on the television screen. Except, now the pictures were very different. Instead of portraits of beautifully drawn faces, they were the victims' faces with scars and bruises, slashes of gaping wounds.

Their eyes were swollen shut from a sudden impact; others had deep gashes that ran across their faces so deep the skull underneath was visible. Blood dripped from their mouths, and their expressions were surprised, mingled with a desperate look of fear. Some looked stunned and terrified; their bloody mouths of missing teeth hung open with astonishment, the children's faces resembled themselves screaming in terrifying pain as if they were being tortured.

Harper looked in amazement and wept uncontrollably trying desperately to reach the pad at his feet. He could not reach the haunted pad. The television's loud volume was deafening making it difficult to ignore the tidal wave of emotions that washed over him. It was the most physical sensation he had felt in years. He clawed and raked at his knees, desperately trying to reach the pad. Weeping loudly, moaning to himself and repeating,

"No. It c-can't be r-real, no, no."

Harper finally gave up on reaching for the book.

He slumped forward, watching each face as the pages turned by themselves. Finally, the last face was shown on the television, then the screen went black. The room was quiet. All that could be heard were the light raindrops that began to slap against the giant window overlooking the dark horizon among Atlantian treetops and skyscrapers.

The page flipped one last time; it was Harper's face on the sketchpad.

He stared at his own face like looking in a mirror through the shaded page; the lines were crisp and neatly drawn, each strand of hair in its proper place, every blemish where it belonged.

His eyes were looking in different directions. His mouth hung open with his tongue hanging out the side of his lower lip. Harper watched as the pad drew the wounds on his throat by itself, the lines and shading magically appearing before his eyes. His throat was split open with multiple gashes. Inside his neck, his spine was severed, as the pad depicted blood pouring down his severed throat, overtop his collarbone onto his chest.

He sat forward, his elbows on his thighs, his hands on his head, covering his face to escape the insanity like a child hides under the blanket from the monster in the closet. Harper realized there was no use and, giving up all hope, yelled loudly, punching at the air like trying to knock out the phantom that sat before him.

He grew tired and sat back in bed, staring at the ceiling, not believing this was happening. His eyes were blurred with tears, his face soaked with sweat. The veins on his neck were pulsating and throbbing from the adrenaline.

The devastating sadness and the depths of his esteem shrunk smaller than a tick - he felt like he had drowned in a morbid sorrow and sat in his bed whimpering, looking over at his nightstand to notice his sharpened graphite pencils.

He Reached over and grabbed two pencils clutching them in his hand.

Suddenly the television turned on again, but the volume wasn't nearly as loud; it was moderate and tolerable. The *Twilight Zone* theme was on the screen, with the opening credits illustrating the giant LED screen. The haunting piano keys of the iconic theme song jingled in the background with the visual of a spinning door among the dark backdrop of space. Rod Serling's voice came on,

"You unlock this door with the key of imagination..."

Harper stared at the screen and then looked down at the pencils he clutched tightly in his fist. His eyelids were droopy, and a spit dribble hung from his bottom lip. He stared intensely at the pencils. He was responsible for so many deaths and pain. He had drawn hundreds of faces, thousands over the years. While Sniffling, and his mouth hanging open, Harper sat in a daze, hypnotized by the show's haunting theme song.

"...in it, you are moving into a land of shadow and substance..."

Serling's voice was distant, but like he was sitting right beside Harper at the same time.

He thought of Shonny and how, in the past, wanted to draw her and her boy, Danny. How much she would have enjoyed that. Now Harper knew full well the consequences *that* would bring.

"That you just crossed over into.... the Twilight...."

Harper wept loudly as he thrust the pencils into his throat.

Blood spurted out, splattering over his white linens. The dark blood poured out of his neck as he continually stabbed and sawed at his throat with the pencils, screaming in agonizing pain. He blubbered gurgling sounds in attempts to cry out, while furiously sawing his throat with the writing utensils.

His eyesight grew darker, the sound of gurgling turning into high-pitched wheezing as he gasped to breathe. The blood poured down his chest like an open spout, spilling over the edge of the bed as he butchered his throat like the grim reaper hypnotized him, forcing him into a steady decapitation.

Finally, his hand fell to his side, and his head hung back. His throat was severed so deep that the back of his skull lay on his rotator cuff, hanging to the side, held on by only a layer of flesh. The blood spurted out of his neck like a fountain, painting the room in the grizzly dark red fluid. The blood on the floor steadily flowed, until it reached the middle of the penthouse apartment.

The graphite pencils fell from his bloody and lifeless hand, toppling over the edge of his expensive hospital bed and landing in the blood pool covering his hardwood floor.

The television turned off. The sketch pad littered with speckles of blood closed shut by itself. On the floor beside his bed, his cell phone vibrated as it lay in the dark warm pool, causing ripples in the surface. It was an incoming call. With each vibration, the phone shuffled on the floor, the blood-speckled screen facing upward, revealing the caller's I.D.

It was Shondra. Calling Harper to check in...and see if everything was okay.

3

THE SAWDUST OF LORETTO

Perched on the top of a forested hill in the township of Loretto, the renovated barn that had once housed a stable of Appaloosas had been turned into a Tavern by the stable owner, who had grown old and died. Keith Boyer's father, Eugene Gustav Boyer, had acquired the lot with the barn and worked on renovating it with his son shortly thereafter. Loretto Tavern was usually hidden among the mist that perched atop the hill, and since being renovated into a country bar, the patrons had begun to dwindle in attendance slowly. The dirt trail leading to its large barn was the only road that twisted between robust Maples and towering Poplar trees for miles, making the trek through the dense underbrush and uneven road a venture not worth taking - especially when drunk. The entrance sign was hidden in the thick brush of branches. The rectangular iron sign was rusted at the edges, with bullet holes in its corners from local teenagers' targets practicing with .22 rifles. The metal-plated sign read,

Loretto Tavern – 100 meters to the left

The road was dusty and torn with fallen branches and potholes. When rain fell, the dirt road turned to thick mud, trapping tiny, incapable cars in its grips. One could see a stripped and tarnished *Volkswagen Bug* along the stamped gravel path leading to the *Loretto*. The *Bug's* interior was removed, and the dulled beige paint that had chipped from years of weather beating had faded away, leaving bubbles along its edges from the rust rising from underneath. Its Interior was now home to sod grass and long vines hanging limply from its openings, some nearly brushing the road's dirt.

The *Bug* was a local charm to *Halton Township*—a type of landmark. For the Rummies and Winos who would stumble out of Keith's bar, the broken-down relic was a sign that they were on the right track, that the highway was just a few miles up the trail, a lighthouse in a torrid storm.

The *Bug* might as well not have been there at all for as long as it mattered to Billy Martel. He knew this trail inside and out, hunting Grouse and Hares in the surrounding forests for years. The path was a gateway to a lunch break glass of Wine or a dinner-time Scotch. Billy Martel reached the front barn doors of the Loretto, and his hand grasped onto the door frame. He took a moment to gather himself and focused on not toppling over. He grunted, then belched, chuckling to himself.

"You *really* messed this one up, huh? Another damn night...." He drunkenly mumbled with a slurred speech. "Another damn...night."

Sawdust covered the floor of the old country bar. Keith Boyer stood behind the long oak countertop polishing the brass rail along its length. The dust had accumulated on the rag, staining the cloth with black spots.

Keith hated himself for procrastinating for so long in keeping the place clean. His father would have scolded him, and he reminded himself of this every time he looked at the black smears on the surface of the once pristine, white cotton rag. Keith finished polishing the brass rail on the countertop when the yellow Edison light bulbs behind the bar began to flicker. It was the usual sign that a storm was brewing. However, Keith paid it no mind. He turned from the counter and caught his reflection in the mirror between two large bottles of a twelve-year-old Scotch and a cheap liquor-store Bourbon.

It was *still* Kentucky Straight. The amber tint of the liquor caught his eye. He thought that any Bourbon shouldn't be considered 'cheap' – even if the price was affordable or the barrels used to age it had been sucked dry of flavour and lost the dark char that infused the distilled *spirit* and gave it a smooth, fruity palate. He stood and looked at his face between the glass bottles, trying to convince himself that having a drink wouldn't be such a bad thing. He quickly jumped from where he stood when he heard the large Barn door to the Tavern slam shut.

The shock dissipated quickly, acknowledging that he hadn't heard the large barn door creak when opened - as it has a reputation for doing. The hinges were old and hadn't been lubricated in years. Another reason for Keith's father to constantly scold him when he was still alive on the importance of upkeep.

Billy Martel stood at the entrance of the Tavern. His hand extended to the wall; his other arm wrapped around his belly. He leaned forward with a pale face, white like a glass of country farm-fresh Goat's milk. His eyes were bloodshot, and his eyelids were a dark ocean blue.

"Oh, for Christ's sake, Billy. How can you show up to my bar plastered as all hell? You better not puke on my floor," lamented Keith.

"Keith, buddy, the sawdust will soak it all up."

"Don't you dare."

"I'm just foolin'." Billy stumbled to the bar dragging his feet.

"What's wrong with you then? Are you going to puke?" Keith asked,

"No, I'm not going to puke. But…the more we talk about it…."

"…You might puke?"

"I might puke." Billy agreed. Keith sighed loudly and reached under the counter for a little wooden bucket. He placed it on the cherry-stained countertop and looked at Billy, saying,

"You know what to do with it,"

Billy nodded and placed the bucket from the countertop beside him on the floor.

"It's there if I need it."

"You usually look this way walking *out* of my bar, not *into* my bar, Billy. What's up? Keith inquired. Billy tucked his hand into his jacket pocket.

"It's nothing, Keith."

"Nothing?"

"Nope, not a god-damn thing." Billy sighed,

"Whatever you say, chum." Keith turned around and flung the dirty rag over his shoulder, hoping Billy wouldn't ask for a drink,

"How about a drink, Keith?"

(Sigh)

Just then, the door to the washroom at the end of the bar opened. Alan McGraw, known as "Big Al" McGraw, the Sheriff of Halton Township, stepped through the doorway, coughing loudly, speckles of his saliva flying out of his mouth. He fixed his belt under his giant gut and came to the bar.

"Jesus. Must have lost a few pounds in there." The Sheriff said. Keith shook his head and closed his eyes, imagining the mess he would have to clean up after closing time.

Billy held his free hand to his mouth and focused on the grains on the oak countertop, distracting himself from having to heave his dinner up after all. Images ran through his head like a movie projection of black-and-white reels of Babe Ruth hitting a homer and galloping to first base. Babe waved his hand to the crowd as they jumped and cheered.

It didn't work. Billy got up quickly and ran to the washroom, nearly knocking the Sheriff over, falling to his knees over the toilet and loudly vomiting into the urine-stained porcelain bowl Big Al Mcgraw had finished shitting in. Sheriff McGraw laughed loudly, with both hands on his ample belly. His brimmed hat nearly fell off as his head tilted back,

"At least I don't have to wash out the puke bucket," Keith thought.

"Ah, Christ, Bill. I bet that'll sober you up real fast!" Al said to Billy over his shoulder jokingly. Billy Martel stuck up his hand, his head buried in the porcelain bowl, holding his middle finger upwards, pointed to the ceiling. This had McGraw laughing harder as he straddled the empty barrel that Keith used instead of bar stools for the patrons. Keith thought the barrels were a bright idea. His father wouldn't have approved – but he was long gone now. McGraw looked over at Keith with a sly grin.

"You were not going to feed him any booze, are you, Keith? I don't want to have to write any reports tonight." McGraw said.

"Is it against the law to serve booze at a Bar, Sheriff?"

"It is - when it's Billy *goddamn* Martel."

"I don't remember reading that in the local by-laws, Sheriff. The last time I checked, serving drinks to my customers wasn't against the law. Even if they are already drunk."

"It's against the law to have him drive home when he's drunk!"

"Drive home? With what car? You had that damned breathalyzer installed in his truck not too long ago." Keith caught himself being confrontational and would usually check himself before causing an argument; he didn't want to hold back this time but thought better of it and did just that.

"Besides, he walked here," Keith said,

"Even still, Keith. He walks out of here drunk as all shit and wanders onto the road; someone swerves to avoid him...bang. That's your ass on the line, son. Best believe I'll be visiting you. Maybe then you can preach to me about *fucking* local by-laws."

"I'll give him a ride tonight, Sheriff."

McGraw could be a real son of a bitch, and Keith had run-ins with him. He knew how shrewd the local Sheriff could be. He had been a ruthless bastard since High School.

"Don't serve him, Keith. I won't ask politely again." McGraw said.

Keith stood behind the bar, his hand wiping a glass cup while he spit on the floor beside himself. *The sawdust will soak it up,* He thought.

Big Al grunted; his dirty white mustache hung over his mouth, hiding the shape of his thin lips. A patch of brown stained the center of his mustache, just under his nostrils, and Keith usually told other regulars at the bar that Al McGraw had gained the brown tuft on his mustache from eating his old lady's ass so often. He usually got a laugh. He wasn't in the mood tonight though, and the brown on Al McGraw's mustache no longer seemed so funny.

"Thatta boy Keith," the Sheriff continued, "Hey, remember I let you off on that DUI on *Concession Sideroad* 15?"

"You don't have to bring it up."

"Huh. Yeah, I remember that too." Big Al McGraw tipped his head back and swallowed the remainder of his whiskey, slamming the empty glass upside down on the polished countertop.

"Well, that'll be it for me, Keith, ol' boy. I'll tell you what; since you're such a great guy to talk with...." He stood up and put on his jacket, which was slung over the bar beside him. "I'll be sure to keep an eye out and perch like a rooster at the trail's end. Watchin'. Do Ya catch my drift? Hope I don't see your red Chevy swerving my way, son." He fixed his eyes on Keith, and Keith's eyes pierced back at Alan McGraw.

For a moment, they resembled prize fighters at a standoff. Keith placed the glass mug he polished on the countertop, then his burly hands fixed on the ridge of the thick wooden bar top in a tight grip as if he would rip out handfuls of hardwood.

"Yeah, I catch your drift, Sheriff."

Billy sat at the bar across from where Keith stood. The colour was back in his face, and his lips had returned to bright pink. He didn't see double anymore but was still lightheaded, and his stomach was full - but he felt much better. Keith placed two glasses on the countertop and poured himself and Billy a shot of Whiskey.

"What happened to not serving the drunk?" Billy asked.

"Fuck it."

"You can get in trouble." Billy caught himself. "Not that I'm complaining," He finished and pulled the cup closer to himself.

"You're walking, ain't ya?"

"Yeah. How did you know?"

"How do I know? *Everybody* knows. It's not exactly a secret. Besides, I didn't hear your car pull up outside."

"Everybody?" Billy asked.

"Everybody."

"No, I mean, who the hell is *everybody*? Why does everyone know my business?"

"Because it's a small town, and people talk." Keith had become irritated at the child's play, "You know why." Billy stared at the floor.

Keith tipped the bottle, happy end down. A stream of Whiskey steadily poured into Billy's cup, topping him up.

"Cheers, buddy," Billy said.

"Cheers."

The cups *clinked* together, and they both tilted their heads back. Their Adams apples jumped as the warm liqueur streamed down their throats. Keith winced at the warmth coating the inside of his chest.

"God damn. Another?"

"Yeah." Billy's eyes narrowed as the burning in the back of his throat hadn't yet withered.

"What are we celebrating, Keith? I'm not a rich man, you know."

"All good, bud. I got a new bottle of this stuff. A good excuse to polish this one-off."

"Jesus, I'm stuffed. I feel like a pregnant lady." Billy said.

"Oh, yeah? The missus cook you a big dinner?"

"Dinner? I wish. Tonight was a liquid dinner." He said glumly, "She didn't cook; got a stick up her ass tonight."

"A stick, huh?"

"Yeah, a sharp one. Stuck so far up, she's got splinters in her lips."

"Is that what you hurt your hand on?" Keith asked. "Her mouth?" It was a nasty thing for Keith to ask. He should have minded his own business but had the nasty habit of shooting from the hip and spewing out whatever was on his mind.

Billy winced and didn't answer. He then swallowed the remaining *Jamesons* in his glass and licked his lips. Billy quickly put his hand back in his jacket pocket. His other hand turned up the collar of his green army jacket to hide the fresh bruise on his neck. Keith snatched the rag over his large, rounded shoulder and began wiping the counter.

"You seen Leah lately?" asked Billy changing the subject.

"Leah?" One of Keith's eyes squinted as he wiped the counter in circular motions.

"Yeah, I saw her last week in town, near old Martha Wilken's diner. You know, the one on 12th and Uhm..."

"12th and Main?" Keith said.

"Yeah, yeah, Main. Whatever."

"Okay, what about it?" inquired Keith.

"Ah, nothin', she's been looking fine, is all. I always had a crush on her, you know? Is she still with that Barry guy? The lawyer from the city?"

"Let me get this straight, Bill. You're drunk. Check. It seems like you have been fighting earlier. Check. Let me guess - You want to bang Leah Giamadi's brains out, right?"

"Maybe." Billy shrugged.

"Check." Keith smiled.

"You don't need to be such a shit about it."

"I'm not. You're the one who brought her up."

"I got a chance. Everyone has a chance."

"The same Leah who goes for the lawyer type. That Leah? The one with the retro *Jaguar* and the big house on Concession 20?

"Hell, yeah, what you say? What's it to you?"

"I'm saying you're drunk, big guy. Stick to making one woman happy, huh?"

Billy spat at the ground beside himself; the spit rolled and collected sawdust until it stopped.

"Have a smoke, Billy. Calm down." Keith said, calming the rough currents. He pulled out a cigarette and offered it to Billy. He hesitated but reached out for it. His long, skinny fingertips were swelled up like fat sausages as they grabbed the cigarette from Keith's hand. His knuckles were cut and reddened. They lit their cigarettes and looked at each other. Finally, Keith broke the silence,

"Another?"

keeping Billy drunk was the only reasonable way to conversate with him. Billy was usually great at conversing, but tonight had been different. Billy Martel had been sullen and apprehensive.

Keith had a pretty good clue judging from Billy's hand, but it wasn't his place to ask about it. So, he didn't. Bill's forearms leaned on the brass railing, leaving smudges on the metal from his oily skin. Billy noticed his Jacket had become noticeably tighter. The sides stretched and pulled away at his shoulders. He took it off and slung the jacket over the barstool barrel next to him.

"Man, I feel fat," Billy said. Keith broke out in laughter. He was reminded of his ex-wife complaining in the mirror years ago when he was still married. He lied to her under his breath, trying to make her feel better about herself. She did get fat, but then again, so did he.

"The hell's so funny?"

"Nothing," Keith gathered himself, "it's nothing." He was feeling a bit light-headed himself. He took a drag from his smoke.

"Seriously. It's weird, Keith. I'm a hundred and sixty pounds, soaking wet...I feel like I'm 210 right now," Billy said, rubbing his gut.

"I don't know what to tell you, buddy. I'm not the type to advise on the matter." Keith patted his large potbelly.

"Kind of weird, don't you think?" Billy asked,

"I don't see a difference, I swear it." Keith chuckled again, putting himself back in that bedroom with his ex-wife.

Billy took a drag from his smoke and rubbed his eyes from the sharp sting of smoke that danced under his eyelids. He swivelled the empty glass on the bar top and hesitated to ask Keith for another top-up. He didn't want to feel like an ass. Keith saw him with the empty glass and uncorked the bottle of whisky.

"Hey, Keith?"

"Yeah?"

"I'd rather have a beer, to be honest. I've been drinking hard all day" Keith nodded, grabbed a bottle from the fridge and twisted the cap off for Billy. The foam rose and drizzled down the side of the brown bottle like a High School experiment the kids did in science class with fizzing Vinegar and Baking Soda.

"This one will cost."

"Shit, Keith."

"I guess beer is a bit lighter, huh? Don't want to lose you're...." Keith couldn't finish the sentence. Billy sat across from him, a smile on his face anticipating the upcoming punch line.

"...don't...d-don't want to...lose your figure!" Keith yelled. They laughed out loud. They were well drunk and lively.

Billy caught his breath and chugged the beer. He could see his stomach protruding past his chest line, slowly growing outward. Keith didn't seem to notice and didn't mention the abnormal growth. He hadn't appeared to take Billy seriously. It was a constant in Billy's life. His wife didn't respect him, Keith considered him an alcoholic, and Billy could never convince himself that he wasn't those things people said about him. He remembered what his wife had told him earlier that night. Her voice was deafening in his ear as if she had sat beside him at the bar.

"All you do is drink; I married a drunk! The kids ask about you all the time. You can't drive, you can't keep a job, your drinking is killing us",

"I'm fine. It's not a problem."

"I should have married that, John Dorsey. He was handsome, and he's still single, you know! Why should I stay with you? Why should I let you keep the kids? I could take them from you and run away with him. He still talks to me, you know!"

"Shut up. You're starting something you can't finish."

"You shut up! You shut up! I hate you! I hate your face and your goddamn drinking! I regret marrying you, bastard!

Billy could feel the edges of the drywall scrape against his hand. The hard wooden stud smashed against his knuckles, swelling them instantly. The impact and sudden pain shot up his arm, and his shoulder pinched in the wrong kind of way. The sting made him angrier and impatient, making him relentless in his fury as he continued pounding the holes in the plaster wall while his children cried out hysterically. He saw their faces. Their eyes welled up with tears, clutching tightly to Aileen, then burying their heads in her arms like frightened Ostriches do when they bury their heads in the sand.

"Are you still with me, bud? You want another?" It was a rhetorical question as he twisted the cap off another bottle and placed it on the damp coaster. Billy took a long drag and flicked the butt into the ashtray, smothering the ember with the crushed Cigarette butt.

"You hear about Linda and Clearance?" asked Keith. He continued, "She caught him cheating on her with her sister. She went crazy, acted like a wild cat."

"Well, what do you expect? What did she do?" Billy inquired.

"She tried cutting it off! You didn't hear?" Billy held the bottle's rim against his lips, and his eyes opened widely, exposing his bloodshot eyes. He mumbled softly,

"Tried cutting it off? Did she…"

"Hell no! He saw her coming at him with the knife and ran out the back door." Keith laughed.

"Christ, that's a hell of a story, man." Billy guzzled the beer. He felt his gut expanding with every swallow.

"You're telling me you don't see that?" Billy pointed at his stomach. "It's huge!"

"I'm not sure if you're messing with me...?"

"Seriously?"

"Uhm...yeah, seriously. You're a skinny bastard." Keith hesitated, "I wish I could be that slim, buddy."

Keith's left eye squinted, and he began to look at Billy with a blank stare. "You sound like a loony Bill." He said, "I know that look when you're nice and *sauced,* and you start prancing off in you're mind with all these imaginings and things. I bet you would pass a lie detector; you believe all that crazy shit."

"Hey, lay off, you big bastard – how can't you tell?" Billy looked down and rubbed his hands on his belly, "How can't you see this giant gut, man?"

"I think it's time to lay off. Think about catching some sleep?" Keith suggested.

"I can't believe you can't see it, man." Billy thought he said it clearly, but mumbling, incoherent slurring came out. Keith shook his head and threw the dirty rag into the sink behind him.

"I got to piss; I'll be back," Keith exclaimed. He walked to the end of the bar and proceeded to the bathroom.

Billy sat on the dark, stained wooden barrel, looking down at his stomach. He rubbed its surface and saw his shirt's bottom seam lay just under his chest, exposing a rounded and hairy gut. He looked with his eyes opened broadly, his brows arched.

He could see the thick, blues veins popping out, almost ripping through the skin. The slivers of dried blood and his black knuckles, swollen and littered with coagulated blood, looked like a fat man's hands. His fingers were plump like sausages, and little dimples took the place of where his knuckles were before. His hand throbbed as his palm clutched at his belly. His other hand met his obese fingers and looked like a starvation victim's hand in comparison.

"God, what the hell....."

His head swayed to the side, and his eyelids felt like they sagged. He waited for Keith to come out of the bathroom for a few moments, then couldn't help it any longer and rested his eyes. He had nothing to do anyway. A little rest was in order. It had been a long day. His forehead propped on the brass railing as his vision, blurred and hazy as it was, faded - then finally - went black.

"It's not the same, Bill. You sit there on the couch all day and drink. We walk by, and it's like we're invisible!" She barked. Her arms were folded loosely like she was cradling an invisible baby.

"I'm here, aren't I? What else do you want? I could walk out of here anytime, and the kids would be fatherless." Bill shouted. "I'd have peace of mind then,"

"Please don't say that."

"It's what I mean to say,"

"You don't mean it, Bill. Please, you don't mean it."

"Shut up!" He shouted again. The poignant sharpness of his words struck her like an arrow in the chest, making her forget to breathe when he shouted. It was the determination in his tone, the pronunciation of every letter, every word, every syllable, and she had learned this from prior arguments – how shrill and mean he could be.

"I should have the right to express myself. I want to be happy." She said sullenly.

"Shut up, I said." Bill straddled off the couch, and she stepped back, anticipating something worse than his words. They both looked toward the hallway as the bedroom door gently clicked in place.

"You're scaring the kids,' Bill. You're scaring *me*."

"I'm not the man you wanted, eh? Not a real man, right?" He walked toward her clenching his fist.

"I didn't say those things, Bill. I'm just saying...."

"What are you saying? You better choose your words, bitch."

"We have no money, and the Hydro bill is three months back. It's hard to get groceries and..." Her hands trembled; she struggled to avoid the shame and humiliation of raising her hands in defence, to protect her face from any sudden blow.

He smacked her square in the jaw with a backhanded slap. Her eyes shut tightly, and she fumbled to the floor. She covered her face with both hands and didn't think of what she thought of herself at that moment, the helplessness, the agonizing anticipation of more pain that would undoubtedly come her way. She only focused on protecting herself from the bruising and welts on her tender skin. Then the ideas of excuses she would say to her little girl when she asked what had happened to her face. Bill grabbed the hand that covered her face and pulled it away, slapping her again with an emanating clap that bounced off the walls.

"Not a real man, eh?" With a clenched fist, he pounded her on the top of her skull, working for every opening to get a clean shot. She desperately kicked her feet to keep him away from her. She flailed her hands, and one of her nails caught Bill on the side of his neck, leaving a deep prick where a droplet of blood started to pool.

Bill heard the pounding on the wall from the kids in the other room. It made him stop suddenly and stand up straight. He towered over her as she cowered on the floor weeping, her arms wrapped around her head to protect her skull.

He took significant strides down the hallway and opened the bedroom door. Trevor was 9, and Martha, the youngest – 4 years old, held each other in a tight bear hug on the bed. Martha's head was buried in Trevor's chest, and Bill saw the wet marks on his son's shirt collar from her tears. He stood in the doorway and watched them. His anger had disappeared and been replaced with sudden regret. His jaws clenched tightly as his eyes swelled up with tears.

Seeing his son's eyes as he held his little sister depressed Bill in a way he hadn't felt since his father had died in a drunk driving accident. There was a sudden blankness in Trevor's stare. The lights were on the inside, but the house was empty. It was a familiar look, a blank gaze, yet deep behind his bright blue eyes; the boy showed disdain and resentment toward his father, much like Bill resented *his* father for dying, not being there when he needed him most.

"Help me, Daddy," his four-year-old daughter said.

"What?"

"Help me, Daddy, it hurts. It really, really hurts," she repeated.

Trevor puckered his lips then his mouth started to gape open slowly. He held Martha tightly and moaned desperately as Bill stood frozen, watching his son's mouth open more prominent like a boa constrictor engulfing its prey. Bill couldn't believe the extent of the opening and watched as it grew bigger still. Sharp teeth started sliding out smoothly from the boy's gums, Trevor's jaw detached at the joints, and Bill felt the piss drain down his leg from the sudden popping and splintering sounds of his boy's jaw bones cracking. Finally, the skin on the sides of his mouth tore, and his mouth split open at both cheeks having the top half of his head fall back on itself. Martha looked up at Bill. Her eyes and mouth were sewn shut with butcher's twine. Each incision point was swollen and infected. She smiled at her father; the stitches ripped from her lips and left them torn and tattered, revealing the severed stump where the tip of her tongue *used* to be.

Bill screamed, and the walls of the bedroom shook. Plaster drywall dust fell all around him, and a giant crack appeared in the ceiling. He closed his eyes and palmed his ears. His sensations were overbearing. He heard the screaming and moaning from his wife and children ringing in his ears. His forehead stung like someone whisked his brain into scrambled eggs.

"No. No. No," he screamed in agony.

"Hey, wake up," Keith shook Billy while standing behind him.

Billy raised his head, leaving a red mark on his pale forehead. His mouth hung open like a drooling idiot as he looked around the bar, suddenly remembering that he was at the *Loretto*. The chairs were upside down on the tables. Keith had shut her down for the night.

"You have been out for an hour, bud. You got to go. Unless..." Keith continued. "Your pretty plastered."

McGraw's voice incessantly reminded Keith that he was waiting for him at the trail's end. Reminding him that he had better not *slip up*. This time the Sheriff probably wouldn't let him off with a warning.

"I think you should crash here. I've got a cot upstairs if you want... promise not to touch the booze while I'm gone, and we're good. You touch my booze; we have a problem."

"Okay," Bill mumbled.

Billy drooled, his eyelids drooped, nearly shutting, and he slurred his speech incoherently. The booze had hit him hard while he slept. He was drunker now than he ever was for the night.

"Good. Do you need help getting upstairs?" Keith asked,

"No."

"Fine. Blankets should be on the cot."

"Okay."

"All right, then." Keith shrugged and walked toward the large barn doors, switching off the overhead lights.

"You know where to go, buddy. Get some sleep," he said as he walked out the door.

The lock clicked, leaving Billy alone in the relative dark; the Edison bulbs hanging from the bar emitted a dull yellow light. Billy squinted and stumbled to his feet.

Keith walked down the rocky path and made it to the Volkswagen Bug, where Sheriff Alan McGraw had parked his cruiser directly behind it in the underbrush of long pine branches and overgrown ferns.

The lights were off on the cruiser, and Keith could make out the large, brimmed hat McGraw wore on his head through the darkness. Keith slowly crept up to the driver's side door and saw the window was rolled down, and "Big Al" was passed out, snoring loudly. As he promised, he had been parked there, waiting for Keith.

Keith stopped to glance inside the cruiser and thought of killing Alan McGraw. He thought picking up a sharp tree branch and sticking it in Big Al's neck would be easy. He would struggle but eventually bleed out, and being out in the woods was an advantage, being so isolated – nobody would hear him struggling or choking on his blood. Keith thought of taking the cruiser with McGraw's body in the trunk up to his property, where he could use the woodchipper to get rid of his remains, then gut the insides of the cruiser, then crushing it at Dustin Gimli's wreckers. Gimli wouldn't ask questions. He would probably help dispose of the Sheriff's corpse if Keith only asked politely. A case of *Pabst* would help, but it didn't take much convincing for "Crazy Old" Dustin Gimli. He also owed Keith for all the nights he ran up a tab and never showed up to pay it. Times Keith shrugged off Dustin's racist tirades and looked the other way when he would tell off-putting stories of his adventures in Thailand with boy-girl prostitutes that sounded too young to be appropriate.

Keith stood at the side of the car, looking in, contemplating if this would be the right call. He looked up the dark path where he came from and pictured Billy stumbling to the cot upstairs and passing out. He wouldn't be a problem after all. Keith could bet money on Bill, not remembering even coming to the bar that night. If anything came out about the missing Sheriff - maybe – Bill would be the perfect suspect.

Keith shook his head and silently walked away from the car, trying not to wake McGraw. He stepped over dark mud puddles and stayed to the side of the path, where treading on the long ferns provided a quieter cushioning to his steps rather than the grinding pebbles of the path.

He walked away, regretting McGraw's childish threats, pondering why this guy had been such a bully in High School and grown into a heathen as he got older. He slowed his steps and looked back up the path again.

Probably not a good idea to leave Billy there. He thought. *That fucking pig might wake up and stroll back in there. I locked the door anyway.* He stood in place momentarily.

Ah, screw it.

He turned and continued down the path. With thunderous waves of emotions rushing through him, he began to imagine the warmth of a hot shower and the foaming bubbles of the body wash on his skin, which helped Keith forget about the Sheriff. The thought had him unconsciously walking faster without realizing it, rushing to get home. The intentions of murder and abandonment soon disappeared.

"Take it out, Daddy, please, cut it out!" Little Martha's voice echoed in Billy Martel's head. It grew louder as he took every sluggish step.

"It *really* hurts." He imagined poor Martha's innocent face desecrated. He thought of the pain she endured. She must have screamed as they inserted the long needle, punching through the smooth baby skin that 4-year-olds still had. He imagined her trying to open her eyelids and tearing the stitches open.

He vomited brown-pinkish bile from his stomach and laboured with every exhausted, huffing breath. He looked down to the floor and saw three pools of vomit at his feet, each pile overlapping until they formed one giant puddle.

He gripped the brass rail, hoping to keep himself steady, and swayed on his toes, then fell over like a giant, rotted pine in the forest. The weight of his stomach forced him to topple forward, where he landed on his knees. The dust from the planks misted Billy's face as it flew in the air from the thudding impact of Billy's sudden overbearing body weight.

His palms were covered in vomit, and worst of all, he felt his belly dragging along the planks and collecting sawdust on his stomach hairs as he crawled around the bar, finally reaching the bar fridge.

He clutched at the top edge and pulled himself to his feet. He was off-balance and nearly toppled backward from the giant cannonball-sized weight in his stomach. He was facing the mirror and gasped at his reflection. His gut was large and rounded, like a 9-month pregnant woman with twins. Dark blue veins pulsated on the surface, and stretch marks – long, thin, and purple - extended from his sides and wrapped around his ample belly in different directions like a road map.

Something inside his stomach kicked. Fist-sized Lumps throbbed outwards, then inwards, like something was inside him, fighting to get out. Billy Martel screamed agonizingly and dug his fingertips into his skin. His stomach was stiff and ridged. The pain was unbearable, and the rumbling sound was loud, like a distant thunderstorm emanating from his bowls. He groaned from the grinding inside his belly, the *thing* tearing at his insides, his organs gripped tightly by invisible hands, then pulled apart. He felt the sting of its sharp fingernails digging into his liver. Whatever the hell *it* was.

It had been born of his gluttony. His irresistible urge to devour any drink before him impregnated him with the evil fetus trying to claw its way out. He nurtured it by feeding the seed its nectar, nourishing it until it got too big, too much to handle, then the inevitable would happen.

Billy Marten ran through the realization in his mind and began to panic. He furiously clawed at his skin, leaving red scratch marks running parallel to the purple stretch lines that had suddenly appeared. He groaned agonizingly, Reaching for the half-empty beer bottle on the countertop. Billy paused, and the pain seemed to cease for a moment. His swollen hand clutched the bottle, trembling. He raised the bottle to his lips. The cold rim was like an ice cube as it touched the skin of his lips. He guzzled the last of the beer.

"That's not what I said, Bill. You're scaring me." He heard her voice say,

With the bottom of the bottle pointed in the air, he sucked at the tip, his lips turning white until the bottle was empty. He belched in a relieving satisfaction as he felt the tiny bubbles prickling down the back of his throat.

His back slumped against the cold door of the bar fridge. He could not see his thighs above the knees as his large gut grew bigger before his eyes. It seemed to inflate like a balloon, unknowing when the skin would tear, and his stomach would burst open. Billy slid to the floor, his back against the fridge's glass door, and he felt a relaxed tingle in his legs as if he had planted himself on the couch comfortably after a long day of being on his feet.

He wept uncontrollably at the shame of being unable to resist the alcohol, beating his wife, letting his children down, and, more so – the aching pain of the thing inside him that caused a nauseous sensation when it wasn't tearing at his insides. His swollen hand clasped over his eyes; he held the bottle with his other hand, the glass shards sticking out of the broken end. The shattered, dark amber glass lay around him. He continued covering his eyes.

"I regret meeting you! Marrying you! Barry is still single; he'll make a good woman out of me and treat me well! Not like you, Billy! He will touch me how I want. He will squeeze me and kiss me, touch me there and have me moaning! Not like you! You Bastard! I hate you!"

"Please…s-stop," he mumbled aloud.

"I regret meeting you!"

"I still love you!" he said, sobbing loudly.

"Why should I stay with you? Why should I let you keep the kids? I could take them from you and run away with him!"

Billy Martel knew he was the laughingstock of the town. People gossiped about him, knew his business, and made fun of him. The drinking had taken his car and his license. His dignity. His respect. It had taken his confidence and his resolution to raise his kids properly, keep a job, or make love to his beautiful wife. It had taken away the eagerness and excitement of coming home to see his kids playing in the living room on the Persian rug he pawned his *.22 Ruger American* rifle for. The drinking had taken it all and left a shell of a man.

"Everybody knows you have that breathalyzer in your car, bud. It's not exactly a secret."

"Is it against the law to serve booze at a bar, Sheriff?"

"It is when it's Billy goddamn Martel."

"I hate your face and your goddamn drinking! I regret meeting you and marrying you, bastard!"

He smashed the bottle on the edge of the countertop, leaving the mouth-end gripped in his hand with protruding points that glimmered in the light.

"I regret marrying you, bastard!"

Her bitter remorse, her hatred of the man she grew to un-love, was the last straw.

He plunged the bottle into his ample gut, and blood sprayed upwards; the falling droplets of blood landed on the cherry-stained countertop like a rainstorm. He screamed and bit down on his swollen hand. His eyes were tightly shut as the blood sprayed on his face. He furiously twisted and jabbed the bottle into his gut ferociously, pulling away chunks of flesh with every stab. He continued thrusting the broken bottle into his belly like a madman possessed, the blood spurting in multiple directions, coating the floor and pooling around him while he gutted himself on the barroom floor.

Billy's mind was dazed, and his thoughts tangled like shoelaces tied with knots. He pictured tossing his children onto the foam mattress, their wonderous giggles when they landed on the soft cushion. He saw his Mother's face, his angel. She smiled at him. He envisioned his father's grip shaking his hand like a man for the first time, the pride in his eyes on the day he married Peggy. He saw Keith's boyish face flash before him, a snapshot of the past, the day he met Keith in sixth-grade Geography class. Keith offered him a spare pencil, kept company with him on the playground, and defended him from bullies like "Big Al" McGraw.

He thought of her lastly. Her white teeth and her little dimples on her cheeks when she smiled at him. He imagined spinning her in the air and kissing her passionately when they made love. Her soft hands, supple breasts, the guilty smile when she used his credit card to buy makeup and doll herself up for him. Her soft voice whispered,

"I love you. Forever."

He whispered back,

"I'm... sorry...."

He dropped the bloody bottle to his side. His gut was deflated. The stretch marks and veins had disappeared and been replaced with a hole in his stomach so profound - his intestines began slopping out and slowly piling up at his side. His heart rate slowed. He could feel his pulse grow faint as the seconds ticked away. Billy's body trembled and shook uncontrollably, the blood pooling around him, being absorbed into the grains of sawdust on the wooden planks. His last thought, as his vision finally faded into pitch darkness, was what he said to the bartender when he teased him about vomiting on the floor,

"Keith, buddy, the sawdust will soak it all up."

4

SHOW ME THE WAY

Jackson Ferreira pulled into the empty parking space near the back of the lot. He turned the engine off and excitedly dug his back into the seat in anticipation. People walked by his car on the way to the front double-sided metal doors that led to the concert hall.

Jackson reached the glove compartment and pulled out an enclosed metal tray that housed his joints and his last few Pall Malls. He lit the joint and blew smoke around him, rolling down the window on his 96 Mazda Protégé to let out the billowing plume. Being enveloped by the thick fog gave him thoughts of what the Jewish population of World War Two Europe had suffered in gas chambers and what must have gone through their heads.

He thought of the suffocating feeling, the desperate clawing at the walls, begging, with every gasping breath. The realization that they were caught in a trap, having been fooled into thinking they were safe. The gnawing ache in their soul when they figured out nobody was coming to help them. That this was the plan all along. He thought how frightening it must have been for those people to lose every breath and know this was their time. Jackson couldn't explain it, but the thoughts of dying people in global atrocities aroused him, ignoring the shame he should have had of it long ago. Jackson shook himself out of the thought, realizing that he would much rather be shrouded in marijuana smoke than Zyklon B.

The can of Coors light was still half full and had lived in the cup holder of the Mazda for the past hour. It was still cold; the frost outside the aluminum can had turned to water droplets.

"Never liked it when you drove drunk, Jack," she said.

"I'm not drunk." He took another pull from the spliff. "Not yet, anyway."

"Please don't get wasted, Jack – we have to get home tonight. Do you want to leave the car again and come back to get it when you're hungover?" She asked, "We both know you're too lazy for all that work,"

"I'll be a good boy, Riley. Stop nagging me. We're here; we're ready to rock and roll." Jack held out a fist like an 80's hair metal band vocalist striking a pose for the latest cover of Rolling Stone. No matter how cliché it was, he didn't care – and embraced the silly action whenever he could. Riley giggled. Jackson always made her laugh; that was his saving grace.

"You could be a goofball; you know that?" She said.

Jackson turned the knob on the radio. Bruce Springsteen and the E St. Band were playing, and he began to bob his head to the drumbeat in a meagre effort to get himself excited for the show.

"This band's going to be killer. I saw them last week in Hamilton – and dude – they kicked ass. I thought the amps would blow their speakers; it was so loud." Riley watched people as they walked to the venue nearby. He continued, "The mosh was sick. I got in, and this chick – like your size – was pushing me around. She was strong, dude, real strong."

"That's cool." Riley said, "You think they will mosh tonight?"

"I hope so – if they do – I'm so in," he said. "I'm not sure if this place will allow it, though. I don't see Security, so maybe."

"I don't see Security either, now that you mention it."

"Yeah – usually there are three guys at the front, two guys in the back, and maybe a couple more inside – probably around 6 or 8 guys," he said, "I scoped it out already. I drove by and stopped for a smoke before I picked you up. Nobody pulled into the club except an old guy and a few waitresses."

"Why?"

"Why what?"

"Why did you scope this place out?"

"Ah, shit." He chuckled. "My bad – I get so into this band. I get too excited sometimes and can't wait for the show to start. I get into this shit."

"Well, it's still early. Let me hit that?" Riley reached for the joint, and Jack pulled it away.

"Get your own." He said jokingly.

"Fuck you, let me hit it."

"Get your own I said."

"Fuck you, Jackson. I don't know why I came out with you – you're such an asshole." Riley sat back in her seat with her arms folded, scolding him with a menacing gaze of hatred and disdain.

"All right, all right." He said. He propped open the lid of the metal case and gave her a newly rolled joint.

"There, you happy?" He asked. She sat with her arms folded and ignored him momentarily to show her defiance, a reason to get back at him later – when he undoubtedly would try to have sex with her.

"Come on, take it. I was just fooling around," he said.

"You see that guy?" she said. Her eyes were no longer furrowed but relaxed as she stared through the windshield at the man who stood at the trunk of a black Cadillac, no more than forty meters away.

"What guy? Why? Who cares?" Jackson said,

"He doesn't look odd to you?"

"We're at a metal concert, Riley,"

"No. just look at him." She insisted.

Jackson took a drag from his spliff, flicked the butt out of the window, and then looked at the man standing behind the black Cadillac. He was tall and slim. He wore a black baseball cap, t—shirt and cargo pants.

"Why is he dressed in all black?" Riley asked,

"Very militant looking," Jack said.

"You don't think?" She finally asked him after a moment of silence.

"C'mon, Riley. That's crazy." He said. He turned down the volume on the radio for no apparent reason at all. They both stared at the man. He smoked a cigarette and looked like he was talking to himself.

"He probably has an earpiece in," Jackson said.

"I don't like the thought of that, Jack. I'm not getting a good vibe." Riley said.

"Oh, chill out – smoke the joint."

"Jack, who dresses like that?"

"We're dressed in all black too, Riley; what the fuck?"

"It's not the same. Our clothes may be black, but it's not like we are trying to hide in the darkness. We have images on our shirts, chains, and our bracelets twinkle – he looks like he's trying to – blend in. Isn't that odd to you, Jack?"

Jackson looked at what he was wearing and thought of Riley's words. He wore an oversized black shirt with *Satan's Angel* written in dripping blood. The cartoon on the front of his shirt depicted a mound of corpses in the background of trees of impaled bodies, which was particularly disturbing. The black, faded, ripped-up jeans that adorned his skinny frame had holes and tears that showed dough-coloured skin underneath. Although he was dressed in dark clothing, the shirt had multiple colours of Reds and Yellows – far from an outfit meant to blend into the darkness.

"Let's stay here a while; then, will you chill out?" Jackson asked.

"Yeah. That would be okay."

"All right." He reached for a cigarette and lit it. "let's hang out until the first band goes up – then we can roll inside." He suggested.

"Yeah, sure." Riley couldn't take her eyes off the man in black.

He looked vaguely familiar, but she couldn't pinpoint where she had seen those eyes before. The deep amber of his eyes mesmerized her – even forty meters away. Perhaps he had kind eyes, she thought. Maybe – he was some romantic idea of a sexy vampire that hypnotized her from so far away to pull her in as his new bride, clutching her tightly and sensually sucking at her neck, like in all the vampire novels she read as a teenager. She felt the heat shoot down into her gut, warmer than grandma's apple pie, fresh out of the oven at the thought. She hadn't felt it with Jackson, not for a long time anyway—a feeling of Horny ambivalence yet mingled with a sense of fear that surprisingly turned her on.

They watched as the man in the black cap reached for the hatch and opened it. People walked past him and didn't pay him any mind, but Jackson and Riley watched him like private investigators on a stakeout.

"You see what's in the back?" Jackson asked.

"No. It's too hard to see." She said, "The streetlamp is too far away; it's too dark."

"Now you got me thinking.", he replied.

"What?" She cocked her head towards him. Her brow was arched, and she looked like she would shrug her shoulders but didn't. "Thinking what?"

"I got my piece in the back. I keep it in the car for times like this."

"What, are you crazy? You're supposed to keep it at home." She said with words that seemed to sting her lips as they left her mouth. "Do you have any idea what would happen if the cops found your gun in the trunk?" She knew the answer to her own question, yet she felt she had to say it aloud to clarify it once and for all.

"Be quiet - don't blow it, or I'll find out the hard way." He said, "What the fuck, Riley?"

Riley went back to folding her arms and seemed more furious than before. Jackson could see the smoke rising from her ears like in the cartoons. After a moment of stewing in hatred for Jackson, she finally spoke,

"What do you mean times like these?"

"Just in case, you know?" he said.

They both averted their glance to the man again and saw him reach into what looked like a duffle bag. He held out a pistol, slid a magazine into the gun, and tucked it in his waistline.

"Are you kidding?" Riley gasped. Jackson had his fingers on the trunk latch with eager anticipation.

The man reached in again, loaded another pistol, and slid it into a concealed holster at the other hip. He looked from side to side, shoving numerous rounds into his pockets. He then slammed the hatch shut and walked quickly toward the door with a crowd of teenage metalheads who didn't notice him sneak into the back of their group.

Riley looked over to Jack with wide-eyed surprise. She had no words, nor did he, as they stared blankly into each other's faces. Jackson pulled the latch, and they both heard the popping sound of the trunk opening. Riley's jaw hung, and she gripped Jackson's sleeve, but he had already pulled away and exited the car.

"Jack, no. Stop. Please, Jack." She screamed. The car door slammed shut, and her cries turned hollow and muffled. Jack opened the trunk lid and shoved the tire iron and a mound of dirty clothes to the side. The large black duffle bag lay in the trunk, sagged at the edges and lumpy in spots. As Jack unzipped the bag, he thought of the weekends he spent on the range training for times like this.

He had been trained at the club for holster shooting and recoil management at ten, twenty- and twenty-five yards, leaving him reasonably proficient with handguns, earning him many merit badges from the club that he proudly pinned on the wall of his bedroom.

He went over the sights of his gun and reminded himself of the instructor at the firing line that imbedded the fundamentals of marksmanship like; lining up both front and rear sights, focusing on his stance, and always looking out for cover to hide behind. He knew there would be panic, and people would scurry if any shots let off. It wasn't the stress of panic and stampeding people that worried him. After so many hours in front of the latest modern warfare video games he spent much of his free time on, he was used to the fast-paced environment he would soon find himself in. He planned for it in his head. He had been through so many trial runs online. He saw the fright on the faces of innocent bystanders as they clutched at his clothing, trying to get past him, the terror in their eyes as they pushed and shoved harder than the punk rockers in the mosh pits he so looked forward to. The more he anticipated the chaos, the harder the blood pumped in his veins until he couldn't help himself, overcome with anxiety for the action he craved so badly. He took a deep breath and tried to calm the sudden rush of eagerness that pummeled him like river rapids in a spring run-off.

Then, there was Riley. Poor, innocent Riley. The one who had been his guilty conscience and had pulled him back from being swept under those currants so many times. He wanted to listen to her. Watching her inside the car struggling to pull the door handle open to confront him and hopefully change his mind. He owed her so much in recent months; she had saved him from so much trouble. He felt obligated to hear her out – but – hear her out only, not necessarily act on her advice.

He unzipped the bag and saw the 9mm pistol sitting on top of pencil cases full of bullets and loaded magazines. He had bought the gun second-hand off Scotty Beckham at the East Aylmer Sportsman's Club. Scotty had explained to Jackson that he had pushed his old lady around a bit too much, and the neighbours overheard the screaming and clashing of pots and pans and called the cops. The police scheduled a meeting to "take his guns away for safety and precautionary reasons temporarily," they told him. Scotty decided to sell as many firearms as possible to make back the money he spent on ammo before the police came to cease his guns. Scotty knew better – he knew that once he was on the *dangerous person* list, he would never see his prized armament again.

"I'll give it to you for $1200."

"That's too much, Scott; I can't afford that," Jackson responded,

"All right, $900 then?"

"$850?"

"C'mon, dude. Nine hundred bucks," Scott pleaded.

"$850, Bro. Even that's too much for me to spend," Jackson had explained. "It's either 850, or I go to Walmart for their twenty percent off, bro. I Can get the same one for a better price. And legit too!"

The magazines in the duffle bag were already loaded. Jackson didn't remember loading them ahead of time and couldn't even remember stocking up ammo, but the rounds were there, and he didn't think too hard about it as he slid the magazine into the pistol. He took another magazine and shoved it in his jacket pocket, emptied the box of 9mm rounds to the floor of the trunk and grasped handfuls of the bullets, tucking them into his jeans pockets. His tight jeans lumped at the sides, and the odd clacking of brass rattling in his pocket made him nervous that he would be caught by Security trying to smuggle live rounds into the concert hall.

Riley's head popped out of the passenger door. A cloud of smoke escaped around her and hung in the air.

"Jack, get back in the car; let's go home. We can call the cops."

"Get back in the car Riley."

"Jack, c'mon, let's go," she screamed.

"Get in the fucking car, Riley!" He screamed back at her.

She swung the door open and stormed from the passenger seat, slamming the door so hard Jack thought he heard something metal snap. She approached Jack and swung an open palm to his face, only to watch it glide through his skull. Beguiled, she tried again, and the same thing happened. It was like he was a hologram, and what she saw as a physical human, conscience, present, tangible, resembled a fog when her hand swept through. He didn't feel a thing. Only a brisk cold gust that swept his hair gently,

"Your dead, Riley. Remember?" He said to her.

"Now get back in the car and shut up."

He knew that the kitchen door was at the side of the building and was most likely unguarded. He had observed the cooks on their smoke breaks, pacing back and forth eagerly sucking back on their cigarettes, anticipating getting back inside as orders were still coming in quickly. He saw the two large metal dumpsters across from the door and thought it was an excellent place to take cover if the man in the black hat had the same uncontrollable eagerness as he did and decided to start shooting before he got in the building.

Jackson had lost track of the mysterious man since he had loaded his pistol and made his way for the entrance to the venue; its large bright sign shined a blinding neon green light that illuminated the front entrance. The sign read, "Cowboy Canyon Steakhouse and Bar." The night's headlining show was a far stretch from the club that promoted itself as a country western tavern playing Waylen Jennings on their outdoor patio speakers as fat older men in cowboy hats smoked cigars and sipped on Miller Light.

The kids at the front entrance with their multi-coloured hair and wardrobes of black leather gathered at the doorway like a line of ants patiently waiting to get in their mounds. Jackson walked briskly towards the venue, and as he reached closer, he saw the two large Security guards patting down people at the door. He followed the outer perimeter of the parking lot and figured avoiding them would be the best and the only available option for getting inside.

The horizon was a dark frontier of black since the sun had disappeared over the hillside. The trees around the venue stood tall but were dark shadows and outlines of extended branches stretching out into the sky with withering twigs. The grass had a mist of dew from the fog earlier in the afternoon; Jackson saw the splashes from his footsteps sprinkle around his ankles, which worried him. He wished it was foggy like it usually had been in the valley to conceal his movements.

Jackson stooped behind a black F150 pickup truck and looked towards the side kitchen door. He saw the cleanly mowed grass mound behind the building shimmer from the wetness and began to shudder with excitement that nobody was smoking at the side door. This was his opportunity. He thought of himself as the anti-hero dressed in black, clutching a black semi-auto like the heroes in the movies or the video games he played daily. It was all working out so perfectly for him, he thought.

"This is a bad idea, Jacks." Riley's voice whispered. She stooped behind Jackson's shoulder; he could smell her perfume and saw her long blond locks hanging gracefully from her shoulders.

"I told you to stay in the car."

"No. I want to see."

"You're not so scared anymore?"

"Of course I am, but I'd rather help you through it instead of watching you fuck it all up."

"Always backing me up, huh, girl?"

"You make me do crazy things, Jacks. I don't know why I go along with it." She said with a slight curl in the corner of her lips.

"What have you got to lose?"

"Asshole," she responded. Her smile disappeared. Jackson closed his eyes tightly and then opened them again.

Riley stood outside the kitchen door, waving for him to come over while holding the door slightly open. A shiver of fluorescent light beamed out of the slit. Jackson looked around at the Security guards and saw they were busy with the lineup of fans awaiting their turns to walk through the metal detectors and have their handbags searched. He made his way to the door, and upon reaching it, he slid in gracefully, closing the heavy metal door gently behind him.

Jackson quickly made his way through the kitchen. He heard a voice from the dishwashing station yell something out, but Jackson was too distracted on making his way to the main hall, that he couldn't make out the words. The cooks were busy tossing onions and garlic, flipping rib eyes on the sizzling grill to notice anyone – especially him – being where they shouldn't be. The servers saw Jackson slip through the double swinging doors into the main hall and chalked it up to someone sneaking in and getting a free show. God knows the twenty-year-old servers have done the same thing at one time or another.

Jackson reached the main hall and was struck with a sense of enthusiastic reminiscence of walking through Dodgers stadium and reaching the end of the long concrete corridor only to gaze at the enormity of the baseball field that was outstretched before him. It was like walking into another dimension, another world. The smell of beer and bleached floors had turned him on, the glazed and polished parkette floors shined, and the stage stood tall and littered with roadies setting up the amps and lighting platforms.

Jackson looked around for the man in the black cap. He didn't see him. He wondered through the sea of gothic teenagers with hair that was dyed pitch black or, to the other extreme, bright pink. Not many people wore hats – that's what Jackson noticed. He figured it would have the man stand out more to him and should have been easier to spot him. He thought of what he would do if he were in the shooter's position. He looked to the bar and saw Riley perched up high on a bar stool glancing at him. She winked at him, and he made his way to her.

"You couldn't spot him, could you?" she asked, then cocked her head back and swallowed a shot of whisky.

"No. Not yet." He looked around,

"Figures." Riley shrugged,

"What does that mean?"

"Nothing. Never mind. Buy me a drink, handsome?" she asked.

She had been smiling more now. She was his secret operative in the field – the one to lead him to the target, provide all the good intel, and the right moment to strike. She had led him through the kitchen door anyway. The side door didn't have a knob on the outside and automatically locked when it shut closed. He pondered how she could have gotten it open. Was it propped open already from the cooks smoking? Had she gone inside – like the spy-thriller phantom she was – and unlocked the door for him?

"I guess we will never know," she said.

"Stop that."

"What?"

"You know what."

"Oh, come on, Jack," she teased,

"Stop getting in my head."

"Why not? You took my body. In more ways than one."

"I said I was sorry – it was an accident."

"Some accident."

"You shouldn't have been standing there. We had a plan. You knew where to be."

"Don't give me that shit, Jacks." She barked, "Shit got wild – people scurrying everywhere. I made mistakes all right, still – "

"Still what?"

"You should have looked – should have seen me."

"I'm sorry, Riley. I don't know how many more times I should say it."

"Never mind. People are clamouring in. If you're going to do this thing, you better hold off a minute." She said,

"No, it makes it harder to find him. I need to spot him now." He said. The bartender finally locked eyes with Jackson.

"What are you drinking, fella?"

"Coors light," Jackson responded,

"Yup, coming up." The barman said. He walked down the counter towards the beer fridge and pulled out a bottle from the refrigerator's top shelf.

Kenny Steward was 45 years old and had later been a witness to the police and detectives investigating the night's events. He was slightly overweight. His body resembled a stocky square shape with a brimming bald spot shooting through curls of gingered-coloured hair. His eyes were beady and dark-coloured, and although they hid secretively behind his glasses' large lenses, those eyes would be the most accurate description of the evil things that happened that night.

Kenny's Steward placed a coaster on the sticky counter and the cold bottle on top. Immediately, Jackson reached for it and unabashedly gulped large mouthfuls of the sudds.

Kenny didn't look up to Jackson when he said,

"$4.50, pal."

He was too busy mixing another drink for the girl with lip piercings at the end of the bar to notice what he was wearing. Later, he had explained to the detectives that he wished he had a better look at the guy that ordered the Coors light. He wished he had taken a moment to notice then, what the guy was wearing, what he looked like, the colour of his eyes, the slender frame of his figure.

"Any idea at all? Anything that strikes you? It will help when you testify, and it's better to be accurate while giving a statement while it's still fresh." The detective would say.

"Shit, I'm not sure." Kenny would say, "I think a black baseball cap?"

※———※

"Maybe you should call the cops? Hello, earth to Jack?" Riley said.

"What are those pigs going to do anyway? They don't do shit other than take notes and get you in trouble. When have cops *actually* stopped these guys? When have they never been too late?"

"Then let's call them and avoid that, Jack." She pleaded, "Put the gun back in the trunk, and we can call them from the car. You could tell them what we saw and what he looked like."

"No. I'm trained."

"No, you're not."

"There's a lot you don't know."

"Stop it! This isn't a game. Stop involving yourself, or the same thing will happen again."

"Don't fucking say it," Jack shouted. The patrons beside him heard his outburst and hovered away from the counter; Kenny, the bartender, arched his eyes suspiciously at Jackson until he heard some guy shout from the end of the bar for a *Michelob Ultra*.

"I've got to wait and see."

"Jack, this is crazy."

"I'm going to check the men's room. If it were me – I would probably think of hiding out in there, and waiting until the time is right. I need you to stay here – or not – up to you."

"No."

"If I see him – then maybe I'll call the cops, okay?" he sat quietly for a moment, watching Kenny serve teenagers that have already been pre-drinking earlier in the night and started to get obnoxious with him.

"I'm not sure I want to go through with this either. I know it's scary." He said.

She looked at him like a hesitant spouse looks at their partner when hubby tries to bribe his wife with jewelry. He had nothing of value to offer her – only the peace of mind of leaving that place in one piece, hopefully without incident. There was a reason for the bribery, and Riley knew that Jackson had been unstable since the accident. He had been regretful, although never expressing it to her, Jackson had made amends to himself rather quickly and vowed to train harder at the range, be there more often, and even dry-firing his empty pistol in his bedroom in his spare time. It was his way of showing regret for his mistake. She could at least appreciate that. Efforts to avoid another misfire or uncontrollable ricochet that would ultimately kill the people he loved the most was the sincerest action Jackson had ever taken with Riley. It was easy to gain Riley's trust. It didn't take more than a bouquet of roses or tickets to a rock and roll show to make her forget the awful way he treated her and what he did. She would succumb to his charm and reasoning the same way she always did when they fought. Even after smashing her head swollen with a glass ashtray, or the time he pressed her against the drywall and left a human-sized hole in the plaster. The scrapes on her back and sides wouldn't heal for weeks. She still had faint scars on her sides that she sometimes confused with stretch marks. Even then – she succumbed to him.

The room filled quickly. The first band made their way up and started to plug in their instruments. The crowd jeered at the sound of the line plugging into the amps, and Jackson felt the same electricity coursing through his veins.

Jackson peered through the crowd, keeping an eye out for Security. He spotted two more guards – big burly ones. One of them worked out frequently and most likely had his fair share of growth hormones and Testosterone injections, telling by the unusual amount of veins popping out from his forearms and the oversized biceps that looked close to tearing his sleeves.

The other was slightly skinnier, wore a black cowboy hat, and had a thick handlebar mustache that Jackson thought comical. Then again, being in this place with these people would be comical to any outsider. The same way country music fans would think him peculiar wearing a shirt that made footage of corpses in Bergen seem like it was rated PG-13.

Jackson made it to the bathroom corridor and became slightly distracted by the corkboard that hung in the dark, dimly lit hallway. One was a flyer for "Blood Guzzlers," a new punk/deathcore band out of Seattle. They had a show in August; the pamphlet was decorated black with skulls and a border of dripping blood. Another post was an article tacked in the middle of the board of a mass shooting at another nightclub earlier in the year. The headline read,

"Massacre at Mythos Nightclub. Suspect at large."

Jackson shrivelled at the curiosity of why that article was pinned up in a country bar anyway. Was it there to tease him? Remind him of fate that he couldn't change? A fate that he would be a part of – one way or another? He read the article further until he froze in astonishment.

"10 dead, 15 wounded."

That article was slightly overlapped by another flyer of up-and-coming Country music concerts like Loretta Williamson and the Memphis Blues band, with Shawn King as the guest appearance—another flyer advertising a restaurant pinned over the top of the last. Jackson wanted to read the place's name that advertised a half rack of ribs for ½ off until he was interrupted by a deep voice.

"You going in, bud?" The bearded man asked. The man dressed as a biker wore a black vest with sewn patches on the chest and a giant skull on the back that read *Black Label Society*.

"What?"

"The shitter, bud. You going in or what?" the giant man asked again.

"Oh shit, yeah. Sorry"

Jackson had been blocking the hallway, looking at the flyers and articles pinned on the corkboard. He opened the swinging door to the men's room and saw it was packed. A lineup of three men were waiting behind each urinal, and *Converse* sneakers and *Dock Marrten* boots occupied the pairs of feet in the four stalls.

He knew it was an unlikely place for the man in the black hat to hide. Jackson obviously couldn't swing open the stall doors to investigate if the killer was hiding there. Jackson gave up on the recon of the men's bathroom.

He turned quickly and went through the sea of bodies that seemed to rock back and forth, like ocean tides rolling in and back out again, pushing each other forcibly and shoulder-shoving like a giant sea with different currents and unrestrained violence. The music was loud, and the drumbeats coursed through his body with each thump.

Jackson made it back to the bar and saw that Riley had disappeared. He stood beside two men conversing with two different girls and found a spot to lean on the bar counter and observe the crowd. The first band played into their set, and Jackson was grateful they didn't have extensive lighting set up. Looking for the killer in the dark with different coloured strobe lights blinding him would prove near impossible, and his anxiety about his time running out made him flustered. Droplets gathered on his forehead, and he could feel the first bead of sweat run down his temple.

The crowd bounced up and down. Some people being flung to the counter (and laughing about it) brought a smile to Jackson's face. It was in the moment of seeing a teenage girl flying out of the crowd, her enlightened, shiny smile filled with exhilaration, a willing competitor in a masculine free for all of different shaped bodies and sizes, caught his attention.

She chose to be here, he thought. She was flung around like a little Annie doll, exalting in the joy that her favourite band hit all the night notes and banged the right drum.

The hysterical laughter coming from her lips in the seconds he noticed her reminded him of his own joyous intentions of coming to the show that night. He wanted to be flung around, arms in the air, tumbling to the floor while enjoying every bruising minute. Her smile, the white porcelain teeth that looked so clean they had to be implanted, made him second guess his hunt. He didn't want to ruin her good time. Her joy made him want to call it off.

Bloodlust was the next band up. The roadies worked their magic on stage as the theatre lights came on and showed the spectators on the floor, still chatting and swarming about while the next set got ready.

Jackson thought he saw the man in black standing behind the long side curtain on stage. He stuck his head out momentarily, almost like he was looking for Jackson himself. That was the impression that overcame Jack while he stood at the bar and straightened up at the sight of the man. Jackson moved along the bar to the side of the stage, where he stepped up and was stopped by another Security guard – one he hadn't seen yet – that was number 5 by his count.

"Whoa, can't come here, man." He said.

"I've got to get over there; you don't under- "

"Don't care." the man said, shaking his head with crossed arms. Jackson peered over the Security guard's glistening bald head and could spot the mysterious man at the other end of the stage.

"I said, beat it, asshole. I tried to be nice." The man shoved Jackson with one hand, and Jack flew back a few steps and nearly toppled over. He felt the pistol in his waistband shift and feared it would drop out and become exposed.

"Don't fucking touch me!" Jackson shouted to the man angrily. His brow sharpened, and his eyes turned to fire like he fed dry maple logs to the hottest furnace of hell.

"What was that? You want to get kicked out, pal?" the Security guard held a finger behind his ear. He was strong. The shove left a red imprint of rounded knuckles in Jackson's chest, and he could feel the slight ache the impact left behind.

"No. No problem," Jackson said.

"Good choice." The large man responded.

He turned around and returned the same route he came while looking in and around the crowd for a floating black hat.

He second-guessed calling it off for a minute. As Riley had said, he thought of just getting in his car and going home. It would be safer. He knew the outcome of leaving and felt a palpable relief at the thought that he would wake up in bed (probably slept in), take a shit and brush his teeth before possibly deciding to go to the range – the usual routine. It beat out waking up in jail because he chose to be a hero. If he left and played it safe, many people would die, but he would be alive, secure, and living his everyday life. He could also stay, see the mission through and become a hero. His face could be plastered on the news and hailed as a saviour. He could get thankful letters from survivors, telling him they owe him their lives and that they wouldn't be alive to see their kids anymore if it wasn't for him. Maybe, they could send some money his way. Jackson wasn't sure which option was the best decision.

Jackson made it to the middle of the parkette floor, which had cleared out somewhat from the smokers who stepped outside into the night, and the piss-filled teenagers lined up outside the washroom doors. The eager motivation had ceased for him. Perhaps, the man in the black hat was a figure of his imagination, as Riley had been. Or was he real? Was Riley *really* a phantom that haunted him? Was she real? He wasn't so sure anymore. The night started with the intention of getting shit-faced and exhausted from mosh-pitting all night – and turned to a search for a stranger Jackson wasn't sure even existed anymore.

Riley stood near the front doors. She had the same look on her face of sullen disappointment as the way girlfriends have when they stand at the door with their luggage about to leave you. The same look that said,

I've told you many times. There's no need to repeat it; I don't feel it anymore. This time you're going too far for me to come along.

Riley locked eyes with Jack as he stood in the middle of the main floor. People walked around him toward her, and she wanted to say, "Are you coming?" But her thin pink lips couldn't make the movement.

Jackson's chin quivered slightly as Riley turned and vanished through the doors. The pit of his stomach felt cavernous, like he felt at funerals when he stared into the open casket and realized this was the last time he would see them. Except for Riley. That's why it hurt so much – she had been with him through it all, even after death. The bile in his chest burned with acidity like drinking lemon juice when he saw her leave him behind and vanish into thin air. He felt the lonesome sorrow of being lost in a place he knew so well but felt the most strange.

Jackson unconsciously walked toward the front doors. He reached the front ticket booth near the main doors and felt a shove propelling him sideways. Jackson looked over and saw the mysterious gunman standing two feet away, staring at him with piercing amber eyes.

Jackson stared at the man, perplexed. The figure who stood before him was an identical twin of Jackson. Like he was looking in the mirror. The man reached for his holster (at the exact moment Jack did) and drew the muzzle of the tanned barrel toward Jackson – two gunshots cracked loudly, and the man in front of Jackson fell backward.

The people stood silent for a moment, which Jackson saw as strange. He anticipated everyone stampeding out the front doors at the sudden blast of the gun. They realized what had happened at the sight of the blood along with the body on the floor and finally rushed to the front door, nearly crushing each other in the bottleneck feed of the crowd.

Jackson swam against the current of hysterical people running towards him and made it to the front of the stage, where he slumped over and gasped. The adrenaline ran through his veins harder and with more heart-thumping and muscle-twitching excitement than any Metal band would offer.

He gathered himself and realized he still held the gun in his hand. He stood stuck in place at the sight of the Security guards surrounding him. They seemed to run out of the crowd, and the same Security guard who had stopped Jack from getting backstage barrelled toward him from Jackson's right shoulder. Jackson turned, looked down the sights, and shot two rounds into the man's face. He slid face-first to Jackson's feet. Jackson then fired at the other Security guards until the slide on his pistol locked back.

With every cracking gunshot, the crowd screamed louder, desperate to get out. Jackson saw them piling all over each other and gasped to see they were all dressed as the man in black, the gunman he had been hunting all night. Every person dawned a black baseball cap with black militant-style clothing.

Jackson pressed the release, and the magazine slid out smoothly, thudding on the hard floor. He reached into his pocket, loaded another mag, pressed the slide release, and nearly urinated at the sense of excitement with the gun's sound when the slide locked forward.

Jackson shot more rounds into the crowd. It wasn't the same as video games. The clothing on the people wore seemed to explode in tiny spots, and people's heads kicked back violently when they took a headshot. Soon there was a beginning of a pile of corpses stacked at the front door while others furiously climbed over and threw themselves through the exit to escape. Some people on the bottom clawed at the floor, trying to escape the mounting bodies falling on top of them and suffocating to death. Soon the blood began to pool around the base of the corpse mound.

The red and blue lights had reflected into the nightclub from the front doors. The lights flickered and strobed over the pile of corpses like they were part of some sick zombie dance party.

Jackson stood in the middle of the floor with dead Security personnel around him forcing bullets into his magazine in a panic. He knew the Swat team or *Tactical Force* as the Police Investigative Bureau calls it – would burst through and wouldn't ask questions; they would put him away. Strangely, amid the killing, Jackson didn't consider the consequences of the police killing him a dire emergency. He was more obsessed with killing as many of the shooters as he possibly could.

He slammed a fresh magazine into his gun, and at that moment, the two cans of tear gas came rolling into the club with smoke streams of white gas trailing behind. Then came two lines of tactical officers with body armour and assault rifles. Jackson looked through the plexiglass visors of their helmets and saw his own eyes – the amber-brown eyes that hypnotized. He recognized the mole on his cheek on each one of them – in the same spot he had on his cheek. He also saw that they all wore black baseball caps with the sloped brim forward – the same type he had on.

"Get down, get down!" was all Jackson could make out. He didn't. He saw the Swat team approach him with their rifles drawn and stood enchanted at Riley, who stood between the two lines of tactical police.

She grinned. She glowed in a way he had never seen before – her bleach blond locks shined, her smile was large, and she truly seemed happy. At peace. She was angelic with the smoke rising around her, the streaks of grey pirouetting around her glow. He regretted letting her go.

She was the last thing Jackson saw. Her glowing eyes had hypnotized so many boys during her life the same way she cast a spell on him once upon a time. She was still his guide, and his shoulders fell in relief at seeing her still leading him, still walking with him, and showing him the way.

"Get down motherfucker!" The Swat team commander yelled, "Down, down, down!"

Jackson didn't realize he started to raise the gun toward the rushing tactical officers. It was too late to learn how far he had gone when both sides of his chest burst open. He could feel the bullets going through his chest and exiting his back. The relative size of the exit wound felt like the size of peanuts, but, in actuality, the exit wounds were more like holes the sizes of tangerines. Two more hit him in the middle of his chest, and a stray bullet kicked his head back, where he fell forward, slumped on his knees, with his arms hanging limply to his sides. One of the officers booted him in the arm, and Jackson toppled over.

His smile was the most haunting of all. It resembled a peaceful serenity as he had never been scared or surprised at the fact he was dying. His mission had been fulfilled. A fulfillment that was unrecognizable to most people until they *truly* died happily.

5

BROKEN PROMISES

The television blared with cartoons, but the sounds from the screen didn't gain her attention. She had been too young to know the difference between the figures on the screen and the ghosts before her. She saw him at the doorway with a confident gaze, and her thin lips curled upwards at the corners.

He hovered at the doorway of his bedroom, watching them. She sat atop the padded mattress dressed in a 'onesie' that he had bought for her at the local big-chain department store three months before she was born. The onesie was decorated with ponies and cowgirls sitting atop leather saddles. He thought it was cute when he saw it hanging from a plastic hook in the store, thinking she would look adorable in it. She wore it now and looked exquisite.

"What are you looking at, baby?" Maria asked the six-month-old. The baby gargled incoherent gaggles and excited screeches, kicking her legs and flailing her arms excitedly at the sight of him. The smell of him. The familiar warmth she felt when he held her tightly not so long before. Maria wrapped her arms around the baby and carried her to her chest. She kissed her on the smooth velvet-like skin that only babies had. The baby they named Esperanza, while on vacation to El Salvador on the saltwater shores of *Playa El Tunco*, named after Maria's favourite jazz bassist, had been tolerable so far. She expressed mannerisms of having a mild manner about her and a quick-learning tendency that began to show itself as she started crawling faster than most babies her age, babbling her baby-talk language and even beginning to stand on her own. Her eyes expressed a child-like adoration to him as he stood invisibly at the doorway. Maria also looked toward him, sensing that she and Esperanza weren't the only ones in the room, expressing a mild perplexity at not being able to see what the baby saw so clearly.

Maria still had his clothes in the drawers. She couldn't bear to throw them out, and on occasion, when she was alone and overcome with sorrow – she held his shirts to her nostrils and smelled the familiar scent that he left behind. It was all he left her. The tears flowed to her chin and finally fell to the sheets when the drip became too heavy to perch itself on her chin, like a bat hanging from the ceilings of a cave. She left his clothes unwashed for this reason – she missed him and hated him for leaving simultaneously.

"I'm still here." He said with a soundless whisper.

She heard him and looked up intently. Not his wife, but his baby girl that had entered his life not so long ago. She flailed her arms and laughed with the adorable tone that infants – filled to the brim with innocence - had.

She didn't have the chance to mourn, miss him, or loathe at the thought of what he could have been possibly thinking that day, bewildered at his decision when he jumped. He thought losing her when she was so young was a good thing. She didn't have to bear the burdens of his uselessness that would surely stick to her like honey. Her mother, whose kiss was as soft as rose petals, was all to expect, and the sense of not knowing any better had been an involuntary and unconscience refuge for her. He felt that she didn't know it yet, but he would be a stranger to her as she grew older, and he preferred that. Framed pictures of Daddy were a solemn recourse to knowing her father in her life, only for him to leave. That would sear deep wounds in her soul. Still, though he thought that baby Esperanza would never recognize his voice, smell his scent, the sensation of twirling the long hairs of his beard between her fingers – she still saw him at that doorway, as if he had never gone anywhere at all.

Ghosts could feel regret. Not in the same way that the living does – as they could make amends and forgive themselves for the ills that had occurred in their past, to ultimately have hope for a better day. The search for shelter in the rain or the warmth of a blazing fire in a dark winter forest was a possibility of redemption for the living. Ghosts didn't have that luxury. It had been too late to make amends. He was stuck in this place where he was still present, still able to observe – but powerless to make a change, unable to speak and be heard. Unable to touch and be felt.

"Do you see Daddy?" Maria asked. "I miss him too, baby – I miss him so much," She whispered, tightening her hold on the baby.

Ghosts can weep as well, and that is what he did, standing in the doorway and watching Maria struggle to hold back the tears. Her chin quivered, and her cheeks swoll at the depressing realization of thinking her tears had dried up after so much crying and being wrong. She had regrets and lived with them every day.

She hated how she scolded him, called him a terrible father and even worse husband, and told him that he wasn't much at all, and the instant regret of her words enveloped her in an unbearable depression that had her chest feel like it was caving in at the thought of him.

Maria's ferocious scolding was taken for granted; they are only words, she thought,

sticks and stones,

She understood now. After the greatest tragedy in her life, she could never imagine it taking place from behind her balcony door, finally comprehending that words have power and should be treated as fire – it either kept her warm – or burned her. The thoughts had raced through her head since she lost him, shouting to God for answers and receiving no response. Was it his purpose when he left? To hurt her? Was it his way of punishing her for what she had said? For insinuating that she would be better off without him or better off alone? Did he know that she loved him with all her heart? She knew it wasn't the truth when she spewed it, only hate-filled anger that escaped her lips when she grew frustrated at him. Still, the words and every letter pierced daggers in his heart and hurt all the same.

She sat on the mattress, holding the only thing he had left behind. She was grateful for that, at least. A reminder and familiarity of him were stuck in the beautiful baby girl he gave her six months ago. She still felt his presence but would constantly remind herself that he was gone, and she was left with a heart-wrenching regret, tearing the soul from her core. Knowing she had a part in his absence, she had driven him to things she could never imagine he would do.

"I'm still here," he said.

"I wish…" she said. "I wish you were still here." Her lips quivered as she held the single tear back unsuccessfully.

"I'm here." He said again, this time louder.

She didn't hear him. He knew there was nothing he could do to make her acknowledge him. He had shouted to the heavens at God, cursed him for being stuck in this middle place, and hated himself for putting Maria through a sorrowful hell.

The baby wiped her mother's tears with her tiny palm, ignorant of the cause of such remorse. Maria knew all too well and also hated herself for her part in the tragedy. She couldn't bring herself to say 'I'm sorry' to the ghost she didn't know was there. Maria knew the meaning of those words too. She couldn't hate herself that much, not when there was a baby girl to raise. If the endless obstacles that came from forgiving herself weren't for her, she must do it for him. If not for his spirit, then for baby Esperanza and her magnificent smile.

"You don't have to cry anymore, baby," he said. "I'm sorry, Maria."

Then he cried.

Ghosts can be heartbroken. Not the kind of heartbreak portrayed in romantic movies or novels, but the kind that Caeser must have felt when he stared into Brutus' eyes, his heir to the throne, his adopted son, as he plunged that dagger into his stomach. The kind of helpless despair steeped in frustration, of running in place, punching underwater, and cursing at the nothingness in the skies, not expecting any answer when it was desperately needed the most. And that's what he did. He shouted to the heavens again,

"I messed up, okay? Why do you punish me like this? Oh God, why?" he didn't hear a response. He never heard a response. Never saw a white light or any angel come to guide him to the afterlife.

"I've prayed to you; I've reached out and forgiven myself, forgiven her. What else do you want from me?"

The baby looked towards the doorway again with an expression of wonder. Maria also looked at the space with a curiosity unknown to her and that she had not felt before. The baby laughed again, and Maria looked back and forth between the baby and the empty doorway. She felt the sensation of his presence. The odour of men's cologne became more robust, and a calm wind kissed Maria's flesh softly.

"What do you see, sweetheart?" Maria said under her breath. The baby waved her hands in the air and gargled in excitement.

Maria stood up from the bed and picked Esperanza up, holding her in her arms. She stepped slowly towards the doorway and could feel the cool mist hit her as she approached. She closed her eyes and imagined his face, loathing the thought that as time passed, there would be a possibility that she would forget his features. She hated the thought. Mortals could only hold on to their memories for so long. He smiled at her. He tried to touch her cheek and wipe her tears away, but his hand breezed through her.

"Oh, Danny." She said. "Why did you leave us, Danny?" she whimpered.

He hadn't the words to say. He had become speechless the way he always had been when they argued or conversated about tough subjects. He had all the words in the dictionary to express on paper, but they vanished before him when it was time to speak. When it was time for her to *hear* him. Maria lowered her head and kissed the baby on the top of the head, then strolled back to the bed and gently rocked her baby as she cried to herself.

Ghosts have memories. They are the most vivid kind. Like a projector that showed him a movie of his life. Memories so real that Danny Boyle felt like he had been transported back in time to experience them again. He reminisced about taking Maria out to dinner when she was still pregnant with Esperanza.

"What are you having, babe?" he asked

"I'm not sure – I have a craving for – "

"Pickles?" he interrupted,

They both laughed.

"Yeah, Pickles. "She said, "It looks like they have deep-fried Pickles as an appetizer; want to share?"

"Share? Uhm, we both know you will devour them before I can get a finger on them."

"This is true," she said with a smile, "but we can try to share, right?"

"We can try." He said to himself as he stood before the bed.

He could have tried to be better; he could have tried to be more loving and open with his emotions. The intense regret of not being able to show it now, that it was too late and there was nothing he could do to fix her.

"I broke you," he said. "I broke you when I jumped. I broke you even before that."

He was transported back to the diner on 44th Street across from the bowling alley they had gone to on their first date. *Get Your Gaming On* was the place's name, and Danny thought it would be fun to bring Maria. The bowling was the biggest attraction, but the deep-fried Pickles were the *real* reason he brought her there. He thought she would surely fall in love with him after she tried the Pickles. He was right.

"Okay, so how is the Thesis coming along?" Maria asked.

"Not so much a Thesis. It's a creative writing course, so I must submit a novella of about 20,000 words."

"I've seen you write more than that," she said.

"Yes. But not of quality, not like this. Mr. Howard expects *top-class* stuff. It's hard to meet his expectations."

"Well, how's it coming along?"

"Pretty good, but I'm stuck."

"Stuck?"

"Yeah. I'm writing about lost love. I know it's *corny*, but I think I got a snippet of an idea."

"Go on. The suspense is killing me," she teased,

"A sailor who wants to confess his love to a baroness, but she's married to the shipyard owner. A wealthy man. She's trapped with him and longs for *true love*. Our hero is forced to go to sea in a last-minute rescue mission and dies before expressing his feelings about her."

"Sounds heartbreaking," Maria said.

"it's supposed to be. It's hard to express an emotion I've never felt before."

"I've felt it." She said. He didn't reply. He knew she meant her father leaving her. He didn't feel the need to bring it up.

"Maybe, you could help me?"

"Yes. I'd be delighted." She said, "Danny?"

"Yeah?"

"Promise me."

"Promise you what?"

"That you won't do that to me. You will tell me all, no matter how hard it is?"

"You mean the truth?"

"Yes. Well - More than that." She hesitated momentarily and unknowingly crumpled the paper napkin with a clenched fist.

Don't leave me, okay?" she asked.

He reached across the table and grasped her hands with both of his tightly. Her shoulders relaxed, and a creek of a smile crept from her lips as he said,

"I'll never leave you, Maria."

―――◆―――

"I meant it, you know," Danny said as he stood by the bedside, overcome with guilt at hearing the hypocrisy spilling from his lips. Esperanza still saw him, and the feeling of delight overcame him when she laid her eyes on his and flapped her arms in excitement. To Esperanza, he was still there in front of her, still present and life-like. Perhaps, he thought, he hadn't left them after all.

Still, it wasn't the same. She couldn't feel him; she couldn't touch him or hear his voice. His laughter had disappeared along with his terrible dance moves and the way he sang every lyric to his favourite songs in the car. She would no longer point out his growing bald spot with a chuckle or poke and prod him because she knew he was ticklish. He was still there, watching, standing near them the way he always had, and though he kept telling himself that he had never *really* left – it wasn't the same.

"You promised me." She said.

"I did."

"You promised me, Danny." She repeated,

"I'm so sorry, baby." It was all he could muster through his sadness.

This isn't what he wanted. It's not what he imagined in the delivery room when Esperanza was born. It was a happy time then. There was no postpartum depression, and there were no sleepless nights yet. There was no feeling of not being prepared for the baby and not earning enough at work to support her. All the pressures had disappeared when he died, but instead, he was left with burdens that dug so deep to his core that he felt himself teetering on the balcony railing again, looking for an escape.

"Stop, Dan. Stop." He told himself. "Just look at her. How much she has grown." He felt a meagre smile enshroud his face. Then he relived another memory. One so vibrant, so real – he wished he could stay there forever.

"I need you to push, honey," the nurse said overtop Maria's agonizing screams. Danny held her hand. It pulsated with sweat as he motivated her like a sports coach aging on a team player to go for a goal.

"You're doing so great, baby." He shouted over her screams,

"You're doing great, Maria; ready for another push?" the nurse said. It seemed to be the common trend in the room. The nurse, her assistant, and Danny said the same things repeatedly that Maria didn't even acknowledge. She was too focused on getting Esperanza out and not falling unconscious in the meantime.

"Oh My god, I see her, baby. I see her!" He exclaimed.

"She's crowning," the nurse said. She looked to her assistant, "Tell Dr. Monroe the baby is almost here. Okay Maria, I need you to breath. A couple more good pushes, and she is out, do you hear me?" she said.

"You hear that, baby? A couple more, Okay?" Danny said to her. Maria's eyes drooped like a boxer's when they caught a clean shot and stumbled backwards, and he worried she would fall unconscious before she could deliver the baby. He reached over to the water bottle and poured a steady stream onto her forehead.

Soon the doctor walked in,

"Hey everyone – looks like the baby is ready to come out." He said.

"Yes. She is." Danny said excitedly.

"Okay, Mom – just one more push and baby is out." The doctor said. He was right. Danny watched as the doctor reached inside his wife and pulled out his baby girl. She cried loudly, and Danny was overcome with emotion. He looked over to Maria, and she lay exhausted, almost unconscious, until the doctor placed the baby in her arms. She smiled.

⇒⇒·⋅+⋅·⇐⇐

"That's when I knew you were okay." He said.

Maria fed the baby with a bottle of formula, as her breast milk had stopped flowing a week before. Maria had felt like a failure when this happened, and heartbreaking for Danny to witness. It was one of the many times he felt helpless, an on-looker. She glumly told herself she wasn't a good mother and couldn't provide for her baby's needs. Those words stung Danny especially. She told herself this often under her breath. It was a depression that was all too familiar to Danny, and he hated himself as he stood beside her. He wished he was there to console her, tell her it wasn't her fault and that it was natural. She was the best Mother Esperanza could ever hope for—the best Mother in the world.

Ghosts can read the minds of the living. This is what hurts so much. There is no hiding anymore; there is no opportunity to pretend that her thoughts didn't exist and that she *wasn't really* thinking these thoughts of failure and insecurity. Maria's voice blared in his head, and he couldn't help but listen to her.

I'm sorry I can't pump for you anymore, Essy,

"It's not your fault," he told her.

I'm sorry I couldn't get your daddy to stay with us.

"It's not your fault. It's mine."

I'm sorry I drove him away.

"Please, Maria – "

I let you down, little girl. I wish I were better.

"...Maria" Danny held out his hand to grasp Maria's shoulder, and she felt nothing.

At that moment, they both wept. Esperanza, suckling on the nipple of the bottle, didn't know what to make of it with her infant mind. She didn't realize regret, sorrow, or pain, not yet. Not like a grown man who had given up so much only to be burdened with the same decisions that got him in the terrible predicament in the first place. She didn't know why the tears fell from her mother's eyes or why her father was on his knees with both hands covering his face. She didn't know she could see him even though nobody else could. She didn't know why Mommy didn't see him too. If only she could. If only she could see the pain he endured, the regret of his actions, the depression he had of not even being able to touch them.

Still, the baby felt him. She saw him. He didn't leave after all, and even though he wasn't there tangibly, she knew who her father was. The man kneeled near her, his knees on the soft carpet, his face covered in salty wetness. She knew his love for her, the overwhelming emotion that flooded his heart whenever he looked at his baby girl. She knew that he was there, forever in her sight, eternally in her heart. She reached for him with both hands outstretched, and Maria noticed.

"Danny?" she said.

"Maria."

"I still love you. I always will." She said.

The white light grew from the corner of the bedroom, and Danny peered into it. He knew what it was. Where it would take him. The light was blinding and warm; it led to a place that felt comforting and peaceful. The glare expressed to Danny Boyle that he was welcome and had somewhere he belonged, a place of paradise.

He refused to go. He made that promise.

"No. Not yet," he said. The light disappeared in a blink, and all three of them smiled.

"I promised never to leave you, baby." He said.

He then stood up from his knees and sat on the edge of the bed, admiring the family he had left behind – yet, intended to stay with.

Forever.

6

BITCHES BREW

The clouds seemed to float like soft pillows drifting underwater in an oceanic current. The sun streaked from rips in the white sky, with the heat blistering a nauseous humidity.

The steaks hitting the charcoal grill made sizzling sounds, and bright flames shot out on either side of the T-bones, the intense flames sparking upwards and grizzling the edges. Robert Pryce and Kevin Desjardins stood on the old porch that seemed to need to be fixed since it was first built by the original owner forty-plus years before. When stepped on, the panels creaked in spots, and the wooden boards were streaked with deep trenches of grains that had stained themselves black from the years of exposure.

"You know we can fix her up. I know I'm only here for a few days – but while you're at work, I can chip away at the backyard gate." Kevin offered.

"Yeah, it leans to one side too much. I meant to get at it." Robert said.

"Well, I get pretty bored; I'm an early bird and find myself with nothing to do most of the day until I go fishing," Kevin said. "I'll start on it. It will keep me busy." He sipped from the *Whiskey Highball* concoction he stirred up in a hurry when he came out into the scorching heat.

"I don't like that tree in the middle of the yard either," Robert said. He took a drink from his beer and pointed the bottle toward the adolescent pine tree, which slightly leaned to one side of his backyard lawn. "It won't take long. I'll cut it down when I come home from work and jump on the gate with you."

Kevin waved the offer away. "I'll cut her down. It's no problem." Robert debated back and tried to sound insistent – but the beer had stolen his enthusiasm for being a good host a few hours before.

"You're here to relax, man. Take it easy. Rent a fishing boat or a Canoe and take the river. The neighbours say there are lots of Pike and Smallmouth. Muskies, too – those taste great. Do you see the smoker?"

"Looks new."

"Yeah, boy – Muskies are mighty fine smoked." Robert took another glug from the Milwaukee lager. "You need a boat, in any case. There are many rivers and lakes up here, but getting access is damn near impossible without a boat."

"I found a boat landing off Highway 480," Kevin said. "When I went yesterday morning to scout out some spots, I came upon a logging trail and followed it down to some lake – I don't know the name. Anyway, I fished from the boat landing for an hour and caught a Pike. Normal size, nothing weighty. I didn't know if you wanted me to bring it home, so I threw it back."

"You should have brought it back - we could have smoked it," Robert responded.

"I didn't need a boat."

"You still need a boat. Trust me."

Robert flipped the steak, and grill marks were present on the thick cut of beef. He was a master of the grill. Robert knew never to touch the meat once you slapped it down until it was ready to flip. That way – the grill marks would be distinctive and clean. He understood the feel of the meat and how it would bounce back, denoting the temperature inside.

"She got more food for the grill, or what?" Robert asked. "I swear she said she wanted to put on the sausages."

"Yeah, she's coming – I saw her seasoning them up."

"Seasoning sausages?" Robert asked quizzically,

"I'm just the messenger man,"

They both laughed and drank.

"What's the point?" Robert asked with a sly chuckle looking over his shoulder so his wife wouldn't hear him gossiping. He couldn't let it go. "They're already seasoned *inside* the casings, for God's sake." He added.

Kevin pulled out a *Marlboro*, stepped towards the porch rail, and glanced at the adjoining backyards. He didn't like to smoke near his in-laws, and his mother-in-law mentioned before that she had been specifically allergic to cigarette smoke. It didn't bother him to step away – he was a guest – and it wasn't his right to argue, even if he was inconvenienced. He observed the neighbours' yards and took in the differences between both. An eight-foot wood-planked fence blocked off each yard and was the only thing both yards had in common.

The yard to the left was a mess. A twelve-foot aluminum fishing boat with the tarp draped overtop was sitting in the middle of the yard with its plastic covering left crumpled and dishevelled. The rusted metal shed in the yard's far corner under the overhanging branches of a large maple tree was painted a dull green. The old shed began to crumple along the aluminum siding and dented inwards from the rough winds in the winter. The gutter on the roof of the single-story house sagged down from an overbearing weight of leaf litter and tree twigs. Kevin noticed the edges of the metal gutter trap cracking and knew it would give way sooner rather than later. The rest of the yard was littered with children's toys, gardening shears, and a lawnmower. They were all left in areas that gave the impression of being placed lazily behind and forgotten about.

The yard next to it had a freshly mowed green lawn with its shed along the adjoining fence to Robert's house. The drying tower was still pristine and newly painted white. Clothes hung from the wires, and they swayed in the gentle breeze. The house was also well kept, the bricks looked as if they were freshly laid along the side of the little bungalow, and the metal siding of the upper portion of the house had frequently been power washed, leaving it to look pristine.

Kevin stood on Robert's porch looking over the fence into both yards, taking long drags from his cigarette and told himself that the house on the left seemed to have dark clouds hovering over the roof and the well-kept home on the right seemed to glisten in the sunlight. At least, that was the feeling that overcame him.

"You get to meet the neighbours?" Kevin asked.

"Yup. Some of them. Nice people. The couple next door has money - they just bought a new boat. A twenty-foot *Utopia Bow Rider* with a 250-horse *Optimax*. Damn fine boat."

"I saw it in their driveway."

"That's the one." Robert said, "They have a pool and a nice gazebo, with an expensive grill and a jacuzzi. You can see it there." Robert pointed towards the jacuzzi, which was covered. The place was lovely – Edison lights hung tastefully around the sitting area, and the fire pit was well-maintained without any soot stains along its edges. Many plants hung from the gazebo, and Marigolds stood along the yard entrance.

"What about across the yard? Meet them?" Kevin asked.

"Kind of, yeah. I've seen the lady on the right side. Always planting flowers and tending to the little garden she has." He glugged the rest of his beer and twisted the cap off a new bottle, "Old lady. Seems like she's in her nineties – but still going strong."

"Damn, that must be nice." Kevin pretended to care. Being thirty-five, he didn't know the aches and pains the body bestowed with age. The sore knees, sharp shooting in the lower back, the loss of balance, and vertigo from getting up too fast. Old age wasn't something he looked forward to, and he couldn't relate to the effects, no matter how much he pretended to.

"She's got a little dog. A black Yorkshire. Chippy little fucker," Robert said, "I'll tell you. Man, that dog comes out barking and barking at nothing every day. Usually at the birds or squirrels in the trees – always barking."

"Hmm. Little dogs are a pain in the ass. I like big dogs instead. They seem smarter and patient even – I don't know, could be wrong, of course." Kevin took a large swallow of the Whiskey Highball he had been nursing. "I'm not a dog guy, but it's something I notice.

"I don't like dogs," Robert responded, then threw on another steak.
"No shit."

"Want a beer?" Robert asked. "Cold ones in the bottom."

"Yeah, sure fuck it. Vacation, right?" Kevin reached into the ice of the *Yeti* freezer and pulled out two bottles, and handed one to Robert. This would be his third in a matter of minutes. Robert placed the cold bottle on the glass patio table and rushed to finish the beer in his hand.

"Thanks for coming." He said, "I know we moved out pretty far, but we like it here. Man, we worked a long time to get to this place. It's nice that you made the trip."

"It's no factor – I've wanted to come up since you guys got up here. Abbie and I want you to spend time with the baby. We'll drive however far for that." Kevin said.

The sweat had begun accumulating on both men's foreheads, prompting Robert to open the patio umbrella for shade. A creaking sound caught Kevin's attention – the old lady's screen door opened slightly, and little black Yorkshire hopped out and trotted towards the backyard fence. It didn't bark at first, but it began its annoying banter when it stopped and sniffed the air.

"Yup. Fucking dog is out again – can't you tell?" Robert said,

"Yeah, no shit." Kevin grinned. "Someone should shoot the damn thing."

"Not me. I'm new around here and don't need that kind of trouble." Robert said.

"I'm just joking, old timer. I'm not going to shoot the dog – that's bad. Just all around bad."

The screen door opened again, and a short, skinny Native American lady slowly walked into the yard. She was of the *Cree Nation*, which had a reservation off Highway 480 heading south towards *Mackinaw Bridge*.

Her skin was tanned and streaked with lines, her skin hung loosely from her jaw, and her eyes seemed to sink into their sockets. Her limbs seemed strong, and although her thin arms were the size of most children's – she showed much strength in them by carrying an overstuffed laundry basket full of clothes.

Robert contemplated greeting his new neighbour. He was good at making friends – he seemed to know everyone in town, albeit having lived in the community for a mere two months. He had gotten to know Ted and Mary Dinowitz, the elderly couple who owned *Freshly Baked*, the modest bakery specializing in Polish pastries, European baguettes, sourdoughs, and Ciabattas. Louise Parker, the town librarian and part-time laundromat attendant; Joe Bossa, a street worker who had been on the Front St. water pipe repair project the town approved a year before; and every barista that worked at the local *Java Paradise*.

"Good day, Ma'am." Shouted Robert waving, "I hope you're having a fine day."

"Oh yes." She glanced up and squinted her eyes. "I'm having a wonderful day so far. How do you like the new house?" she responded in a graceful tone,

"We are enjoying it. It took us a long time to get here – but here we are."

"Yes, here you are. Well, welcome to the neighbourhood – I should bring you a pie or some pastries. Mary Dinowitz has these wonderful chocolate croissants." She placed the basket on the grass beside the drying tower and stood with her arms at her hips, a permanent smile on her face.

"Oh my, you don't have to, really. It's a pleasure just talking to nice folks." Robert said.

"Aren't you kind? What do I call you?" she asked.

"Robert. My wife's name is *Mable* – she's inside seasoning sausages, would you believe?"

The old lady giggled and held her hand to her lips to stop the laughter from coming out. She had the grace and gentle mannerisms of a seasoned royal dressed in house clothes. She giggled modestly in a way that the *bourgeois* higher classes would in public, desperately hiding their humanity for an image of ancient breeding and class.

"Yes," she said. "Sounds yummy."

"Hey, you can come on by if you're hungry. We have Steak, Chicken, and lots of Veggies – we have a ton of food." Robert insisted, pointing the metal tongs to the meat sizzling on the grill.

"Oh, that's nice, Robert – but I have my chores." She said, "I'll tell you what – let's get together for tea or a cocktail sometime, and I'll bring treats. I make a mean apple pie, Robert!"

"Yes, Ma'am, I'm sure you do," he responded.

They both concluded their conversation without saying any more words, and both went on to do what they were doing before. Robert flipped another steak, and the old lady went about taking down the dried blankets, then hanging up wet clothes like she hadn't even spoken to Robert at all.

"She's a very nice old lady," Kevin said.

"Yeah, she is. Very nice. You notice the dog stopped barking when we talked?"

"Nah, I didn't."

"That's the secret. Just talk to the old lady, and the dog stops."

"Hell of a strategy, Robert. Think you can keep up with it every time?" Kevin asked.

"If she comes out when the dog does, I can. Hell yeah."

"Who was that?" Mable's voice came from the sliding mesh screen. She held a metal bowl of sausage links and another small bowl of the barbeque sauce she had made herself.

"It's the old lady across the yard," Robert said.

"Oh, that's nice. how is she?" Mable asked.

"Nice." they both shrugged their shoulders in agreement, and that was the only word that had to be said to be understood.

There was silence, and Kevin noticed the sense of awkward silence and couldn't help but spew information to eliminate the feeling,

"Seems like a nice old lady. Said we should do tea or cocktails. That she would bring pie, she's the little old lady from the movies." He shrugged again as he was at a loss for further description, "Just like the nice granny in the movies."

Thanksgiving was starting the following day, and Katherine had done all her chores in preparation for her adult kids and grandchildren coming over for the family's traditional Thanksgiving feast.

She had folded and put away the clothes, laid fresh sheets on her bed, finished washing the dishes, and finally prepared the nine-pound butterball. Pots were on the stove filled with mashed potatoes and chives, green beans sauteed in butter, corn that she drizzled pure Manuka honey on top of, a pasta salad that was mixed earlier in the morning, and for an added sweetness, in the fridge was the cranberry sauce prepared the night before.

She was ready for her guests, and when she slid the turkey into the oven, she leaned back on the kitchen counter and lit a cigarette. She took a long drag and exhaled a large plum of smoke into the air. She looked out of the kitchen window and noticed her shed. The shed Ted had built her just a few years ago after he decided to replace the wooden one that had become rotted and soft.

She reached into her apron and uncapped the bottle of *Percocet*, then downed a few of them, chewing vigorously with her dentures, letting off a crunching sound that had the little black Yorkshire tilting its head to the side in curiosity. The pills took effect immediately. Her vision started to focus in and out, and her shoulders slumped forward slightly. She stood staring through the window at the shed, thinking to herself,

You had to go on and die - leaving me with your damn dog that I never wanted in the first place. Having me acting out to the new neighbours – God, I hate pretending - why do I pretend? Why can't I mind my business without the new guy starting a conversation? She began to speak out loud,

"Bill was better - he wouldn't talk to me. He kept his own damn business to himself and wouldn't bother me with mine. Motherfucker had to go on and die too." She shook her head contemptuously. She looked down at the dog and shooed it away with her foot. It whined, trotted off to its floor mat, and buried its head in its paws.

"Leaving me with your damn dog," she said aloud. She downed a few more pills and put out her cigarette in the teacup saucer while staining her long, withered fingertips in the ash. The doorbell rang, and knocking on her door soon followed. The dog barked annoyingly then she heard the doorknob turning open and her son's familiar voice with her grandkids yelling in the yard.

"Hey, Mom. We're here." Ted Jr announced.

"Oh Christ, here we go." She mumbled.

"Yeah, I'm in the kitchen; take your stuff off and help me with all this shit."

Kevin sat on the back porch before a typewriter he had found in Robert's basement. It was a *Royal Deluxe* from 1956, and although the Magic Margin keys and the Shift key didn't work, it was still enough for Kevin to sit in the dark, luxuriated by candlelight and kick out a meagre attempt at a first draft to a short story.

On the glass patio table to the left of the typewriter was a glass ashtray littered with Marlboro butts, a cold beer on a coaster, and a pack of cigarettes lying next to the bottle. He typed away. The clacking of the keys was like a calming symphony for him, and every clack motivated him to punch the keys with a calming rhythm that regular computer keys could not provide. He started fine. He was beginning a story about a boy of 15 years who is waiting at a bus stop in the early morning dawn for a bus of ghosts to arrive. It was a shred of an idea – but still, something to explore.

He became distracted by the dim yellow light emanating from the old lady's shed. He noticed it from the corner of his eye as he was writing. He hadn't heard anyone come out, the dog that would surely bark, or the metal shed doors screeching open. He thought that perhaps he had been in a trance and tuned it out. He drew a slight curiosity as to why the lady would be in the shed at ten o clock and why the dim light looked a lot like the light that emits from candles and not light bulbs. The same kind of light that illuminated the features of his face.

He debated between going over to the fence for a look or staying put. Finally, after much rocking on the legs of his chair and staring across the yard, Kevin got up quietly and snuck closer to the fence. He hid in the dark and took wide steps, his heel touching the grass softly and the rest of his foot rocking forward with noiseless refinement.

He reached the fence and peered over it. The stink from the yard was putrid and smelled like cases of tinned Mackerel filets that had rotted in the sunlight for days. Kevin held his breath as he looked over and heard the faint rumblings of a conversation in the shed. The light shining out of the slit in the doors flickered, confirming to him that it was candlelight after all.

He heard a loud cackle and nearly fell back from the fence. The hysterical laughter shocked him, and he could feel the cold chill snake up his spine. He tried to stay silent, and when he looked over the fence again, he saw the Yorkshire Terrier's black outline sitting outside the shed. He sat on one side of the candlelight and didn't bark. Instead, he whimpered and looked at Kevin as he stared back at the dog's tiny face over the fence.

The conversation went on until the light quickly went out, and he heard the rusted screeching of the shed door slide open. He ducked his head and paused. When he listened to her slippers grazing along the concrete path towards her side door - he looked over again. The old lady opened the screen door to her house and walked in. The Yorkshire sat calmly in the dark; the tip of his small tongue dangled from his mouth, the long whiskers curling under his chin dripped with what Kevin hoped to be water and not drool. The dog's eyes pleaded to him, and Kevin felt a sense of pity in him. He knew it tried to communicate to him but was also aware that he had limited knowledge about dogs to understand their body language or delicate mannerisms. The dog didn't seem threatened by Kevin's presence but looked to be accepting of it instead, and even inviting. But as Kevin peered over the fence at the dog, its manner portrayed a look of warning. The dog's eyes told him to get out of this place. His tiny black eyes buried under long lashes communicated to Kevin that this place was not what it seemed.

※

Katherine's family sat around the large dining table.

In the middle of the table, lined up in a row, was all the food with spoons in each bowl for everyone to serve each other. The children had their table in the living room, where they shouted, laughed, and chased each other around the table the way children do when their parents are not supervising them. Katherine sat at the head of the table where her late husband, Ted, would sit every Thanksgiving. She felt she had taken the throne after so many years of sitting beside him.

"How's everything about the town, Mom? You been getting out much?" Katherine's daughter Aileen asked. Aileen poured a glass of water from the pitcher and did not necessarily care for the answer but wanted to gain an impression of her mother's mood.

"Who cares?" Katherine responded. "Always with the stupid questions." She lit another smoke.

"Towns fine, Aileen; your mother had been taking walks, killing time. keeping busy." Cindy said, "The days get hot, but she gets her exercise in."

"She didn't ask you, Cindy – she asked me. Goddammit, you always have to be the center of – "

"She's just being nice," Michael said. Katherine slammed her fist on the table, and the glasses jumped.

"Don't you *fucking* interrupt me, boy! You marry my little girl and think you have a right to speak up to me?"

She took a drag from her cigarette. The room fell silent at the sudden clattering of the glasses on the table. The living room, where the kid's table was, turned into a ghost town.

"I'm sorry I asked," Aileen said. Michael sat with a brooding stare at Katherine but also reserved himself from causing a further commotion.

"You seem to be in a good mood, Mom," Ted Jr. said,

"Your Father left his rods. You want them?" Katherine asked,

"I'm sorry, what? His fishing rods?"

"Do you want them or not?"

"I've got Rods at home." Jr. responded, "You keep them."

What the hell am I going to do with them? Do I look like I'm in any condition to go fucking fishing?"

"You look great, Mom; what condition – " Cindy asked,

"Oh, blow it out your ass." Katherine interrupted, then laughed like a drunk does when he talks to himself, clutching a bottle of rum – or in this case – a stomach full of Pills.

"You're too damn kind, baby." She said to Cindy, "I didn't teach you to be stupid, did I?"

"You don't have to call her stupid," Aileen said. Katherine ignored her.

"Well, she is, ain't she? Asking stupid ass shit, almost like asking me 'how's the town,' like anyone gives a hot shit! Give me a break. You're too damn soft!" her voice rose again, "- too damn soft, and when hard times hit you good – you won't make it out alive. Soft!"

"Well, I can see dinner's going planned as usual," Ted Jr said with a snicker. Michael chuckled and ate a spoon full of mashed potatoes. "Let's just have a nice meal; what do ya say?"

"Stop it. Don't talk to me like I don't know any better. I know better!" She growled, "It's *my* house. You come to *my* house, that means *My* rules, and I shouldn't have to pretend to be polite or nice to any of you, God dammit."

"C'mon, Mom. I know it's been hard – " Ted Jr said, looking at his plate and shaking his head.

"Aileen, how's the new office? Uncle Joe mentioned something." Michael said, eagerly changing the subject.

"It's nice. Better than the last place." She played along.

"She had a turban-head boss," Katherine said,

"Yes, Mom. Well, it's better anyway – I work fewer weekends and late shifts, and everyone seems nice."

"Your father worked hard. Didn't complain. Always hung his coat up and left the job behind when he came home." Katherine said, "He had to work weekends for years, then get switched over to night shift out of nowhere." She chuckled,

"Shit, I hadn't felt some dick for a year after that."

"Mom!" Cindy blurted wide-eyed with shock,

"Jesus Christ," Michael whispered.

"What? Can't I have my needs? I need to get *fucked* too – "

"-All right, I hear the stuffing is good – is it your recipe Aileen? The world-famous stuffing?" Michael asked,

"Yeah, I put some bacon and some red peppers that I roasted on the grill. It's an added little flavour."

"Like that new man you're slutting yourself out for?" Katherine blurted out,

"No, Mom – there isn't a new man."

"Yes, that – Oh Jesus, what's his name?"

"Josh?" Ted said, snickering. Cindy's eyes turned to slits, and her gaze pierced Ted Jr, making him chuckle louder.

"Josh! Yes. A real *faggot* name."

"You can't say that, Mom, please."

"All right, all right – so God-Damn sensitive."

"I wish Dad was here." Ted Jr said aloud though he didn't mean to. The thought of those words in his mind, and they proved too powerful to be kept inside for so long."

"Spare me, Jr. Don't give me that." Katherine's eyes turned to slits, and she could taste the venom on her lips, "When have you called? When have you visited? For god's sake, you didn't even come to your father's viewing." She spewed. "He would be so ashamed of you. You'd break his heart – You'd break it into pieces."

"Mom, please, it's time to tone it down," Cindy said. She placed her hand gently on Katherine's arm. Katherine put out her smoke in the dinner plate with the other hand and exhaled another large plum of smoke above them all.

"Grace, why don't you tell us about your new school? She got into university." Aileen said to her daughter, who sat beside her with her head down, staring at her phone screen. She didn't answer.

"Grace, honey," Aileen said in a louder voice. Grace propped her head up and answered. "Yeah, I got in. It's a nice school, I didn't make any friends yet, but I'm sure I will."

"You won't, staring at that fucking phone all the time," Katherine said.

"What are you taking, Gracie?" Ted Jr asked.

"Agriculture and Environmental studies. I'm going to be a *Climatologist*, I think."

"What the hell is a Climatologist?" Katherine asked.

'It's someone –"Grace replied but stopped speaking as Katherine waved her hand impatiently. A gesture of saying 'never mind' without saying so many words.

"There are jobs for it; I know that!" Cindy said. "We are all very proud of you, Gracie."

"You *could* marry a good man like your grandfather was. A damn good man." Katherine said. Her speech began slurring slightly.

"I'd rather her have a career Mom," Aileen said.

"Well, why don't you let the girl make up her own damn mind?" Katherine lit another cigarette, "What happened to all the women's rights bullshit you're always talking about, Aileen? A woman's choice to choose and speak for herself. Equal this, equal that." She giggled a lazy laugh, "For fuck's sake."

"She wants a career too, Mom." Jr. poked in.

"Where is Ben anyway?" Katherine prodded with one brow furrowed.

"Mom, enough!" "Aileen and everyone else at the table had grown tired of the room's tension. It caused a sense of hyperventilating, which was overpowering and suffocating.

"Did he run off with another whore? Like he did in Arizona or Maine or wherever you live now." Katherine chuckled as she spoke.

That's enough now, Mom," Ted said. He put his fork down and placed his hands into fists, squeezing them with every pulsating heartbeat. "You know why he isn't here – there's no need to bring it up."

"Oh, but you Bring up your father any chance you can, can't you? Don't you think it hurts me to talk about him? In the same way, I'm sure it hurts her to talk about Benny, *the big dick* cheater?"

"We didn't bring him up, Mom," Aileen said,

"That's because you didn't give a shit about him. Like you didn't give a shit about your husband." She screeched. Katherine pointed her finger at her daughter with scorn. "Men don't just go off with another woman, you fool! If only you gave it up more often, he'd be happy and wouldn't *need* another woman."

"Mom, please, we don't want to talk about it. Not here." Cindy pleaded under her breath.

"Of course, you don't, honey – it's too hard to talk about," Katherine made of gesture of wiping tears away from her cheek that weren't there. "A word of advice to you, Gracie-poo. If you want a man, you must suck him and fuck him at every turn – especially a rich man – or he will find it somewhere else. Just ask Mommy."

"Mom!" Jr. shouted, then caught himself and looked over his shoulder to the kids in the living room, not trying to shock them with his anger. He heard a faint laughing coming from the garage and realized the kids had found solitude away from the conflict at the table. "That's enough of this garbage. You know you're out of line and being inappropriate. Please, we just came here to see you and have a good time. There's no need to ruin it."

"I'm going to the bathroom," Grace said. She scooted her chair and walked away abruptly, swinging her arms and clutching her smartphone.

"Yeah, run away, girl, like your daddy did," Katherine said with a smirk. "Just - fucking weak." She looked at Jr. as she spoke.

"Shit, no wonder nobody looks forward to these things," Michael said. Everyone seemed to snicker at the comment except Katherine.

"And how long have you been in the picture Mike? Or is it, Michael?" Katherine asked, taking a long drag from her smoke.

"Mike is fine. I Met Aileen about six months ago. I guess she didn't tell you." He glanced at Aileen with a forgiving look, 'All good; I get it.'

"No. You see, Mike, what you will come to observe - is that my kids don't tell me *shit*. They avoid me at all costs. I'd rather the privacy, but it still matters to know these things."

"I think you make it hard, Ma'am. If I'm allowed to be honest."

"*I think you make it hard, Ma'am.*" Katherine childishly imitated him. There was a silence, then Katherine continued, "Do you know hard, Mike? Do you know what it's like to have it hard, Sonny? Having three *fucking* Brats clawing at your teets all the time?" Cindy placed her hand on Katherine's arm again and pouted.

"So? Do you?" She barked,

"Yes, I do know *hard*. It's not worth mentioning, though." Michael said.

"Yeah? Not worth mentioning? Well – I'll mention that I had to sell my pussy a few times to keep the lights on – I'll mention that. I'll mention the nights of only having a can of tuna in the cupboard for dinner. I'll mention the years of a rummy husband that had bastard children with other women. You think you know hard?"

Michael didn't respond. He felt Aileen's hand grasp his and squeeze tightly under the table—her way of apologizing for having to put him through this.

"Jr.'s right. We came here for a good time, Mom," Aileen said. "You should be grateful that we are all here. We don't get together often."

"Yeah. And what's your excuse? Late nights at the office, dear?" Katherine said.

"Yes. Exactly."

Katherine nodded her head. "I'm done. I lost my damn appetite. I'm going to the kitchen for my *Vino*."

"I'll have some Wine," Michael said.

Katherine stopped and looked at Michael. "You got some balls, don't you, boy?" she smiled. "I like him, Aileen. Don't let this one fuck around." She then walked to the kitchen, uncorked a new bottle of *Merlot*, and brought it back to the table.

"Who wants *Vino*?' Katherine asked, throwing back two more pills.

Nobody answered. Grace sauntered back to the table, sat down beside her mother, and asked,

"Can I have some?"

"No, Grace, you 're too young," Aileen said.

"God damn, she's in *fucking* University, Aileen," Katherine screeched. She stood up and poured a large glass for her granddaughter, then poured herself a tall glass. She placed the bottle in front of Michael. "Pour yourself, new guy." He did. Then ran a glass for Aileen and nodded to her.

"Shit. When I was her age, I was doing some crazy things, I'll tell you." Katherine said.

"Please don't," Cindy whispered,

"You know..." Kathrine pointed her long, skinny index finger to Cindy, "She had always called every day to check up on me after Teddy died. Don't get me wrong, Cindy – you can be annoying – but it's a nice gesture. She's the only one who called! Made an effort!" Katherine scowled at the rest of her family at the table.

"It's because I love you; we all do," Cindy said ashamedly,

Katherine nearly choked on the glug of wine in laughter. "Yeah – sure. Thanks, Cindy"

"Mom - I think we got to be heading out – the kids look like their getting tired – " Ted Junior said, wiping his hands with the napkins.

"Yeah, sure, Jr, Sure they are," Katherine responded. She helplessly giggled in the trance of being high and slightly drunk. She didn't care if they wanted to stay or go. She knew the effect her attitude had taken and wasn't ashamed of it. She was alone now and could do what she pleased, say what she wanted, and act out as she saw fit. Ted wasn't around anymore to make her slow down with the pills, even though he was a rummy himself and was the biggest hypocrite she had ever met. Still, she loved him. Still, she missed him. She thought of the shed, and a genuine smile crept on her face, causing the lines of her cheeks to crinkle, having her resemble an illustration of a wicked witch with a bump on her pointed nose. All Katherine needed was the broomstick to knock the effect out of the park.

Her family sat beleaguered as Katherine rocked slowly back and forth.

They watched her escape before their eyes, the haze of the drugs and wine overtaking her and transporting her into another realm where they weren't there. Her kids didn't sit at the table with her, the cigarette smoke didn't hang in the air, and the cursing had subsided.

Ted Jr. told himself that he pitied her, that she had missed him so much and was so lonely that drugs were the most effective reprieve from the dull loneliness she had found herself in the past year. Aileen thought the same way as she pictured a warm blanket of sorrow wrapped around her mother as she mentally hurried away to another place. Katherine stared at the chandelier in the dining room with ecstasy in her eyes, lost in a haze.

They got up one by one, like leaving the room of a sleeping infant, tiptoeing away, avoiding the creaks of the laminate hardwood floors. Grace was the last to leave the table. She sat and stared at her grandmother with a blank observing kind of stare. Grace felt her mother's palm on her shoulder, and she left the table. Her head bowed in remorse at her grandmother's state and how the evening had turned out.

Kevin sat on the front porch the following day, watching people walking down Darlene Avenue towards the New Methodist Church. He saw parents holding hands with their children, dressed in their best Sunday Church attire of freshly pressed blazers and dress shirts, the girls with their clean white dresses accompanied with frills, and he wondered why he had stopped going to Church himself. He remembered he had taken it for granted when he was younger and grew tired of the hypocrites in the congregation that gossiped about their friends behind their backs, only to put on a kind face when approached, as if they had said nothing wrong at all. He knew these people were the same way. All people were the same way. They had to be.

Eddie Bower was walking his dog, a big German Sheppard with an extraordinarily long tongue flapping from his mouth. Eddie was a burly man with a pot belly that resembled a pregnant lady protruding from his waist, nearly popping off the buttons of his shirt. Eddie strolled with a wobble, and his suspenders were held on so tightly they seemed to imbed into his skin. Eddie Bower noticed Kevin on the porch, and when stopping to pick up his dog's fecal matter, he decided to converse and gain an interest in the stranger sitting on his new neighbour's porch.

"How are ya?" Eddie called out from the sidewalk. His black mustache was thick and covered his top lip, and Kevin found it amusing that he couldn't see his lips move from under the hairy awning.

"Not bad. Pretty good morning if it wasn't for the fog." Kevin responded.

"Yes, the fog," Eddie said. "If it were October, it would be perfect for the kiddies in their Halloween costumes." Eddie chuckled. "I noticed your car in the driveway – did you just move in?"

"No. I'm just visiting my in-laws. They moved here about a month ago, and my wife has been missing her mother, so I decided it was a good idea to take a few days off and spend it up here with them." Kevin shrugged as he finished his response. He thought he had given too much information to the stranger, but he seemed nice.

"Well, that's kind. Believe me, the older you get – the more things like that mean to people."

"I agree," Kevin said. "I noticed the *Bowrider* in the driveway – 250 horsepower?" Kevin knew the answer to his question but felt he had to ask anyway to keep the conversation going. He didn't understand *why* he wanted the conversation to continue – Eddie seemed friendly enough and enthusiastic, and perhaps that seemed to be enough.

"It's my first one. It's funny – like getting a new car – you wipe her down every day, make sure she smells nice, and everything is in tip-top condition – then the novelty wears off. Maybe I take it for granted. I'm lucky, is all I mean to say." Eddie said.

"Yeah, I do," Kevin said. He sipped from the mug that read 'World's Oldest Grampa.' "Say, I got a hot pot of coffee here if you're interested?" Kevin asked.

"Yes, sir, I sure am." Eddie strolled up the path and sat beside Kevin on the front porch of Robert's house. They watched the churchgoers exit the lineup of cars on either side of the street and walk down the sidewalk in the thick fog.

"I met Robert. He's nice. Much better than Bill. He lived here before." Eddie said.

"What was he like?"

"Bill? A good man. He kept to himself often and didn't like talking to folks much, but that doesn't make him a bad guy. I like my privacy too." Eddie continued, "A big fisherman. I bet you've found his tackle box by now. He had these giant deep-sea lures and fancy reels that I could never figure out how to use for the life of me. Sometimes he would come by and give the wife and me an extra muskie or Pike he had caught. Once, he brought over a nice-sized Pickerel. I guess he was in a good mood those days."

"Muskie is nice. I haven't caught one yet. The shoreline is very wooded. I can't get any good fishing done unless it's from a boat landing or a dock – even then – just not the same without a boat."

"No shit. You won't have any luck shoreline fishing around these parts. It's so remote out there that not many people have wandered and created natural trails and openings to fish from the shoreline." Eddie sipped his coffee with a loud slurping sound. He continued,

"I'll tell you what. I don't know how many days you're here for, but we can get on the new cruiser if you want. Maybe tomorrow or the next day – up to you."

"Sure. Sounds fine. I don't think I introduced myself. I'm Kevin" He stuck out his hand, and Eddie shook it firmly.

"Eddie."

"Pleasure to meet you, Eddie. We came up from the city, and you rarely get to meet strangers and shoot the shit for a while. Get to learn about folks. It seems like times have changed – I remember when a community was *really* a community, and everyone looked out for each other. I don't mean to complain."

"Oh Lord, it's still that way. Just not so much in the big city – everyone is always so busy, has something to get to, or somewhere they are late for."

"Yeah, I hear that. It's peaceful out here. Almost like time stops, and you got all the time in the world to relax and do what you want." Kevin sipped from his mug again, "it's nice meeting new people. We met a lady across the yard yesterday, and this morning I met you – it's nice."

"Katherine?" Eddie shook his head.

"Who?"

"The lady across the yard. Old lady, skinny arms? I think she's Cree?"

"Oh yeah, Robert chatted with her a bit yesterday. She promised to come by with some pastries or pie or something."

"Hmm," Eddie grunted,

"Something I should know, Eddie? The anticipation is killing me over here, buddy."

"I'm not sure what to say. She's pleasant enough – sometimes too nice. so nice that it seems – I don't know – almost phony." Eddie said sullenly, which raised suspicion in Kevin's inquisitive nature. "I can't pinpoint it, but the missus always had a bad feeling about her. I do too."

"There's a weird smell coming from the shed," Kevin said, trying to pry more information from him.

"Yes. I saw you last night, you know. Is that why you wandered toward her yard? The smell?" Eddie asked. Kevin was slightly shocked that he had been caught spying on a little old lady for reasons he was unsure about.

"You saw me?"

"I don't mean to pry," Eddie said, chuckling. The fat rolls under his buttoned-up white shirt seemed to juggle under the fabric. "I was having a smoke out back last night and saw you sneak up to the fence. Shit – I don't blame you; I would have caught a peep too."

"So, you saw the shed? The smell?"

"Never got *that* close, but I've heard her neighbour complain about the same thing lately. Warren Hunt lives right next door to her, and I usually chat while walking Snapper... much like we are doing now."

"Snapper? That's a hell of a name for your dog." Kevin said with a giggle. He leaned down and scratched the dog on his forehead while he lay beside him patiently.

"Yeah, it's more like a joke. Like calling a 6'5 bodybuilder 'tiny.' It's funny." Eddie said. "Anyway, Warren says the same thing. It's like an invisible wall of rotten fog when he gets close to that side of the yard. 'It's enough to make you faint,' he says. It's been three weeks since the smell appeared."

"I wonder what it is," Kevin said, "I chalk it up to a dead raccoon or opossum in there, tucked away in some corner. That would make sense – but the smell, though – must be more than one dead critter in there." Kevin pondered aloud.

"Or it's Ted," Eddie said.

"Ted?"

"Wouldn't that be a hoot? That would be like something out of those true-crime television shows, eh?"

"I guess Ted was her husband?"

"Sure was, yeah."

"That would be *fucked up*. Excuse me."

"No, your right – it would be right *fucked up*," Eddie chuckled, "I'm just joking. Ted was a fine man. A rummy, but still a fine man. Helped me bag my first Moose north of Kapuskasing. Even when he was licked harder than a sailor at port, Ted was a hell of a shot." Eddie pulled out a cigarette and handed another to Kevin, "That was a hell of a trip. Ever feel like the most fun times of your life were a pain in the ass while you were taking part in them? Climbing those hills and weeding through the thick brush was a nightmare – but when I think back to that trip, I tell myself, 'Yeah, that was fun as shit.' I would do it again in a heartbeat, even if we didn't bag a Moose. Funny, eh?"

"Yeah, I know the feeling. Counter-intuitive, but I get it."

"Sure. That's mainly why I went to Ted's funeral. He was a nice guy. He may have cursed a hell of a lot, but he was a blue-collar guy, and though he would seem annoyed, he would still help change a tire for your wife or watch over the kids from his yard while they played in the back. Jesus – it's a shame how they found him. Sad, even." Eddie took a drag from his smoke, then sipped the hot coffee immediately after exhaling. The steam rose to his nostrils and then dissipated in the morning fog. "Apparently, Ted went fishing one morning with a bottle of *Jim Beam* – a cheap fucking Bourbon if you ask me - and didn't come home. Police say he got too drunk, fell overboard, and drowned. The Dingy was found the same night he disappeared, floating in the middle of Sparrow Lake. Ted's body washed up a week later on the shore near Crow's Landing."

"Makes sense. Accidents happen." Kevin said.

"Sure, accidents happen. One thing I do know is that Teddy could hold his drink. He was the only man I knew that acted the same way, drunk or sober – it was astounding."

"Are you saying you can't believe that he fell overboard?"

"I don't know." He paused. "Ted was an all-American swimming champion in college, then went on to coach the men's national team in the Pan-American games. He won lots of trophies and medals, and he was good. Real good. So damn good; it's hard to believe he died from drowning. After his swim career, he worked in the Nickel mines south of here for another thirty years. The money was too good; he said," The dog looked up at him as if he knew what his owner was getting at. "He hated fishing. Loved the water and could stay nights in the bush hunting but hated to go fishing for some reason. He complained about how boring it was sitting there waiting for a bite. Impatient, I guess." Eddie shrugged his shoulders.

"I'm sure patience is a virtue when hunting, isn't it?"

"Yes, it is. He was a bit odd, I suppose."

"I see," Kevin muttered.

"Great swimmer, hating fishing, yet he fell off a dingy while fishing?" Eddie said.

"Yeah, it doesn't make sense." Kevin added, "How was the service?"

"Nice. a good send-off. Katherine was in a terrible state. Moaning and weeping – her husband died, of course." Eddie seemed to bite his lip under his mustache and finally blurt out the words he wanted to say, "*Crocodile tears*?"

"Really?"

"Mmhmm," Eddie muttered. "You know, there was this time, our customers plane had maintenance problems in *Haiti*. About four years ago. We went down and drove through some pretty shady parts of town on the cab ride to the hanger." Kevin didn't know what Eddie was getting at but listened intently. "- And as we drove through, I hung my arm on the cab's windowsill as I usually do on hot days. The driver turned to me and asked that I put my arm in the car. I thought it was because I was a white boy, and the gangs would see me as an easy target to rob – I suppose that's also true – But the driver explained that if I kept my arm in the car - it looked like I have my hand on my rifle or pistol." Eddie said. "Probably best if you don't, Pry. Probably best if you keep your arm in the car." He said, "Don't get me wrong – do what you want, your life and all – I'm just saying I got a bad feeling about her. Probably nothing. But a feeling nonetheless."

"No, I understand. I get a bad feeling about her, too," Kevin added.

"Well." Eddie rubbed Snapper's head. "I'm afraid I scared you off this place. A spooky story to put you off our little town."

"Hell no, not at all. It's interesting." Kevin said.

"Well, good then. It's best I should be on my way. You're a good conversation, Kevin."

"Thank you, sir. It's a pleasure meeting you. Hope I see you again." Kevin said.

"Yeah, if you're around, we can use my boat. There's a ton of fish in these lakes for the catching."

"I'll take you up on that; thanks, Ed."

※ ⋯ ⋅ ⋯ ※

The night came fast and cold. The stars sprinkled the black sky, and the moonlight was in its crescent phase. Kevin found himself at the back porch again, sitting by candlelight with a pack of smokes and a bottle of cold *Milwaukee* on the tabletop. The ashtray was piled high with butts and ash.

The writing wasn't on his mind anymore since chatting with Eddie. He was waiting like a hunter awaiting his prey to arrive at the bait he left out - except there was no bait - only his curiosity about the woman that would find her way to the shed and continue her strange rituals.

He waited patiently in front of the typewriter like it was a decoy for Eddie if he were to catch him in the act again. It was dark enough. Not as dark as the night before, and Kevin thought that if he snuck up and spied on her again, his cover would more than likely not be as concealed as it was the night before. The thought hadn't stopped him or slowed him in the slightest.

After three hours of recon at the glass patio table, he heard the screen door of the old lady's house slam shut and the sound of dragging slippers on the concrete path. He listened to the old lady's shed door slide open, then close and saw the faint glimmer of candlelight shoot out from the slit in the shed doors.

He snuck up the same way before. He reached the short pine tree, took a few breaths, and slowly stepped to the fence. This time, he paused to look backward toward Eddie's yard. The patio lights weren't on, and he was not sitting and smoking. Kevin took advantage and snuck closer to the fence, propping his head over. He heard her chanting, which turned into a faded and muffled conversation. He had to get closer. He had spent the day thinking of how he could sneak up to the shed and hear what she was saying, maybe even get a look inside.

He thought of jumping the chain-linked fence to the side but knew it was too loud. He thought of coming around the front of the house, staying close to the hedges, and making his way into her yard, but that would have looked criminal if other neighbours had seen him. Instead, he found himself in the same place as the night before - on the fence with the same impatience the old lady's late husband must have had when fishing, and he eventually decided to climb over the same fence he stood on.

He propped one leg over and rolled his body over the top, landing gracefully on the lady's backyard lawn.

The black Terrier met him. The dog looked at him with its head pointed to the side. Kevin reached up to pet the dog, and then he let out a burst of barking. Kevin leaped up, ran to the shed's side, and hid in the dark. The shed door slid open, and the looming candlelight covered the yard. The dog stopped barking and looked up at Katherine as she took a few steps, then booted the tiny dog in the rib cage.

"Shut up, you little fucker." She said with a menacing tone.

The dog whimpered and hobbled towards Kevin in the darkness. He hated her at that moment for that. He wanted to walk in there and lay a booting to the old bitch the way she had with the tiny Yorkshire. He stood in place, and the door slid shut again.

Kevin was dizzy from the putrid smell. It was stronger now that he was next to the shed and knew it was coming from inside. How can she bear that smell? He thought. He gagged, dry heaved a few times quietly, then gathered himself and shimmied closer to the shed door, trying to hold his breath as long as possible. As he got closer, he heard what she was saying.

"...always pretending with these fucking people. You always told me – you must try, and if you can't do it, then pretend. Well, I don't want to pretend anymore, Teddy. You loved me for who I am, so why can't other folks? Why can't they leave me be? Always shooting the shit. Fuck these people, fuck them all."

(pause)

"Okay – I get it, Teddy; you don't have to be such a prick."

(pause)

"Yes, fine. I'll call and apologize. I know it was a bad time. It's my fault; I know that. Shit, I knew it when I spewed all that poison to the kids." She paused again, and Kevin heard a shuffling from inside the shed, making him freeze, fearing being caught. He expected the door to slide open, and he would be made like a spy behind enemy lines.

The door didn't slide open. Just the angry response of Katherine's menacing and aggressive voice,

"It's not the fucking pills, Ted. Fuck you! You're dead and think you can tell me what to do. You had enough of that while you were alive!"

Kevin leaned around the front corner of the metal shed and looked inside. He saw her standing, facing the back of the shed but couldn't make out more than that. He noticed she wore a blue knitted sweater and pyjama pants. He could feel the stink tingling his nose hairs and encasing him all around.

He decided to retreat over the fence and climbed it quietly. As he got to the top, the shed door slid open, and Kevin rolled over the top and landed on his back on the other side. He knocked the wind out of his lungs and struggled to breathe. He hadn't felt this way since he was a kid during the great snowstorm of 89' where he and his friends would jump from ledges doing back flips and landing in the snow until the snow had gotten so pressed down, it might as well have been concrete. He scurried up and returned to the small Pine tree in Robert's yard.

He caught his breath and huffed into the night air. Next door, he saw Eddie sitting on his back patio with the Edison bulbs above his head lit brightly, with a glass of wine in one hand and a cigarette in the other.

"Keep your arms in the ride, Buddy."

"Hey, Ed," Kevin responded. "Playing detective got the best of me."

"No shit." Eddie chuckled, "You find anything out?"

Kevin walked closer to the fence line, where the neighbours wouldn't hear what they were saying. He clutched his belly like he was keeping his intestines from falling out. His back ached, and a sharp pain in his leg had become apparent.

"I learned that the smell is coming from the shed. She's also talking to herself. Like she's talking to her husband."

"Shit -maybe he *is* in there." Eddie chuckled. "You shouldn't Pry Kevin – but hey – it's your life, buddy."

He had been up all night after sneaking into her yard the night before. He tried to write but couldn't keep the experience he witnessed from the forefront of his mind. The odd stammering of the old lady, the one-way conversation with what seemed to be her dead husband.

He had laid on the basement couch thinking, what could have been there? Who was she really talking to? What was the smell? Was it her husband dug up from his grave in the shed or the early onset of dementia in an elderly lady who had exhibited a sense of sincerity to Robert and everyone else she had spoken to?

The night turned into dawn, the morning sunlight streaking the skies with slivers of orange and pink hues. That's when he decided to fake an excuse to get closer to what was in the shed.

Katherine awoke the following morning to the dog barking. She moaned loudly and looked to the wall where the clock read nine o clock. She intended on sleeping in, but the dog had stopped all that. She shuffled to the side of the bed, slid her feet into the blue slippers at her bedside, and dragged her feet to the kitchen. The dog was at the door, barking furiously. She entered the kitchen, turned on the kettle, and poured ground coffee into the French press Ted had gotten her for her 70th birthday.

"Shut up, you damn Mutt." She said to the dog. He continued barking. She slammed the bag of coffee onto the counter, and refined grains spilled onto the countertop,

"I said shut the fuck up!" she yelled. The dog continued. She quickly walked out of the kitchen toward the front door and met the dog. It was facing the door barking and yelping. She looked through the peephole of the front door and saw nobody there. She turned to the dog and said,

"Shut up! Shut up, I said!" She could hardly hear her screams amongst the annoying yelping. The dog didn't stop barking.

She stomped the dog on its back with her heel and exaggeratedly pushed down with all her weight like she was stepping on a hard-shelled tortoise, trying to break through the shell. The dog's back let out a loud crack, and it lay on its stomach, withering in tremendous pain. She stomped the tiny dog on its spine and head until it stopped making noise, and there was nothing left but fresh roadkill on her living room floor. The blood puddled around the dog's corpse and slowly oozed from beneath it. Drops of her drool fell on the dark glass-like liquid like rain splatters.

"That'll shut you up, fucking – "

Knocks at the door startled her.

She panicked, looking back and forth between the dog's mangled corpse on the floor and the front door as it shook on its hinges from the pounding. She took a deep breath and turned the knob, slightly opening the door to see who it was. Standing in front of her was Kevin Desjardins.

"Oh, good morning to you, young man." She said in a cheerful, enthusiastic tone while crumpling up in shameful frustration inside,

"Good morning, Ma'am. I'm sorry to bother you so early; I hope I didn't wake you." He said,

"Oh gosh, no. I was up already making my morning coffee, that's all. Your no bother. How can I help you, son?"

"Well, I figured you were such a nice lady after we met a few days ago while you were drying your clothes on the drying rack - and I hate myself for it - but I thought you would be nice enough to help me out?"

"Yes, of course; how can I help?"

"You see, my father-in-law hates the Pine tree in his backyard and tasked me with cutting it down. I looked in his shed and his basement, but for the life of me – I couldn't find an axe or a saw to cut the tree down with. Do you have either one I could borrow? I think I wouldn't be more than 10 mins – it's not a very big tree at all."

"Bill planted that tree years back; you want to cut that one down?" She asked.

"Well, it's not me, Ma'am - I'm just the worker. I couldn't care either way. but I'm trying to help the old timer out." He explained.

"Of course, how nice of you." She responded. The hatred in her chest bubbled like molten lava, and she could taste gun-metal on her lips. Behind the door, her fist clenched where the knuckles turned chalky white.

"You're a very nice young man – polite. My late husband had an axe in the backyard. You can feel free to use it if you return it."

"Yes, Ma'am, of course." He said.

"Right. Just go back there – "she was interrupted by the faint clawing of the dying dog on the hardwood floor. "Excuse me a minute."

"Of course,"

She closed the door, turned to the dying Terrier, and stomped it on the head again, grinding her heel tenaciously like she was stamping out a cigarette on the floor. A gushing sound on her heel delighted her slightly; she kicked her slipper off to avoid leaving bloody footprints. Its paws stopped moving. She turned and opened the door again with a gentle smile.

"I'm sorry – kettle was boiling over – anyway, you will see a stump and a wooden racking of firewood in the back. The axe should be there. It's not in the shed; it's near the stump." She said and smiled.

"Near the stump. Got it. Thank you so much, Ma'am."

"Please call me Katherine or Rudy. My friends call me that. Ma'am makes a lady feel old."

"Rudy. Thanks again, Rudy. I'll be quick and silent as a mouse, I promise." Kevin said. He waved his hand and stepped back. She closed the door and turned to look at the puddle of blood seeping closer to the living room rug and was overcome with a menacing irritation for realizing she would waste good dishtowels soaking up the dog's blood.

"Always a fucking pain in my ass. Dead or alive." She muttered.

Kevin scampered to the backyard. He faced the shed head-on, and to the left, he saw the stump and the racking of firewood neatly stacked beside it. There was no sign of the axe close to the firewood. He watched the kitchen window to see if she was spying on him. He didn't see her or the kitchen drapes move in the small rectangular window, but he could feel her prying eyes watching him from a distance. He inched closer to the shed door. His heart pounded in his chest; he began to sweat.

He reached for the shed door and slid it open, slowly trying to avoid the screeching from the metal roller hinges.

Inside was dark, and the smell slammed against his face, nearly making him vomit, forcing him to cover his mouth with the back of his hand. Like the night before, he felt the stink attach to his skin like the rancid odour had suction cups, and he felt the toxicity seep into his pores. He tasted the copper-like rot glide along the roof of his mouth. It smelled of a cemetery—a scent of dampened sod and grave dirt.

He stepped inside and closed the door behind himself, leaving him in the dark, panting mists of cold air from his breath. It suddenly became frigid in the shed, and the beads of sweat on his forehead had frozen and dissipated. He flicked the Zippo lighter he had stolen from "Casper Mulligan" in High School twenty years before. The flint sparked a few times, then finally lit.

He shrieked at the sight of the rotted corpse in front of him. The dead husband was sitting on a small wooden chair, his head tied back to level and nailed to the shed's back wall. His skin was grey and decomposing. It looked hard and dry, like beef jerky. His mouth hung open, and the white porcelain dentures sparkled in the light. They were the freshest object in the shed. The body was dressed in khakis loosely fitted and hanging from the boney frame, looking as if it were to fall off the corpse if not for the suspenders slung around the nearly skeletal shoulders. The white dress shirt was stained with a dark Brown substance from the collar covering the torso. Kevin was unsure of what it was. Blood? He thought. Wine?

The eyes were the most haunting of all. They looked alive, as the corpse in front of him was a conscious human being trapped within the exterior of rotted flesh. The baby blue eyes pierced daggers into Kevin's heart and seemed to read him. The lines under the lids were much like Robert's old, withered fence's deep and blackened planks.

The door slid open with a blistering sound of metal screeching; the loud bang at the end shook the shed on its foundation. Kevin looked behind him and saw the dark silhouette of Katherine standing at the entrance. His Zippo had suddenly run out of Butane, and the morning light behind her was blinding him – all he could make out was a dark shape of a thin and bony woman with what looked like a long-serrated bread knife in one hand.

"I told you it wasn't in the fucking shed." She said with a growl. "You people don't listen, do you?"

She stepped closer to Kevin, and the words he wanted to spill from his lips didn't come out. He was frozen at the sight of the old lady stepping closer. He saw her eyes in the darkness as she came close to him. Her brows were furrowed, and her pupils dilated to pinpricks amongst a background of jaundice-coloured corneas.

He stepped back and felt the corpse's foot on his heel which made him stumble, finally crying out loudly. Katherine leaned forward, swiped the blade toward Kevin, and tore a large slit in his neck. He grasped the wound quickly with both hands and could feel the blood oozing between his fingers. He scurried on the floor of the shed in panic. It was harder to breathe. He gasped at the stink surrounding him and prayed that there was enough oxygen to keep him from going unconscious. She chuckled and moved closer to him. She was patient and controlled. A smile had appeared on her face, and she seemed excited as she stood over him. He took his hand away and held it out in front of him. The blood poured out of his neck like an open faucet. His vision became blurry, and all he could see was the shape of the old lady hacking away at him.

The blade caught his fingers, slicing them off. She hacked at his arms and face with the knife in a furious rage, like she was clearing a path with a machete in the *Amazon* rainforest. Kevin tried to scream, but the slashing cut off his voice as she continued furiously slicing him as he struggled on the floor. His cheek opened from a deep cut, and his tongue hung out of his face. He moaned loudly and gurgled large bubbles of blood; his legs trembled like the tangs of a tuning fork.

She drooled as she chopped Kevin mercilessly with the blade. Like the dog, Kevin had ceased to move or make any sound after enough blood loss from the constant butchering.

Splatters of blood covered Katherine's face. Her white apron was stained with warm, sticky blood as she stood over Kevin's body, huffing large breaths and her skinny arms trembling from the over-exhaustion of forceful blows to her victim.

Kevin's mangled body lay in front of her dead husband. The corpse's bony fingertip, where the flesh had decomposed, revealing a boney fingertip, began to tap at the arm of the wooden chair. She picked up the lighter, flicked the roller, sparking a dim blue light, and showed it in her husband's face. His porcelain dentures were more visible now than before as the dead body smiled profoundly at her. His bright baby-blue eyes looked down at the bloody corpse and moved side to side gleefully at the chunks of flesh strewn across the bloody floor. Katherine breathed heavily, gasping, her chest rising and falling with long breaths of putrid stink,

"We got more parts for you, Teddy." Katherine leaned down and picked up a severed index finger. She placed it in her mouth, sucked off the blood from the pale, dead skin, then stuck the finger in her deceased husband's mouth. She used two of her fingers to force it down his throat. She caught her breath,

"Always want to pry, always want to get involved." She muttered. She flayed a chunk of flesh from Kevin's arm with the serrated bread knife and began to feed her dead husband, forcing the meat down his throat with her long bloody fingers. The corpse's eyes bulged with delight at the taste of fresh meat.

"You like that, Teddy? We have enough to get you back to tip-top shape." She said. She looked down at Kevin's body and spoke to him as well with a grave voice,

"Wasn't such a good idea, was it fucker?" she leaned closer to Kevin's butchered face. His eye blinked twice. "Hey Teddy, looks like we got a fresh one here. So fresh that it's still alive. Like a flapping Muskie." She chuckled, "Think I didn't know you were creeping on me; you dumb son of a bitch?" she stood up and chuckled.

Kevin's eyes blinked again, and as she carved more flesh from his arms - his gaze finally turned blank and cold.

The darkness had provided a respite from the smell, the awful stink of rotting human flesh, the cast-iron metal taste in his mouth, and the warm blood spurting from his wounds. He was free from the pain of the knife blows, the shocking realization that he was dying, the embarrassment of being killed so suddenly had disappeared, and the shame of getting himself in this mess by not minding his own business evaporated like steam rising to the blank sky.

The Zippo lighter flickered on his mangled face, and he didn't feel the heat from the lighter, the glow of its luminescence, or the blunt tip of the knife digging into his eye socket – popping out his eyeball.

She forced Kevin's eye into her husband's mouth, and his jaw started to grind it to mush slowly,

"Oh yeah." She said. "I forgot to tell you, Teddy." She licked her lips,

"I killed your dog."

7

LOOKING FOR ROGER

The rain drizzled from the looming clouds as Darian Miller strolled down the concrete parking lot trail leading to *49th Street Memorial Dog Park*. In the usual circumstance, the weather was enough of an excuse to stay inside and avoid the rest of the strangers who glared at him with such peculiarity. If only it weren't for the run-away dog, he could have found himself in the safe seclusion of his home, away from the prying eyes and rude chuckles of those who poked fun at him, dressed in his cartoonish pyjamas, playing video games on his duel screen computer.

Miller walked through the chain-link barrier up to the gate, using the side of his closed fist to unlatch the northern entrance gate door, walking with a leash in his hand but without a dog on the end of it. Shutting the gate behind him with a back kick like an angry mule in heat, the gate slammed shut with a loud crack that startled the morning joggers who used 49th Memorial as a training ground for the upcoming city Marathon. They were stretching when Miller came through the gate, and they couldn't help but wonder and squint an eye at the lanky stranger who entered a dog park without a dog, whistling loudly, causing such commotion so early in the morning. The songs of Ella Fitzgerald and Ray Charles stuck in Miller's head all morning as if his skull was a transistor radio playing all the classics at the whim of a thought. He nodded to the ladies and older retired gentlemen as he strolled along the gravel path, swinging the empty leash in big circles beside himself like a cowboy would loop a lasso.

"Hi, there! Beautiful day we are having, aren't we?" he said to the older couple, who glanced at him suspiciously.

"If you say so," the older man responded, clutching his wife's hand tightly, leading her away. Miller shrugged and kept Strolling along. He had seen it before, being shunned like a leper as he had been his entire life.

He had been avoided by others in high school and college in his earlier years and saw himself as a loner because of it. What was it with Darian Miller that pushed people so far back from him to leave him exposed and prodded at like an animal in a zoo? He didn't know the answer to that question, but what he could realize was that he could feel the painful electricity of the cattle prod of insults and stinging punches to his ribs. The bruises faded away from the surface of his pale skin, but the humiliating scars left behind in his self-esteem didn't. The shame of taking it silently hurt more than the aches, scratches, pointing fingers, and hysterical jokes that scalded him. The glares and menacing whispers didn't bother Darian Miller after long into his childhood. After years of trying to fit in, he wondered why people avoided him and finally concluded that he didn't care if people accepted his odd mannerisms and awkward conversation. If these strangers were not on board with his upbeat, pleasant manner, melodic singing or enthusiastic greetings, they might as well stay away from him altogether.

It was best for everyone. Most of the time, it was better to be alone anyway, he thought.

After all, his physical persona didn't shiver up people's spines. He had no physical disfigurements like vintage horror monsters of classic cinema or vulgar speech that would tend to push people away during a conversation, but the cheery melody that Darian whistled while walking in the damp, sodden mud of the overcast day gave the impression that he was the kind of person who would be gleeful during the most inappropriate of times. The type to crack jokes and laugh at a funeral, chuck out cheesy pickup lines to the bride at her wedding, or suddenly grasp a stranger's child and start playfully tossing them in the air without the parent's permission.

"What the hell is he so happy about?" was a common phrase among people in Miller's life, including his co-workers, family members and what seemed to be an ever-dwindling supply of friends with enough tolerance to put up with more than a few seconds of small talk—the guy with the dog leash and no dog. The guy with the bounce in his step and the swing of his hips that gave the impression that *all was good*, when it hadn't been.

His arms swung in long strides as he walked down the path, occasionally leaping over small puddles in the gravel with enthusiasm similar to Fred Astaire twirling around lamp posts in the rain. His happiness was overbearing to some, having his wife's friends gossiping to themselves about how they loathed the guy who was so lively and upbeat.

"Roger, where are you, boy? Roger." He called out. His feet dragged slightly at the heel, kicking up tiny stones in his wake. He scanned side to side, occasionally glaring across the north entrance hill.

He contemplated climbing the steep slope used as a toboggan hill in winter and working toward the western field through the park. The usual route was where most visitors to the dog park strolled along with their canines in the early weekday mornings. Though he ignored them and told himself that people would whisper to themselves about him as he walked by, as they usually did, he didn't want to feel the darting stares and melancholy attitude of folks that weren't as *chippy* as he was. If he could keep to the shadows and stay out of sight, the others who paddled their dogs along would rush past him, looking straight forward and purposefully avoiding eye contact like he was the *Invisible man* and wasn't there at all. Today, he preferred that. To be in his universe, where he could be himself and look for his lost dog in the only place he thought reasonable for the runaway Doberman to escape to.

He walked through the shallow valley on the East side and around the back through the clearing that was later transitioned into a sandpit by city officials and volunteers alike. The grass was wet, and the tips of each shard glistened with fresh dew from the overnight rainstorm.

"C'mon, boy, where you at?" he called again, his hands cuffed over his mouth.

As he made his way toward the low valley, the dip in the trail steadily became covered in fog. He saw silhouettes of a Golden Retriever and a Malamute playing in the distant mist. As he got closer, he saw that the Malamute had its poufy white fur covered in mud as the sprinkles of dark muddy water splashed around the canines as they jumped on their hind legs and hopped around each other, in a playful wrestle that excited dogs do when they play with each other. Both dogs jumped and danced in circles, their mouths open with the occasional grunts and growls as their owners stood to the side, leaning on the East entrance gated fence.

They watched and chatted away as they looked at their pets, enjoying themselves like children at a playground. They held doggie bags filled with shit and jawed away about the latest morning news, mumbling incoherently until one of the men blurted out,

"Crazy bastard: got to watch your back nowadays..." he said as the other nodded in agreement, his eyebrows raised, and his lips pursed tightly together.

"Hey there," Darian greeted. He hated the fact that he had to say something to the men.

They nodded back, then quickly looked back at their dogs like they were in a trance. Watching their canines in meaningless conversation was more important than greeting a stranger at the park. Miller told himself he could appreciate the struggles of the lonely housewife: being shooed away disrespectfully while their husbands focused on the big game in front of them. The overwhelming disgust pumped through Darian's veins at the sense of more people ignoring him, cutting their eyes off at him like he was a biblical leper or had a sign around his neck reading,

"Judas! This man betrayed the only son of God!"

Miller walked by the men engulfed in the fog, reassuring himself of the security the thick mist provided him. It was hard to see their faces through the thick haze. He enjoyed the feeling of being hidden. He could watch others and not be seen, and he found the thought exhilarating. He avoided the dogs as he strolled past, then stopped suddenly as if an idea popped into his head. He turned around with a finger pointed to the sky and asked the two gentlemen on the fence line,

"Hey, did you guys happen to see a Doberman stroll by here?"

"No luck, pal." One of the men said. Miller could have sworn he heard a *"now, fuck off, buddy,"* but that could have been his imagination. They quickly looked back at their dogs and continued mumbling to each other. Darian wondered if they were whispering or gossiping about *him*. He stood momentarily, puzzled at the scene of the two men obsessively occupied by their wet dogs jumping around and playing with each other.

Like watching strippers take their tops off... he thought, *look how so little can have them staring so hard.*

He snickered and continued walking, calling out for his dog.

"Hey Roger, c'mon' boy. Where you at, Roger?" Cupping the side of his mouth with both his hands now, trying to create a loud echo in the dense fog of the valley, he walked in. He hoped Roger would hear his voice in the distance, echoing in its ultra-sensitive ears like a steel tray falling on a tile floor.

The air smelled Dewey, like fresh autumn rain, and the heavy moisture hung in the air as the showers finally reached a standstill. He continued on the gravel path until it turned muddy. On the East side of the park, where the gravel would gradually shift to a dirt trail that wandered through a tiny, forested area, he could feel the mud stick to his soles and pull up out of the ground with every step, like wet Velcro ripping off its mating fuzzy patch. Darian Miller walked on the muddy trail approaching the large clearing, leaving deep footprints behind him. The frigid drops that fell from the tree leaves landed on his shoulders and gently rolled off his sleeve. He peered through the trees on his right, slumping down to look through the wet bushes for his lost companion.

Where the hell did he run off to? You're being a bad boy, Roger. He thought,

To his left was the fence line, and the lake was coming up. He could see from a distance that the waves were choppy and rough, the white tips rolling furiously and crashing to the shore with a thunderous rumble.

I wouldn't want to go out in that. I bet these rich assholes are sitting back in their fancy Yachats, drinking their morning tea or whatever the

hell rich people drink in the morning. Champagne. He shook his head in disgust. *Be nice if they fell over the rail and nobody was around to yell, "Overboard."* The corners of his lips crinkled upwards, then quickly disappeared when he realized he was only being jealous and reminded himself that he shouldn't envy other people, not knowing what kind of problems they might have had,

Well, at lEast I got to find a lost dog. Better than losing a ton of money in the market. Still, I'd like a yacht with champagne fed to me every morning by my supermodel trophy wife. Growing impatient, he yelled out louder,

"Roger! Roger, where are you? Roger!"

The wind eased, leaving a cool breeze grazing Darian Miller's damp face. The water particles could be seen in the bright rays of the sun floating like dust particles illuminated in light, and the evaporating steam rising from the ground with the smell of earth pine freshness made the sand look as if the surface was slightly simmering. The tall natural pine trees towering above were apparent and surrounded Miller as he strolled along the path carefully. Like giant wooden skyscrapers swaying with the wind, standing high above him, he occasionally glanced up at the trunks, interested in how tall the trees had grown over so many years and how few had died, toppling over to the hard wet ground he stood on.

Darian reached the sandpit, where wooden picnic benches were scattered along the perimeter of the tree line and the fence. People sat and chatted, holding their morning coffees as they watched their dogs play and run around. Two boys along the fence line tried jumping over the chain-linked fence in a race to see who could get to the other side first. A mother with an all-terrain stroller sat on a bench in the corner, warming up a bottle of milk in a canteen with what appeared to be filled with boiling water. Miller couldn't distinguish the steam from the canteen lid from the mist rising from the dampened sand. He could feel the growing frustration disappear with the smiling faces of children running around. Their giggling and off-balance steps as they chased their family pets around, their legs still underdeveloped, reminded Darian Miller of his young children at home.

I bet he's here somewhere. It's a matter of time before someone asks me if I'm missing a dog and that they've seen a Doberman trotting around. Hopefully, they can point the way to me. I don't see him anywhere around here, though. He thought.

He combed the perimeter for Roger but didn't see his dog trotting around. He reached the damp picnic bench where puddles of cold rainwater gathered in large blots on the wooden surface. He perched himself on the table with his feet on the seating planks. He didn't mind the wet puddles on the table, as his pants were already wet from walking around in the rain; he could feel the water puddling soak through his sweatpants, chilling his hamstrings. It was almost refreshing if it wasn't unbearably frigid.

I'm sure he will show up. The dumb dog will stroll by, not expecting to see me, then I'll guide him in with a bacon treat and leash him up.

He unzipped his jacket pocket and pulled out a damp pack of cigarettes. The creeping rainwater that snuck into his jacket softened the pack, leaving the white Marlboros flimsy and malleable. He carefully flipped open the thin cardboard lid of the pack and gently pulled out a cigarette. He anticipated the cigarette being soaked or broken in half from the state of the cardboard packaging. It wasn't. He took a sigh of relief and placed the smoke in his mouth. It dangled from the corner of his lips, and he pictured himself looking like James Dean in that famous photograph before he died in that car wreck. Closing his eyes, with his head tilted back, he imagined the inner dwellings of his front jacket pocket as his hand fumbled and toyed with the contents within, finally pulling out an orange plastic lighter. He lit up and sat on the bench with his elbows on his knees, slumped forward, observing the people with their dogs around the clearing.

I'll get him home, give him a big bowl of his favourite food, and forget this shit ever happened. I hate when he gets out... he took a long drag, the ashes building up quickly on the end of his cigarette, dropping his lighter back into the deep cavern of his jacket pocket again. He heard the *clang* of the plastic lighter bounce against the other object he had in his pocket. He had hoped it hadn't been obvious. The way his pocket sagged from the weight.

"Hey, buddy." A voice appeared from behind him. He snapped out of his trance and looked over his shoulder, almost biting through the cigarette butt with the jump scare. The back of his mind reassured him that some concerned dog owner had finally noticed his lost dog and thought of asking if the friendly Doberman had belonged to him. It wasn't what he imagined at all.

"Oh jeez, I didn't mean to scare you. I noticed you have a leash and no dog... He run off from you?" A voice asked from behind Miller. The voice seemed stern and gave away a hint of knowing the answer to his own question yet asking anyway. Getting a good look at the voice behind him, he was surprised, then realized he shouldn't be. Of all people to address him, a Police officer – another bully that terrorized him more frequently than he felt appropriate.

The man with burly eyebrows and sunken eyes slowly approached the front of the picnic table. Miller saw the shiny golden badge and glint from the shine of the metallic handle of the holstered Glock 19. Dressed in his dark blues, the Cop looked relatively dry, like he hadn't been out in the rain for long; his golden badge pinned on his dark blue jacket shined and sparkled in the light like it was intentionally polished earlier in the morning and Darian found the badge mesmerizing, a mirror finish almost hypnotizing as Miller responded to the Policeman in a kind of trance.

"Yeah…a Doberman; you see one around?" He sat up straight and peered into the Policeman's eyes.

"I haven't seen one on the loose, no. I'll keep an eye out for you. You got a name, stranger?" He asked.

"Blake, Blake Worthy." A Lie. His go-to fake name when anyone suspicious asked. Before, it was Michael Hunter, but Miller realized it sounded too much like an action hero's name; insultingly evident for anyone to take seriously.

"Well, Blake, a hell of a shitty day to be outside, don't you think?"

"I don't think so. I enjoy overcast mornings; besides, the sun's starting to come out, making me feel…. happy."

"Good to hear." The Cop squinted one eye at the strange response, "You got a Doberman, huh? How long have you been out here looking for him?"

"Not long." Miller felt the Policeman was getting nosy and wasn't just polite. He was suspicious, and it was evident by the look on his face that it was all too familiar. Darian Miller had a brooding warmth in his chest and could feel the acidic bile in his gut bubbling.

"I see. Say, ten minutes or maybe, an hour?" he asked, "I'm sorry – I don't mean to be so inquisitive. I suppose I got a little too comfortable with the job after so many years. It makes it hard to speak to some folks when I sound like I'm interrogating them."

"I don't think so. I get it. For the record, I didn't feel like you were too forward."

"Yeah, that's good." the Policeman said, "I just haven't seen you around here, is all." He placed his hands on his hips as an unconscious show of authority. "I just got on the shift and figured I'd stroll around." He shrugged his shoulders and continued, "I like this park this time of year; I bring my dog on my off days, even during my shift sometime. I'll go home on my break and pick him up. You come here often, Blake?" Darian was pleased that the Policeman started to open up to him. Miller took another drag from his smoke and pondered suspiciously at the possibility of the Cop being gullible or, most likely, an old Cop's trick of a ruse to fool the stranger at the dog park into confessing his crimes through genuine and pleasant conversation.

"I've come here a few times. I think the last time was about six weeks ago, on a Tuesday. Roger loves this place. I figured since he ran off on me – he would most likely go to the place he felt most comfortable in. Alas, here I am."

"He ran off on you?"

"Yeah, from the yard. There's a slit in the side fence that I've been meaning to fix. He got through there when I let him out for his morning potty time. He must have spotted a cute little critter and just took off after it."

"Did you try the Shelter or the local Rescue?"

"Not yet. Figured I'd check this place out first."

"Well, I got a Husky, so I know about big dogs and how they can take off on you. Even rip the leash from your grip if you let them. He's Four's years old and still acts like a pup. I like it that way for now, at lEast. That is until he gets old and lazy and doesn't care every time I walk in the door anymore,"

"Ha," Darian chuckled enthusiastically, "When has a dog never cared when you walked in? That's what makes them so great! You know the one about the woman and the dog in the trunk of the car, right?" Miller was taking a risk with this one, and he knew it. He proceeded anyway,

"You lock your woman, and you're dog in the trunk...leave for an hour, then return. When you open the trunk...who's happy to see you? The woman or the dog?"

The Policeman blurted out laughing, slapping his leg with amusement,

"I'm telling that one to the boys; that's good. What do you do? Are you a comic, Blake? It would be good to know a Comedian on my off days when I bring Buster; I could use the laughter."

"I'm here all week; tickets still on sale," Miller continued, imitating playing the drum symbols with imaginary drumsticks. "I suppose Buster's your dog?"

"Yeah, my wife named him. Typical. I wanted to call him *Scar*, you know? Something cool since he's *man's* best friend and all. But what are you going to do? *Happy wife, happy life*, right?"

He seemed gentle and a genuinely lovable man. Miller saw him as a grandfather in years to come, sitting on his front porch, the Cicadas chirping in the distance, with all the life lessons and wisdom to teach his grandchildren as they joyfully bounced on his knees. His speech was soft, and though he imagined the Policeman speaking assertively or becoming aggressive, he found it hard to imagine the same man becoming a relentless brute when he had to. Those kinds of mannerisms seemed against his nature -which Miller saw as a weakness for a man in an authoritarian role.

Is this the guy to cover my ass when some creep comes after me with a knife? He thought,

Will this guy find my murderer when I'm cold and dead?

He saw the Policeman's gentle mannerisms as a crutch, no matter how sympathetic the Policeman had been towards him. It was possible; The Cop had a genuine friendliness about him that came from a good place. Nevertheless, he made Miller feel an uncomfortable itch, a feeling he wasn't used to. A sense of gratitude. He couldn't help but contemplate the uses of taking advantage of manipulating the Cop. He imagined circling Hyenas and heard their cackle as they excitedly surrounded wounded prey. He despised weak people—especially those supposed to represent themselves as protectors and uber-masculine.

"Do you live around here? It's a nice neighbourhood." The Cop asked, "Expensive, but friendly."

"Sheppard Ave. I've got a basement apartment just behind that taco place...Uhm, Taco Paradise...or taco...something...."

Oh, Taquitos! I love that place. Ask for Juan; he makes the meanest quesadillas, I'll tell you. It makes me *not* want to call immigration on that guy." He winked his eye. "Listen, I'll keep an eye out for your dog. If I see him, I'll grab him and bring him back here, and if you're gone by then, look for precinct 22 on the corner of Quantum Ave and 34th. I'll keep him there until the end of the day; if you don't claim him by then, he's off to the Shelter downtown. They're good people over there; they will watch him until you show up."

"Well, thank you, I appreciate that. You off to walk the beat?" Darian asked.

"Yeah, we've been getting a lot of calls near the Marina. Residents have been complaining of some creep stalking around, making people uncomfortable. Anyway, I probably won't see anyone, but I got to look - it's the job in the description." The Policeman said. "I don't mean to put you off. It's usually nothing."

Interested, Darian inquired some more. His mother's habits of prying into other people's business had rubbed off on him. Pulling the curtains back to peek at the commotion outside or pressing her ear to the wall to hear the neighbours argue. Any information was good information.

"Probably some spooked-out old lady?" Miller asked,

"Yeah, probably." The Cop said. "If I don't see you around, it was a pleasure meeting you. Good luck finding your dog."

"Yeah, will do. Thanks for the tip," Darian Miller said. The Policeman nodded and walked away, his hands in his jacket pocket, his shined boots caked with mud. Strolling along the tree line, he turned back to Darian Miller with a confused look,

"Roger, right? The name of your dog?"

"Yup, Roger that," Miller responded with a smirk. "That's a major 10-4."

Keep walking, keep on walking away, he thought.

Miller turned his back, smoking his cigarette and hoping the officer would keep walking. He listened to the incoherent voice on the Police radio fade as the friendly Policeman walked farther away. He patiently waited to make sure he was gone for good.

Miller always became nervous around Cops even though Miller felt like he had nothing to hide. The chill of the cold rainwater soaking into his clothes was less frigid than the look on the Cop's face when he stopped to confirm his dog's name. The way the friendly Policeman said Roger's name was very disconcerting for him. He hadn't remembered if he had mentioned Roger's name and didn't seem to remember bringing up an excuse in the conversation to say it, only that Roger was a Doberman.

Miller made excuses to reassure himself that the Cop hadn't been suspicious enough to come back and interrogate him with his friendly banter. He still wasn't sure of the Policeman's welcoming and approachable tactics. Was it a way of getting him to loosen up and confess to being that stalker guy he was looking for? A method of gently prying the lock open instead of bashing it with a sledgehammer?

Christ, I'm just here looking for my dog. It isn't illegal to sit here without a dog. So what? People look for their lost dogs all the time, right?

Still, no matter how reassured he felt, he thought that everyone was guilty of something and who better than a Cop to weasel the skeletons in the closet out of their hiding place, then judicially punish him after the exposure of his darkest secrets to the world. Authority figures always had his heart beating faster and his natural comedic charm to signal on, hopefully insinuating he was no threat because he was funny and had a quick wit; that was enough for the Cop to stop thinking about him as a threat.

That "Roger that" line was pretty good. Miller thought,

It made him keep walking after all...but why did he stop in the first place, I wonder? How did he know Rogers's name? Weird.

Miller sat, pondering to himself, as he watched the people standing around drinking their coffee, the steam from the rain rising off from the sand like they were on the surface of a volcano or hot sands in the desert. It was becoming humid, and Miller felt the beads of sweat pooling on his brow. He glanced to the sky, squinting his eyes from the blaring sunlight, and mused,

Wonder how the winds are up there?

He remembered his pilot training program when working toward his PPL (Private Pilot's License). The first time he flew with his instructor Theodore Wallace, he fondly remembered how Wallace gave the checks, with Miller, in turn, confirming every command. He transported himself back into that bouncing aircraft as it gained speed on the runway. The ATC radio chatter in his headset was hard to make out, as the voice on the Cop's radio had been. Still, he could hear the squawk clearly, the loud humming of the rotary engine puttering along the taxiway, and the smell of diesel fumes seeping into the cabin through the slit in the side window. Miller closed his eyes and was transported into his memories, as clear and tangible as the hard wooden bench table he sat on.

"All right, keep her steady; we're going 20 knots, now 30…" The hangers from his side storm windows passed by faster and faster as the two-seater Cessna 150 accelerated on runway 52 West.

"Flaps at zero degrees," the instructor said,

"Copy zero degrees," Miller would respond. "Oil temp and pressure in the green, Ailerons into the wind and Elevator about half back from the gust lock hole."

Darian Miller would Check the gauges, and everything looked right. The crash axe was above his head. The blade was shiny, polished metal, and the point on the opposite end fell into a sharp tip to punch holes in the aluminum structure in case they crash-landed and had to cut themselves out. He learned that in ground school, and the idea of the axe and its purpose thrilled him, and he even dreamed of escaping a plane wreck in the Bolivian jungle while everyone else around him lay dying or already dead. Darian admired the gloss white paint finish on the blade and thought the handle's wooden grip was too long. It resembled more of a lumberjack's long axe, heavier than a crash Hachette should have been.

"Applying smooth, full power, check for at lEast 2300 RPMs, oil temperature, and pressure in the green. Do you Copy?" Wallace asked,

"2300 RPMs check, oil levels green, we good to go," Darian said.

"Good, good. Maintain runway alignment with the Rudder. Can you feel it on the pedals"? Wallace asked,

"Copy. What a feeling!" Miller responded excitedly as the aircraft picked up speed. The howling wind outside the cockpit whistled loudly through the seams of the storm windows. The plane shook as it sped down the runway."

"Okay, good stuff. Now, decrease Aileron deflection as we accelerate. Forty knots, Copy?"

"Aileron deflection carried out, check,"

"Now, at 55KIAS, pull the Elevator back to pull the nosewheel off the ground and place the top edge of the cowling on the horizon; you will feel the aircraft lighten up; that's when you know we are airborne."

"Check," Miller's hands were sweaty. His legs shook as he sensed the wheels rolling on the runway's gritty asphalt.

"50KIAS, 53, 54, okay, starting to pull back," Miller advised. The needle on the gauge slowly moved past the numbers and ticks on the analog instrument panel.

"Gentle, son, don't have to yank it." Pulling back on the column, the nose of the aircraft pulled upwards, and suddenly, the feeling of the landing gear wheels rolling on the asphalt was gone; the plane swerved side to side slightly. It felt like the aircraft were as light as a feather as the instructor, and his pupil tried to keep the plane from banking too much- the feeling was exhilarating, but the focus on checks was still present,

"Establish Wind Correction Angle to stay over the runway," Wallace said,

"Copy, angle corrected, sir," Miller responded.

Darian laughed and whooped out loud like a football player who had just won the Superbowl. He was ecstatic, clenching the control column tightly; he could feel the rubber grips squeeze between his fingers; he looked over at his instructor, and Wallace was bearing a huge grin at Miller like a proud father would when his kid hit the game-winning home run.

"All right, kid, we are not out of the woods yet; keep the top of the cowling on the horizon and the wings level. Climb Speed 70-80 KIAS," he said.

"Yes, sir," he stared at the gauges while the aircraft climbed toward the clouds,

"I'll keep an eye on them and let you know when to level off. Take a look around, son. Enjoy this."

The buildings and roadways shrank as they gained altitude. The people on the ground disappeared. Miller looked out of the storm window to see different sizes and colours of square and rectangular patches, rows of grape vineyards, and the big city in the distance – the world looked like a miniature model. Darian Miller felt like a God staring down at it.

He told himself that he would never forget the frightening strength of the winds in the sky at 5000 feet. The winds up there were not the same as on the ground, like a whole other world. How the plane bobbed up and down with every gust, the way the wingtips dipped up and down, side to side, as he tried to hold it level. Every minor adjustment could be felt. His adrenaline spiked, the nauseous feeling in his stomach disappeared, and his heart pounded against his chest cavity as he experienced natural turbulence in a small aircraft behind the captain's seat for the first time. He opened the storm window to hear the ferocious howling and the cold air infiltrating the cockpit. The things that scared most people and made them sick - he relished.

Miller flicked out his cigarette butt into a wet bush and decided to carry on walking. Enough reminiscing about flying - which had developed into his true passion - he had to find the damn dog. He stood up from the picnic table and stretched his arms, groaning loudly. He felt his hamstring muscles tighten as he stretched. He pictured himself like the old couple whom he had passed. Frail bones, thin and easily breakable. Weak, like the stupid Cop who had spoken to him. The pit of his stomach felt like a bubbling cauldron of disdain at the thought. He walked along the tree line, watching the kids playing as he strolled past. The sand was heavy and not as loose as on a sunny day. He felt his feet sink into the sand, but not as deep as they should have been, which gave him more traction, and he walked faster.

Darian Miller was beginning to lose hope. He hadn't seen Roger around, and nobody was going out of their way to ask him about the large Doberman they saw alone with no leash. Darian's head felt heavy at the disappointment. His chin lay on his chest, and he began to whistle as before, desperate to stay optimistic. It was the one thing the rain or a lost dog couldn't take away. He whistled his version of *Honky-Tonk Woman* by The *Rolling Stones* and occasionally mumbled the lyrics to himself.

He walked along the sand pit until the ground turned muddy again, and the trees cast shadows over him. Turning the corner where the Cop previously made his way up the pebble path, a Doberman ran up to him, sniffing his boots as it wagged his black stump of a tail. His ears perked as his dark black eyes stared at Darian Miller. The dog then sniffed at the sagging pocket of Darian's rain jacket, backed away, and looked up at him curiously the way dogs do, his head tilting to the side.

"Sorry about that; I didn't see you there."

A young woman outfitted in a sundress with a denim jacket ran up from the dense bushes. She was grasping a slobbered orange ball in one hand and a blue leash in the other, reaching over optimistically to grab the dog by its navy-blue collar. Miller looked around, noticing that the distant voices at the sandpit sounded like they were getting farther and farther, like being underwater and screaming, only to have the muffled sound faintly blotted out.

"Sorry. If I knew you were there, I would have kept him on the leash; I hope he didn't scare you." She continued, panting with a broad, friendly smile, leaning down to rub the Doberman on his forehead. Blake looked around until he met eyes with the young brunette,

"Oh, no worry at all; Roger loves me." He said.

"Roger?" she tilted her head quizzically, much like the dog had. A look of bewilderment became apparent quickly as she stood in a confused spot. Her smile slowly disappeared, "No. This is Daisy."

Darian placed his hands on his hips and replied.

"I'm pretty sure that's Roger. Isn't that right, Roger? Want to come home with Daddy?"

"I think you are confused." She said. "Where have I heard that name? Roger."

"The Newspaper. the *Creeper*? That's where you heard the name." Darian Miller said, "The guy who kills folks while out looking for a dog named Roger…. I think six or seven people so far; I'm sure you heard…." He explained calmly, barely holding back his pride.

She stood stunned. Her grip tightened around her dog's collar - she didn't know if this guy was joking or if he was serious. He glared at her through every word like it was typical for a crazy lunatic to be out killing innocent people. He spoke like he was discussing the weather or the lottery winnings from the night before, yet his eyes were broad and nearly bulging from their sockets as they strangely pierced through her.

Miller stood smiling with his hand out, pointing at the Doberman, "Yeah. Roger, I'm glad you found him; the girls will be so happy…."

"I'm sorry, I think…" She looked behind her to see if anyone else was around. The blood pumped furiously through her veins. She stepped forward to try and maneuver around the strange man with the odd and sick sense of humour.

As she took another step, her hand gripped tightly on the dog's collar; he reached into the open pocket at the front of his rain jacket and pulled out a small hatchet (the gloss white paint on the handle smothered with splatter marks of maroon, dried blood), and whacked the girl in the side of her neck. Her eyes widened broadly from the surprise and fright as the blood squirted from the hatchet blade stuck in her neck. Her mouth hung open, yet no words came out - wanting to scream, her vocal cords were severed, and instead let out a gurgling squeal. Red bubbles blew out between her fingers as she attempted to grasp the object he hit her with, not completely knowing what it was. She didn't feel the pain yet—too much adrenaline. The pain would shoot up her legs momentarily once she realized he was whacking her. She touched the blade protruding from her neck and felt the cold, wet edge with her fingers. Then, the pain rushed in. As soon as her brain clicked that it was an axe, her legs turned to soft Ramen noodles, and her knees buckled.

"Trying to take my damn dog, eh?" he yanked the cleaver from her neck and whacked her again in the forehead. The blade caused a loud thumping sound that surprised him as blood splattered on his face. Turning his head to the side and squinting from the blood getting in his eyes, it stung, like salted sweat dripping past his lashes. Miller's heart was beating rapidly. He tasted the iron on his tongue as it hung out of his mouth, like a child trying to catch snowflakes in winter snowfall.

The dog was taken aback and started to bark as Miller continuously hacked at the woman's head with the hatchet. He laughed as he furiously butchered her with an evil grin, chopping her repeatedly like a frenzied madman hacking through bones. With every blow, he pulled away faster, then struck her again, as there wasn't so much skull left to have the axe blade get a wedge in anymore.

This will teach you for taking my dog, making me look everywhere for the damn dog. Looking in the Marina, in people's Yachts, in their boats...in their homes.

The sound of squishing with every blow to her head, splitting her skull open further, and her brains poured out as she tumbled lifelessly to the floor.

...little old ladies calling the Cops on me...

(Whack, whack, whack.)

Pieces of skull and brain matter flew in the air as he pulled the hatchet away with every swing. He furiously butchered her skull with a sound that resembled smashing a cantaloupe with a hammer.

Take that, take that, take it...

Breathing heavily, with the dog barking loudly at him, Miller stopped, stood momentarily, and watched the girl lying in a pool of blood. Both her legs were shaking vigorously from her body going into shock. He had seen it before and became erect at the sight of the bloody scene. Pieces of her skull and hairs lay scattered, clumps of brain falling out of what's left of her primarily cavernous skull. Now soaked in dark red blood, her sundress lay wet in the sand as the grains absorbed every ounce that poured from her head like an open water tap. She lay with her eyes open, looking blindly out into the empty, devoid of life, her mouth wide and tongue hanging out to the side. The blood was dark and looked sticky and warm.

Darian Miller panted heavily. His chest rose and fell with every breath; his lungs burned from breathing so hard, like he had just finished sprinting for gold at the Olympics. He looked at the crash axe, admired the blood splattered against the white paint job on the blade, and glared at it glimmering in the sunlight.

Wow, what a rush! he thought,

He stood looking down, smiling at his handy work, then raising the hatchet to his face like King Arthur raising Excalibur and admiring the weapon as the blood streamed from the blade's edges, down the handle and pooled at his feet.

That will teach you, bitch. He looked down at the Doberman, barking loudly at him, and nodded. He put the bloody hatchet in the waistband of his sweatpants, tightened the string, and took off his bloody raincoat, wiping his face with it and tossing it to the side under a bush, kicking mud and dirt over it to hide it under the brush.

"Hey, Roger. I've got your treats, buddy… you're favourite…." He reached in his pants pocket to pull out a zip lock bag of "Mr. Barks" brand dog treats he stole from the local pet food store. Miller took a knee, hands shaking with a constant tremor of adrenaline coursing through his body, and he held out pieces of chewable bacon-flavoured dog treats- the tiny pieces sat in his bloody palm.

The Doberman tilted his head and stopped barking as he stepped closer to Miller, sniffing, intrigued at the scent of Bacon. Miller, feeding the dog out of his hand, slowly put the leash on the dog's collar, looking down at the corpse of the girl he hacked to death, patting the dog on his hindquarters and then scratching his back. The Doberman looked down at the bloody mess and whimpered,

Well, she's the first one to shake like that. Interesting. The flight instructor didn't shake. Neither did the guy from the hardware store…or that cackling old bitch behind the apartment building…huh, I guess there's a first time for everything. He chuckled aloud, tugging at the leash as he turned and strolled up the hill.

"You got to stop running away, Roger; this is like, what, the seventh time now? Eighth? Come on, buddy; the girls will start to suspect something."

Miller strolled up the hill, his faithful new companion beside him, kicking back the tiny pebbles that made up the trail of the artificial garbage hill that kids used for tobogganing in the winter. The sandpit was to the south of him. Lake Ontario's sparkling, cold water, the hallmark view of the dog park, was also behind him now.

Miller wondered about the circumstances and thought he might have missed Roger if he didn't stop at that park bench and conversate with that Cop. He tugged at the leash, and "Roger" gracefully trotted beside him. He whistled the same cheerful tune he did when he walked in, except there was no rude old couple this time. No asshole bystanders who stared at their dogs playing, like eyeballing strippers as they removed their clothes. There was no Cop to interrupt his peaceful serenity as he sucked back his cigarette. This time, he had "Roger." He had *his* dog. At lEast until the canine ran away, leaving Darian Miller to look for him again.

8

WALKING WITH GHOSTS

Northern Alberta, Canada
18 /Feb / 1954

My dearest Eleanor,

I've arrived at the cottage. The train ride was pleasant, and the food they served was... well, - not so much. I could tell the *Chicken Cordon Bleu* was previously frozen, and the faintest sense of freezer burn was present. The cottage is smaller than in the pictures, which is not quite what I expected. It is cozy; let's put it that way. The walls are made of logs from the surrounding forest, and the floors are hardwood planks. The large area rugs are excellent; I can tell they are old and handwoven. The living room has two large bookcases littered with classics, like Dickens and Twain. I can't wait to sit by the large fireplace and become lost in *A Tale Of Two Cities*. This Cottage is lovely and looks old. There is much to explore, both within and around its walls.

The walk from the cottage to town wasn't a long one—about 2 miles. Yes, I know, a brisk walk, but the surrounding wilderness is lovely and serene. As I strolled toward town with Frankie, I noticed a deer ahead of me. Can you believe it, Eleanor? It was trotting alongside the river while we were on a gravel trail. The deer was elegant. I think it was a female (I believe the males have antlers). It looked up at me and took off through the half-frozen river into the forest. The way it galloped into the woods was graceful, as they say in school textbooks. It quickly disappeared out of sight. I know now why hunters say deer are easily spooked and hard to get a clear shot on. As we strolled to town, the little waterfalls and tiny rapids gave off an incredible sound of rushing water. It's clear- I bet we could drink straight from the river (don't worry, I won't). I know better than to catch some parasitic disease that would make my trip unbearable; imagine that. Taking time off and spending so much money, only to be stuck in the bathroom most of the time. I bet you would get a laugh at that. It would be *just my luck*, wouldn't it, Ellie?

The town is cute; I noticed the cobbled road with indented tracks from the horse-drawn carriages from the past. The old road reminded me of our trip to Rome a few years ago when we walked along the *Appian Way*. Remember how deep the indents in the stones were? Imagine, people have travelled these roads for thousands of years before us. In the case of *Grande Cache*, I doubt people have been here *that* long, maybe a few hundred years or so, but still, it's impressive.

The town consists of one main street with shops like Bakeries, a Deli, and a little local farmers market that I mentioned before, taking up the middle of the square. Also, Victorian-style homes on either side of the main street were built in the 1800s. Some even have rusted old plaques dating back to 1805-I didn't think civilized people were here that long ago, especially out here in the woods. Still, the small-town charm is adorable. The homes have been renovated and kept up; they still look impressively new. They must have been well cared for by their owners over the years. The main street ends with a dirt road leading into the forest. The same dirt and gravel road winds down and eventually turns into the trail I walked on to get back and forth to the cottage and town. (Cab driver was friendly enough to help me with my luggage to the house, in case you are wondering. But he took off quickly. He was practically running away as soon as we got to the front porch).

I picked up lunch from a cute little mom-and-pop shop, *Grand Cache Market and Deli*. Oh my god, Ellie, the BLT sandwich was so fresh; I loved it. I know it's just a sandwich, but the ingredients are to die for, and the produce I see at these markets shines with vibrant bright colours. We don't see fruit and veg like this in the city.

Grande Cache has a river that runs beside it as it snakes through the town. The Smoky River. Grande Cache is quaint, but I'm not used to its size. It's tiny. I think I read the sign on the cab ride over saying it was a population of 210 people. I look forward to visiting the coffee shop and boutiques tomorrow after I unpack all my things tonight and cozy up beside the fireplace with a good book.

I'll update you in a few days, as my adventure is only beginning.

I hope its an eventful one,

Yours forever,

Claire,

Beans & Roast Coffee Shop,
Grand Cache, Alberta
20 / Feb / 1954

Elenore,

You won't believe it. The little coffee shop I'm writing you from this morning is lovely. It's nothing that I expected. The building is built of different-sized stones and shapes that interlock perfectly with each other. (Like buildings of ancient times. The kind archeologists wonder how they constructed them with so little modern machinery). The shop is suitably placed in the middle of Grande Cache, surrounded by an old Anglican church on one side of the shop and a boutique with an awning that reads, "Grace's Graceful Gallery." I find it cute.

Beans and Roast is smack dab in the middle of the town square like it was planned to be the gem of the town - and my god, the coffee is *fantastic*. The scent of freshly roasted beans flows down the main street approaching the shop. The old stone chimney exudes thick smoke from the roasting beans, enchanting the town with the smell of fresh java- it's delightful. You walk in to be greeted by a handsome young gentleman – another reason I look to stop in more frequently (don't judge me), and the artwork that hangs on the stone walls is plentiful and unique.

The canvases depict pleasant streetscapes of Grande Cache and natural landscapes painted by local First Nations artists from the past and present. The walls are also adorned with framed photographs of the early industrial period in Alberta. Pictures of men with giant handlebar mustaches and chimney stack top hats cutting the ribbon for the grand opening of some of the shops that still exist today. There are photographs of the mayor at the time, standing proudly beside the first railway access and artificial dam.

The large windows gave me views of the little town with backdrops of the Boreal forests and the Rocky Mountains. The only thing I could complain about is that they won't let Frankie inside. I peer through the giant front window at him as he waves his tail and stares back at me through the glass. His long tongue hangs from his mouth as his warm breath fogs the window in front of him. The gentle snowflakes land on his golden fur, only to soak in and disappear from his body heat. I feel sorry for him, so I'll try and write faster - so I can take him for a stroll. Before I do, though – listen to this,

I got a hold of the landlord yesterday. I don't believe I told you in my first letter. On the nightstand beside the bed (which is exquisite, by the way. Made of cedar, it's solid, which reminds me of the bed's headboard. It has a unique engraving that seems to tell a story, although I can't quite describe it now, for I haven't figured it out yet....). The letter read,

Dear guest,

Please enjoy your stay in this beautiful 18th-century built log cabin. At the entrance, you will find a jar of fresh maple syrup my family has produced from local maple trees for generations. The linens and blankets are freshly washed and pressed, and please take advantage of our fireplace in the main den. To our delight, the cabin you are staying in was built in 1789 by my ancestors, one of the first colonists to land here so long ago. The add-on to the cabin, for instance - the second floor, with your bedroom and the upper floor den with (I'm sure you noticed by now) the 12 sq ft tempered glass window overlooking the majestic Rocky Mountains, were, in fact, built some fifty years after by my great uncles who were fur traders and known for travelling on the winding rivers to Montreal on the famous voyageur routes.

My family and I hope you enjoy and have a pleasant stay in our family's cottage. If any assistance is required, the telephone is in the downstairs dining room; our phone number is under the receiver's base; please do not hesitate to call.

Enjoy the maple syrup, and by the way.... we left you a bottle of our homemade cider in the refrigerator. (Beware, the alcohol content could be a bit much, we advise watering it down as per your discretion, of course,)

Cheers,

The Holloway family,

You would love it here, and I dearly miss you. I know you are going through a lot after Derek, but I wish you had taken me up on my offer for this winter getaway. Take your mind off it and all - Even for a moment.

I'll be returning to the cabin now with Frankie, and I look forward to hiking and exploring the nearby forest with him on his daily walks. This place is like a wonderland. I'll stop by the post office to send this in.

I Miss you, Ellie; with every moment that passes,

Your dearest friend,

Claire

Holloway Cabin, Alberta, Canada

21/Feb/1954

Dearest Eleanor,

You won't believe it. This place is like *Alice in Wonderland*! After leaving that fantastic coffee shop, I walked Frankie into the forest behind the cabin. The old-growth trees and the stunning vistas of the mountains and deep valleys are marvellous. I understand why artists have come here over the years to paint landscapes - this place is heavenly. I could only imagine what it would look like in the summer, but the winter does not disappoint. The trees are encased in snow and ice, making them look like ice sculptures, and the valleys covered with fresh powder look so smooth. Untouched.

This place would be magical to escape to for writing your next novel Ellie (which you better be working on! I NEED to know what happens to Marie LeBeouf. I don't appreciate how you left that cliff-hanger at the end, yet, I still respect you for it. I digress.)

One mysterious thing. Frankie took off on our hike today. He doesn't usually do that. I thought I had almost lost him, but I followed the barking in the near distance ahead of me. I trekked through the overgrowth and thorny vines for over an hour, following him as he stayed what seemed ten or twenty feet ahead of me. I wouldn't have found him if it weren't for his constant barking. I nearly fell down a cliffside, for heaven's sake!

When I finally did catch up to him, I found him sitting kindly on a hillside overlooking what looked like an outcrop of stone buildings in the valley below us. I thought I saw some buildings through the thick trees. The mountains surround this place. It would be treacherous due to winter avalanches and mudslides in the summer and rainy seasons. The winds started picking up at that point, making the snow drifts blinding in the distance, and it was hard to make out the structures below us. I'm not very good at guessing distance, but I would estimate 600 yards ahead of us.

The trees were also overgrown down there, so it's hard to make it out—something to explore tomorrow, I suppose. Still, Frankie barking, staring down at that mysterious outcropping, was unusual. He's a quiet dog. I felt like he was guiding me to that place, or he was being drawn there. Maybe you could explain, being an animal lover yourself. Some things you know that I don't. That's why I love you.

Anyway, I'll write tomorrow. Hopefully, the weather will clear up so I can explore some more,

I look forward to hearing from you, Ellie,

Claire.

Holloway Cabin, Alberta, Canada
25 / Feb / 1954

Dear Eleanor,

A lot has happened since I wrote you last. Some delightful, some very curious. I'll start with the day after I wrote you last, which was Tuesday.

I walked down to the market in Grande Cache. I must remind you that the walk is more of a rugged hike. Holloway Cabin is located in a valley between Mt Sprague and Camelid Peak, situated on the shores of the Smoky River. It's simple enough to get to town by following the river, but I fear hiking back with groceries would be a nuisance. So, as I got to town that day, I stopped by a little home with a sign out front of it advertising wilderness outfitting survival gear for sale. A large awning hung from the front porch, and the windows had displays with snowshoes, winter clothing, mukluks, and yes - toboggans and sleds.

Walking in the front door, hearing the cheerful little bells chime above my head, I spotted a red plastic sled in front of me. I felt like I was having a lucky afternoon and checked the tag to see it was two bucks—a bargain. This place is satisfying in every way, Ellie.

The elderly lady selling the sled asked where I was staying, as I wasn't familiar with the town. Grand Cache is so small and all. I told her I was staying at Holloway Cottage, and I noticed her smile disappear as I explained how beautiful it was and how I was enjoying my stay. You know when you explain something to someone, and they aren't paying attention to what you're saying and thinking something else? Yeah, she pulled one of those on me. Her eyes narrowed into contemplative slits. Curious as to why she noticeably seemed distressed, I asked what the matter was, and she turned and strolled back behind her desk, saying,

"Nothing, nothing, dear. It's just ...that place has a history. It's ancient; it was built so long ago; I'm just worried about your safety, is all. How long are you staying?"

She seemed to be prying, like a salesperson at Tiffany's who asked what you were looking for, only to know that behind the questions, they assumed you couldn't afford the item in the first place. She seemed to want to know the answer so she could arrange a cab to get me out or maybe talk me out of staying. Her line of questioning was strange.

I told her I was staying another week since I called the Holloways on their phone number, explained how I was enthralled by the cottage and surrounding area and asked to stay another week. Shaking her head, she seemed disappointed.

"Please be careful, honey, it gets lonely out there, and I would hate to hear of anything happening to you. Please, take this sweater and mitts I made last week," she continued, handing me the light blue crocheted sweater and mitts. "It's dangerous out there, a young girl like you....be careful, please." She said worryingly. I handed her some cash, and she gently pushed the handful of bills toward my chest,

What a wonderful old lady, like my own grandma. I remembered thinking to myself. I walked out of the little shop, curious about what she meant and her concern—pondering what she said about the cottage having a history. What did *that* mean? Chalking it up to the environment and the weather outside, alone in the wilderness, I'm not worried.

Please write back to me and let me know your opinion. She was a sweet lady, but she genuinely seemed concerned.

Anyway, The hike back on the frozen river to Holloway Cabin wasn't as bad as I expected. The sled trailed behind me with paper bags of groceries to keep me equipped for the following days, and

Frankie, my beloved golden retriever, led the way. The sun was shining through the clouds over the tips of the Rockies. The sunlight hitting my face offered an incredible sensation and warmth. The simple things Eleanor. The simple things.

The next day, on Wednesday, I had some news to report. However, I wanted to call you to hear your voice. I do very much miss you and am starting to grow lonely. Of course, Frankie is an excellent companion, but I could never again take human interaction for granted, especially yours.

I tried calling you on the telephone in the cottage, but there was no dial tone. The power must be out, and I was curious if the weather had also toppled the telephone lines in town. There is no other electricity in the cottage. As exquisite as it is, the house is quite humble when it comes to modern entities. There is no television and no light bulbs, can you believe it? The fireplace and shelves of old literary classics are my entertainment and should give me much solace. The oil lamps and candles situated on the walls are my reading lights. A hand pump provides water from the nearby well, and the toilet is of the composting kind.

Fun.

The Holloways told me not to worry about it on yesterday's phone call, as they would cater to the sewage when I left. I am a little embarrassed knowing strangers would clean up my shit (excuse my language). I feel like I'm living on the frontier, like the pioneer village we visited outside of Toronto. I sometimes feel the need to purchase a bonnet and raise farm animals. I joke, Ellie (of course), but still, it is very primitive here, and it reminds me that simple things are essential - we must not take them for granted.

That night, I did try to make out the carving on the main bedroom headboard—a curious one. I'll try my best to describe it as I didn't bring my camera (I'm an idiot, I know).

Starting from the top left corner of the headboard was an illustration of a church and schoolhouse with what looked like children dancing and playing on the grounds before it. As I stared at the carving moving to the right, I could make out the Rockies carved above with scenes of a priest giving an outdoor sermon in front of the church as parishioners sat before him, following his every word. They Looked like kids, and I couldn't make out any adults. His hand raised to the sky, pointing up with two fingers; it was like he was in the process of performing the sign of the cross. More engraving of what looked like children and kids dressed in native garb transitioned into more catholic or modern attire: collared shirts and buttoned-up dresses. The kids with long hair were now trimmed short below the ear lobes—I'm not sure what this is supposed to depict.

I must admit that the artwork is impressive. Whoever carved this headboard was immensely talented and an experienced engraver. The details of the figures and the trees in the scenes deserved to be in a museum. I continued to examine the carving for a while, sitting cross-legged, facing the headboard. I almost dropped the oil lamp I was holding as I heard Frankie. He was lying beside me on the mattress. He growled slightly, then sat up hysterically, barking at the bedroom door like someone was on the other side. After barking a few moments loudly, he laid back on his belly, his paws covering his head like he was hiding, and he began to whimper—so weird, Eleanor. I began to become concerned. The room became bitterly cold as I stared at the bedroom door in the dim yellow candlelight. Frankie has never acted like that before.

I didn't sleep well that night, either. After deciding to call it a night and trying my hand at the carving another time, I snuggled up to Frankie under the heavy quilt of the bed, trying to keep warm as the bitter cold was present all night. Another weird thing happened that night; I must relay it to you.

I awoke in the middle of the night to see Frankie sitting politely at the foot of the bedroom door staring at the wooden planks that made up its construction. He was looking up like he was sitting before someone. He patiently awaited a treat, his tail brushing the large woven rug side to side. It was pretty odd, Ellie. I called him to the bed, and he came without a hitch. I grasped onto him tightly, absorbing his body heat while he kept me feeling safe.

Other than that, not much took place on Thursday and Friday. On both days, the snow came down hard, and I stayed near the fire reading Hemingway's short stories, then *Fathers and Sons* by Turgenev. I roasted some sausages on the fire and took Frankie for a stroll playing with him in the snow.

I slept a little better, but I thought I heard leaves rustling outside Thursday night as I lay in bed. Probably a raccoon or coyote or something. (I am in the wild, after all). Didn't think much of it. Oh, I almost forgot to say that I awoke on Friday morning to the scent of burning sage. I'm not sure where it came from, but it was soothing. I hope you can read my handwriting as I found an old quill and bottle of ink at the desk in the living room library. I'm trying to practice with it, so please forgive my sloppy chicken scratch.

This is a long letter, Ellie – I will cut it short. Like always, I always think of you, and I'm sorry if I worry you with my exaggerated imagination. It's getting a bit lonely up here, and my mind wanders.

I didn't have the opportunity to explore the woods yet, because of the weather and deep snow. I think I'm going to invest in some show shoes at that little old lady's shop tomorrow,

I'll also send you a gift when I mail this letter to the post office, Claire.

Holloway Cabin, Northern Alberta, Canada
26 / Feb / 1954

Eleanor,

I finally made my way to what I thought were the stone buildings I saw in the distance while hiking with Frankie. They were not stone but dilapidated wooden buildings. I discovered them as I walked through the woods and trekked down the valley.

The trek was arduous; I almost fell down a cliff edge (again). The snow was high, reaching my knees in-depth, and I was exhausted when I got down from the mountain pass. I'm unsure how to describe what I saw, but I will try.

Before I left, I saw how hard the snow was falling and knew Frankie would have a terrible time, if not with the depth, at least the temperature; his paws would freeze quickly, and I couldn't bear to watch him suffer with frozen pads. As for myself - I did buy the snowshoes; they were much help. I admit, walking into the store, the old lady was glad to sell me the snowshoes, and yes, she asked how much longer I was staying at the Holloway cabin. She can be sweet, Ellie - but the line of questioning is getting quite annoying.

The trek was arduous; I almost fell down a cliff edge (again). The snow was high, reaching my knees in-depth, and I was exhausted when

I got down from the mountain pass. I'm unsure how to describe what I saw, but I will try. It took me hours to climb down the mountain slopes, and when I got to the base of the rugged mountain, I had to trek another kilometre through dense vegetation and old-growth trees. The snow was deep, and I became more exhausted with every step. I felt like my knees would touch my chest with every lumbering stride. The snow drifts were so deep. For this reason, I'm glad I left Frankie at the cottage.

I finally made it through the dense forest and came upon a clearing. Situated in the clearing was an ancient wooden building that resembled a church. It had a tall tower with a point and an iron cross still perched on the tip. I wondered how the wooden structure still stood. A very long building with wooded tiles on the rooftop lay beside the church. The wooden planks were previously painted white, but the paint was chipping off, missing in chunks after years of degradation. I got closer to both buildings and noticed that the walls had caved in on the south sides of both structures and bushes were littered around the foundations, with dead vines creeping up the walls.

I managed to access the inside of the long wooden building through an opening on the south side. It was a schoolhouse. I saw desks and chairs littered, lying on their sides, and wooden stools broken in pieces from a sudden impact. With every step I took within the building, I could hear a creek from the floors, and I felt like I might break through the boards. The winds outside whistled, and I could hear them blowing through the cracks and holes in the walls of the wooden structure. A large chalkboard was still hung up, and many books and Bibles were littered around the floor. I tried to grab one of the books to bring back and read, but I was afraid I could not reach any of them as the large beams and fallen walls blocked my path. There was not much else to see, and with mounds of rocks and snow, leaning planks of wood resting on the vertical east wall that looked as if they would give way any moment - I couldn't move any farther within the building.

I walked out of the schoolhouse, surrounded by a sudden chill. It was very dark and eerie inside that place; I exited it as quickly as possible. I tried to gaze inside the church, but unfortunately (maybe not), I couldn't get inside. The walls were caved in, not offering me a hole or nook to crawl through. I did manage to peek inside a crack between two planks of fallen debris, but I couldn't make anything out in the darkness.

I walked around the clearing some more and suddenly fell into a ditch. My heartbeat was so fast that I swore I would have a heart attack. My panic also grew when I realized how deep in this pit I was and knew I would struggle to get out. I stood there in a ditch, up to my waist in snow, gathered my wits, and as I climbed out, grasping onto the top ledge, I was reminded of climbing out of an empty swimming pool when we were kids. The walls were flat, and the ridge was sharp, dug at 90 degrees. As I hoisted myself from the pit, I sat on the edge, examining the hole in astonished wonder. I looked abound and thought I had made out the extent of this ditch. It was huge, Ellie. The size of a football field, at least. The giant hole showed no evidence of it being natural—sharp corners, like a huge rectangle of land removed from the ground. Like a massive grave.

I was astounded at the size of this pit and wondered what it was doing there. It was located at the north end of the church and schoolhouse, which would have been the back of the buildings. A sudden fright came over me; I could hear a wolf howl in the distance. And I could feel the winds pick up, blowing snow in my face. The sharp prickles of snow ticking on my flesh stung. I was worried that, being in a valley surrounded by mountains, I would get caught in an avalanche and be buried there forever. The whistle of the wind was haunting. I swear, Eleanor. My heart raced the whole time I was there. It was hard to breathe.

That place was haunting, and I remember being overcome with a feeling of pity and sadness. I left the clearing feeling nauseous. My emotions raced and were many. I still can't make sense of it. I'm not sure about this place, and I don't want to return to these ruins in the woods.

Ellie, I still don't have any electricity at the cottage, and the trail is too deep to make it to town. If I'm lucky, I can walk over the river as it tends to have less snow on its surface. If you can, try and find out about this place and what it was from back home. I'm sure the local library has newspaper clippings or articles to work with. This place is about 14km north of Holloway Cottage, which would be 2km from the town of Grande Cache—a total of 16km northwest between *Mt. May* and *Camelid Peak*.

Please let me know, as I am gravely curious. What happened here? If I could make it to town, I would ask around. Maybe that lady in the shop? If I can't, please post me whatever you find.

So many questions, Eleanor.

Claire.

Holloway Cabin, northern Alberta, Canada

28 / Feb / 1954

I found out more.

I sat around the fire all night when I returned from the clearing. After writing you and sealing the letter, I could not find any more paper or ink to write you further. I trekked to town the following day (yesterday); I followed the frozen river as soon as the winds and snow let up. I did speak with the old lady at the outdoor store.

Her name is "May." She said she had never heard of any schoolhouse or church deep in the forest, although I think she was lying. I mentioned what I had found, and she immediately denied the church and schoolhouse, turned her back to walk away, and tried to change the subject. She wanted to offer me vacationing brochures and horseback riding pamphlets. Why didn't she want to talk about that place, I wondered. After pestering her, she finally gave in and told me a tidbit of information. She did know about the descendants of the Holloway family and was very hesitant to tell me any details. I prodded her and practically begged, so she finally told me more.

She told me that the great-grandfather Thaddeus Holloway was a devout god-fearing man and a priest. He had a local legend around him that went as follows.

Thaddeus Holloway was born into an incestuous family, his mother and father being brother and sister! Disturbing.

There was a rumour that Thaddeus Holloway was born with a cleft palate and missing the "sense of a normal man." He was violent, and she described him as being filled with rage. A rage so furious he was known to scream at strangers and townsfolk for being sinners and non-repentant blasphemers. He would beat the native children and chase teenagers away, waving his bible around. Legend described him as disgusted and having strong disdain toward his mother – not because of her marriage to her brother (Thaddeus's father) – but because he was a Catholic like his father before him – and she wasn't.

His mother was Lutheran. She felt and tried to explain to Thaddeus that God's word was meant to be interpreted by his loyal followers and not necessarily from the words in the bible. He disagreed and hated his mother as she beat him for the aggressive tone he had developed toward her. Once, his mother beat him with a pipe and knocked him unconscious. She was suspected of causing so much head trauma in Thaddeus as a child that he would have constant migraines, and soon after, he reported hearing voices from the skies. The voices of the angels Michael and Gabriel. Both his parents blamed the imaginings on childish imagination and ignored the result of the constant beatings. Furthermore - his mother, especially, became depressed from the guilt of causing her child further head trauma than he was already born with.

After years of emotional and physical abuse, Thaddeus was once beaten by his mother bloody with a rusty pipe in the library of the family cabin (where I'm writing this, Ellie) until his father stopped her and threw Thaddeus out into the wilderness. It was said that Thaddeus survived the first few nights in the woods feeding off mice and bugs, and eventually, starving, he cut off his pinky and ring finger on his left hand, suckling on the raw meat for nourishment.

He lived in the woods preaching the gospel out loud to himself and yelling profanities and curses to the skies at night so his parent could hear him, losing sleep and staying awake to listen to the harsh and deliberately vulgar sermons from their estranged son.

One night, Thaddeus snatched the axe from the wood-splitting log outside the house, crept up the stairs, and stood silently staring at the main bedroom's closed door for hours. Finally dragging the door open, he stepped carefully toward his sleeping father, hacked him to death first, then hacked his mother with the same bloody axe. The legend goes that Thaddeus sat on the floor, carving his dream of a schoolhouse and church on a wooden plank and making a headboard out of the carving. He then installed the headboard over his parent's mutilated corpses and slept between them for multiple nights as their bodies stank and rotted away.

This is the same headboard I told you about. Now that I know more about this cottage, I hesitate to stay here longer. It all started to add up to me. Frankie sat at the door that night like he was looking up at someone. Was it Thaddeus Holloway's ghost? The headboard - was that carving depicting the place I found in the forest? If it did, what happened there?

As the old lady told me all this, she refused to tell me more as I begged her to go on. Whatever happened to Thaddeus? I asked her. She shrugged and said it was all rumours and legends. Some people told tales of Thaddeus living the rest of his days in the cottage peacefully; others told more sinister stories. She wouldn't go on. She insisted that I leave that place, grasping my hands while pleading with me to go home.

I'm not sleeping in this Bed, Eleanor, after knowing what happened here. I swear to you, I saw an axe outside leaning on the woodshed, and with all I know now, I look forward to leaving this place immediately. I'm not saying it's the same axe, but one can't help but wonder.

I fear I may be trapped in this haunted place if this Blizzard doesn't let up soon. I'm sleeping with Frankie on the couch downstairs in the living room tonight, but I doubt I'll sleep any tonight. I look over at the bookshelves and picture Thaddeus Holloway's mother beating him with a rusted pipe. I imagine a boy screaming and holding his hands up to shield the blows as she swings wildly, thumping him with the heavy rod. I picture blood splattering on the walls and the books behind her. I almost hear him screaming the bible verses aloud as she brutally beats him.

I'll pack my stuff in the morning; I hope this reaches you in time. Ellie, I will come home soon. Please write back; the phone does not give off a sound. I fear it is entirely disconnected, and the snowdrifts are higher than ever. The snow is still coming down, and I have no other communication with the outside world. I hope to find a way to have this letter posted soon.

Toronto, Ontario
02 / March / 1954

Dear Claire,

I just received all your letters. The post was delayed by a significant accident on the Trans-Canada Highway from Alberta. In your last letter, you found the abandoned schoolhouse and church. I think it was dated the 28th. I'm unsure if it's the last letter you wrote, but it's the most recent one I received anyway.

I researched at the university and found out about the place you described.

First, Claire, please leave that place once you read this letter! That place is dreadful, and I should never have let you go. I wish I could send a telegram sooner, but I don't think *Grand Cache* has one. When you read this and know what I know now, I hope you will return to me immediately. Go to Edmonton; I will cover the cost of your flight. This is what I found out from old articles and news clippings from the *Edmonton Herald* and local native tribe stories in that area,

The place you found was founded by some guy named Thaddeus Holloway in or around 1838. Not much is known about what happened there, but local native lore speaks of a white man who kidnapped local native children and brought them to this place. He would shave their heads, dress them like white people, and beat them bloody. Local chiefs say some parents of the missing children would find them in this church, where they were tortured and killed in terrible ways. The parents would escape the grounds, returning to the reservations mutilated, one case of a father crawling back with his intestines wrapped around his throat, only to die from blood loss upon reaching the reservation.

Natives and townspeople from local towns, including Grande Cache, gathered and torched the Holloway cottage. Right down to the foundations. Thaddeus Holloway was never found, and the mysterious church and schoolhouse were also never located by local authorities at the time. Claire... the Holloway cottage... was never reconstructed. Not only that, but the Holloway name also died with this Thaddeus guy. There are no reports of a wife or siblings to carry on that name, so who were you talking to on the phone when you got there? Where exactly are you staying? Are you sure you know where you are?

I am worried. I am sending this post expedited. I tried calling the post office and businesses from Grande Cache only to find out they have not heard of you or seen any young college-aged girl with a golden retriever.

I'm sending this post to the return address from your past letters, hoping this finds you soon. Very soon.

Please come home, Claire; your parents and I are distraught. If we don't hear from you in the coming days, we are booking flights and coming to look for you.

Eleanor

Dear Blessed Eleanor,

I pray this correspondence finds you, as my master finds your inquiries obscene and hideously blasphemous. He is immensely frustrated at your accusations. Do not hither any further as you will suffer great agony if you choose to pursue me. I am in the hands of Christ our lord, the holy spirit, and, alas, the virgin mother. I dwell in her loving and gentle embrace, suckling at her teat with the aspirations of a heavenly paradise near her side.

I have repented my sins and shone in Christ's light, only to see myself in a new view, a unique sight like being born once again. Holloway church and boarding home are not dreadful but magical, enlightened places of God. These savages must know our ways and repel their misgivings and sinful nature. If they do not, they will learn to pray thee by the ends of my lash. I offer these children paradise at the feet of Yahweh, and they cheer in my abounding presence for offering them his glorious honour.

Do not seek me, as I am content in this place. In repentance, I must share the truth with you and confess my past sins, though I have not had the chance to speak truthfully to you. I pray my confession will keep you away and leave you to your omens - to find him as well.

Brian, your fiancé - was my lover for many moons. We fornicated as you slept in the dwelling next to us. He learned the truth of my passion for you, Eleanor, and with my refusal to fuck him any longer, he could not bear the sincerity of my heart, and he committed the atrocious sin of suicide. He was pathetic; alas, I rejoice in his pain and can assure you he is burning in hell, suckling at the bosom of Satan. I care not how you feel about this confession. I pray you find Christ and repent to our lord seeking his divine forgiveness.

Once again, do not seek me hither. I leave you with a verse from Mathew, praying you to find God or suffer the anguish of your repulsive existence,

"Again, the devil took him to a very high mountain and showed him all the kingdoms of the world and their splendour." | Matthew 4:8

Yours in Christ,
Clarissa Kathrine McKenna

"A gruesome discovery in the woods near Grand Cache. KJBW is on the scene, with Fredrick Watkins reporting; we must advise that Viewer discretion is advised as this report contains graphic description unsuited for sensitive audiences."

"Good morning, Kelly,

Yes, early morning, 18 km north of Grand Cache, Alberta, on the outskirts of Edmonton, police have said they found the body of missing college student Clarissa McKenna, known as "Claire" to her friends and loved ones.

It all started with police in Edmonton being contacted by McKenna's parents, worried about her well-being as letters from Claire to her best friend and roommate were found to be increasingly alarming and worrisome. Constable Danial O'Brien was the first to inquire from the locals in Grande Cache, a small township west of Edmonton known for wilderness retreats and ski slope resorts. The letters written by McKenna describe that she was staying at the infamous Holloway cottage and inn—a wilderness retreat located deep in the rocky mountain wilderness. The story from here becomes increasingly mysterious as aerial views show no evidence of a dwelling in the location described."

"Fredrick, do we have any information regarding the Holloway homestead?"

"Yes, we have learned since arriving here that Holloway homestead was Rumored to be the home of the serial killer and child abductor Thaddeus Holloway in the mid-1800s. Holloway, a self-proclaimed

catholic priest, was rumoured to have killed hundreds of native indigenous children from the neighbouring reservations."

"Chilling. What have we come to learn about this place?"

" Local legends have told tales of the infamous killer Thaddeus Holloway for years, with many authors writing about the Holloways and, even most recently, haunted guide tours of the grounds where Holloway Cottage once stood. Locals and guides describe the townspeople and indigenous tribes teaming up to burn down the Holloway homestead at the beginning of the twentieth century. Locals and police never found the schoolhouse and church grounds where the grizzly murders occurred until later in the 1930s, when reports of a group of hikers stumbled onto the church grounds in 1931.

The dilapidated church and schoolhouse, overrun by a massive avalanche in 1850, stood on the grounds before the mass grave for over 100 years as indigenous tribes were left in the dark by the provincial government about their missing relatives.

Upon the discovery, local tribal chiefs invested thousands of dollars in radar ground penetrating technology that led to the discovery of the mass grave. Shortly after that, 14 km from the Holloway homestead, Excavations revealed a mass grave containing over 500 bodies of missing children from the local area. The church and schoolhouse were demolished after removing the remains in August 1933.

The schoolhouse and church were later described as the foundation for residential schools, funded by the Canadian federal government and Catholic church authorities. Residential schools have run since 1886. The schools throughout Canada were notorious for their brutal treatment of first nations children in an effort to convert them from their native heritage to the catholic faith. They were beaten and malnourished, forced to change their appearance and religion, forcing the children against their will to conform to a strict catholic education system that left many depressed and suicidal. The federal government has yet to acknowledge or apologize for the schools. The 'Holloway mass graves,' as was later to be known, was the first of these Residential schools in recorded Canadian History, predating the government-funded schools by thirty years."

"What have authorities told you about the remains?"

"Well, I have to warn our viewers about the grizzly nature of Mckenna's remains. If there are children in the room, please have them escorted out, as the details of what occurred here are quite disturbing,

Claire McKenna was found on the former grounds of the former Holloway homestead just a few kilometres away from the town of Grande Cache. Coroners report her arms and legs severed off, probably with an axe or hatchet. Her torso was tied to a Maple tree wrapped in barbed wire, where her back was split open, her back ribs broken, protruding out of her side, and her lungs flipped over her shoulders, portraying the gruesome look of an angel with spread wings. Very similar to the Medieval Viking torture-killing method called the "Blood Eagle." Her eyes were also reported missing. Coroners had not determined if her eyes were removed from the time of death or if wildlife got to the corpse before authorities did. Her arms and legs were found in the nearby woods days later, most likely dragged off by wildlife. On the discovery, her left hand was missing two fingers, which were confirmed to be removed at the time of death and later found in her stomach. We have with us Aileen Jankowski from the Edmonton Coroner's office. Aileen, what can you tell us about the victim?"

"We are still to determine if this was a homicide or a tragic accident. Telling by the wounds on the body, we can suspect malicious intent but haven't concluded our findings to label this as a homicide officially. What I can say is that the investigation estimates that she was most likely tortured and killed this way while still alive – but – as I said, it's still

early in the investigation. It must have been excruciating for the poor girl,"

"Do we know what exactly the cause of death was?"

"Do you mean what caused her vitals to fail?"

"Yes, exactly,"

"It's my opinion that she most likely died from shock while the torture took place. It's hard to say; We estimate she was in the woods for approximately ten days until the discovery, and the body has started to decompose, making the investigation complicated."

"Thank you, Aileen. I spoke to some detectives combing the crime scene, and one of the detectives on the case told KJBW that, when local authorities found her, Claire Mckenna was dressed in religious garb - a black priest's robe with a white collar.

There are no suspects, as forensics investigators have yet to conclude on facts of this case.

Claire McKenna was 21 years old. More to come in the proceeding days.

This is Fredrick Watkins, reporting for KJBW Edmonton.

9

Comforting Places

It was yesterday, it feels like, that I got my first Tattoo. It was through the same door I stand in front of now, with the same neon sign that enticed me to enter the first time I noticed it in my younger years. I remember a sense of Anxiety as I stood before the door. The nervousness had gradually faded, but the initial visit to *Dragons Den Tattoo and Piercings* had my legs quivering and the loose-leaf sheet of paper in my hand fluttering from my trembling hand. I remember being seventeen, looking down at the sheet as I stood in front of the doorway and second-guessing if this artwork that I had drawn myself in Mr. Fink's class was good enough to have plastered on my forearm for good.

I spent two solid classes drawing a giant purple octopus with its twisting arms wrapped around three skulls that I told myself (in a morbid justification) represented Mom, Dad, and myself. There were scribble marks, and faint pencil graphite smudged on the page in meagre attempts to erase squiggly lines and redraw them with a stiffer finger.

The drawing was messy, but isn't that what artists were for? That's what Scotty called himself; after all, they all did –*artists*. I never debated them. They were *artists*, all right, just not in the practical sense that people like my grandfather would imagine when you brought up Tattooing to him. Grandpa Jake imagined artists in the class of Michelangelo or Caravaggio but wasn't a stupid man – he knew that anybody could call themselves whatever they wanted. *Real* artists were few and far between.

"They certainly didn't include 'street rats' and 'gutter trash' on street corners plastering ink into people's bodies and calling it art." He would say.

Grandpa Jake had been around. He joined the Navy at 18 and sailed around the world. We called him the "Great Old Shark" at home. He didn't debate it. He took it with pride. Before Grandma died, she said that she couldn't keep him out of the water when he was a young man – that if he should be reincarnated, he should return as a Fish in the Ocean. That would make things right.

Grandpa had seen his fair share of Tattoos in the Navy. He told me when he and Herb Cooper, Jessie Watkins-Keefe, and Teddy 'Big Bear' Owens had visited red light districts in every Port they touched down. The fun and itchy regrets from fumbling with prostitutes and the head-splitting hangovers from cheap wine. He did mention the pier in San Francisco and the first time he saw a Tattoo shop under the bright red, blue, and yellow lights that seemed to carpet the hard concrete of the road and sidewalks.

He had gotten one after Teddy's constant berating and nearly begging Grandpa to get one with him. He got an anchor (which was fitting) inked on his forearm. It was small compared to the Tattoo I would get on my first visit, but the experience was enough to have him accept that this *new thing* would catch on –still, he didn't consider it 'art.'

"When I want to see art – I look at the Mona Lisa or the Sistine Chapel," he would say, "not a goddamn anchor or sparrow drawn on the skin. The god-damn thing hurts so much; I wonder why these fools get them in the first place."

I always found the cliché funny of bringing up the Mona Lisa or the Sistine Chapel. He knew of other masterpieces but always brought up the memorable ones that everyone would understand when he mentioned them.

"Even if it was of quality – the drawings – skin still gets wrinkled, ink still fades away, and we die - so how long will this art last anyway? A lifetime? It doesn't seem everlasting to me."

"Is art meant to be everlasting, Grandpa?" I asked.

"I would think so. That's what makes it special. I could look at a Caravaggio that was painted 500 years ago. It hangs in Italy somewhere, I forgot where – but I've seen it with my own eyes. That's art!"

"For someone who appreciates art, I think you would appreciate Tattoos. It's the new thing – skin is the new canvas."

"Ah, a bunch of bullshit."

"Well, the silence of an empty Chapel is exchanged with the loud buzzing of an electric Tattoo gun and the smell of oil-based paints. "I tried to explain to him, but instead, he sarcastically responded,

"- the smell of Whisky coming from the artist's breath, more like it,"

"Well, yeah, I guess."

"And you admire this?" he asked.

"No. I acknowledge that times are changing. I like how Tattoos have caught on – I see what is now and what used to be, that's all. Like Bob Dylan said, Grandpa – *the times are a changing.*"

The bells clattered together, and the bright fluorescent lights in the shop brought a vivid picture to my mind as I walked in. I had been here before, and everything was in its place, the same place it had been twenty years ago. There were posters pinned up to the walls. Classic pin-up girls and Sailor Jerry-type flash, Japanese dragons and Koi fish decorated each canvas. The radio in the back of the room playing Jimi Hendrix and The Doors resonated mildly and warmed a satisfying heat in my chest once I heard Jimi's *Fender Strat* wailing to 'All Along the Watchtower.'

One large poster was decorated with skulls and snakes. Another was strictly pin-up girls, cartoonish but still attractive. Another had old sailor Tattoos like flying sparrows, compasses, anchors, and north stars. Grandpa would appreciate that kind – even if he was a stiff old man. These were the type that always attracted me as well. These old sailor Tattoos had gotten me obsessed with the art form in the first place.

As I looked around in the waiting area at the posters on the wall, I admired the faint tint of the yellowed pages crusted at the edges that had maybe been around since Gramps was on board the USS Harry Truman. It wasn't the quality of the artwork that was so attractive. I didn't realize it then, but somehow, I felt I was channelling my dead Grandpa and reaching out for the same style that was beginning to become popular in the 1950s (The only style at that time) when he was in the Navy. Sometimes I swayed myself into thinking that I had taken the mantle from him. He had started with the anchor – and I carried on with my arms patched randomly from shoulder to wrist with the same anchors and sparrows, Jaguar heads and Pin-ups in Nurse's outfits depicted on the shop posters.

The metal chairs with maroon leather cushions that had ripped at their edges sat in a row along the wall, and across from them was the front desk. I thought about sitting for a while and realized I no longer needed to. I looked to see that I had both my legs again. The left hadn't been amputated, and the right hadn't been covered in cold sores and scabs. I was dressed in my Pajamas, the pants littered with superhero characters like *Ironman* and the *Hulk,* the same type children would wear. I always thought it was cool to have those Pyjama bottoms. I even wore them as an old man. The top was just a white undershirt that didn't have juice stains on the collar or chilli splatters on the front. It was the same thing I wore at the hospital.

I realized then, in frightening horror, that I didn't remember getting onto the bus to get here. I didn't remember deciding to come here either, and the last image that came to my mind - was laying face up in the hospital bed, looking up at Madalyn and the kids. I felt her lips on mine. I couldn't move them to kiss her back, but I felt her still. I remembered Madalyn leaning down to kiss me. I remember the sorrow on my kid's faces, although my death had not been unexpected. I've been sick for a long time. Then, I remember being blinded by white light, and I was here.

"It *is* everlasting, you know." A voice said from the end of the shop. "Tattoos. One way or another, they *are* remembered." The man sitting on the stool said, his back turned towards me. "The only question is, who remembers them, and can we re-create them?"

"Can't we say that about any masterpiece?" I asked, but I couldn't feel my lips move. I suppose in this place, they didn't need to.

"You're right. They don't need to. Not here. Are you coming over or what? I've got other clients coming in." Scotty said, spinning around to face me.

He was a younger man – younger than I remembered him to be. The last time I saw Scotty, he had grey streaks that ran the length of his ponytail – which was always tied at the back tightly like the hairs were nearly ripped from his scalp – they had disappeared. His wrinkles across his forehead had vanished, and the loose skin that hung from his jowl, like a bulldog - was gone. I witnessed his youthful appearance from a time when I had never met him, what he must have looked like in his adolescent liveliness. The neck Tattoos, dragons, and spiders that reached down to his chest were vivid and bold - like they had just been freshly applied, but without the redness or swelling.

"You coming, dude?"

"Yes," I said.

I walked over to him, felt like I had taken a single step, and found myself sitting in the chair across from him. He had a metal tray with little cups of ink, his Tattoo gun, a mound of Vaseline, paper towels, and a bottle of Isopropyl Alcohol sitting on top.

"How ya been, Benny?" he asked. He smiled, and his gold-capped tooth shined brightly.

"I'm good, Scotty. It's been a long-time brother." I said.

"Yeah, too long. I guess that's not your fault, though. Only so many places on your body I can ink up, right?"

"We had good times. Lots of them in this chair." I shrugged my shoulders as I spoke.

Scotty wiped my forearm with the soaking paper towel, and the coldness of the alcohol gave me slight goosebumps. It was a sensation I hadn't felt in a long time.

"What am I doing here, Scott?" I asked, half knowing the answer.

"You came in for a *tat*, bro. Except this place is a bit more special, my man." He reached over, placed a stencil on my arm, and rubbed the paper to make it stick to my skin. Then he peeled it away and left the blues lines of the drawing. It was the same drawing that I brought in the first time. I was excited. I looked down at it and smiled, thinking this would be a good time.

"What is the last thing you remember, Benny?" Scott asked.

"My kids and Madalyn. They were looking down on me. I was dying." I felt my back and ass cheeks with my free hand for the bed sores and bruised flesh and didn't feel anything.

"I've been there a while, in the hospital, that is. The doctor said he tried to save the leg, but the infection spread, and he had no choice but to amputate it. I'll tell ya, Scotty – Diabetes is a son of a bitch – especially when you get old."

"Rough," he said. He then rubbed Vaseline on the blue lines and examined the drawing with his head tilted.

"Yeah, looks good. You ready?" he said.

"Always am, Scotty."

"Right on, bro."

He picked up the Tattoo gun, plugged in the adaptor, and stepped on the pedal several times to check the gun. Upon his satisfaction, he dipped the tip of the gun – the fun side, where the needles protruded – into a cup of black ink and proceeded to start on the first line of the drawing. He spread my skin tightly with his fingers, and the tiny needle began injecting my arm at a rapid RPM.

"How's that feel? All good?" He asked. Every artist asked that. I appreciated the gesture; the first line was always a run-up to what to expect for the rest of the session. The loud buzzing and the sharp prodding of the tiny needle felt exhilarating - if I had felt anything at all. The question "All good?" was pointless. My anticipation of that familiar stinging pain had dwindled when I realized I didn't feel a thing. I saw the needle glide down on the outline of the octopus but didn't feel the same stinging and vibrating sensation I had gotten so accustomed to.

"Tell me more." He said. "What else do you remember?"

"I remember the feeling of Madalyn's lips. It was nice, Scott. Soothing."

"A good way to go out, huh?" he asked

"I suppose. Is this what - this is?"

I could help but ask. Scott knew what I meant. I could see it in the way the edges of his lips crept upwards into a faint smile as he focused on another line.

"Do I have to answer that?" he asked jokingly.

"I think so. It would clear up a lot, don't you think?" Scotty didn't respond, and I told him about the last moment I remembered. "I saw a white light."

"Ahh, the famous white light – you were there, now you're here. Doesn't that kind of tell you something?"

"I died." My cheeks swelled with heat, and my vision became hazy momentarily at the realization.

"Ding, ding, ding, get the man a prize." He chuckled.

"Why didn't you just tell me?"

"It's not part of the deal, brother." He leaned back and wiped the excess ink and blots of red blood that had begun to seep from the Tattoo with a paper towel, and again, I didn't feel the sting. I didn't feel the aching soreness or my forearm muscle twitching slightly as the cold, damp towel wiped the slate clean. He examined the newly inked lines and nodded his head,

"Yeah, nice," he said aloud to nobody in particular.

"What *deal*, Scott?" I asked.

"You always ask questions you have the answer to, Benny; that's what you do, I guess. I think it's because you want confirmation and to ensure you're on the right track. It's fine. It's not a problem for me. Some people get annoyed, but I don't – I get it."

"You *can't* tell me? This is something I have to figure out myself...."

"Shit man, if I had a trophy or a medal – or better yet – that Korean hooker from *Chapman's Massage Parlor*, you know, "*Ming Park Sun?*" Oh boy – she would be your prize." He laughed heartily, "You're a smart one, eh?"

"I guess. Still, there are so many questions." I told him, not knowing if my questions were even relatable to the place I was in. *How did he know about Ming?*

"They all are. Ask away, my friend, and I will enlighten as much as I can."

"Okay." I hesitated at the feeling of a stupid question I was about to commit to. "what's the meaning of it? Life, I mean."

"That's a tough one, Benny. Ever think that there was no meaning? That we were there for a brief moment in time like all the other organisms that ever existed?" he asked. "I'll tell you what, bro. I don't have the answer to the meaning of Life thing because nobody ever shed light on that subject for me either. Believe me, I asked and got no response. What I can tell you... "

Scotty arched his brows towards the stack of drawings pinned up to the corkboard on the wall. "You see those drawings? Each drawing is someone's life – like this octopus is a drawing that represents *your* life. Now, believe me, each life that comes through that door – including yours – has sat in this chair at least thirty times over and had the same Tattoo inked on them. The same questions and answers, all oblivious to the fact that they had been where you're sitting so many times before."

"So, I've been here before? Dead? I don't get it."

"Of course, you don't. I don't expect you to. Not yet, at least," he said. He dipped the needle in the ink cup again and spread my skin tightly with his free hand, and the buzzing continued.

"Listen, you have a choice. Do you remember the bathroom here? The one downstairs?" He asked.

"Yes." The vision flooded my mind of the countless times I had gone down there 20 years ago to urinate between breaks. I remember the steps being old and creaky. I remember the scent of body odour and a musky mildew smell as I took each step down the stairs. I saw the single light bulb that hung over the cot in the corner, the olive-green bedsheets piled on top of the mattress and piles of dirty laundry on the floor that resembled a steady slope reaching the edges of the bed. The bathroom was a single toilet with no shower and no sink.

"I remember the 1980's style *Hustler* pages stuck to the wall. With big hair and clean muffs, the girls opened their lips with two fingers. Romantic stuff," I teased, "I remember them plastered on every surface." I told him.

"Yeah. Well, those girls are still there," he said with a snicker. "If you choose to go there, downstairs – you come back reincarnated." He said, "You will experience the same life. You will be pulled from your Mother's womb by a female doctor named "Marie Bourgerette," a French woman who was a nurse in the war. You will still be born in Hempstead, where your Douche-bag father leaves your mother, and your Navy Vet Grandpa takes up the reins instead. You will move to Baltimore, attend the same high school, and enlist in the Air Force, where you meet "Madalyn Lawrence" on deployment to Hawaii. Laura, your first child will be born on January 15, 1972, at 18:40 hrs – just like before."

"How do you know?" I felt that had been a stupid question, but I had gotten used to the idea of those.

"Because it's always the same. You sat in this chair already – you asked the same questions, had the same dishevelled look and always – I mean always – chose to go downstairs. Fuck, this is going to be a badass *tat,* dude."

"Then why give a choice?"

"I don't make the rules; I just explain them. Wouldn't you rather have a choice?"

"What's the *other* option?"

"A clean one. You would be surprised how many choose to walk out the front door – to end it all – go black, once and for all."

"So, what happens then? Let me guess – I've asked you before, right?"

"Yup. Nothing happens. At least, I don't think." He responded.

"Heaven, Hell, what?" I asked.

"Nothing. Call it what you will. Some folks like the serenity of nothingness and think it heavenly; others hate the silence, want more."

"So, a light switch gets turned off?"

"Exactly."

"I can see why I always choose to come back."

"Yeah, but you have gotten close to going out the front door a few times." He said. "Never did, though."

"And how did you end up here – in this *Purgatory*?" I asked him.

"You brought me here. You envision what makes you comfortable. For some people, it's chatting with grandma over a cup of tea; for others, it's conversating with their Father at the Carnival they loved as a kid. For you – it's here, with me."

"I wouldn't think it," I said, perturbed.

"Yes, I know. Still, every time it's us going over the same thing. You sit there, and I sit here, the same octopus, same skulls, same, same, same. I have to ask – about Madalyn. Tell me how you met her."

"I don't want to."

"Yeah, but you end up telling me anyway. So cut the shit, Bro." Scotty's tone became dark.

"If you already know, why ask? I don't remember you being such an asshole."

"It's for you, not me." He said sullenly. After a moment, I began,

"It was in Melbourne. We had touched down from Malta, where we moored to help locals stack grain for the migrant refugees coming in from the Horn of Africa. When getting to *Valletta,* we were itching to get off the *Nimitz* – me and Tommy Wilkens," I explained. "Anyway, we finally stepped off the ship for a weekend leave at night – I think it was about 8 or 9 o clock local time. The red-light district wasn't far. Tom kept asking to go to the bar and shoot pool with Mitchel Franks and Fitch D'Amato, who had already gotten to the *Empty Crab* and were waiting on Tom and me to show up. I gave in, and we shot pool and drank beers for about three hours, and that's when I saw her."

"All right, the good parts. How romantic." Scotty was finishing the skulls he outlined on my arm.

"She was gorgeous. She wore a tight-fitting blue dress, and her hair had been done up in curls. I thought she was a street girl because of how she stared at me."

"And her friends?"

"Mindy and Kathryn. Yeah, I remember them. She came in with them, but I didn't care much about those floosies."

"Floosies?" Scotty chuckled.

"Well, we sent over drinks, and they finally came over. Next thing I know, the six of us rented a hotel room to drink and hopefully fuck the night away."

"And that's what you did," Scott said in more of a comment than a question.

"Yes. You know we did. Why am I telling you this?"

"Go on."

"No."

"You should. It makes it better for you." Scotty sighed. "You have to come clean, Brother. You tell me anyway." He shrugged, "Humour me, would ya?"

"She was warm." I said, "We were in the room, and the dress slipped off easily. I loved how she acted so shy. The excitement shot through me just at the fact that I had this beautiful woman in front of me."

"She wrapped her arms around you."

"Yes. When we got going, that is - At first, she was a bit reserved. I know she felt insecure taking off her clothes in front of a stranger. I suppose she thought her stretch marks or slight muffin top would drive me away and leave her humiliated."

"Since when has a man walked out on a naked girl? Regardless of what they looked like." Scotty chimed in,

"Exactly – she didn't realize I won the lottery. I felt lucky because she was there with me – I had already won the prize."

"So, when you gonna get to it?" he asked.

(sigh) "I don't want to."

"Did she wrap her arms around Fitch and Tommy boy, too, when they took turns on her? Did she look into their eyes and smile at them as they thrust their – "

"You don't have to be vulgar." I interrupted.

"Well?"

"No, she didn't. I don't want to talk about it. It wasn't *date rape* if that's what you're thinking."

"No?"

"No, God Dammit!"

"Of course not, Benny. Of course not," Scotty said sarcastically. "Most dudes wouldn't marry someone they, well, – you know. Anyway, I'm curious; I have to ask – why did you marry *her*?"

"Because she was still special to me." I hesitated momentarily, "And because I felt responsible. Obligated to take care of her, almost. I still loved her, you know."

"I know you did, Benny."

"Then why do you want to know this stuff?" annoyance and deep-rooted shame flooded my body with resentment toward this son of a bitch. I began to hate Scotty, loathe him for bringing it up – making me tell him the shit I had forced myself to forget so long ago.

"Hate me all you want, brother." Scotty leaned back in his chair, and the roller wheels squeaked a little. He yelled over his shoulder,

"You hear that, Ralphie? He *hates* me. *Loathes* me." There was no response, and I wondered who the hell Ralphie was. Then I got the sarcastic humour.

"Tell me more about why you married her." He insisted.

"I told you why. I loved her. Still do."

"How do you know?"

"Because every deployment, every OP, every new country and airbase – I missed her. I thought of her always. We kept in touch through the post. I got to learn about her. Her abusive father and delinquent mother. She wanted to escape Malta and how she had masked herself with dresses and makeup but couldn't hide the shame of that night. Of what we did to her."

"Didn't talk much to Tommy after that, huh?"

"No, not after the fight. I nearly threw him off the deck – I did time in the Brig for it."

"If you could go back – it would all be the same. The bar, the dress, the room – if you could go back and re-live it all again, would you?" As he dipped the needle again, Scott didn't seem to care for the answer.

"If it meant I would marry her again and have Laura, Mike, and Judith grow old with her? Then *Hell Yes*, I would."

"Even if you had to go through that night again? Watching her get fucked by your friends? Would you have that?"

I didn't answer. I wanted to change it. For so long, I wanted to go back and relive that night. I imagined pulling them off her but didn't know if that would happen if I lived through it again. Would I know better and try to change things? I've been haunted for so long, hearing her cries and the image of her giving up and lying quietly sobbing while Fitch was on top of her. I remembered her looking at me for help – and I just stood there. I stood there and watched.

"Not so sure anymore," I said.

"Outlines are done, Bro – check it out" Scotty sat back and admired the line work. He stared at the crisp dark ink embedded in my skin and admired the skulls and how they stacked neatly, with each long Octopi arm wrapped around the base of each skull.

"I always liked doing this one. I get jerkoffs coming in here with shitty little scrolls that say "Mommy and Daddy" or a poem by some long-dead white guy telling me it *'means something to them.'* That's why I like you, Benny – a lot of your art doesn't have a meaning – sometimes a spider is just a spider – not a representation of something deep and heavy. You know what I mean?" Scotty asked without expecting an answer. He took a moment and glared at the outline on my arm, and repeated,

"Yeah. I like doing this one."

He unplugged the gun and placed it on the paper towel lining he used as a sheet to cover the bare metal tray he placed his tool on. He leaned back in his chair (that awful squeak again), pulled out a drawer behind him, and reached for another gun – this time with more needles at the tip – for shading.

"All right. What colours do you want?"

"Purple for the octopus, black and grey for the skulls," I said

"Maybe some white accents on the skulls? Make it pop a bit more?" he asked,

"We've been through this before, haven't we?"

Scotty stared at the outline and smiled at my remark while unconsciously plugging in the gun and dipping it in the same black cup of ink he had been using all along. He proceeded to shade the Octopus head a dark purple. I found this place inexplicable. He didn't have to pull out more ink cups; the same little plastic cup housed all the colours of the imagination.

He dragged the needles in the same spot between the eyes of the Octopus, and I could see the micro specks of dead skin brush away, and the slow, steady seeping of blood slowly started to gather in its place. I watched him wipe the area he shaded with a wet towel, and the beads rose within the purple, making the tint of both the blood and the Tattoo darker – darker than it should have been. He went over the same spot like he was torturing me steadily if it wasn't for the fact that I felt no pain in this place.

"Let's fast forward," Scotty suggested.

"What?"

"Tell me more about Laura, your firstborn. They were happy times, right?"

"At first, yeah. But then, Madalyn developed a serious case of Post-Partum Depression. That's what the Doctor called it. She would be calm as a pond one minute, then bouncing off the walls the next. She never really came out of it. Once, I asked my buddy at the plant, Bruce, what to expect when the baby was born. He told me about the depression *his* wife got, and she never really came out of it either. Then, he told me I wouldn't have sex for a while after the baby came. I asked how long. He laughed and said, "Shit, it's been six years for me.' We both laughed pretty hard."

"He was right, wasn't he?"

"Yes."

"Is that why you did what you did?" Scotty leaned back and smiled. Then rolled his chair forward a few inches and carried on the shading.

"What?"

"You heard me. Are we still on this?"

"On what?"

"The lies, the bullshitting. Go. On."

"You *really* have turned into an asshole, Scotty; what the fuck? This is supposed to be my comfort place, remember?"

"Go. On." He took a momentary pause between each word. My fists clenched tightly into a fist, my fingernails dug deep into my palm, and I could feel the blood trickle and drip to the floor.

"You're messing up my floor, dude. C'mon," he said. "Are you going to spit it out, or will I?"

I said nothing. The silence was awkward, and I felt wrenchingly that he would tell me what I had done so long ago. I contemplated spitting it out and beating him to the punch. I knew I could sugar-coat it and make it seem like it wasn't so bad – reasonable even.

"Okay, fine." He said, "Madalyn didn't let you touch her for a while. You got tired of stroking off to *Hustler* magazines and started to prowl the night. Red light districts were your thing, another comfortable place you walked into and sighed in relief. The scent of dried piss and vomit excited you – reminded you even – of all the different ghettos you searched in, all the different countries and their whores. All the 'good times you had with them."

"Stop," I said. I wanted to pull my arm away, but he had a tight grasp on me. So tight that my arm felt stapled to the chair's armrest – I could not move, and the feeling of being trapped in the chair made my stomach queasy. He continued,

"-So, you came on down to the dirtiest place in every town and made your way through all the whores, didn't you? Shit - even got a case of syphilis a few times. Never went away, did it? Don't answer – we both know. Anyway, there was this one night. Shall I continue?"

"No."

"No?"

"No. I will." I said remorsefully, "There was one night that bitch gave me a hard time."

"Oh yes, tell me more."

"She was having a bad night, I suppose. The hooker, that is. I don't blame her – it's a hard life. I felt bad every time I went out, away from Madalyn and the kids, but a man needs satisfaction too."

"Preach, my brother."

"Stop the shit." I was beginning to be severely annoyed with Scotty's attitude. He had changed from what I remembered of him. It seemed like he was a shell of a familiar friend from 20 years ago – like a costume or decoy that dressed the part to make me comfortable or lower my guard - but there was something else inside – something unfamiliar. "She was beaten up. I saw the bruises on her ribs, and the side of her face was reddened like she just took a good hard slap." I said.

"What did she say?" Scotty asked.

"It wasn't what she said. She was withdrawn, never really looked me in the eye."

"Pissed you off some, huh?"

"Yes. It started to, but I pushed it down." I responded.

"You started to get close to her. You held her by the waist, then took her arms and wrapped them around your neck – "

"Yes. But she pulled back when I kissed her. It had been too soon for her, I guess. I was probably too forthcoming."

"Bullshit. She was disgusted. Call it what it was. She jumped back and spit on the floor. Then she felt the bile rise to her throat, and she ran to the john and vomited." Scotty laughed with a maniacal gargle foreign to him and any other creature I knew of. Hyenas didn't even have a laugh like that.

"Fuck you, Scott," I told him, hoping he would cut it out.

"Not even the fat old guys with missing teeth and rotten breath did that to her. You must have been special. You were furious. You snuck up behind her... "he said.

"Shut up," I yelled. He wouldn't stop.

"Small, careful steps so she wouldn't hear you. You could feel the heat in your chest; your mouth gaped open, and you even drooled a bit."

"Shut up, you fucker!"

"Then you pushed her head into the toilet. All your man strength you developed with years of lugging and hauling in the Air Force did you good. She had no chance. Poor girl – drowning in her vomit like that."

Scotty shook his head and looked up at my face. I wished I could smack him, get up, and throw him around the room. Surely, he saw the anger in my expression, but what puzzled me was the white puss that had begun dribbling from the corners of his eyes. The same kind of puss that St. Bernard's excrete. It had a foul smell– like rotting flesh and grave dirt. He smiled and then carried on shading the rest of the Tattoo like the puss wasn't there, blinding him.

"Why are your eyes like that?" I demanded. He didn't answer. I peered around at the corners of the shop. The walls were painted an industrial green that started to peel at the edges of the plaster before my eyes. I noticed the wet stains on the ceiling and damp asbestos panels and watched the wet stain spread on the surface until some panels started to drip with red water that looked like diluted blood and sagged in the middle of the boards.

"Those are gonna drop on us," I said.

"Don't worry about them. You got away, right?"

"Yes. Nobody saw me come in or get out. Madalyn was asleep when I got home."

"How convenient."

"Scotty."

"Yeah?"

"This isn't a type of purgatory. This place isn't what you said it was, is it?"

"Dude – check it out, all done." He pushed away from me and rolled back in his chair a few inches, admiring his work. "Killer man. You know I always enjoyed this one. Take a look – what do you think?"

I looked down at my arm, and my body was in shock. I fell off my chair and scooted along the floor like I was trying to escape something in front of me, suddenly realizing the horror was the Tattoo itself. My arm looked like it had rotted. Where the octopus and skulls were supposed to be was a cavernous legion with skin that had turned green; the surface of my flesh bubbled like water in a cauldron, my skin sizzled loudly, and steam rose from my arm.

Scotty sat in the chair with a frightening laughter that shook the room. He pointed at me with a long, withered finger, his mouth gawking open with what sounded like faint screams erupting from his gullet.

"Look at you. Ha-ha – don't you like it? Ha-ha-ha," he couldn't help himself. I got on my feet quickly and raced to the front door. The walls shook around me, and the wet ceiling tiles fell to the floor and splattered with red liquid on their surface. The panels had been soaked with blood, and the thick scent of gun metal enveloped my senses.

"Look, Ralphie," Scotty yelled, still maniacally laughing. "He's about to do it."

My fingers wrapped around the iron bars of the front door, and I witnessed the steam rise from between my fingers. I paused and turned to look at Scotty. His face was caked in white puss like he dipped his head in a bucket of cream cheese icing. He was still laughing at me. Both hands were on his belly like he was trying to keep the laughter inside. His large gut expanded and boiled like hot tar on the surface, looking like an over-inflated balloon about to burst.

I started running away from the front door – knowing what was behind it – and staggered sideways, trying to gain my balance. It was like standing on a sailboat in the middle of a storm. My arm began to throb painfully as I reached out to grasp the walls, although they crumbled before my eyes. I slipped on the bloody panels and fell on my face crushing my nose into the hard tile. I crawled furiously on my elbows toward the basement door – to the gate that would bring me back. I made it to the wood-panelled door to the basement steps and gripped the knob.

"Hey. I'll see you next time, buddy." Scotty waved his hand at me; then his gut exploded – his intestines and organs plopped onto the floor and let out a heavy splatter. Scott waved his hand at me and smiled through the thick layer of puss on his face, his guts piled at his feet.

"Come back soon." With a cheerful optimism.

I pulled the door open, and the same white light I had experienced when I came here blinded me as it shone on my face again. It was clean, and a pure feeling came over me – a relieving sensation like all my burdens had lifted from me as I stared into the white light. I stepped through the doorway, and all the noise ceased immediately. Scotty's laughter faded, the collapsing walls and ceiling panels didn't rumble, and I couldn't hear the screams from Scottie's gut anymore. It all disappeared when I walked through that door.

10

1918

The dried leaves fell from the towering maples as the force of the gale wind pushed the mighty trunks back and forth like they were in a swaggering dance. Jake was there. He observed the pine needles that lay at his feet, the dead leaves that trotted away towards the lake's sandy beach like the points of their flowers had feet, being pushed along with the wind.

"It's probably not a good day," Robert said.

"It's always a good day. Any day outdoors is a fine one." Jake responded.

"I don't know about that."

"What's the problem? I haven't heard you complain too much. Not since we left anyway."

"It's too damn windy. I don't feel comfortable if a doe or buck shows. I'm afraid -"

"You won't get a clean shot? Leave it to me." Jake said. "Have a drink."

Jake reached into the lime green rucksack and pulled out a rectangular glass bottle with half its content emptied from a late night at the lodge.

"Don't think that's a good idea either."

"Oh, cool it," Jake said. "Have a drink, loosen up. I'm not sure why you're so hesitant. It's not the first time you shot something."

"That's a pretty good reason in itself not to shoot anything else, isn't it?"

"If you take it that personally, I suppose it is. You wanted to come along, didn't you?" Jake asked,

"Yes, but it wasn't to shoot." Robert groaned and shook his head, looking down at the wheel of Jake's wheelchair. "I'm rusty, that's all. You're right; sometimes, I take things so damn close to heart. It's just fresh, is all, but I'll get over it. Only one way a man gets over things, and that is to face them head-on isn't it, Jake?"

"You don't have to shoot, Robbie. I'll do it."

"I haven't felt the same since we left. I hate that I left her in such a state." Robert said,

"Which state was that? Angry?"

"Yes."

"I don't know why such a row. She could have tagged along, you know? It was your own fault to leave her home." Jake said.

"This is no place for a woman." Robert poured the whisky into a tin cup and topped it off with water from his canteen.

"Says who? I've brought Marge before—many times. Women have a great time doing things men like to do. It makes them feel involved. Equal even."

"Equal?"

"Yes. It's not such a terrible notion."

"You are one of a kind, Jake, I must say. In all the endeavours I have partaken in – I've never brought a woman."

"*Jesus.*" Jake whispered to himself, "Have another drink."

"I admire you, Jake; you know that?" Robert said.

"Why is that?"

"C'mon, you know why. I don't want to talk anymore about it." Robert said.

"Then why bring it up?"

"Because I speak too soon, Jake, you know why, C'mon."

"I'm not a cripple. I can still -"

"Yes, Jake. I know." Robert interrupted sullenly. Then they both drank from the tin cups. The rifle sat in Jake's lap and pointed toward the floor as he looked aimlessly into the forest. Robert occasionally glimpsed through the eyepieces taking in long steady breaths of air as he was known for doing. The long exhales were like their own prolonged, whistling gusts of wind that stirred the fabric of the tent flap in front of him.

The sides of the tent rippled like beach tides with another sudden breeze of autumn wind. The surrounding trees still had various colours of red, orange, and yellow leaves that hung at the fingers of the branches dangled from the stem. They sat in the tent atop plastic stools watching the odd leaf float to the ground. Jake admired the grace of each maple leaf as if it rocked side to side in the dead air between gusts, kissing the air with each swoop until gracefully landing on a padded floor of pines.

"Season's almost over. You think this is our last one?" Robert whispered,

"Maybe not. I try to be optimistic."

"I'm not sure if we have enough rounds with us."

"Why do you say that? All we need is one – or maybe two rounds at the most – I intend on a clean shot."

"As do I, of course. another drink?" Robert said. His shoulders slumped after a sip from his cup.

"Yes."

Robert topped off Jake's tin cup, and Jake watched the whisky rise to nearly the top of the brim.

"No water for me?" Jake asked.

"Shit."

"Take it easy. Save the water – it will help to sober us up."

"Coffee is better."

"Save it."

"Okay."

They sat in the tent's opening and peered into the long grassy corridor where large trees graced the lane. Robert raised the binoculars to his eyes and saw the bait of fresh strawberries and plums still lying on the floor 300 yards away. He saw through the lens; Fruit flies hovering around the pile of fruit, mosquitoes and other insects flying around throughout the forest, occasionally landing on the men as they sat quietly in the tent.

"This is a good distance," Jake said. "He won't hear you, smell you, see you. A good distance indeed."

"Only if we are capable," Robert responded.

"Well, bully for you – look how you've changed. Of course, we're capable. This isn't the first time, as I said."

"No. I'm just trying."

"You really left her in a bad state, didn't you?" Jake asked,

"It's nothing worth mentioning. The relationships between men and women are far too outlandish and will cause too much noise in the woods. We might spook the deer."

"Causing a row with capabilities, won't? A hell of a thing to say."

"I'm sorry, all right? Is that what you want?"

"I don't need to be questioned on something I've done many times before," Jake continued.

"Take it easy; I said I was sorry. I spoke too soon and regretted it, Jake."

"I'm capable," Jake said. "Capable of much farther shots – whether it's a damned Hun, a buck, or a Hare. I'm damn capable."

"You are Jake. You are." Robert said. He poured another glass. "How's the Rye, Jake? I picked it up from a little place in Antwerp before we shipped home. I saved it for us."

"It's Swell. It's getting me a little tight, but it's damn fine. I prefer Sherry."

"Good. Don't get too drunk – I need you to shoot for me if it shows up – your no use to me if you are seeing double, especially from 300-"

"Oh, would you cool it? You're the one serving me, and dare ask me to take it easy?" Jake said jokingly. "I'm not a damn rummy."

"Didn't say you were, chap. Hand me one of those sandwiches." Robert responded. "Sometimes I find we act like a damn married couple."

"Mildred always says it." Jake chuckled while reaching into the rucksack.

"Says what?" Robert asked,

"That since the war, I've been drinking too much."

"It's true, isn't it?"

"Yes."

"And...?"

"And I God-damn hate it when she accuses me of such things. How can I be a drunkard? I work my ass off every day at the stockyards and come home to her every night, sober and clean. Do you know how hard it was to get picked? Do you know how lucky a guy has to be there? I have no time to be a rotten drunk."

"Then why does she accuse you of being a rummy?"

"Because she's a woman Jake. They are all the same. They find something about you and hold on to it. The same way you hold on to a trout when it kicks and flaps on your line. Once, she caught me looking at her sister – I didn't hear the end of it – still don't."

"Nobody's perfect," Robert said.

"God, I hate it when you listen to my banter. You're damn good at it, and sometimes it torques me up."

"Too bad. We are friends – since *Vimy* – we have been through hell together; I would think I have earned the right to annoy you."

"Ay, yes, you have." Robert said, then whispered, "Son of a bitch."

They locked eyes and hid their laughter from the distant echoes of the forest, like two children who told a dirty joke in church and tried to hide their laughter from the prying and judgemental eyes of the congregation.

"I wish I were here with you, Jake," Robert said,

"Me too, Robert."

"Do you remember that day? In Paris? The time we...."

"Yes. I remember. How can I ever forget Robbie? Best time of my life."

"Yes." Robert nodded. His cheeks were swollen and flushed with warmth. He wanted to smile but hid it back. There was a sullen pause in conversation as the two sat beside each other, staring down the corridor lined with Maple and Poplar trees. Jake was the first to break the silence,

"I wish you were here with me too, Robbie," Jake said as he poured another glass of whisky.

"There's only one shot left – do you want it?" Jake asked.

"No. I'm torn up already." Robert said. He took a long breath and exhaled with exaggeration. "I have regrets, Jake. About us. Paris."

"I only regret not having more time," Jake said. He lifted his finger and brushed Robert's cheek with a tender semblance of affection."

"Me too," Robert said.

Robert looked at the tree branches' awning cover and admired the ever-changing skeleton it represented as each leaf fell. "I regret the last thing I said to her before I took off."

"You don't have to get into it, Robert. Your drunk. Just leave it alone."

"I won't."

"Please," Jake said.

"All right," Robert concluded. He reached into the same rucksack, pulled out a box of .308 rounds, and loaded Jake's rifle.

"I can do it myself, you know," Jake said.

"Yes. I know."

"I'm not useless."

"I know, Jake."

The sunlight peeked through the withering branches and glared off Jake's wheelchair. He had tried to keep the glistening metal in the tent's shade to avoid spooking any bucks – even from 300 yards away.

"You were a hell of a shot, Robert. Do you know that? A hell of a shot. Do you remember that Kraut in Toulouse? The one who ran across the Soy fields wearing an American overcoat?" Jake asked.

"Yes. We hesitated at first." Robert smiled. "Didn't know if he was friendly or not."

"The spike on his helmet gave it away," Jake said.

"Yes, it did."

"Must have been – what – 400 yards?"

"Around that, yeah. I don't remember exactly." Robert said. "Hell of a shot with iron sights, Chap. Hell of a shot."

"A lucky shot."

"Hell, that's true," Robert gulped back his last drink. "Well. If we don't see a buck in another couple of hours – we better call it."

"Yes. We will." Jake responded. "God, I wish you were here with me."

"Ay, me too," Robert said. After a sullen pause, Jake said,

"She still loves you, Robert. She hasn't forgotten." Robert sat quietly and didn't respond. "She tells me all the time,"

"I still watch her, you know? I watch her sleep; I watch her roll around at night when she has dreams about me. I watch as she gets ready in the morning and how she fixes herself her breakfast – fried eggs with buckwheat cakes." Robert said tearfully.

"Don't forget the fresh syrup from the tap in the yard."

"How could I ever forget the syrup, Jake? How can I ever forget the damn syrup?" They both laughed.

"She still comes by to visit Marge and me. We try not to bring up the past or the war. She still misses you, Chap. We all do."

"The war took its toll on the both of us, didn't it, Jake?" Robert said.

"Yes. Yes, it did."

"When was the last time you slept well?" Robert asked.

"Not for a while. Marge helps – holding her at night. Her warmth reminds me that I'm not in the trenches anymore. I startle awake almost every night, but when I realize she is beside me, I remember not being wet or scared. Not being covered in dirt and sinking in the mud. Her warmth reminds me that I'm safe."

"Ay, that's a beautiful thing. And, if you don't come home tonight, Jake? What then?"

"Well, I suppose Marge will get over me. I hope she does, at least."

"She won't." Robert chimed in. "The same way Mildred still misses me, I suppose. Love is a fascinating thing, isn't it, Jake?"

"Yes," Jake responded.

"It must be the strongest emotion – the only one that can make good men do bad things."

"And hate? Anger?" Jake asked.

"Not as strong as love. We can get over hate and anger. But love – that's something in itself."

"I don't know, Robert. In another life – another time – could we be together again? Could we love without hiding? Without sneaking away and pretending there was nothing about it?"

"Maybe another time, Jake – but not in ours."

"I miss you, Robert," Jake said without particularly expecting a response.

"As do I, Jake."

Robert grazed his index finger on jakes cheek, and Jake could feel the shiver run up his spine mixed with the flustering warmth that filled his cheeks. It was a familiar feeling he hadn't felt since Paris – since he lost Robert and the last shred of decency he felt when looking at his reflection in the mirror.

"That goddamn war took so much – my legs, my mind - you," Jake whined. He couldn't hold the quivering in his chin any longer. The deepening sorrow in his chest overtook him, and he couldn't control the words pouring from his lips.

"If I could be with you again, Robert – would you take me?" Jake asked, holding his salty tears from raining down. "In a place where I wasn't limp, where we can embrace each other and not hide? Say, if there was no Mildred or Marge – if they never existed, or if we never met them – would you – "

"A place like Heaven?" Robert asked.

"Yes. If I could be with you now." Jake looked at the barrel of the rifle.

"Please, Jake," Robert said remorsefully, "don't think that way – for me – please don't."

"Fine."

The buck straddled toward the bait in the distance. Jake had a clear shot, raised the loaded rifle toward the deer, and looked down the iron sights. His sweaty index finger gently messaged the face of the trigger, and when he was to squeeze it – he saw the buck look at him. It stood proudly; its eight-point rack towered above him, brooding in majesty. Jake lowered the rifle, realizing he found himself in the tent alone. The empty bottle at his feet stood on its base, the ring of amber left over in the empty glass.

Jake looked at the empty bottle and then glanced back at the buck. It had leaped into the woods and was gone like so many things in his life.

The war had been enticing as a young man, enthralling himself with thoughts of victory on the battlefield, the glory of his triumph. That was gone by the time he first went over the trenches. The lust for his wife after being in *The Somme* for so long, only forgetting her face, her voice, having her replaced in his mind with French pinups on water-sodden pages of torn leaflets. The pornography was gone, the wife who didn't know him anymore – she was gone - and Robert. He was gone as well. Though Jake knew Robert was with him occasionally, in those times, he dared not bring up what happened to Robert at *The Somme* or even think about it. He dared not wake from his dream.

Jake was alone like he had been so many times, even in bed with Marge during those frigid winter nights when the blizzards knocked out the transformers, and they were left with only body heat to keep each other warm. She didn't know that when Jake grasped her, holding her tightly – it was someone else he imagined – someone he had missed for so long. It was the same one to whom he regretted not confessing his love, forsaking all that he deemed acceptable for the simple grace of an unburdening love.

11

THE MASKS WE WEAR

Gary O'Hara felt he had gotten to know her on those calls that became more frequent as the days dragged on. She was kind and seemed enthusiastic when Gary chatted with her, which made him comfortable finally meeting her in person. She made him chuckle, which was a surprise at first and made her instantly become stimulating to him, like someone out there who was the only one who could prod Gary's humour. The preverbal 'where have you been my whole life' phrase he had often heard in movies repeated in his mind thousands of times. He had felt the same familiarity and relaxing comfort about the last few dates he had with other girls, yet for some reason; he couldn't figure out why this one thrilled him the most.

Cones of light flew past as the *Toyota Corolla* flew down Wilkens Ave until the stop sign appeared in the headlights. Gary rolled through the sign quickly, hardly stopping, thinking he'd better get to her place and not be late. It would make a wrong impression. He hadn't met her face to face yet; the anticipation of meeting her had overcome him with a numbing excitement when he had gotten off the phone with her just two hours earlier.

"My parents aren't home," she said. "My dad is away on business, and Mom is getting drunk at Laura D'Amato's house. She goes over there a lot."

"How long will she be out? Will she be home soon?"

"No," she responded, chuckling. "She'll probably crash over there. She usually does. Mom can't handle her liquor."

"I don't know. It seems pretty risky for me to come over there. Don't get me wrong; I'm at the point of jumping in the shower and getting ready, but still...."

"Please? Please, *Daddy*, come see me?"

The way she called him *"Daddy"* made his chest warm and stomach flutter like butterflies were trapped in his gut. She knew all the right things to say to him, the right tone and punctuality. It wasn't the same as the *dirty talk* they had consumed for weeks. It wasn't the same filthy innuendo he had with the other girls he'd texted back and forth with. The pitch in her voice had the sense of longing, and when he heard the word *Daddy* escape her lips in a tone of persuasive sensuality, it made Gary jump from his bed and strip his clothes off, marching to the stand-up bathroom shower.

"I'll be over, okay? It'll be about two hours. I have to shower and get ready; do you want me to pick up anything on the way?" He asked.

"No. Just you." She said innocently.

Gary pictured her biting her thin pink lips as she spoke to him, her loins burning in the same horny eagerness that Gary felt when she called him *Daddy*.

For a moment, he felt like a kid again. He stuttered when they spoke and blushed like a virginal teenager when she said nice things to him. He didn't need the sexual imaginings or filthy talk coming from her; he was contented with her politeness and friendly enthusiasm that raised his self-esteem and had his chest popping out a little more than usual.

The sex he awaited eagerly was only a bonus – but still an important and necessary one.

The passenger seat was littered with fast food receipts, and letters from the *Revenue Agency* spread around the surface of the seat cushion. Under the documents were a pack of little blue pills and a pencil case that contained a miniature vibrator, three condoms, and another batch of pills. These were for her to take the morning after or preferably right after they were done.

Gary had arrived and drove past her house. He wanted to scope the place out first before he parked his *Corolla* down the street and strolled up to the front door.

The coast looked clear. The small bungalow sat between two large multi-story homes. The large window at the front of the house gave him sight into the living room, the lights were on, and he could glimpse into the home as he scuttled slowly in his car. The curtains were drawn open, and the place looked empty.

He parked his car and sat briefly, staring at the house. Adrenaline had been shooting through his veins when he drove closer to the address. Sitting just a few houses down now, his heart thumped against his chest, and his palms started to sweat more than before.

He reached into his pocket and pulled out his phone. He sat reading the texts they had exchanged before. His eyes enlarged like dinner plates as he read what she had said. She wrote about all the deplorable acts she wanted him to do to her and the things she would do to *him* excited Gary as if he were reading them for the first time. He looked at the pictures she had sent him. The nudes of her bare body, the close-up shots of her pink nipples and her face staring back at him with a giggly smile, a sense of doing something naughty like an experienced escort but with a sense of adolescent guilty pleasure.

"Yeah, you like breaking the rules, don't you?" He whispered. He began rubbing his member through his denim jeans, then stopped at the realization that he had subconsciously settled at the meagre act of self-pleasuring himself without thinking it through rationally,

Why? He thought,

When the real thing was so close.

She was just a few dozen steps away, and this moment had finally come. His hand throbbed, and his leg bounced rapidly with restless anxiety until he shut off the screen and took a deep breath. He then smiled.

"All right." He whispered to himself. "Here we go."

"Yeah, I think that's him, Father," Joey said as he sat in the passenger seat and twisted over to glare out of the back windshield.

"It *is* him. Stay down. Don't get seen, Joey."

"I know, Father, I'm just anxious."

"Don't be. And stop calling me *Father*. We are not at *St. Agathas* now, Joey. Call me by my name." He continued, "...this is after-school shit - We don't need formalities." His hands were clutched at the steering wheel so hard that Joey thought his fingers would indent the soft rubber grip of the wheel.

"I chose you for a reason, Joey. You know we must keep this between us. As we discussed." He shook his head slightly, "Christ, this isn't a good idea."

"I know. I'll be good." Joey said.

"Write down his description. Height, weight, hair colour, what he's wearing...."

"I know, Father," Joey responded, stumbling for the notepad in his lap.

"Mike."

"Yes, Mike. Sorry," Joey clicked the end of the ballpoint pen and scratched the notepad cover to confirm the pen would work.

"Don't be nervous. Calm down. You won't be anywhere near him *as long as* you stay quiet and keep your head down. I won't let him come close to us. Imagine us as angels or spirits, Joey; we watch and gather information from afar. For now."

"When do we call the cops?"

"We won't."

"What?" Joey growled. "That's not what you told me! I thought we were doing something about this shit. I thought we were going to change things – "

"We don't have to, Joey." Michael interrupted. "You must trust me. When you see the outcome of this, I pray...." He stopped his speech and loosened his grip on the steering wheel. His voice had a tone of parental authority mixed with an overwhelming sense of reason. "... I pray you understand, Joey. I pray it doesn't burden you."

"What's the plan, then? I didn't sign up for this to watch!" Joey nearly shouted, "We agreed we would do something about this."

"You're very young. I'm not sure this is a good idea." Father Michael saw movement from the corner of his eye, "Just trust me, Joey... quiet." Father Michael said and shooshed, placing his finger on Joey's lips. Joey could smell the Pall Mall cigarettes Father Michael had been chain-smoking nervously on their drive from St. Agatha's.

"He's coming; keep your head down and write notes. I'll read them out to you. Ready?" Father Michael said in a harsh whisper.

"Yes, Father. I'm ready." Joey opened the notebook and then pointed his phone toward the house to video record every moment.

"Okay. He looks about 5 foot 10, blonde hair." Father Michael stared as Gary walked along the sidewalk toward the house and explained his description to Joey. He sat beside him, scribbling the information legibly in bubble letters like a girl would. A girl about the same age as the one Gary was here to see.

"He exited a black *Corolla,* gloss paint. License plate LXM 386. You got that?"

"Got it," Joey responded, focusing on scribbling on the page in his lap.

"He looks to be about 200 pounds, has a clean-shaven face, he's wearing a dark blue golf shirt tucked into brown Khakis. He seems to be carrying something... hold on," Father Michael said and stared through the lenses of the binoculars silently.

"Looks like a pencil case?" he said.

"Probably has something in it he shouldn't have," Joey spurted out from the corner of his lips.

"I'm sure. He looks like he walks with a limp. Take this down. It's important."

"I'm writing. Slow down a bit. I'm trying to catch up. Why is his limp important? For the cops?"

"No. I told you – no cops."

"Then why?" Joey inquired again. He hesitated questioning Father Michael, but the words still slipped out of his mouth.

"When you hunt, taking down injured prey is much easier."

"When you hunt?" Joey asked. "We're hunting?" Joey began to seem intrigued. "I kind of like the sound of that."

"No," Michael said. He placed the binoculars in his lap and looked at Joey.

"We're not the ones hunting."

Gary strolled down the sidewalk. He walked briskly after immediately shutting the car door behind himself, then slowed his pace as he drew closer to the white-painted aluminum siding of the bungalow. He glided along the neighbour's lawn, staying out of the illumination of streetlights until he reached the hedges along the side of the house. He stopped and nearly buried himself in the tall brush to hide from peeping neighbours or people driving by. He tucked the pencil case he was carrying in his hand into his back pocket. He stared down at his phone screen and texted,

"I'm here."

He patiently waited a few moments then a green bubble appeared on the screen that read,

"Yay! Come in. The doors open. I'm getting dressed."

Even the words typed on the screen turned him on. The ways she smiled at him and giggled in her photos brought a sense of innocence to her deplorability that enthralled him.

He walked toward the front door and saw the shorter hedges that aligned the front lawn. He wondered for a moment,

who had trimmed them so neatly? If Poppa Bear was always on the road and her mother was in a drunken stupor?

He hurriedly walked to the front door and twisted the knob, walking into the house while looking back to the dark street to observe if anyone saw him sneaking in.

The home was elegant inside and exhibited a classier impression than the already impressive rows of neatly manicured hedges that aligned the front lawn.

The walls were painted white and adorned with medium-sized framed paintings. The carpet on the floor was a light grey colour that had never collected a dust mite or juice stains and was comfortable on Gary's toes when he took his shoes off at the door. He dug his feet into the carpet and observed the tasteful paintings adorning the walls. They were oil paintings of French landscapes. Countryside hilltop villas, scenes of *Patisseries* with chalkboard menus, and quaint Artisan bookshops lining a refined cobblestone square. Some others were paintings of Notre Dame and the Basilica of the Sacré-Coeur sitting atop Montmartre. They looked ancient but preserved with strict obedience. The side tables and lamps were modern styles. The tabletops were glass, and circular-shaped pot lights were buried into the ceiling. It smelled like French Vanilla with hints of Cinnamon that drifted around him. Gary breathed it in and exhaled a deep sigh at the elegant scent.

"Hello? Kaycee?" He stood quietly, hoping to hear her voice and *only* her voice.

"I'm coming down," she said from upstairs.

He smiled. Then rubbed his sweaty palms on his tanned Khakis and looked around.

He strolled forward, and to his left was the living room. The large window had its curtains drawn open. He had noticed that before. He stood at the foot of the room and decided not to go in. Gary took slow, measured steps down the hallway. He passed the carpeted stairs on his right that Kaycee's voice had come from and found himself in the kitchen. He was impressed with the layout and organization of the cooking utensils and sets of knives that hung on the surface of the white-tiled walls on magnets. The island in the middle of the kitchen had a marbled top with two crystal vases on either end. Long dark-red Roses stood out of the vases gloriously. Between them was Kaycee's phone. He gazed at it and furrowed his brow at the thought of how she could text him if she left her cell phone downstairs while changing in her room.

"Hey, stranger," the voice behind him said merrily.

She shocked him; he jumped slightly at the surprise. Gary turned around quickly and saw her standing in front of him.

She wore a loose-fitting t-shirt, two sizes too big, with a Korean K-pop band on the front of it, with pyjama bottoms that were pink with flowers. She wasn't wearing socks, and he could see she painted her toes a bright pink. Her hair was tied in pigtails and hung down to her shoulders. It wasn't the attire he was expecting and not the sexy outfit she had promised him in all those text messages. The most perplexing to Gary was that she was wearing a baby's bib at the collar. It was white with a little cartoon sheep at the brim.

"Don't be disappointed, baby." She said. She pursed her lips into a frown, then smiled broadly. "I'll be out of these soon." And chuckled a bubbly laugh. "Come to the living room. I'll close the curtains."

"Sure. Where can I sit?" asked Gary as he rubbed his hands together.

"You can sit anywhere you like, dear," another voice said.

The voice had appeared out of nowhere. Gary stumbled and planted himself on the white leather couch then the curtains slammed together. He didn't see who slammed the curtains together so furiously and intently looked up at the older woman standing before him.

She was holding a white porcelain saucer in one hand and was sipping at (what smelled like) French Vanilla coffee in a teacup with the other. The steam from the cup rose in front of her face, nearly disguising her appearance, but Gary focused on her through the haze.

Her hair was white as milk and tied in the back tightly, her scalp pulled back at the hairline. Her outfit was a long black leather dress buttoned to the collar with a dark rouge corset strung tightly at the waist. She was adorned in gold metals like the type generals get for their military achievements, but these were different. They were rusted and eroded at the edges. Gary wondered what kind of Halloween costume this lady was wearing. He sat frightened and gasped at the adult whom he was not expecting to be home. He regretted how he let down his guard and didn't scope the interior out first.

His eyes bulged as he stared at her and began breathing heavily. This was a mistake, and Gary could feel the sinking feeling in his stomach that people feel when they have been caught in the act of doing something grotesque and atrocious.

"Who closed the curtains?" Joey asked, trying to gain assurance of what he had witnessed.

"Nobody; I didn't see anyone. They closed by themselves, I think," Father Michael said in a low murmur.

"How are we going to see inside? Did this happen before? What do we – "

"It always happens every time I come here," he said. We need some surveillance inside, but it's hard. I don't want to spook them."

"What is the worst case? If we get caught, they are the ones in the wrong. They're the guilty party, right?"

"What are you saying, Joey?" asked Michael with one eye squinched.

"I'll go up there – "Joey said. "I'll put my phone on record and lean it against that side window. I think I can get it open. I think I can sneak around the side."

"No, Joey. No."

"Yes. It's the only way. I'll lean my phone at a good angle and get audio from it too. Then, I'll come back."

"It's Trespassing." Father Michael said in a furious whisper,

"But..."

"No matter the reason. We can get in serious trouble."

"I've been in trouble, Michael." He made a point of saying his name, "Besides, you're here. You can cleanse me when all this is done. You told me this was dirty, and I know that - You asked me if I was prepared, remember?" Joey felt more confident as he worked to convince Father Michael that he should go. He knew it was foolish and realized that his rap sheet from previous issues would land him in a holding cell overnight if he had been caught.

"It's too dangerous. I won't allow it." Father Michael was adamant and final. His irritation with the kid who wouldn't stop trying to be a hero was apparent with burning fury in his eyes.

"I'll be fast," Joey said quickly, and he opened the passenger door and sped out of the car. The interior light that had come on when he opened the door momentarily blinded Michael as he had been sitting in the dark for two hours waiting for the next predator to appear.

Father Michael sat speechlessly. His hand hung out like he was trying to pull Joey back, but no one was there.

He watched through the car windows as Joey snuck quickly to the tall hedges at the side of the house. He paused for a moment and got down on one knee. The shadows of the night had him disguised well. A curious passerby wouldn't spot him if he didn't move and stayed still. He snuck along the hedges toward the backyard, where he found an opening. He jumped the waist-high chain-length fence and crept toward the house.

Michael couldn't see Joey anymore. He contemplated leaving the car. He questioned his morals by staying in his seat while the 17-year-old kid with a record the length of a grocery receipt did all the dirty work. He hated that Joey ran off and took that kind of responsibility, took on that kind of danger, yet felt palpably relieved at the thought of attaining audio and visuals from inside. After all, he didn't have to go inside and was safer in the car. That's what he tried to convince himself. The voice in his head told him the truth that seemed to pound the words into the deepest core of his intellect. *You're scared. You know you don't want to go back in there,* like a little red devil perched on his shoulder chanting in his ear. He didn't feel the weight of the angel on the other shoulder. He hadn't felt the angel in a long time.

Joey snuck through the side yard, nearly tripping on a snaking garden hose. He came to the side window which led into the kitchen. The view wasn't perfect. Having been blocked by a pillar blurring part of the view, he could still see into the living room due to the house's open concept.

Joey peered through the window while standing in the dark and saw Gary sitting on the white leather couch with a little girl perched on a wooden stool and beside her, an older woman with her back turned towards Joey. She was holding something, but he couldn't make it out. He focused on his fingertips, prying on the splintery windowsill. He forced the window up slowly and was slightly relieved at how smooth and quietly the window glided up the seams. He raised the window just enough to perch his phone on the corner, propping up the window simultaneously. He breathed heavily with a long exhale as he pressed the red button on the screen to record.

Michael clenched two fingers around the driver's side door handle, then loosened them. Michael closed his eyes and gasped at the scent of French Vanilla in his memory. He began breathing rapidly and hyperventilating when the passenger side door opened, the interior light forcing Michael to open his eyes. Joey enthusiastically closed the door behind him, his chin high, smiling broadly like he deserved a prize.

"See? Told you I'd be fast," he said, then suddenly paused at the pale skin complexion of Father Michael. His smile quickly disappeared,

"Hey, Father, are you all right?"

"We both know why you are here, don't we, Mr. O'Hare?" the old woman began saying. "I've seen the text messages between you and my granddaughter, and I must say - quite perverse stuff."

"I don't know what you mean."

"You don't? Oh my. Shall I read them out to you?"

"No."

"Let's not pretend that you aren't here to do naughty things to a 13-year-old girl Mr. O'Hara." The woman said plainly.

"Don't call the cops. I've got a lot of money." He said,

"That's very well. I don't want money. You see, my darling Kaycee must feed, and you have produced yourself to be the perfect bait."

"Bait?" Gary asked.

"Yeah, bait. Like fishing, you know?" Kaycee said in her childlike voice. She wasn't smiling anymore. She wasn't endearing like she had been the whole time conversating with Gary. She sat with a straight and hard expression on her face, perched on a wooden stool like a buzzard leaning forward and sniffing the air. She looked over at the older lady and said,

"Grandma, it's happening again." She held her hand up and pulled away her fingernail. The nail separated from the cuticle smoothly, leaving a long strand of blood in the air between the edge of her dismembered nail and her fingertip. She pulled off the others, pouting and flicking them to the floor.

"You see, Mr. O'Hara. She must feed."

"What the fuck? I have to go." Gary shuddered,

The lights shut off suddenly, leaving just a single pot light that cast shadows on everyone in the room. He looked to the wall and saw the mirage of the old lady's shadow, a mirror image of her holding the saucer and teacup.

Kaycee's shadow was frightening. The cold swell of goosebumps appeared on Gary's back as he stared at the black silhouette on the wall. The shadow was tiny, like a children's doll sitting on the edge of the stool. It wore a long-coned hat that became slimmer towards the tip with what appeared to be a fuzzy ball or a jingle bell on the end. The shirt collars were exaggerated and protruded far from the shoulders, they also had bells on the ends, and the tiny shoes the shadow wore, were long and pointed like that of a sultan from *1001 Arabian Nights.*

Gary gasped and couldn't take his eyes off the shadows on the wall. Kaycee sat swinging her legs, the sound of bells rang throughout the house with every kick and swoop of her feet blaring in Gary's eardrums like his hearing had been amplified ten times over. His legs were frozen, his feet planted to the carpet like his toes had grown long fangs and dug deep into the floor, and the trickling of sweat from his forehead stung his eye as the salted bead dripped past his lashes.

"You seem frightened, Mr. O'Hara. I truly understand your predicament. I know you didn't intend on me being here – that's obvious – and I also realize that you're scared and are surely contemplating the consequences of being here." She sipped from the teacup, then continued, "I must offer you the options, however. I don't want to dig too deep into the matter, but you must hear it. You must. For your own good."

"I want to go. I can pay you if you don't call the Cops, alright? We can pretend this never happened." He pleaded.

"Is that what you would think if you were successful tonight, Mr. O'Hara? Would you walk away with sticky undergarments, the scent of her juice on your lips, and a smile telling yourself that this never happened? We both know you would never forget what would happen tonight if you didn't get caught. Nevertheless, you are caught - aren't you, Mr. O'Hara?" She smiled a grotesque grin at Gary.

"Caught in the sickening act of rubbing her in all the wrong places. You can pretend you didn't mean any harm, telling yourself that you wouldn't hurt her. Pretend all you want. You can beg and convince yourself of your innocence, but we both know the truth, don't we? That you – a grown man - intended on coming here to *fuck* a little girl." The older woman's vulgarity stung more coming from her lips. Gary shuddered at the thought that the fragile old lady wasn't delicate but the opposite, made of lead - dense, concentrated and toxic.

"Please, I have a lot of money.... "

"I don't want money; please stop this nonsense, Mr. O'Hara. I've been polite with you thus far; I expect the same respect. Please keep up."

Gary sat quietly. He decided to himself that it wasn't worth pleading or begging. He told himself that he wouldn't be going anywhere. The realization slammed him as he looked at the expression on the older woman's face. Kaycee sat blankly, staring at Gary, which was scarier than what the older woman said to him.

"You have two options, Mr. O'Hara. Indeed, you won't be going anywhere tonight, so let's please not bring up the subject, if not for a waste of valuable time, then for the sake of good breeding and politeness. Your first option is to slit your wrists. It will sting briefly; rest assured that you will grow weak until you finally sleep."

The woman spoke with a straight face as if she read from a script. She made it sound so easy – like the act wouldn't happen to him but to some character in a movie or novel.

"I value this option and suggest it strongly opposed to option 2." She sipped from her coffee. Gary sat still, listening to her with squinted eyes.

"Option 2..." she continued, "you can cut your throat. It's a faster death - but messy. Many people panic and start clutching at the wound and flailing around, splattering blood all over. Most of them don't even cut themselves deep enough to bleed out. They sit and struggle, too scared to make death so much easier to come by. They only end up bleeding all over my carpet." She sighed deeply. "Mr. O'Hara, as you can see, I have exquisite taste in furniture. It's all imported from *Marseille* and *Lyon*. I certainly don't need them stained. However, the decision is entirely up to you. Kaycee is hungry and hasn't eaten in 2 weeks. She's falling apart, don't you see?"

Gary nodded, sweat dripping from his chin.

"I won't pick either." He said. Kaycee jumped from the stool and stepped toward Gary, pulling the white bib and her neck collar down to expose her neck. A long and jagged scar that ran along the front of her throat. She smiled and explained to Gary,

"I didn't get to choose an option. A bad man like you gave me mine. At least you have a choice."

"N-not much of a c-choice," he shuddered in a low voice, almost mouthing the words without any sound coming out.

"I was raped, beaten, raped again, then he cut my throat. He sawed so deep he severed my spine. Do you have any idea what it feels like, Gary? To have a serrated blade tear at your throat?"

Gary shuddered at the thought and curiously gazed at the scar. The bells jingled again as she propped herself back on the stool.

"Enough of this, Grandma; I'm hungry." She pleaded. They both looked at Gary then their eyes drew to the thin boning knife that was rusted at the edge. It sat at Gary's feet with the round wooden handle pointed towards him. He hadn't seen it before. He didn't notice it when he sat down and didn't remember anyone placing it on the floor before him.

"Which will it be, Mr. O'Hara?" Kaycee's Grandmother asked,
"None."
"Fine." The old lady sighed deeply and looked over at Kaycee, who was grinning widely. Tears of blood had started to drop from her eyes, leaving a dark stream on her cheeks among a canvas of porcelain white skin. She bit her lip so hard the pink turned white, then severed, and red blood swelled the surface of her lips.

"You may feast, Kaycee. *Bon Appetit.*"

"We won't see what's happening until I return for the phone. I should have stayed there," Joey said

"No. It's good you came back. You don't want to know what will happen in there." Michael responded.

"Yes, I do; that's why I'm here."

"No, you don't. I know better. Believe me, Joey – I know better." Father Michael seemed tired. He was mentally exhausted from arguing with Joey for so long only to have the boy constantly question him and ultimately ignore his requests, contemplating why he brought him in the first place and the shadow of his conscience that toyed with his heart and convinced him that he had to bury his secrets deep within himself. Joey (or anybody else) could never know.

"Then why bring me here? Why choose me? You seem to put on more than you know, Father. I have the right to know."

"Listen - you will see for yourself when we grab the phone." Michael looked up and closed his eyes, making an invisible cross with two fingers. He instantly regretted what he said.

"When?"

"When what?"

"Do I grab the phone? Do we wait until he comes back out?" Joey asked, annoyed.

"He won't come back out. Unless he's lucky," Michael responded. He was staring at the house. He recognized the white light coming from the slits of the curtains.

"It's bad. Real bad, Joey." Michael said.

Joey didn't respond. He sat back in the seat, closed his eyes, and tilted his ball cap forward to cover his face.

"Okay, let me know when to get the phone back," Joey said.

Father Michael watched as Joey fell asleep and began to snore silently. When he was confident Joey was completely passed out, he looked down at his hands and lifted one of the cuffs. He rubbed his thumb along the scar on his wrist. It protruded upwards with bumpy ridges, and Michael shivered at the sensation.

"Yeah. I will, Joey." He whispered.

"Joey. Wake up. It's time." Michael gently shook Joey's arm.

"Yeah? How do you know?" Joey asked, rubbing his eyes.

"It's been an hour. It's time."

"Okay, just give me a minute; I dozed off deep, Father."

"Stay here. I'll get the phone. I can't stand letting you go back out there." Father Michael reached into his pocket, produced a Timex stopwatch, and began to fiddle with it nervously, "I was wrong to let you leave the car the first time. if anyone should do it, it's me." He said.

"I'd love to debate with you, Father - but I can't argue with that."

"Good. Joey, I need you to listen to me. I want you to start the timer on this stopwatch as soon as I leave the car. If I'm not back in 10 exact minutes, to the second, I want you to run down the street, hook a left, and you will arrive at Front Steet. Keep going south; stick to the fence. You will see a row of Taxi cabs...." Michael explained.

"You want me to leave you after ten minutes?" Joey seemed surprised and angered at the same time. "I can't do that."

"You must," Michael said. He grabbed Joey's shoulder tightly. "You get the hell out of here and never come back."

"And what do I tell people? The Priest of our Parish goes missing; don't you think they will ask questions?"

"Then tell them the truth. Tell them why we came - what I told you. It won't matter to me. I'll be dead."

"Dead?" Joey's brows raised in an arch; his mouth gaped open at the shock of Father Michael's revelation.

"When you see the cabs, Joey, get in and go home. Do you understand?" Michael shoved his hand in the cupholder, pulled out crumpled bills, and gave them to Joey.

"Yes. But why don't you think you will be back? Just grab the phone and go." Joey said,

"I hope, Joey. I hope it's that easy".

Father Michael had made it to the side fence in the break of the hedges. He had snuck quietly, although his back tightened, and his legs burned from the lactic acid build-up as he slumped forward and ran, trying his best to stay low to the ground. He huffed large white clouds of frozen breath. He saw the plumes coming from his mouth and controlled his breathing to remain undetected. He struggled to make it over the fence, but he did. He snuck up to the side window and discovered it was shut.

Michael looked around in the grass for Joey's phone. He couldn't see it. It was dark, and he depended on his eyesight adjusting in the pitch-black night to locate the phone but wasn't finding it. His vision also took a long time to adjust to the darkness. He looked through the window, hoping it didn't stumble and fall inside. He raised his head slowly to peer through the faded glass and looked at the kitchen tiles in front of him on the other side. There was no sign of it. He looked around the dimly lit kitchen and saw a phone on the island with two crystal vases of roses on either side.

Great. How did it make it over there? Someone found it for sure. Michael thought.

He turned his back to the wall and slid down slowly, planting his rear in the wet grass. Michael thought he could smell French Vanilla seeping under the window seam. He closed his eyes and focused on his breathing. He didn't want another panic attack as he did in the car. He needed to focus on getting the phone back. He needed to know what they *would have* done.

The window slid upwards smoothly like the tracks had been greased. The side window wasn't large, but it was enough for a man of Father Michael's size to squeeze through. He tried to be quiet and imagined himself imitating a Boa Constrictor, slithering through the open window and gracefully easing its way down to the floor, where nobody would hear him or notice he had crept in. Michael came through the window headfirst and used his waist as a pendulum, rocking himself forward until his hands grasped the cold white tiles. He pulled himself through and found himself in the exact place he never wanted to be again.

Michael didn't hear anything coming from the living room. He saw that the single light was still on, and he hesitated to glimpse into the room, afraid of what he might see. He reached over to the phone and grabbed it. He looked at the back of it, and the phone case had a large purple flower decorated with other stickers that read "suck it" with cartoon fangs adorning the slogan. He looked at his feet around the kitchen and couldn't see Joey's phone. He must have picked up Kaycee's phone.

The pit of his stomach rumbled with bile, making him shrink at the thought. He put the phone gently back on the countertop and moved to get out of the house. Then, the phone vibrated on the marble top that instant. Michael leaned forward and saw the caller's I.D. on the screen.

It read,

Joey Graziano

"Joey?" Michael said aloud, not even realizing he had broken the house's silence. He picked up the phone, pressed the green button, and said nothing. The voice that came through was familiar but very angry.

"You didn't think I knew?" Joey said over the phone. "I have you where you deserve to be, asshole! You won't escape this time. You deserve what you get, and hey Mike...my brother Justin's rectal stitches have healed. He says, '*Paybacks a Bitch*', you piece of shit!" The phone clicked and hung up.

Michael stood in the kitchen staring at the phone screen go blank when he heard another familiar voice.

"Hello, Father. I have sinned. I've been a naughty girl."

She stared at Father Michael; her eyes seemed distant and empty. Like looking into a dark room, knowing nothing was there. Her mouth and the entire front of her K-pop band t-shirt, including the bib, were covered in blood. Her skin was pale like chalk dusting had covered her face behind the dried blood stains smeared around her mouth, resembling a child gorging on strawberries. The warm, sticky drips hung from the edge of her chin. Flies buzzed and swirled around her head.

"Don't I still look pretty, Father?" She asked as she slowly took steps toward him.

Michael's elbow hit the crystal vase, and it tumbled to the floor. The crystal smashed, and bits of glass spread out among the surface of the ceramic tiles. Michael stepped backward, caught a piece of glass in his shoe sole, and tumbled, his back landing in the shards of glass. He screamed an agonizing terror. Kaycee stood laughing at him like she was watching *"Jackass"* reruns on television, but her maniacal laughter was muted by the loud buzzing of the horse flies that landed on Michael's arms and began tearing away chunks of flesh.

"Nobody ever escapes, Father." She chuckled louder at his desperation.

Michael crawled backward, the shards of broken glass embedded in his palms. The pools of blood crept from Kaycee's feet as she stepped towards him, the cracking sound of broken crystals crushing from the weight of her heels. Michael shrieked as he heard the crunching footsteps and the striking pain of glass digging into his elbows. He finally got up and stumbled into the living room.

The carpet was clean and a light grey. The fabric had streaks along the surface as if it had just been freshly vacuumed. He saw the shadow of the doll-sized figure walking toward him on the wall. The jingle bells rang in his ears, along with the buzzing of the flies with each step she took toward him.

Then suddenly, he felt the sensation of his hair clutched with a firm grip, then he felt the skin of his throat split open, and blood poured from his neck onto his chest with the ferocity of river rapids during a Monsoon storm. He felt the meat and fat of his neck tear and imagined it splitting. Michael heard the horrific gurgling of blood as he tried to scream. The hissing of breath escaping from his severed windpipe. He Panicked; he clutched at his throat and felt the sharp blade cut further into his neck. The crunching of bone echoed in the house with every knife stroke. Michael could hear through the gurgling, his spine splintering and splitting apart. The pleasureful grunting of his killer was distant among the sound of his head being taken off.

Michael's arms finally dropped to his sides, and his body fell over once his head detached. All seemed calm and tranquil at that moment. The silence had returned to the serene bungalow.

Michael saw his body fall over at the last moment and let out a plopping sound as it toppled forward and landed on the floor. He also heard Kaycee chuckling. The little girl chuckled loudly, holding her belly and pointing her finger until the sounds faded, and his vision slowly faded into pitch black.

12

A Deal They Can't Refuse

It had been hard for Brian to approach the salesman at the tiny booth.

Placed in the middle corridor of the outlet shopping mall, Brian nervously twisted the bottom brim of his t-shirt. He began pacing behind the shopping mall pillar, mustering courage and beating down his teenage anxiety.

Finally, he took the first step and approached the stumpy East Indian man and pointed to what he had taken the bus so far to come purchase. The newest Android phone was all the rave in his high school. Other kids had been flashing them around and making video blogs about high school life and posting them on social media outlets, even earning money, which was an incredible idea to Brian.

The seller seemed nice. An older Indian man with a white beard and purple turban seemed to smile through every word and every sales pitch. He burst with an aura of being kind and Friendly enough to convince Brian the red-light special on the ripped and tattered box was worth the investment. Brian handed over his Mother's credit card to the teller at the phone booth. The East Indian gentleman swiped the card, and the tiny screen on the *Interac* machine read "approved."

I guess your Mother sent you here to get yourself a new phone?" asked the Indian man in a thick accent as he waited for the receipt to come out of the machine.

"Yes. She did. She's, uhm... a little sick today." Brian responded. He looked through the glass case as he spoke. He had hoped the Indian man behind the counter wouldn't notice he was lying and that he had stolen the credit card from his Mother's purse earlier that morning. The Indian man's furry brows raised, not in shock but with amusement – as if he knew better.

It wasn't the man's place to do anything about it, Brian thought to himself. *What does he care? It's all about the Benjamins to him anyway.*

The box was unusually bigger than the standard-size phones released late last year. All the kids in school had the latest, and Brian didn't remember the phone being so large when he saw Lucy Willingham and Paulo Gutierrez staring at their screens during school lunch break. Brian examined the white cardboard box. The scratches on the side and the ripped plastic sheet in the corner gave a hint away that this wasn't exactly off the shelves from the manufacturer's facility. Instead, it seemed like this particular box had fallen off the back of some truck on its way to a big box store. Brian had his suspicions, but since his Mother wouldn't go out of her way to buy him one, he didn't particularly care where the phone had come from, As long as he had his hands on one.

"Why would I spend all that money on a phone? What's wrong with the one you have?" She would ask over dinner when Brian gathered enough nerve to ask her for it in the first place.

"Besides, there will be another released next year. Maybe then, I'll get you one. Not now, though." He shrunk at the memory of her voice when he slipped her forbidden credit card into the side pocket of his denim jeans.

Brian slid his finger across the silky plastic covering and examined the tattered plastic and the dent on the corner of the box that would explain the reduced price. Cut nearly in half from what the other kids at school had paid, or more accurately, what their parents had paid. He was convinced that he had gotten such a good deal that he was, in a way, stealing it. Brian stood waiting for the receipt, his legs shaking and his palms leaving moist handprints on the surface of the glass counter. The man handed the receipt to Brian, who sighed in relief once he felt the box in his palms.

"There you go, young sir. Enjoy, and remember; it's *the final sale*. Unless it's returns, but no refunds, okay?"

"Yes sir, thank you," Brian said in a whisp as he hurriedly rushed away from the booth clutching the white box to his chest. He had made it twenty steps and thought he had heard the Indian man in his thick Punjabi accent shout something over the blurred voices and echoes of the shopping mall patrons. He glanced over his shoulder while still walking frantically and saw that the booth was gone.

Weird. Could have thought I wasn't that far away. Maybe I walked faster than I thought.

With an extra bounce in his step, he walked over to the Coffee shop at the end of the mall's hallway, where he pushed open the heavy glass door and sat at the closest available table. His anxiety faded, and he sat momentarily examining the other customers who sat near him. The guy with the laptop and a stack of pages beside him was a blogger or a writer of some sort. His glasses were thick, and he was skinny, wearing a tight-collared shirt. Brian glanced at the chalkboard menu that all trendy Coffee shops had nowadays and gasped at the prices for the Coffee that smelled like it was brewed in a shithouse in a construction yard. Brian wasn't much for Coffee, but those Latte milkshakes, on the other hand, would be very convincing if they didn't charge 7 dollars for a small.

The plastic came off quickly. Brian pinched the torn corner with his nails and pulled the thin plastic veil away from the white cardboard box like a ribbon. He opened the flap and pulled out the inner tray that housed the phone and its charger. The scent glided up Brian's nostrils, and he sat amused at the smell of new cardboard with a hint of Lavender. He wondered if the Punjabi man had sprayed the box with some sort of perfume to make the purchase more appealing to the customers' senses. Even Brian knew that was unlikely, but the Lavender was still present, and he thought,

Well, you never know, I guess.

This box excluded the manual, which was more unusual than the hint of Lavender. Brian squinted his eye and pursed his lips. Lifting the plastic tray from the box, he couldn't find the paper anywhere. It wasn't a big deal; he knew how to work the phone, that is, if this one was like other phones from the past. He didn't take long to ignore the missing manual and peeled the sticky covering off the phone to expose its shiny plastic casing. He pressed the side button, and the screen lit up. Bubble letters appeared on the screen that read,

"Hello Brian"

Funny. How does it know my name? Maybe the Indian guy at the booth programmed it for me already. Pretty neat. Brian thought.

His eyes glistened on the illuminated screen as the white light bounced off his eyes, already scrolling through the setup and configuring his phone when a friendly voice grabbed his attention.

"Hey, stranger."

"Oh, Lucy," Brian responded with an air of surprise.

Lucy was beautiful in a wholesome way. Her long brown locks danced on her shoulder, and her light blue eyes brightened up when she spoke. They were mesmerizing to Brian, which he initially found attractive about her. He thought to himself and debated if they resembled the tint of turquoise waters off the coast of *Cuba*, or if they were light grey, similar to approaching spring rain clouds. Lucy was bubbly and enthusiastic when she spoke. Her addictive gaze brightened when she talked to him. It made him feel like she wanted to engage in thought-provoking conversations with him particularly and that she wasn't just being polite. That she was *into* him the same way he was *into* her. Her radiance was distracting, and her cheerfulness made the sun shine brighter, flowers stand taller and the radiance of their colour illuminate objects around them. There was also her perfume that stung his nostrils. She had always over-sprayed herself with her Grandma's husky perfume, the kind in a glass bottle with a tube and bladder to squeeze. Brian smiled and responded to her.

"Have a seat; check out what I got."

"Oh, I heard about these. What did you spend on this? Your college tuition? I heard these things are crazy expensive."

"Not really. Well, yeah, it is expensive. I got a deal. A red-light special from the Indian guy at the phone booth just up the hallway."

"...Phonebooth up the hallway?" Her eyebrows arched as she looked over Brian's shoulder through the glass doors, trying to glance in the direction he was talking about.

"Yeah, I got it for, like, half price. There's no way I could afford it otherwise. The Bowl-a-Rama only pays so much, you know?" Brian said.

"Yeah, I totally get it. I wanted one for Christmas but wouldn't feel right asking my parents to spend so much on me. Especially for a phone that will go out of style in the next year..." she caught herself. "Oops, sorry." She covered her mouth like she was blocking any more offences from sneaking out. Brian noticed the coincidence that his

Mother had said the same thing to him the night before at dinner. He finally understood when people would say that you are best to marry a girl like your Mom. At first, he found it gross, but now he understood. With Lucy, he could tolerate it; he welcomed it and found it cute that she was so opinionated and lacked a verbal filter.

"All good." Brian chuckled. He was too excited at his new toy to let anything Lucy had to say offend him or turn him off from the cell phone. He stared at the screen as the apps started to load in front of him. As he stared at the screen, he continued talking to Lucy in a trance.

"It's *pretty* cool! It said my name when the screen first came on."

"Your name, huh?" She said. "I never heard of that one before."

"Red light special, I guess. I bet the guy programmed it for me."

"Which guy is this you are talking about? I just came from that way and didn't see any phone booth. I need a case for mine; I'm sure I would have noticed."

"Check it out. It comes with games already installed...." He interrupted, ignoring what Lucy was saying.

Lucy signalled the waiter to come to their table. She wanted one of the newest Lattes the shop was promoting. Lucy's Mother felt like she was still a bit too young to drink caffeine, but Lucy told herself that a Latte would be okay.

The young man strolled over, a white apron tied around his waist and a black collared shirt with the top button stylishly loosened to show off his two strands of chest hair. His left breast had a name tag that read "Jimmy," and under his name, like a subtitle for a novel read, "I like Cookies and Chocolate."

"Hey Lucy, Uhm, it's nice to see you. Can I get you anything? Brian raised his head at Jimmy's voice. Brian knew Jimmy Callahan worked here and had gotten along with Jimmy just fine in group projects for

English class. He recognized his voice and immediately remembered that Jimmy had a *major* crush on Lucy, which made Brian's blood slowly heat up.

"Hey, Jim. Yeah, can I get one of those Lattes on the board there? They look good." Lucy asked in her upbeat and positive manner.

"Sure, Lucy. Can I get you maybe a cookie or a Muffin? The chocolate chip Muffins just came out of the oven, and...."

"I'll have a Muffin, Jimmy." Brian's voice was hoarse and assertive. "I'll also have a large dark roast. One cream and a lump of sugar. Thanks, bud." The waiter nodded and gazed to the floor as he walked away towards the counter to fetch their order. Brian looked back down at his phone. Lucy stared at Brian as he sat hypnotized.

"Coffee?" she asked. "Since when do you drink Coffee?" she asked. He didn't answer her, only glaring at the phone screen.

"So, Mr. Bradford was asking about you today. Wondering where you were." Lucy said,

"I slept in. Mr. Bradford could chill out a bit. I had a late night."

"What were you doing?" she asked.

"Working... At the bowling alley...oh cool, check this out." Lucy didn't seem interested in the phone anymore. She prodded him further, catching a hint at the blatant lie. Brian wasn't much for lying. He was terrible at it. Lucy knew it wasn't like him to lie or not pay attention when someone spoke to him. What had attracted her on the first day of school when they met was how polite and considerate Brian was. He always offered to walk her home and help with her math work and never made a move to try and slide in a touch or a feel. He was a real gentleman for a teenage boy with sex on his mind nearly eighty percent of the day and hormones that made him uncontrollably erect at the worst of times, like in the middle of Calculus or anytime he spoke to

Lucy. Hell, anytime he even thought about her or her hypnotizing blue eyes.

"You were supposed to present the Essay today. He seemed *pretty* disappointed," she said.

"That's too bad. I forgot."

"Don't you care?"

"Not really."

"You know that kind of attitude won't get you very far." He heard his Mother's all too familiar voice again through her lips; this time, he didn't find it cute or sincere.

"Thanks, Mom," Brian said under his breath.

Jimmy was back with a circular metal tray. The Coffee and Muffins sat on top, and he nervously placed the coaster on the table in front of Lucy. He stared at her as he leaned forward, trying to avoid spilling her drink. Transfixed on her like Brian was transfixed on the phone, Jimmy's gaze battled back and forth between Lucy's short-cut shirt that exposed the start of her cleavage and her eyes, where he hoped she would not notice where he was *really* looking. Lucy could quickly see where each boy's priorities lay.

"Hey, Lucy," Brian asked. "Wanna go out on a date? I could get you some dinner and chill at my place. I'll make sure my mom won't be home; it will just be us. Alone." Brian looked up at Jimmy as his eyes pierced the floor once again. His smile shrunk away, and his lips clenched tightly, his upper lip growing a pale white from the pressure of his thin lips pressed tightly together, contrasting the flush red in his cheeks. Lucy didn't answer Brian, knowing what he was doing. She crossed her arms, and her leg bounced up and down under the round Coffee table. Jimmy walked away quickly, his head bowed and his arms straight to his side. Lucy's eyes followed Jimmy as he walked away in defeat, her heart thumping against her chest, her jaws growing sore from the tight clenching.

"That's a real asshole thing to do, Brian!"

"What did I do?" he answered sarcastically.

"You know what you did, and I don't like it. Enjoy your Muffin." she slid the chair back, and the feet on the metal legs scraped against the hardwood floor. Her brows furrowed. She glared at Brian as he continued to stare at the phone screen.

"I hope that phone treats you well, Brian. I hope it doesn't replace your friends." It was the only thing she could muster up. She stormed off in a hurry like she suddenly had an appointment she was late to get to. She pushed the glass door open, kicking up tiny pebbles behind her as she scurried out of the Coffee shop. She was gone just as quickly as she had shown up. Any other time, Brian would be left embarrassed and regretful. Today, however, the phone was on his mind, and he could give a damn about Lucy or anyone else at the moment.

"Whatever." He muttered.

She had forgotten her Latte. Brian reached over and picked up the paper cup, putting it to his lips, taking a sip, and pulling back quickly at the burning sensation on the surface of his tongue.

"Ah, Fuck!" He said as he struggled to swallow the hot molten down his throat.

He had burned his lip on the scalding hot Coffee and stood up with the cup facing Jimmy, who had come back to Brian's table to inquire what the outburst from Lucy was all about.

As Jimmy approached the table, he was blinded by the scalding brown liquid splashing on his face and felt the burn sizzle on his skin under his collared shirt. Brian had gotten up and thrown the hot Coffee at Jimmy in frustration, covering him in the sizzling liquid that seared his flesh. Jimmy screamed in agonizing pain. He imagined his skin melting off and drooping from his bones, making his heart beat faster. His skin began to steam like he had walked out into a winter evening from a hot jacuzzi, and tiny white blisters had miraculously appeared on his forearms through the redness. Jimmy jumped up and down, wailing like a *Banshee*. The patrons sitting close by shrieked and shook their heads at Brian in disgust as he laughed hysterically. One man got up, rolled his newspaper into a tube, and pointed it at the door.

"Get the hell out of here, you little punk!" He shouted.

Brian slumped forward with laughter, his face flush from struggling to breathe.

As Brian turned to walk out, the screen from his phone glowed furiously. It had seemed to light up, its glow pulsing brightly in rhythm with either Brian's laughter or Jimmy's screams.

"I don't understand. He's usually a lovely guy. He seemed to change into something I haven't seen in him before." Lucy said as she walked home with Laura.

"Maybe he was always a *dick*, and the phone brought it out in him. Maybe, he was just impatient and wanted to play with his new toy." Laura responded, shrugging her shoulders.

"Maybe. I don't know. It's just not what I expect from him, is all."

"Not what you expected?"

"He asked me out, but not how I imagined him to. Jimmy was waiting on us at the shop, and Brian became a real asshole. Like he was trying to bully Jimmy."

"He was jealous, for sure. He sees that Jimmy loves you off, which is his way of *claiming* you. I find it kind of sweet." Laura said, again shrugging her shoulders in her way of suggesting something dirty innocently, disguising the fact that it was what she truly felt.

"I don't. Especially from Brian. He reminded me of those jocks in the movies, Ya know? The ones everyone hates, the stereotypical musclebound idiots that always get the girl."

"Well, you want him, don't you?" Laura inquired.

"Yeah, but not like that. Not that side of Brian. Where was the boy who helped carry my books to class? Walked me home after school every day? The Brian I know is charming; he's kind and compassionate."

"Oh, he's still there. He's just willing to do those things when it suits him." Laura said

"You don't like him very much, do you?" Lucy stropped her pace and looked at Laura, her purse strap falling off her shoulder.

"I've been defending him this far, haven't I?" Laura responded. "Besides, it's not that I don't like *Brian* per se; it's all guys. I think they are all idiots. I read some of these romance novels I found in my Mom's bookcase, and the men in those stories...oh my god, Lucy, the men. *Real* men. Not boys. The romance is beyond belief. It's kind of putting high expectations on these morons that go to school with us."

"Romance? Sounds corny," Lucy said, her binder clutched tightly to her chest. "I hope it's not the kind of novels Moms keep from their kids, you know, the dirty ones."

"No, not that kind. I mean, those are fun too." Laura chuckled, "I mean real romance, the kind women lust for. The kind only we can relate to. Love from a woman's perspective. The kind where the man is willing to die for her." She continued, "The kind of things you're saying. The things the men say in these books are almost too good to be true."

"That's not real life, Laura. Those are fantasies some feminist authors drew up of their ideal man. It's not real. I understand people aren't perfect, but at least they are human, not some character in a book."

"If only, though, right?" Laura chuckled as she said it. Lucy laughed, and they continued up the street,

"Yeah, if only."

"Brian, your teacher called again. What's going on? Why did you skip today?" Brian's Mother asked as she leaned on his bedroom door frame. Her finger tapped at her side, impatiently waiting for an answer. Brian lay on his bed, staring at the phone screen.

"Sorry, Mom. I just wanted to get a hold of the Science project I'm behind in. Mr. Flakes' class had to be sacrificed for time."

"Sacrificed for time, huh? Why are you on your phone, then? Shouldn't you be working on catching up on Mr. Bradford's assignments? Are you caught up on *those*? What about your Science?"

"Yeah"

"Yeah, to which question, Brian? Mr. Bradford or Science?"

"Both"

"Brian...listen," Vivian sighed. Her white nurse's scrubs had spots of some unknown substance she had carried on her from a long and arduous night shift. Her ankles throbbed, and her shoulder became numb from pressing all her weight on the door frame.

"I know it's been hard lately, but that's not an excuse to skip class. It isn't like you. Why didn't you just ask me if you could stay home to catch up?"

"I told you why I skipped class."

"It's not the *why* Brian; it's how you went about it. Did you *really* skip to work on your Science?"

"Yes." Brian didn't take his eyes off the screen; his face was a bright white from the light that illuminated his face.

"Yeah, but I don't believe you, though." She shrugged. "Are you going to tell me the real reason you cut today, or will I have to pry it out of you? I sure know I can't afford that phone you got there. Let me guess…." She patted the large side pockets of her scrubs and didn't feel her credit card, and upon realizing it was missing, with the truth consequently flooding into her mind, she stepped into the room and walked over to Brian. She reached over and snatched the phone from Brian, and he exploded.

"What the hell, Mom? I told you why I skipped! I'm caught up on everything, okay?"

Vivian stepped back with her mouth gaped open at the surprise of Brian suddenly turning into Mr. Hyde.

"Then show me." She responded defiantly. Brian sat on the edge of his bed, his fingers clutching the sheets, crumpling them within his palms. He had no answer; he sat with his eyes narrowed into slits, his face growing a bright red.

"That's what I thought. Show me the work, and you get the phone back." She walked out of the room and turned around before gently closing the door behind her. "You ever turn on me like that again – I'll slap the shit out of you, do you hear me?"

He didn't answer, just sat huffing rapidly with the slits of his eyes darting a menacing stare at his Mother.

In her stained hospital scrubs, Vivian Spenser stood at the foot of her bed with her arms crossed, trying to process what just happened -trying furiously to understand her son's state of mind and how he had changed into somebody else she didn't recognize so quickly. The teenage boy she birthed only 14 years ago grew fast, and quickly developed into a man before her eyes. She couldn't believe that she was carrying him in her arms just a few years ago and swinging him in the air on the playground. Now he wanted privacy and to go out with friends instead of cuddling with his Mom in front of the big screen and watching a movie.

"He's a nice boy; I never really had to raise my voice at him like that or punish him."

That is what she said to Gladys in the Rapid Assessment Wing. Gladys was the resident head nurse three years past retirement and always had stories to tell about how compassionate and kind her grandchildren were and how she could relate to children growing up before her eyes.

Morning meetings would consist of Gladys putting her Peppermint tea on the counter in the nurse's quarters to flaunt Chrissy, her most prized and special little grandbaby.

"Well, let me tell you what little Chrissy did yesterday. So adorable..."

Was he a man now? She thought,

Did I have to treat him more like a colleague, a friend, or a patient? Jesus, this is like learning to be a parent all over again. She sighed heavily,

I really don't need this kind of shit.

The teen angst was a lot for her to bear at that moment, and more still, the strangeness and unknown answers to the question of doing the right thing by taking away his phone had occupied the forefront of her mind. She missed her little boy. Brian had been the only one to keep her company for so long. That company was starting to be sorely missed as every day passed more rapidly, hardly witnessing the subtle changes her little boy was going through.

Vivian tucked the phone into her sweater pocket, got her beach towel from the linen closet, and began anticipating the soothing heat of the Sauna downstairs.

The Sauna was empty when Vivian walked in through the large wooden door. A towel wrapped around her, she poured water on the hot rocks and watched the water sizzle away and transform into steam. Drips of moisture soon enveloped the oak-panelled room. She had the Sauna all to herself, and although the thought of privacy would be a welcoming thought to anybody else, with Vivian, she had been lonely for so long that being by herself was like any other day. The boredom of it yanked away and tore chunks off her soul.

She lay on the bench and placed two cucumbers on her eyes. Unaware of her blue sports sweater that hung on the locker hook. The slits from the vent holes of the locker glowed a mesmerizing blue light. Inside, the drooped sweater pocket glowed from the opening. A blue light pulsated like a lighthouse signalling a lost ship to shore. Inside the sweater pocket lay Brian's new Android phone; the screen read,

"Hello, Vivian."

The needle on the Thermostat gauge slowly crept up as the heat inside grew to an unbreathable temperature. Vivian found her throat starting to burn with every inhaling breath, the burning in her chest becoming apparent and bothersome.

She sat up, poured the Aloe Vera water on her skin, and leaned forward with streams of sweat falling to her feet, creating a pool around her toes. She loved the relaxation the intense heat offered, but this was a bit much.

Suddenly, she heard the door click. She was unaware there was a lock on the Sauna door, as it would have been an obvious safety concern for the condominium.

Was that a lock? She thought.

The sound reminded her of when her husband Danny turned the lock on the front door behind him that night when he left. His face flashed in her mind for a moment, but after fourteen years, his resemblance had blurred in her memory, forgetting the little features that made him indistinguishable from other men.

She wondered for a moment if this was the start of the anxiety and stress taking its toll—the beginning of a nervous breakdown. Is this the type of thing that happens? She thought

the click was obnoxiously loud, and she abruptly stood, peering through the door's window, looking down at the handle on the other side. She pulled at the handle, and the door rattled but was indeed locked. Her eyes opened broadly, and her mouth hung open as she saw a large plank running through the Sauna door handle, trapping her inside.

"Are you kidding me right now?" She said under her breath.

She wiped away the mist from the door window with her sweaty palm and looked again at the latch that locked her in. She stared at the wood plank through the window and squeezed her eyelids shut – trying to wake from this dream.

"Wake up, Viv. Wake up."

The plastic dome covering of the thermostat had started to stain a dull yellow, and fifteen minutes had passed as fast as what seemed like seconds ticking away. The needle on the Thermostat had moved from 80 degrees and reached 200, well past the red *danger* indicator on the gauge.

She pounded and shook the large wooden panelled door by the handle. Her heart began to beat violently in her chest.

She had stopped sweating; her skin turned dry and began cracking like the sunlight caked dried saltwater to her skin, withering it like dried fruit. With every pull and tug of the handle, she grew weaker. She breathed harder, and the burning in her chest sizzled her lungs. As she continued to tug at the door, a face appeared in the door window.

It was Brian.

He smiled at her and waved his phone at her through the glass, showing Vivian he had broken into her locker and stolen it back.

"Why? Did you lock.... help me. Brian...please," she whispered. It was all she could muster from her cracked lips. Every word from her lips sizzled, and she could feel the hot breath leave her with every straining word.

Brian stared with a giant grin watching his Mother roasting through the fogged window of the Sauna door. His eyes were covered in a dark blackness; his teeth appeared glazed with brown saliva that had the colour of a dark amber Molasses.

He was drooling as he stared at his Mother struggling inside the Sauna. The long brown sticky strand of drool drooped to his feet. His revenge for her taking his phone, his satisfaction, and his lack of empathy introduced a heavy chill in Vivian's skin cutting through the dry heat of the Sauna at the realization that the face that stared back at her was not Brian. It was not her little boy.

"Slap the shit out of me, right Mom?" he said contemplatively. She could hear every word through the thick wooden door of the blistering Sauna.

"This is what you get. Bitch. Whore." He growled. He didn't have to whisper anymore, didn't have to hide from her.

"This is what you get!"

Vivian swooned. Her legs were wobbling, and her vision was spinning. She felt like a fighter that had gotten caught with the perfect punch, and her senses were a mess. Her breath had grown shallow, and suddenly, the Sauna floor seemed like an excellent place to rest. Although knowing it would be her last resting place if she gave in to the temptation of lying down and shutting her eyes.

Her leg gave out, and she fell backward, hitting her spine on the ledge of the wooden Sauna bench. The pain shot through her bones, but she was too drained to cry.

Brian looked inside at her. His black eyes glanced up at the inside thermometer. He looked back at Vivian and winked. The Thermostat was at its peak, and her eyelids grew heavy, then they slowly closed. She mumbled incoherent words to Brian, who stood on the other side staring at his Mother through the window. He was cackling so loud that the sound emanated throughout the condo Sauna and locker room. She heard him from the inside as she took one last look upwards at the door's window; to see the screen of Brian's phone read,

"Goodbye, Vivian."

Students piled into the hallways like ants. Friends gathered in their usual spots and walked together toward the high school Cafeteria, gossiping about the latest news.

In the early morning, the *CQBW News* reported that Brian's Mother had been found in the condo Sauna with 3rd-degree burns all over her body. The coroner reported that she died from severe dehydration and heatstroke. She was found sitting slumped on the Sauna floor like a robot who had been suddenly unplugged. Her skin was covered in blisters and was withered, resembling the same texture as a dried Apricot or Beef Jerky. Her eyes were open, and her mouth gaped like she had died screaming.

The kids looked over their shoulders as they talked about the tragic news. They looked around for Brian, but he didn't show up to school that day, which was absolutely predictable to students and teachers alike. The Principal on the morning announcements didn't bring up the tragedy due to respect for the family. He knew just as well as anyone else with common sense that the kids would know the details from their parents driving them in or the radio newscasts. Chances were, if he didn't keep up with the constant updates from local newscasters, and the constant barrage of social media posts, the kids would know more details about it than he would. Technology was a tragic occurrence in the modern-day; it didn't relieve grieving families from the tragic news of their personal lives. It didn't offer privacy anymore. Instead, It shoved it in their faces.

"I bet he took off and ran away." One kid said.

"I bet he did it. How did she become trapped in there." Another chimed in.

"Why was the *Homicide unit* there? If it were an accident, they wouldn't be involved."

Most kids felt pity for Brian and tried calling his phone to inquire about his whereabouts. Some genuinely appreciated the circumstances and wanted to offer their condolences and grieve alongside him. Others simply wanted to know more, to gossip about his Mother's death to their friends. Either way, no calls went through; they all went straight to voicemail.

Lucy sat at one of the long Cafeteria tables alongside many other students. Across from her was Jimmy, and they were conversating together with grim looks on their faces. It was not a one-sided conversation, as few words were spoken, and most of the time was spent thinking about what would be appropriate to say in the first place. There were so many questions with few answers.

"I feel so bad, Jim. I was just with him yesterday, and I gave him shit."

"Do you?" answered Jimmy, thinking that Brian deserved more after scalding him for no apparent reason. Jimmy had 2nd degree burns on his face and chest from the hot Coffee Brian threw at him.

That moment felt like it had changed Jimmy's life, crippling him with patches of red burn markings on his pale skin, and he felt the warm glow of satisfaction that Brian was getting bit in the ass by that bitch named *Karma*. Jimmy would never say it out loud, but to his credit, Brian had been a bully to him and acted like a predator once he sensed Jimmy's gimp-like feebleness over Lucy.

"Of course, I feel bad. It's terrible. I knew her. She was hardly around but was very nice when she was." she caught herself again. "...when she was around." The gravity of speaking in the past tense gave Lucy a nauseousness that had her starting to focus on not throwing up.

"I know he asked you out yesterday to get under my skin...." Jimmy blurted out with a sly grin.

Lucy didn't answer. It was a common discomfort she was starting to feel as she grew older. She had noticed the dirty old men who stared at her while she waited at the bus stop. She had mastered polite denials to cocky boys who asked her out to impress their friends. She was starting to witness the dread of looking like a piece of *ass* instead of the intelligent and compassionate person she was. She decided it was acceptable to ignore Jimmy's question. Lucy went on sticking to her point.

"I didn't know he would be going through so much. I tried calling him but no answer. I guess..."

"He wants to be left alone." Interrupted Jimmy. *Fuck Brian*. He thought as he grasped Lucy's hand.

"So? Are you guys going out anyway?" he asked. It's been a question he had wanted to ask for a long time.

"I said *no* to him, Jimmy. Not in those words, but I'm pretty sure he saw I wasn't interested." She answered.

Jimmy smiled and blushed. It was hard to tell from the red mapping burns across his pale white face. Lucy admired Jimmy's dimples in his baby-fat cheeks when he smiled, and it had become apparent to her at that moment. It was cute. It put him in an attractive new light.

Staring into the Cafeteria from the steel meshed window leading to the playground view outside, Brian stood against the concrete wall with his arms crossed. He was watching Lucy and Jimmy sitting at the table together,

They are talking about me; I know it. That little Brat keeps making a move on her. She wanted me to go out with her, and I asked her, didn't I? Why the hell is she sitting with that loser?

Are you going to let them treat you like that, Brian? For all the things you've done for her. You helped her with her homework, walked her home, and took it slow with her. Then you ask her out, and she sits with that loser behind your back? Nice guys finish last, isn't that the saying?

No, it can't be that simple. I'm sure there's an explanation. She feels sorry for him, that's it. Fuck, I shouldn't have done that to Jim. We were friends.

No, Brian. They are going behind your back. How does it feel? No wonder she wants him, Brian. Look at them holding hands, that fucker. How does it feel to have the girl you love so much go behind your back and cheat on you with that loser? Do it, Brian. Show her...

No.

Can you picture it? Lucy Stradling him and moaning, her tits jumping like fried eggs in a skillet? That should be you, Brian, not Him!

Stop it,

Kill that cocksucker!

No. I can't...I'll get caught.

Brian froze and stood at attention like a drill sergeant was chastising him. His eyes rolled slowly to the back of his head and turned a foggy grey until they transformed into pitch black. He marched towards the school doors, passing students by as they covered their mouths at the sight of him.

Yes, Brian. Kill him! Kill him!

Some kids pretended not to see him; others did not pretend. Some called out to him, but Brian still marched on. He swung open the doors and ran down the hallway, crashing into students and teachers, knocking them all over like an oversized running back, plowing over the smaller bodies with rage that burned deep in his stomach like the hottest pits of hell. He repeated to himself with a deep groan,

"Yes. Kill him."

Jimmy held onto Lucy's hands cupped within his own, his thumb gently brushing her skin. She felt the tickle of his nail grazing her skin and enjoyed the shivering sensation. Jimmy's knuckles were cracked and peeling away like a snake shedding in season. Staring at her intensely in her eyes, he spoke softly to her in the way he had learned from his Mother's favourite daytime soap operas, the same techniques he had picked up and practiced in front of the bathroom mirror. He spoke slowly with an air of honesty and sophistication like the burly, hairy-chested protagonist on "*Days of Our Lives.*" As he talked to her, he imagined himself as the mustached protagonist, a kind of *Casanova* of romantic lore.

"I know you like him, Lucy. It breaks my heart, but I know that sometimes you can't change some things no matter how badly you want to." He said.

How wise. He thought to himself sarcastically.

"I don't want to be mean, Jim. I like you; I do. I've known Brian for so long and had a crush on him for a while now. It's just that... yesterday, when he acted that way toward you, it put him in a different light." She explained.

Jimmy sat looking at her intently. She continued,

"I feel like I can't begin to hate him because he was an ass. I don't want to say it, but if you base a relationship on *only* good times, that relationship won't last long. There will be times when you are fighting with each other." Lucy explained to him.

"He burned me, Lucy. It's more than just a bad attitude. He's dangerous." Jimmy said. His eyes shone in the overhead lights and reminded Lucy of Jimmy having the nicest puppy dog eyes she had ever seen.

"If I were your man, I'd try my hardest to make you happy. If you were ever to get mad at me, I just don't know what I would do. Beg? Get on my knees? I shouldn't be saying this, Lucy. I'm sorry."

"No, don't be. I want to hear it. It's sweet." She gripped his hands tighter.

"Listen, this Brian thing; it's not like I devoted my life to him. I know he makes mistakes, but I feel myself weening away from him anyway. That doesn't mean...

"That you will jump into anybody's arms right away? Jimmy interrupted.

"Yes."

"All good. I understand." Jimmy smiled.

"I'm glad I talked to you, Jim...." She continued, looking straight at him. "You're not just *anybody* to me. I just need some time."

Just as she finished her sentence, the Cafeteria doors burst open like an explosion of dynamite had let off.

A DEAL THEY CAN'T REFUSE

Brian stood at the opening, his face red and his eyes pitch black. He sprinted towards Lucy and Jimmy. The crowd of students at the tables rose and spread out as the Red Sea parted for *Moses* at Brian's furious oncoming rage. He thrust his arms forward vigorously, clutching something unrecognizable in his hand, his arms pumping so fast it was hard to make it out. He leaped on top of the long adjoining tables and dashed towards the both of them, knocking over trays of food with every frantic stride.

The crowd stood silent, not believing what they were seeing. Some called out to Brian and cheered him on, thinking this was just him acting out or the beginning of an innocent high-school squabble. The lunch supervisor yelled at him from across the Cafeteria, but Brian didn't hear any of it over the odd cheer and prodding of other students *stirring up the shit*.

He finally got to Lucy and Jimmy. Brian leaped off the table and tackled Jimmy to the floor. Brian sat on his chest, dark spit spraying from his mouth like a ruptured fire hydrant. He screamed in Jimmy's face covering him with the dark brown substance emitting from his bowls that resembled soft baby shit or diarrhea.

Brian began furiously pounding Jimmy with the object in his hands. The thumping sound of the impacts was blaring, and the crowd of students gathered around suddenly gasped in awe at the ferocious violence they witnessed in front of them. The cheering stopped once the thumping began. Jimmy covered his face with his arms, but the hard object in Brian's hands crunched and splintered Jimmy's forearms, leading Jimmy to cry out in agonizing pain, and eventually, his arms fell to his side, mangled and swollen.

The screams disappeared soon after, with every thrusting impact on Jimmy's face. The dense thumping sound had turned to a splattering as Jimmy's skull crushed in with each blow. His legs stopped kicking and instead started to twitch. The sounds of his brain matter being mashed were all that was heard in the Cafeteria, the splattering sounds of Jimmy's head being struck enveloped in Brian's screaming, then his laughter. His maniacal, evil laugh as he smashed Jimmy's mushed skull into a further bloody pulp.

Lucy was on the floor, on her knees, gasping at what she witnessed. Speckles of blood covered her face, and the pool of dark sticky blood had made it to her, staining her tight denim jeans with Jimmy's blood. Students and teachers stood frozen at the sight of blood spurting from Jimmy's head and his brains flying in every direction.

The crowd stood silent, an air of continuous gasping that had the presence in the Cafeteria feel heavy and dark.

Brian finally stopped his attack. He sat on Jimmy's corpse, panting hard. His bloody arms now hung to his side. His dark yellow teeth blared in the overhead Cafeteria light. The saliva on his teeth sparkled the same way sunlight twinkles off glass. He sat straddled on Jimmy's bloody corpse, and looked around to see students crying, holding each other, and vomiting at the sight of the horror he had caused.

"My God." Gasped the Phys-ed coach, Mr. Tracy, as he ran into the Cafeteria. His feet suddenly became rooted to the floor when he reached the scene, his sneakers letting out a loud screech like he was doing sprints on the gym floor at the sudden stop.

Mr. Tracy gathered himself and lurched towards Brian carefully as if walking on the ledge of a high rise. Brian smiled at him as he got closer; he held his phone covered in blood and dented from the impacts on Jimmy's skull. The screen flashed its eerie blue light, pulsing excitedly like it was enjoying every moment of Brian's evil. It read,

"Goodbye, Jimmy"

"Yes, I just got this one in, sir. I can offer an excellent deal."

"I like the sound of that. Is it refurbished?" asked the tall, middle-aged man.

"No sir, nothing wrong with the phone, it's just like new. It was previously owned, But the owner gave it back. He said something about it not suiting his needs." The Indian man explained, his long grey beard dangling from his chin with a few tiny brown curds hanging from loose strands as he spoke..."

What are you willing to offer?"

"I can offer it for half of the market value. I believe you will not find a better price, sir," he explained.

The brown morsels were distracting to the man like a bad car wreck had just thundered before him, and he couldn't look away. He struggled to keep his focus on the phone the Indian man was selling. He glanced at the tag on the plastic sheeting and nodded at the sight of the price markdown.

"And it works just fine?" he asked,

"Oh yes. This model is special. It has features that you will not find on any other phone."

"Yeah? How so?" the man's hands went to his hips like the shroud of an overbearing tutor examining a math proof in front of his pupil.

"Well, sir. For one, I guarantee you will be obsessed with this particular phone. I know technology these days can be distracting, but I can guarantee the phone has apps and programs already installed on the device that you can't get on another phone, for instance. It will have your name memorized in its encryption; it will welcome you as the screen turns on. It is very, very personalized, sir. A lot of people enjoy this."

"Hmm, ok, well, I don't see why I can't get it. It's for my son anyway; I don't know much about these new phones and what they do. It can make phone calls, right? Text message?" The tall man asked.

"Oh yes, sir. It can do very much more, sir." The Punjabi man shook his head from side to side and smiled.

"Do I need to sign up for a plan or something?"

"No, sir. I only sell Phones and gadgets. No obligation."

"Great, do you take Credit card?" The tall man reached into his back pocket and pulled out his wallet.

"Yes, sir, I do." The Indian man responded gleefully.

The neon signs behind the booth flashed pink and green as the fluorescent lights bounced off the glass display of the Indian man's stall. He didn't make appearances often, but he seemed to make a *killing* in sales when he did. Not only in "special" phones but also in various other gadgets and trinkets. They all held exceptional value to their owner and offered their unique intricacies. Returns were always welcome, but when it came to refunds, the booth would vanish from their outlet shopping mall, as if the Indian vendor knew about its unsatisfied customers approaching ahead of time.

It was usually a mystery when people asked about the booth and the man with the long grey beard and purple turban. Nobody had heard of him or even seen his booth. However, when someone needed that particular gadget, that newest technology that was all the rage, he seemed to show up—waiting for his prospecting customers to offer them a deal they couldn't refuse.

13

Mother's Milk

Martha Chimalski's back rested on the torn fabric of the old black and yellow cab, sinking into the cushion with relief and an exaggerated sigh.

Looking out of the cab window, she watched the dark clouds hover above. The large flakes of snow glid blissfully to the surface of the window and turned to streaks of water droplets that made the view outside blurry; the frost on the surface of the glass, clouded with tiny ice crystals, blocked the silhouettes of the buildings and street signs rendering themselves unrecognizable through the mirage of melted snow. The cab ride from work had been the best part of the day.

Her legs ached from lugging around the oversized steel-toe boots that felt like she had cinderblocks attached to her feet. Her back was stiff like splintering plywood from bending over constantly to pick up and stack heavy boxes onto skids. Her eyelids drooped heavily in a familiar way that reminded her of passing out in front of the television while trying her hardest to stay awake and finish watching "A Farewell To Arms," which had been playing on *Turner Classic Movies* the past few nights. The blisters on the soles of her feet indicated that she wasn't a young girl anymore, and the years of hard labour reserved for burly men twice her size had taken its toll on her body. Still, with all the aches and sores, the popping sounds her knee made when she stood up too fast, and the collapsing weight of exhausted limbs, her struggles of fatigue were better than dealing with Randall Martin - her supervisor.

She couldn't help but think of him while she sat in the cab, thinking of the evolution of Randall Martin's harassment. He had been obsessing over her for a few weeks now.

First, it started with extreme politeness. He exaggeratedly opened doors for her and looked her passionately in the eye when he spoke to her with a soft voice like a comforting pillow on a heavy head. He offered her snacks from the vending machine, picked up what she dropped at her feet, and handed it back to her to save her from bending over herself.

Soon she was aware of his eagerness. She saw through his *politeness* and noticed all the strings attached to it. She quickly recognized the ploy of setting the bait for her to loosen up until he hunted her down like a big-game hunter creeping in the bushes. After long nights dreaming of her, thinking of what he wanted to do with her in the bedroom and the fantasies of her lustful exuberance at his hands, Randall Martin began touching her when nobody else was around. Whether alone in the lunch Cafeteria or the last ones to finish their smokes on break, he found a way of getting comfortable, getting too close to her, lost within the delusional fantasies that enchanted him. The touching began with accidental brushing like he was making his way through a crowd, his hand casually gliding against her thighs or *accidentally* brushing his hand against her breast. Soon he began getting much too close. Randall Martin knew it was wrong, but she had been nice to him, and her friendliness was confused with attraction toward the recently divorced man who hadn't seen a naked woman before him in years. He had begun staring at her. His gaze was piercing, and she could feel him watching when her back was turned. Every time she looked away, Randall Martin wondered if he repulsed her or if she felt the same way he did, only not wanting to make it evident to her other co-workers that she was interested in her supervisor. He told himself it was her way of playing hard to get, that he had to push forward relentlessly with his perverted advances until she finally gave in. He told himself he was on the right track.

Martha Chimalski was grateful and even proud of herself for avoiding his advances. Albeit, it had been difficult at times to show face and avoid causing a scene. Times when he had told her obtuse and vulgar things he wanted to do with her. Brushing her hair to the side and telling her how he would enjoy bending her over the table and having his way with her, or the inappropriate mentioning of how he liked to pull hair and choke the woman he had sex with. He bragged to her about the bruises left behind on past girls and how they were a mark of pride, a type of flag planted in the sand. She ignored him as much as she could but was often overwhelmed by his advancements, often using the "lady's room" excuse to escape him.

She usually found herself folded between the toilet and the graffiti-littered side wall with meagre attempts to muffle the sounds of her weeping, blanketing her mouth with balls of toilet paper. In these times, her mind unravelled like a ball of yarn, and, although vulnerable and destitute on the urine-sparkled floor, at the most bottomless pits of despair, she mumbled to herself that she wasn't a victim.

"I am not a victim," she repeated, first, with a shallow whisper, then with each turn of the phrase, she grew more confident.

She was worth more to someone who recognized that she had a value greater than the price of flesh, the trembling ecstasy of orgasm, and was undoubtedly in a class above the hard calloused touch of a perverted man like Randall Martin, who tread heavily on the grounds of his authority with relentless harassment. She repeated to herself that she wasn't a victim through the muffled cries and salt-stained tears. That's what she had – and all she needed to survive each day.

"3425 Banner Hill Ave. Is it okay if I drop you off here?" The cabbie asked.

"That's fine. Thanks." Martha responded, handing the cash over the seat to the man and opening the cab door.

The cushioning of the snow had been like walking on pillows compared to the cold and hard concrete of the factory floor. The snowflakes landed on her face and vanished as quickly at the moment of contact. The cool, brisk winter air was relieving to Martha, who was overheated and beginning to sweat in the back of the cab. There was nothing like the winter's air. The sudden shock of the cold had a way of clearing her mind and pressing the reset button on her emotions. It kissed her skin gently and froze all the heated thoughts she had earlier in the dark and hollow bathroom stall. She smirked at the thought of rolling over to the cold side of the mattress and how the nighttime air provided much of the same contentment. The cold winter was a frigid lover who provided solace to her soul, held her tight to its frigid bosom until she couldn't help but take it in, holding the cool night's air with the same relentless comfort it provided her, and she held on to the thought,

"I am not a victim,"

The winter's night had come early this time of year. The thought of leaving for work in the early morning dark, then arriving home at the moonlights glare every night, had begun to feel depressing amongst the other ills of her everyday life. She dragged her heavy boots through the snow, the cold wetness soaking into her leggings until she reached the front door of the tiny corner bungalow and walked in. The place was quiet. She placed her keys on the glass dish that had served as her Mother's ashtray since she was a child, and the tingling sound the keys made in the glass dish made her instantly regret not placing them gently on the hook perched on the wall instead. If she weren't so tired, she would be paying attention. She would remind herself to grip the keys tightly together, slowly hook them on the wall, praying that her Mother didn't hear them and come blazing out from the living room.

"Who's there?" Martha heard coming from the next room. "Martha, is that you?"

"Yes, Mom. Sorry if I woke you." Martha responded.

She slid her feet out of her boots and imagined the flesh from her legs peeling off as she lifted her foot out of the heavy steel toes, much like a reptile sheds its skin. It felt that way. She dragged her wet socks on the hardwood floor, leaving slug streaks of melted snow behind her until she reached the living room, where her Mother sat on the couch knitting.

"How's your day, Mom?" Martha asked,

"I'm sorry?" Her Mother responded. She paused, knitting momentarily, and looked towards Martha like a stranger was in her presence. As far as she knew, it was the truth. The momentary lapses of familiarity had begun to be frequent, the same look that resembled a dog tilting its head to the side with confusion.

"It's me, Mom. Martha. How's your day?"

"Oh yes, Martha, of course." She looked back down and continued knitting.

"How's your day going, Mom?" Martha repeated as if she was talking to a deaf person. She sat beside her Mother and sank into the leather sofa with relief.

"It was fine, I suppose." She said. "Dishes need to be done. I don't know why you didn't do them in the morning before you left - or even last night. Last night would have been the better thing to do."

"I was tired, Mom. I'm always tired."

"Tired hell," her Mother snapped. "You don't know, *tired* girl."

"Sorry, Mom."

"Sorry, Mom." Her Mother repeated, "your one of those people, aren't you? The kind that says you're sorry when you don't mean it, always trying to be polite. Are you sorry, girl? Are you really *fucking* sorry?"

"Yes, I am. I *really* am."

Her Mother pouted while her gaze stuck onto the needles twining the pink twine strands on each other, "My Daddy would whoop me a good one if he heard me saying I was sorry for anything. Anything! He taught me to be brutal and damn right. Sorry, she says. Take your sorry's and phony – "

She suddenly stopped mid-sentence and looked up at Martha, perplexed, "What was I saying, dear? I think I lost track. What was I saying?"

"You were saying how happy you are that I finally came home from work."

"Oh yes, of course. I am thrilled. How was work? I'm sure it was a swell time."

"It was, Uhm, normal. Yeah, just a normal day, Mom." It was the best way to put it out loud to anyone who asked. It was her way of avoiding complaining to folks about how dreadful her day had been. It didn't provide enough information for people to draw conclusions and assumptions about how terrible her life was, or at least, for how Martha could drag on in such misery – if only they knew the truth. Regular insisted on a sense of 'just being another day,' nothing more, nothing less, a forgetful working day with nothing remarkable happening. As she sat and thought about it, she smelled the faint scent of Randall Martin's rotting breath, the perfume of body odour and sweat, feeling her stomach start to stir.

"The dishes need to be done, Martha. The plates are stacking and starting to stink. Not worse than your god-damn feet, though." Her Mother said.

"Yes, Mom. I'll do the dishes; I just want to relax for a minute."

"God-damn always complaining. My Daddy would whoop me a good one if he caught me moaning like you. I messed up, you know?" she said, "I should have whooped you kids good like Daddy did. You would have thicker skin and be tough like him or me."

"I'm glad you didn't, Mom."

Martha dreaded the direction the conversation was going. She sensed the air around her grow thicker and dense, nearly hyperventilating until she spoke aloud under her breath, intending to keep the thought in her head,

"I'm sure Tristan would have left sooner."

"Who the hell is Tristan?"

"What?"

"Tristan. You said, Tristan."

"No, I don't think I did." Martha insisted, "You're having a spell again, don't think too hard about it."

She wanted to spew the words to her Mother, her saliva splattering on her Mother's wrinkled face, the toxins burning her thin lips that seemed like slits and blinding her sunken eyes that had darkened in the sockets. She pictured herself standing triumphantly in a rebellious exuberance that had her towering over her overbearing Mother and finally screaming the words toward the older woman who looked on with surprised astonishment, horror, and a sense of shame mingled with burdening guilt,

"Tristan was your son, Mom! You're First Born! He called you Ma and tucked you in every night when Dad left. He held your hand a stroked your palms softly, telling you the same stories Dad told us as children when he was still around. Before he got fed up! Before you ruined your marriage and made our lives hell!"

She wanted to say it with the hiss of an angry hellcat. Her face flushed, and her cheeks became warm with a toxic repulsion toward her Mother and all the damage she had caused. Yet, she didn't. She sat quietly beside her Mother as she knitted away in a world of her own, overcome with a tiresome and despairing hope that Alzheimer's would take her Mother away, even for a peaceful, unobstructed moment.

"Tristan." Her Mother said repentantly, "Who leaves their Mother so young? What happened to Tristan?"

"He died, Mom. You know this."

Her Mother stopped knitting and stared into the empty space of the living room, "Oh yes. He died." She said, then resumed knitting with a blankness that made Martha realize that her Mother had disappeared into the limbo of her mind once again. A place that was empty and cold, where she was stuck, yet content at the same time, unaware of her reality. A place of faded memories and the blissful ignorance of her regrets.

Martha pulled herself from the sofa and nearly toppled over from rising too fast. Her vision blurred slightly, and her legs wobbled with fatigue.

The glass coffee table had multiple teacups half filled with coffee, and the surface of the glass table was littered with her Mother's medication. The pill bottles stood like skyscrapers, the taller bottles standing side by side with shorter ones like skyscrapers in Manhattan, their labels like white banners pasted on orange glass, the white twist-on plastic lids like a rimmed ceiling were missing and laid beside the bottles like a rooftop that had been blown off during a hurricane of addiction. Some pill bottles were toppled over like Corinthian columns from the ruins of the Roman Forum, once complete and absolute, majestic in their splendour with the power each pill bottle held within, now empty and void, the little white pills scattered around the living room carpet.

"I need more meds, dear." Her Mother said.

"I know. We have to wait until the 15th. I don't get paid until then."

"Bitching and moaning." Her Mother said, shaking her head. "Did you do the dishes? The plates are stacking and starting to stink. They stink worse than your God-damned feet!"

"Yeah, I know, Mom, you said that already," Martha responded.

"I did not, you little shit!" Her Mother barked, throwing her knitting needles at her daughter. Martha didn't even flinch. The needles bounced off her as a tennis ball bounced off a concrete wall, and she was glad it was a sensation she didn't feel. Not like her feet or lower back - or worse - the bruising imprints of Randall Martin's sausage-like fingers on her waist.

"I'll do the dishes, Mom. Take it easy." She returned the needles to her Mother and went to the kitchen.

She flicked the light switch on and walked to the sink. It was empty. The stainless-steel basin was polished with lustrous shine, and the kitchen counter's drying rack was stacked neatly with plates and glasses. Martha looked in the oven and saw a burnt pie on the rack. She immediately turned the knob, and the bright red glow of the oven began to die down.

"Mom, I told you that you're not allowed to cook anymore," Martha shouted from the stove,

"Why can't I cook? I made a pie for you. It's done. It's on the counter." She responded.

"Christ, Mom, you'll be the freaking death of me," Martha said under her breath.

"What was that?" She heard her Mother ask from the living room.

"Nothing. The pie looks good."

"What pie?"

"Never mind." Martha sighed.

She took the pie out of the oven and set it on the counter. The crust's surface was a darkened black, and the middle of the pie had boiled over like a miniature volcano. It was hard to tell what her Mother put in the pie. She had come home before and seen her Mother make a pie except with all the wrong ingredients. It had been a long time since Martha had her Mother's famous Rhubarb and Blackberry pie. In a matter of weeks, the ingredients had been swapped for quizzical items, like mince meat instead of fruit, dishwashing fluid instead of Cinnamon, and shards of something unknown (probably broken glass) that Martha couldn't quite make out that was substituted for sugar. It was a clear sign of the relentless days to come. It was a clear sign that her Mother was changing, and her memory was failing faster than before.

"It's only going to get worse," she said aloud.

Martha fixed her Mother a sandwich with her limited ingredients in the fridge. The week-old Bologna and a jar of yellow mustard had developed a film on the surface.

She carried the plate with the sandwich to her Mother, placed it on the coffee table amongst the spilled meds, knocked over pill bottles and half-drunken coffee cups, and sat beside her.

"Oh dear, you made my favourite."

"Yes, Mom. Eat up so we can go to bed."

"What time is it? Is it time for bed already?" her Mother asked. Martha looked outside into the darkness, knowing it was only 6 pm,

"Yeah, it's getting late."

"Is this Bologna?"

"Your favourite."

"Yes. It is."

Martha didn't remember if her Mother had taken a bite of her sandwich. She sunk into the couch, and her legs felt numb and lightweight. Her eyelids became heavier until she began to snore. She dreamt that she was young again.

She was in Highschool, and Scotty Buchanan had asked her to the Thursday night dance. He was handsome. Boyish, but he had the signs that he was developing into a man faster than the other boys and stood out to her in those days as being much more mature and tolerant. Scotty was kind, and his voice, which crackled when he spoke, made her shiver with delight as she found the transition from a pubescent young boy into a strapping young man. He reached his hand out to her, and she grasped it with hers. His palms were smooth and weren't littered with scars and cuts from working with them for years. His nails were neatly filed, not caked with dirt, and his skin was soft like velvet. She awoke and jumped in shock. Martha looked from side to side and saw her Mother wasn't beside her.

"Mom?" she called out. There was no response. The kitchen light was turned off, and she didn't remember switching off the light herself.

She stood up and rubbed her eyes, looking at the clock and reading 3 am. She thought she must have gone to bed and felt relieved that she didn't have to drag her elderly Mother to the bedroom like she did every night.

Martha shuffled her feet lazily to the kitchen, and in the darkness, she froze at the ghastly sight that caught her immediate attention.

She made out a slender figure in the corner. She felt the plums of breath exhale from her lips frantically. Martha was too damn tired to run, her legs shook, and she felt like she was walking on stilts. Still, she was close enough to the light switch to expose the stranger in her kitchen, and when Martha flicked the light switch on and saw her Mother dressed in her nightgown, her arms at her sides facing the corner of the kitchen wall, she let out a sullen gasp.

"Mom?" she said.

Her Mother's head turned slowly, and her shoulders followed. As she turned to face her daughter, Martha stood in horror at the face that appeared before her. Her Mother's eyes were missing and left with empty black craters in their place. Blood streamed down her cheeks from her eye sockets, and her mouth hung open in a silent scream. Martha shrieked but couldn't move. Her feet felt like she was wearing her steel-toe boots, and when glancing down, she, in fact, saw her shoes on her feet, the wet puddles of melting snow spreading out in front of her. She looked up again, and her Mother stood inches from her face. She screamed,

"COME BACK, TRISTAN! COME BACK"

Martha's nostril hairs tinged at the scent of the putrid rot of Randall Martin's breath, and upon feeling the dry and blistering heat on her face, she woke up.

The sweat poured from her face and dripped onto the collar of her shirt. She found herself on the couch, where she fell asleep with her Mother beside her, knitting. Martha glanced at the clock, huffing long, exasperated breaths and saw she had only fallen asleep for an hour. She pinched herself on her arm to ensure she wasn't stuck in a nightmare and quickly sighed with relief at realizing it had all been a terrible dream. Her Mother knitted away and finally looked over at her daughter and asked,

"You finish up the dishes yet?"

———•———

The pharmacy in the township of Erin Mills was a small one. It lay in the middle of a strip plaza that consisted of a Bakery, a Deli, a Slovakian grocery store, and a Ukrainian Bank. Since the golden age of Erin Mills, "Old man Jack Sawyer" had run the place for the past forty years, where nickel miners and plant workers swarmed the long abandoned diners and pubs in the early 70s. The shouting and drunken hollering had echoed into the night in those days. Gamblers stooped in front of cinderblock walls next to the front door of the convenience store. They threw dice against it, watching them tumble and clack against the hard surface, revelling in the utter excitement of triumphant rewards and the disappointing groans of financial loss. Women were more frequent in those days too. Some were prostitutes prodding lonely men into the upstairs apartments where the distinct, false sense of lovemaking was smeared on every bedsheet along with bedside trashcans filled to the top rim with crumpled tissues that had frozen in shape like white and yellow stained boulders atop a cliffside, nearly toppling over to the base the can stood on. Some women tended to the patrons as waitresses, constantly peered and chastised for their uncontrollable femininity, and exhibited a lack of remorse when they shunned away the rummies who became too touchy and overbearing.

Even still, with the misogyny of those days, the drunken fighting, the bruised egos and drained pockets, the liveliness of the place was exuberant. People had relished the merriment in their squalor; the thought of being broken and the burdens that came with it were left to the imagination – this was the place to be, for a moment, even if it wouldn't last, it was a place of excitement and sinful thrills.

That was then. Now the same pubs and Diners stood abandoned. Windows and doors were boarded up with plywood sheets, which were littered with graffiti on their surface. Much had changed since then, indeed.

The workers had moved to the big city and had left the women in Erin Mills outnumbering the men six to one. Even those women migrated to better opportunities in the bustling metropolises of the world, leaving behind the damp dreariness and sorrow of abandoned small-town degradation. Old man Jack Sawyer was still around that old and lonely Pharmacy. He stood in his place behind the counter as he always had for years, doomed to his existence like a marble statue planted in the rotundas of Florence and Rome for what seemed like an eternity.

"I know it's expensive, Martha, but I can't come down any lower in price," Sawyer said,

"I know you can't, Jack; that's why asking is so embarrassing." She said sullenly, "I Just figured you would let me the off the hook a little for old time's sake and all. Mom's getting worse, and Dr. Bennett doesn't seem to understand. I know this Alzheimer's thing is new to us all, and we are still learning about it, but the meds he keeps prescribing don't seem to help."

"I'm very sorry to hear about Abilene. You know, I've known your Mother for years, and well, she isn't exactly the easiest person to deal with on a good day. Still, I'm sorry she's having a hard time." Jack Sawyer said. He looked down at the slip of paper through his glasses' soft, corrected lenses and noticed the different writing styles on the bottom of the prescription slip.

"Why do I get the feeling that Dr. Bennett didn't prescribe Percocet?" he said, his eyes glaring upwards to Martha for a response in the way a Father waits for an excuse from their child, knowing there was none that was legitimate. She didn't answer him. She looked down at the lottery scratch tickets on the countertop and hoped he would forget the question all together.

"They're not for Abilene, are they, Martha?" he inquired,

"No, Jack. No, they are not."

"You feeling some discomfort?" he asked.

"Yes. My knees are shot, and I feel like I'm walking on Ramen noodles all day. My feet hurt, and blisters appear on the bottom, and some ripped open."

"I suggest soles for your shoes Martha. Drugs like these just make things worse."

"I get the feeling that anything is better than the pain, Jack."

"Did you tell Bennett about the pain?"

"Yes, but he thinks I'm just trying to score a cheap high."

"Are you? I'm not one to judge, you know."

"I'm not. I've never touched drugs in my life – you have known me long enough to know that, Jack."

"Yes, but it's not me you need to convince. I'm just the fellow that gives the stuff out – Dr. Bennett is the one –"

"I know, I know, Jack." She interrupted. "It just hurts so damn much."

"Even if I give you the drugs, Martha, it's still too expensive. I suppose if I used my employee discount or..." he hesitated momentarily, "...even removed the Percocet from the bill altogether, it would be easier to pay for."

"I only have so much money, Jack. The plant has been laying guys off, and I'm worried my turn may come soon. I don't have much right now. Can I owe you?"

"You can owe me if it's just for your Mother's meds, but not the Percocet. I can't risk losing my license over it."

"I understand." She said sullenly.

She reached into her coat pockets and laid out three crisp bills on the counter on top of the glass casing of lottery tickets. Knowing it was all she had, he sighed and placed the bills in the register.

"Sharing is caring." Martha heard from behind her.

"Mike. My god, I didn't know you were there." She exclaimed,

"I'm a sneaky fellow, Martha. I couldn't help but overhear. I can help, you know?"

"What do you mean?"

"Well – the *Percs*. I'm getting some for my arthritis and don't mind sharing. That's the thing with pain – only *you* can know the real extent of it and what it does to you. I'll give you some of mine but don't tell Jack, don't make it obvious."

"You don't have to."

"You want some or not?" he bragged.

"Yes. I suppose I do."

"Great. Let me get them, and I'll walk you home. I don't know in all hell how you made it here in this storm – the damn snow is nearly chest high – how did you do it?"

"I'm not far from here, just behind the plaza. The snowplows have been running all night and cleared the parking lot, so I took the shortcut and made it here as fast as I could while the snowfall eased a bit."

"I bet that same parking lot is knee-high again – at least," Mike said.

"Yeah, I bet it is." She responded.

They didn't say anything when Jack Sawyer returned to the counter with a neat white bag professionally folded at the brim and handed it to Martha.

"I'm sorry, Martha, I really am. I added my employee discount to save you some. I wish I could do more; it's just that my hands are a little tied on this one. Wish your Mom the best for me, would you?" he asked.

"Sure, Jack. I will – and thanks."

"Right." He said. "Mikael Petrovic, I can see your back again, are you? How's the Arthritis?"

"Shitty, Jack. The usual."

"Yes, it never seems to ease up, does it?" Sawyer looked down at his hands and watched them tremble. He had much experience with Arthritis and how it painfully froze his hands into claws.

"Let me see the slip." He said, peering down at the white paper. "a little more than usual, I see. Well, the doctor knows best, I suppose."

"Yeah, sure, Jack, Bennett's a real angel. I give him about another two weeks until he keels over."

"I'll take that bet." Jack Sawyer said, chuckling. "He may be an old man, but by god, that man can keep on trucking."

"Old – no shit." Mike said, smirking " I bet that old bastard still has his pet dinosaur buried in the backyard." Both chuckled.

"Don't we all? I'll be back with it; just wait a moment." Sawyer said. "Hey, Martha – you need anything else? Want me to call a cab?" he saw she was hanging around.

"No. Mike offered to walk me home – it's pretty bad out there."

"That it is. Okay, Mike, give me a second." Jack Sawyer walked to the shelving unit and turned his back to them both. Martha had been looking at Mike and admired his politeness. He didn't have to offer her anything, and she didn't want to seem desperate. She knew he needed the pills even more than she did. On their lunch break at the plant, he had complained about not being able to close his fists most days and how his fingers felt like they were made from stone. Even now, in line waiting for his pain meds, both his hands shivered and looked like withered tree limbs in the scary movies.

"All right, here you go, chap. That's $18.97."

"Take a twenty, Jack – keep the tip," Mike said.

"Oh my, so generous – a whole three cents."

"Well, if you had made an exception for the young lady, it could have been more," Mike said.

"Have a good day Mike; always a pain in my ass seeing you."

"You too, Jack," Mike responded.

Mike Petrovic and Martha walked along the plaza pathway. The concrete was salted, and the overhanging roof protected them from the mountains of snow that had accumulated around them and on the roof above them. Still, the wind gusts blew hard enough to blind them momentarily with fresh powder as they walked, turning around the corner of the Ukrainian bank and proceeding to the slit in the fence that acted as Martha's "shortcut" home.

They stopped next to Fung Soo's Hairdresser and stepped into the dark stairwell entrance that acted like access to the upper-level stores or, most often enough, a place for the junkies to hide out and get high. They had found themselves to be not so different from those drug addicts that slithered into dark seclusion.

Mike had sprinkled a few pills into the open palm of his glove, and his hand resembled a claw with his fingers arched upwards and frozen not from the cold but the arthritic pain. Martha plucked each pill, one by one, from his palm and tucked them into her coat pocket. She supposed that no matter how much she wasn't addicted to the pills (at least not addicted yet), she couldn't relate to the addicts that hissed at blinding lights that exposed their infested layers, the harsh shunning of onlookers that pointed at them and threatened to call the police, or the relish of the rushing tides of toxicity, the warmth that blanketed them every time the plunger pushed the poison into their bloodstream. Perhaps, Martha had not been so different; standing in the dark stairwell, scoring free pills from her co-worker, she felt the paranoia of being caught participating in the forbidden taboo. She placed the drugs in her coat pocket, and they began to walk again,

"Thanks, Mike. I owe you. When we get paid, I'll settle, I promise."

"Oh, save it, Martha. I don't need the money, and you need the meds." He explained, "The god-damn prices went up so much over the years that it's hard for anyone to afford meds. I hope the government settles it and makes these damn things more affordable to folks like us."

"You're kind Mike, but I insist." She said. "How's Maggie doing anyway? I forgot to ask."

"Ah, Maggie left a few months back. No notice, not a word, nothing. She packed up and left while I worked a night shift at the plant."

"My god Mike, I'm sorry, I didn't know."

"Nothing to be sorry about, I suppose. She's sick. She hasn't been well for a while now, and I'm afraid it's taken its toll." He hesitated to say more, but the way Martha's eyes shined in the darkness told him that she would understand more than anyone, that she wouldn't judge him on his wife leaving him, enshrining a feeling in him that it was all right to open to her, no matter how obscene or perplexing the reasons had been.

"She ran away to some convent called the *Survivors of the Apocalypse*. Some bat-shit crazy cult that believes aliens are coming down to take a selected few to heaven and decimate the rest. It's those damn books she was reading, I think. Shit, I don't know. Last I heard, she wrote to me from some farm in East Elgin. Ten "survivors" had bought the place, and each pitched in. Maggie threw in five hundred bucks to get a space."

"I'm sorry Mike, I really am. You're a good guy. Maggie was very lucky."

"Thanks," he said, "You know, being home alone gets lonely after you reach about 45. I regret not having kids; Maggie never wanted any."

"You just wanted to make her happy, Mike."

"Yes, I did. I forgot to make *myself* happy, though – I suppose it's the result of being married so long; you tend to forget what makes you happy and focus on keeping the relationship alive. I guess – ah, never mind."

"What?"

"Well, I guess Maggie found a way to make herself happy in a way I couldn't. She found something bigger than herself – bigger than what we had – and jumped right on board. I can't blame her for that. Now, I have nobody at home. No kids, grandkids, wife."

"It's no excuse to throw it all away. God, I feel shitty about it, Mike."

Martha pulled out a cigarette and handed an extra one to Mike. "It's selfish, you know? You've been married for so long, so many good times, only to give up on all of it and join some cult full of lies."

"I don't know. Maybe, she found something that defined her. a meaning she had never experienced before. Can I blame my wife, of all people, for giving up on me and going toward her happiness?"

"It's not happiness. It's a cloud, a smokescreen. It's like that kid that just bought the newest comic book – he will avoid everyone and anything locking himself in the room and taking part in what he thinks is his "happiness" until he gets tired of the book and takes it for granted. Then the excitement wears off, and the novelty fades away. He tosses that same comic to the side, never to pick it up again. I bet it's the same thing, Mike. I bet Maggie will come back once the novelty of this crap wears off."

"I'm not sure she will, though, Martha. And why should I wait around for her to get better and treat me well?" he asked, not waiting for an answer, "I tell myself the same thing sometimes – that she will be back, I mean. Still, my heart hurts over the fact that she thinks I'll just lie broken, waiting for her to make up her mind. I'm not some rag doll or comic book. I'm worth more than that, I'd like to think."

"I know the feeling. I got an idea."

"Oh, here we go," Mike said sarcastically.

"Well, I would like to get away. Mom's been getting worse, and I need some time to myself, and I don't feel like being alone. It would be nice to have – a friend?"

"You asking me out, young lady?" Mike teased.

"Maybe. I'm not so young anymore, you know?" she began slurring her words in nervousness.

"Yes! I'll answer yes before you change your mind." Mike said with a chuckle. "I suppose I am a pretty lucky guy, huh?"

"And I'm a lucky gal, too."

They reached the front door of Martha's home, and before Mike walked away, he grasped her hand and stared deep into her eyes,

"Thanks, Martha – for being so lovely to me. It's an unfamiliar feeling, and –"

"I can't wait to see you, Mike, *really*." She smiled and then leaned over to kiss him on the cheek. His smooth face felt nice against her lips, and she felt the heat rise in her chest – a feeling she hadn't felt since high school when Scotty Buchanan asked her to the dance. It was a warm feeling, a feeling that words couldn't express. The heat rose to her cheeks, and keeping eye contact with him had been too much. Perhaps he would see right through her, know her soul and her darkest thoughts, her most embarrassing feelings and girlish excitements that she hid away to show herself as a mature woman on the outside who didn't think such idealistic imaginings as little girls with fantasies of big weddings and ballroom twirling, the glass slipper fitting just right on her foot – no-one else's.

Yet would it be so bad? Exposing her soul to the man who hurt so much from having too much love and even sacrificing his own happiness or contentment for someone who didn't feel the same way toward him. He could open up to her, and though it hadn't been easy for him to do so, he did it anyway, which showed a new affection towards Mike, one of desperate sensuality and an eagerness to please, and be pleased himself.

Martha walked through the front door thinking about Mike and how he skipped along knee-high snow drifts like a giddy teenage boy that had just gotten his first kiss on his first date. She felt the same way. Asking him out gave the equivalent feeling of being asked to Prom. She never had such experiences, having moved away after Tristan died, swearing never to return to Erin Mills County. Yet here she was - dragged back in by the burdens of her past, the chapters yet to be written, and the lack of closure that her Mother would need to provide her when she finally died. It was a harsh thought to imagine, but she didn't feel remorse about it. Although her menacing Mother was a constant reminder that the pits of Hell in her run-down bungalow existed, she felt trapped in a hole that had been dug so deep, the ledge of the hole out of reach, desperately yearning for an escape.

She began to revile her Mother the more she thought of the past. She had spent years thinking of ways to run away – which she did – at 17, only to come back and care for the same Banshee that had caused her so much pain.

Martha found it ironic how she wanted nothing more than to stay away from the woman only to come running back after hospital care workers had called her and told her about the kitchen fire. Her Mother had put her down as an emergency contact, and for the life of her, she didn't know how her Mother had even found out where she was living and her phone number, which hadn't been listed for a good reason. She hated the fact she was here again. She wanted to go and stay away, yet she found herself as a live-in nurse caring for her Mother as Alzheimer's set in.

She optimistically thought it hadn't all been that bad all the time. Mike was lovely and could have the opportunity to be the muse that she craved so desperately. A muse that could whisk her away from her Mother and Randall Martin, a dead-end job plagued with the injuries of exhaustion and over-working. He was a protector who shielded her behind himself like a Spartan warrior, lifted her in his arms like the cover graphics of many romantic novels, and finally took her away somewhere far and never returned.

So far away, over the rainbow and lush green fields, deep canyons, rushing rivers and the endless depths of oceans, to a place where she could breathe and feel like a giddy little schoolgirl skipping along knee-high snow drifts. Just like Mike had done.

※

The bath water was warm. Martha had let the tap run extra hot to warm her skin from the deep freeze outside. Her feet stuck out from the end of the tub, and the water had become murky and fogged from the Epsom salts she poured in and the dirt that sat finely on her skin that had otherwise been invisible if it wasn't for the opacity of the bathwater to remind her of how dirty she was.

This is soothing, she thought.

The salts tickled her skin under the water, and her legs lay under like lifeless limbs, and she imagined the loose folds of cellulite on her inner thighs stretching and becoming tighter around her thigh muscle.

She hated growing older. Her skin wasn't taut as it once was, and her breasts sagged from age. The lines became more profound, and her hair thinned; a once luscious flow of blond locks had slowly turned into thin slivers that grew into a darker brown the older she became. She softly grazed the scars along her breast with her fingertip. They were deep, protruding with subtle peaks like a mountain range observed from space and were still a dark magenta colour as if they were freshly healed though the lashing had taken place when she was a teenager. She regretted the ugliness of them. The scars were a memento of her helplessness, her inability to protect herself from the constant beatings she endured as a kid. A reminder that she was born to the wrong couple. Two people so volatile she couldn't remember a time of happiness under the Christmas tree or celebrating happily when Dad came home. She hardly remembered him at all. She became anxious in the tub when she thought of how Mike would react if he saw her naked, or worse, the dreaded resentment she felt towards her Mother.

How would he react to her if she explained the dilemma she found herself in with such an essential aspect of her life? If she explained to him that she patiently waited for her Mother's lapses of memory to occur so her Mother would forget how much Martha disappointed her, how would he react? She sighed with relief at the effects of Alzheimer's. She relished in delight when her Mother forgot who she was, how she despised every action towards her, every moment she breathed, every thought she muttered, her existence altogether. How unnatural for a Mother to hate her child so much – both her children, she thought; the involuntary realization that had embedded itself in her psyche after so many years of learning of its existence pricked at her conscience with the awful sting of how terrible it must be, to pray for her Mothers debilitating disease to take effect, while she found solace in its grips.

Was she a bad person? Would Mike forgive her for her guilty pleasure? She didn't know the answers to those questions, but she had an unapologetic optimism that the world would become brighter if she stuck it out longer. It had been a deep hole, but she could always find a way out.

Martha often thought of the *Sisyphean* tragedy that her life had become. Doomed with the absurdity of pushing an enormous boulder up the hill only to watch it roll back down. Hoping for better days had been a struggle; occasional victories guided her eagerness to push harder. Successes like leaning in for a kiss, asking Mike out on a date, his enthusiasm at the request, his excitement and that childish pleasure of innocence lost at the romantic adoration that Cupid ensured when he stuck his arrows in them both.

She savoured the thought and tried to hold on to it until the bitterness set in, of the inevitable despair of the boulder rolling back down the hill, staying perched on the top for only a slender moment. Randall Martin's voice set in. His breath reeked worse than an open can of sardines left out in the sun, his overgrown mustache untendered, the hairs fraying in different directions like the ends of loose wires, scratching the back of her neck when he leaned over her to whisper in her ear. She couldn't shake the awful scratching feeling on her skin, and she unconsciously rubbed it like she was trying to scrub the leftover scent from her pores. She could still feel his boulder-like stomach rubbing on her side, his thick and calloused fingers gripping her waist tightly, and a sudden resentment overcame her. The bitterness of the enormous boulder gaining momentum on its descent.

She began to sob. The droplets of tears splashed in the bath water, and the relief of a relaxing, hot bath had disappeared. She knew her Mother was downstairs. She felt the scorn of knowing that she was responsible for it all. Martha knew that Tristan had had enough as well. She knew well why he ran away at 14 years old, and she hated her Mother every time she pictured her little brother in the ditch of Highway 413, his body mangled, his head tilted in the way human anatomy didn't allow – a victim of a late-night hit and run.

"Martha."

She cocked her head toward the door, nearly cracking her neck in the meantime,

"T-Tristan?" She muttered.

She heard nothing else. The silence overcame the atmosphere with a thick air that frosted the bathroom mirror, the dew and steam on its surface transforming into a crystallized sheet, in a type of ungodly metamorphosis, nature didn't allow to happen so quickly. Martha heard a thump coming from Tristan's bedroom, next to the bathroom.

"Hello? Mom?" She heard no response.

Martha exited the tub and wrapped herself in a baby blue coloured bathrobe. The fabric brushed against her skin and was soothing if she didn't imagine the scars under the fabric hiding from plain sight.

She exited the bathroom, frantically opened Tristan's bedroom door, and flicked the light switch. His room had been left the way it was when he ran away. The Power Ranger bedsheets were tucked into the twin mattress, and the Jimi Hendrix and Quiet Riot posters were still crisp, like being unrolled yesterday. His desktop along the room's wall had been preserved, and the top of its surface was devoid of loose papers and pencils littered on the floor. It smelled clean.

The room didn't feel as heavy as she stood at the doorway. It had been as it always had been, the place of excitement and playfulness for her little brother. She saw the faded ghosts of her memory lying together on his bed, his head against her breast as she read Dr. Suess to him. They laughed with the kind of unconditional love that is impossible to manufacture artificially.

She hadn't expected to see Tristan in his room. He was dead, and she knew that very well. But she still wished to find him on his bed reading comic books. Every anniversary of his death, every time his birthday came around, she wished for it.

She sighed, switched off the light, and closed the door behind her. She heard the sounds blaring from the television downstairs. She made her way down the carpeted stairs, expecting to see her Mother sitting in the living room watching "Murder, She Wrote" while continuously knitting as if she had never moved from the spot on the sofa.

"I saw you know." Her Mother said, not looking up from the crochet pattern,

"What did you see?" Martha asked,

"I saw you kiss that boy. I didn't raise you to give it up so easy."

"Relax, Mom. He's not a boy, and I'm not a little girl anymore." Martha said, strolling to the kitchen. " You made sure of that when I was a kid. I grew up real fast, thanks to you."

"Don't you talk to your Mother like that?" She scowled,

"I'm sorry; I didn't mean anything by it." She did, in fact, mean every word. She meant to say it under her breath or, better yet, keep the thought in her mind, but she couldn't help the words escaping from the brim of her lips. Her Mother didn't respond, and Martha hoped that the memory loss would kick in at that moment. At least, her Mother was tolerable when it did. It was better than getting the woman she had put up with for so long. Someone so malicious and obtuse towards their own daughter. She wondered if she had put on a play. She wondered if her Mother transformed into her natural self when the memory loss occurred – more forgiving, polite, courteous, and Motherly.

Why put on a show? Martha thought, *Why delight in being purposefully rude and mean?*

Perhaps, she thought, that her Mother found a kind of solace in Martha's abuse, feeling the same relieving sensation of sitting in a Sauna, taking out her frustration on a punching bag or squeezing a stress ball between her fingers every time she chastised Martha or whipped her with that dreaded leather belt.

Martha poured water into the kettle and pressed the little red button to start boiling when her Mother strolled up to the sink and began to run the tap.

"I'll do the dishes in a bit, Mom. Just leave it alone. Go relax and watch the show."

"I'll do no such thing." She spewed, "Stop treating me like I'm a cripple. I'm capable of doing much more than you think."

"I'm sure, but Doctor Benne- "

"Oh, screw Dr. Bennett – that perverted old man. You know he tried to reach under my dress once? Oh, when I told your Father, he changed his mind real quick. I'll tell you that."

"I don't want to talk about it, Mom."

"I'm doing the dishes, and that's it."

"Fine."

Martha also poured herself a cup of tea and one for her Mother. The tap ran hot, and the steam rose high into the air, and Martha couldn't help but think of dunking her Mother's head in the rising basin of water to shut her up once and for all.

"That boy is married, you know."

"You don't know anything about it."

"Sure, I do. Mikael – the Serbian. His Mother and wife go to the same church as I did until your ungrateful ass dragged me out of it and kept me from going. Anyway, I know he's got a wife, and you go kissing a married man there. You're disgusting."

"She left him, Mom."

"Only to come back. They're still married. You would know better if you found a good man to marry yourself – then you would know all about taking vows and keeping them."

The fierce heat rose in Martha's chest. Her jaws clenched tight, and she thought her teeth would chip at the pressure.

"Like that Scott Buchanan boy, you brought home as a little girl."

"Don't talk about him."

"I'll talk about whomever I damn well please!" She shouted.

"You're the one who kicked him out of here and chased him with a belt." Martha couldn't hold back the tension in her voice. "Then you took the belt to my ass and shredded me up good."

"Yes, well, I hope I taught you something. All that boy wanted was to reach into your panties."

"He was nice."

"Sure. Sure, he was," her Mother cackled, "a real nice boy."

Martha ran her finger through the scars on her breast through the bathrobe. Her vision started to blur with a deepening fury. Her Mother rubbed the dish with a wet rag and continued,

"He ran like the little bitch he was."

"That's enough, Mom!"

"You don't tell me when it's enough, you sorry- "

Martha shoved her Mother's head into the basin and watched as she frantically clawed around the sink, knocking over the drying rack, and dishes crashed and splintered on the tile floor. She struggled, but her strength wasn't there – unlike Martha remembered – she was an old lady now, and her words were harsher than her lash. Martha's hand was enveloped in the blue-grey strands of her Mother's wet hair; she forced her down and watched the bubbles rise from the scalding water in a strict fascination. Martha heard her Mother screaming underwater, which turned her on, made her push harder and even considered bending over for a broken shard of glass dinnerware to slit her throat. She considered it if her Mother kept up with the fight. As seconds passed, her Mother's clawing became weaker and increasingly desperate. The tension from her head trying to pull up from the water made Martha realize that the elderly lady was nearly dead. Keeping her Mother's head underwater was essential until she stopped moving altogether.

Martha stepped back from the sink, and her Mother's body fell to the tiled floor, her head causing a loud thumping sound as her skull struck the laminate. Martha was baffled by the expression on her Mother's face. Her mouth gaped wide open, her eyes bulged, and the skin of her face was a bright red from the scalding heat of the water. Martha stood frozen at the sight of her Mother, and as she peered around at the broken glass, the overflowing basin, and the corpse at her feet, her heart sank to her stomach, and an overwhelming sensation of nausea overcame her. She ran to the trash bin, nearly slipping on the wet tiles and dunked her head in the rim, spewing acidic vomit from her insides.

She felt better. She walked over to the sofa, sat down, and began nodding off. It was the most relaxing feeling she had had since initially getting into the tub. Martha unconsciously rubbed at the scars on her breast and didn't feel them anymore – like they were never there to begin with. She had time to take it all in and knew it well.

The snowstorm was at its most horrendous, and she knew she would be stuck inside with her Mother's corpse and that a visitor in this weather was highly unlikely. It was unlike her Mother to have any visitors anyway. There was nobody else who cared as to why she had been her Mother's primary caregiver.

Martha sighed expressively and smiled, relishing that she would finally be alone. She wouldn't hear the complaining and the dreadful words from her Mother's lips anymore. She closed her eyes and pictured her Mother lying in the kitchen with her arms spread and legs twisted, the puddle of blood pooling around her head, and Martha let out a slight chuckle.

Martha thought to herself that her Mother must have realized *this was it*. The horrifying realization of drowning with the hot tap water pumping down her throat, filling up her lungs, the desperate gasps for air that wouldn't come, and finally, the terrifying realization that she would indeed die in that kitchen sink, at this moment, by the hands of her daughter, and there was nothing she could do about it. With that thought, she dozed off.

Martha awoke to a knock on the front door. She didn't startle; she felt like she was in a hot Turkish Sauna and that moving away from the couch was probably the last thing she wanted to do. The pounding continued.

"Who the hell?" she muttered and slowly got up from the couch. Her knee gave a popping sound, and Martha stopped for a second and extended her leg, assuring herself it wouldn't fail her. She limped slowly to the door and opened it, forgetting the snowstorm outside would blow cold wind and snow into her face. She pulled the door open, and Mike stood at the doorway.

"Hey – can I come in?"

She stood frozen at the surprise of Mike showing up at her door. She pinched her leg to ensure she wasn't having an ultra-realistic nightmare again.

"Yeah. Yeah, of course, Mike." It had been an involuntary response. The words spilled out before she thought to stop them or think of an excuse not to welcome him inside. Then she thought of her Mother's corpse in the kitchen.

He stepped in and stamped his boots on the thick mat at the doorway. He was covered in snow like a human size abominable snowman, and Martha helped dust off the wet snow at the door, where Mike took off his snow jacket and hung it on the hook on the wall.

"I thought I'd pick you up. It's terrible out there."

"Wish you called Mike."

"You're right; I'm sorry. Maggie hated that I was so unpredictable. I only have good intentions, I swear." He chuckled.

"It's fine, come in." she looked over her shoulder and saw in her periphery that the kitchen light was off – a slight relief, yet a chill darted through her limbs at the thought of Mike discovering her Mother's corpse in the kitchen.

"Uhm. Have a seat, Mike." She said, guiding him to the sofa couch where she slept.

"Thanks, Martha. It's crazy out there. I won't lie to you; I was thinking of taking a rain check on our date. Until I got the old Mustang running earlier today and thought – well, hell – wouldn't it be nice if I picked you up in a classic car."

"You mean that you got covered in all that snow just from coming up the walkway?" she asked.

"Yup. It's crazy."

"You drove a Mustang in this weather?"

"I guess I like you, huh?" he continued, "Maybe we should just stay inside tonight. I know it would be nice to go out somewhere fancy, but it might be safer if we stayed inside. We could order Chinese food too if you like. I'm sure you don't feel like cooking."

"No, I don't," she looked over her shoulder to the kitchen. "I sure don't."

Martha tightened the strap of her bathrobe, "Jeez, I'm not even dressed. Give me a second, and I'll put on some clothes, just....stay there a second, would you? Do you want something to drink? Tea?" she thought of the scalding water in the basin, how it must have had streaks of blood and vomit from her Mother drowning in it. "The water just boiled. Can I make you a cup?"

"Yeah, sure – one sugar though – I got to watch my figure." He chuckled; she didn't.

"Yeah, okay, just don't move, okay?" She tried her best to crack a smile, but it had been more complicated than chipping granite with a spoon.

She raced to the kitchen and froze at the entranceway at the sight of a wet floor, shattered glass, a pool of dark red sticky blood, and nobody. What was left was a trail of bloody footprints leading to the adjoining dining room. The prints meandered off into the dark room, and Martha shuddered at the thought that her Mother was alive.

"Can't be." She muttered,

"What's that?" Mike asked,

"Nothing – running low on sugar."

"All good, no sugar then."

"All right," she whispered while peering into the dark dining room. Her skin trickled with sweat as the cold beads ran down her neck, causing her to shiver all around, the goosebumps standing high like mountain tops on the surface of her skin.

She poured Mike a cup of hot water and dropped a tea bag in the cup while staring into the dining room. She anticipated her Mother running out, her arms stretched out in front of her, her long fingernails rushing toward her face like daggers. The seconds passed by and felt like hours. Nothing came out from the dining room. There were no moans or screeches, no trembling voice, no dragging sounds, nothing – only darkness with blood-red footprints disappearing into the pitch black of the room.

"You need help in there?" Mike asked,

"No, you stay right there, handsome." She replied. He didn't listen. He had already stood up and made his way to the kitchen, where Martha was staring into the dark room.

"Hey, you all right?" he asked with a slight shudder. "Kind of weird how you're staring into that room, Martha – are you sure you're all right?"

She looked at him as he stood in the kitchen with her. She looked down at his feet and saw a clean tiled floor with no blood or spilled water, shards of broken glass, or footprints. She stood perplexed at what was going on. Was it all in her head? Was it a dream again? If so, where was her Mother? She thought.

"I'm fine – I just - thought I heard something," she said. She shook her head and handed Mike the cup of tea. "I'm just going upstairs to change."

"No need." He said.

He placed the cup on the counter and came close to her. His hands grasped her waist as he stood beside her. She could feel him smelling her hair, and he pulled her closer, his hand reaching through the slit of her robe and feeling her breasts. She liked it for a moment – the warm, soft hands caressing her, the stink of cologne he wore, the soft words coming from his mouth as he whispered in her ear,

"No need," he said. "I want to bend you over that table –"

She jumped from his grasp and looked back at him, astonished. She saw Randall Martin, with his oversized belly and messy mustache, standing before her. She gasped and held her hand to her chest just under the swell of her breast, where a long gold chain adorned with a crucifix hung from her neck,

"My god." She muttered,

''What is it?" She heard Mike's voice say through the lips of the dirty fat man.

Behind him, she saw the slender figure of her Mother in the living room, standing in the corner near the living room window facing the wall. Randall Martin's face looked perplexed and ashamed from moving in too fast. The dark figure turned around slowly, and all the while, she heard her Mother's voice in her thoughts,

"Tristan…"

"Tristan, come home."

The ominous figure in the living room turned slowly around, revealing her Mother's sharp-toothed grin at her daughter's look of horror. Her teeth were small sharp fangs that protruded from her lips in a ghastly grimace, her gums black like used motor oil, her eyes were red like bright flames of a burning fire, and her skin was grey, rotting, and pulled tight to her skull. Martha was speechless. Her Mother's voice echoed in her thoughts louder than before,

"Tristan, come home, Tristan-boy."

"STOP!" Martha shouted. Mike stood in place, shocked at the sudden change in Martha's demeanour. She repeated,

"STOP! STOP!" She yelled, her hands cupping her ears like earmuffs,

"JUST DIE! JUST FUCKING - DIE!"

"Calm down, Martha!" Mike shouted with his hands held out in front of him.

Her Mother was standing in the corner, cackling loudly, black blood dripping from her mouth and pooling around the tip of her chin like a bloody liquid beard. She squealed loudly, and still, Mike couldn't hear it; he didn't see her and was baffled as to why Martha was acting this way.

He understood he may have stepped out of line, coming over, grasping, pulling her in, and saying something dirty he thought she would like.

Martha took more steps backward into the darkness of the dining room. Her eyes bulged, and she mumbled to herself; her hands trembled as she stepped back, where she disappeared into the black.

Mike saw her fade away and heard silence coming from that dark room. The ominous sound of silence seemed louder than horns blowing into his eardrums. He listened to his heart beating and tasted the gulp of saliva he nervously swallowed down, the chill that gave him goosebumps on the surface of his skin.

The deafening silence became unbearable until he heard loud thumping from the dark. He hesitated walking into the dining room, but his curiosity enveloped him, and he couldn't resist investigating what Martha was doing in that dark dining room. What that awful monotonous, metronome-like thumping was coming from. He thought he could help. He thought he had seen bat-shit crazy with Maggie, but Martha seemed to top it. He felt like being at the scene of a car wreck – he should have left, run out the front door – but he had to see what was going on – what that loud, deepening sound was.

He stepped into the dark room and felt a bitterly cold air hit him. He shivered slightly but regained himself, reaching out for the light switch. The thumping was constant,

(Thud)

(Thud)

(Thud)

He finally flicked the light switch, and what he saw took his breath away. He stood astonished at the dining room doorway, grasping the doorframe in case he fainted,

"M-Martha – Martha, s-stop!" he said in such a low tone he could barely hear himself,

"M-Martha..."

The large dining room table sat in the middle of the room, and seated in the chairs were Martha's Mother, a teenage boy, and Martha sitting at the head of the table, violently smacking her face against the hard oakwood. The Vase at the center of the table shook and rattled, nearly toppling over with every hard impact of Martha's face on the tabletop. Her face was bloody, her thin long hair stuck to her face, but he could see she was smiling while she constantly thumped her face against the table with such ferocity that her teeth were scattered along the surface, some even embedded into the hardwood.

(Thud)

(Thud)

Martha's Mother sat beside her. She had a glass China plate in front of her and cutting utensils in her hand like she was waiting for her supper. The only thing on the plate was a sprinkling of Martha's splattered blood accumulating with every thudding impact.

(Thud)

(Thud)

Mike looked at the teenage boy, and his wounds were gruesome. His head was turned at an unimaginable angle, his neck clearly broken. His skin was grey and putrid, pieces of flesh missing from his face and exposing the white bone underneath. He heard the buzzing of flies but couldn't spot any flying around. Worst of all, he smelled the rancid scent of grave dirt. The freshly dug mud and clay stuck to the little boy and protruded from him like he had been covered in the aura of death. Mike shrieked at the sight of the dreadful family at the dinner table. He wanted to scream, but no sound came out of his mouth. He felt the warm stream of urine streak down his legs and pool at his feet and felt the wave of humiliation rush in, taking him back to when he wet his pants as a child, the teasing and pointed fingers, the lashing from his Father from being sent home.

"Martha, stop!" he screamed.

She didn't. The hard thudding sound sounded like a Cantaloupe bludgeoned with a baseball bat. Blood pooled across the table, and with every impact, the splatter would land on her Mother's face – as she smiled at Mike.

The little boy began to clap his hands and laugh maniacally. He bounced in his seat like a toddler being bounced on its parent's knee.

Martha's skull had begun to cave in, and her brains began to pour from her shattered skull. The smell hit Mike's nostrils and was sudden and intense. He began to vomit. His legs turned to withered vines, and he collapsed to the floor, spewing bile and his lunch excessively on the carpet. He finished, then huffed and when finally gathering his breath, he stood up and saw Martha's Mother was gone and the boy too.

Martha stood in front of him, only inches away; her face was dark and sticky with blood, her mouth gaped open in a large toothless smile, blood pouring from her lips like an open spout, brain matter dribbled down her cheeks in chunks, falling off her chin and plopping to her feet. He smelled the thick scent of hot iron around him and felt the putrid heat from Martha's breath. If he had any more in his stomach to throw up, he would, but he didn't, so he dry-heaved and finally stumbled backward out of the dining room, where the light turned off and became a dark blackness again. He crawled backward toward the kitchen stove and propped his back on the oven door. He furiously breathed, his eyes like spherical planets in his sockets, the tears flowing down his white stricken pale face.

The room was quiet again, the same deafening silence that kept him in a state of horror; in some ways, it was more horrifying than the scene he had witnessed. A sense of the unknown, and what he saw was only a taste of what would come. The anticipation made him moan loudly, impatiently waiting for the hounds of hell to run out of the dark and rip him to tatters. All that could be heard was his mournful moaning and cries - until he listened to her voice. The words came out sloppy, an exaggerated lisp, and the mouthful of blood he heard,

"Mike." She said softly, "Mike. Come to bed with me, Mike."

He got to his feet and ran out of the front door as fast as possible. He didn't bother reaching down for his boots or grabbing his winter coat (which had the car keys in the front pocket). Instead, he ran barefooted out into the blizzard, dragging through the waist-high snow, getting as far as he could away from that place, out into the middle of the street where he froze at the sight of an ample white light suddenly blinding him – then a loud car horn – the sound of a skidding tire on wet slush - then he heard nothing, except for that deafening sound of silence.

14

Acknowledgements

I want to thank my editor, Chris Urie, for his (greatly appreciated) opinionated perspectives on these stories and his incredible work in helping this collection come to fruition. My gratitude to Margaret Basile, Monica Van Es, Sonia Da Costa, and The Reesdy online platform, for the opportunity to find and collaborate with the editors of this work. Also, Bookbrush cover design online platform, Atticus writing and formatting software and Amazon KDP for making the self-publication process of this work a tolerable one.

Most of all, my deepest gratitude and appreciation to my wife, Vitalia, for suffering through the countless hours of my absence in writing these stories and for being the driving force of my family, which she plays the most pivotal role in the process of keeping our family functioning while I slave away on the computer screen. This work could not be possible without her.

15

AUTHOR BIO

F. Miguel Da Costa was born and raised in Toronto, Ontario, Canada. He is an honours graduate from Sault College, with a Transport Canada Approved Certificate in Aircraft Structural Repair and a Transport Canada AME-S (Aircraft Maintenance Engineer, Structures rated) licence holder. He could be found near Pearson International Airport, where he works as an Aircraft Structural Repair Technician on various aircraft. He was born in 1986 and resides with his wife and two children in Mississauga, Ontario Canada. *"The Shadows In The Pines"* is his first publication.